THE
SPRINGBORN

CARRIE ANNE NOBLE

OLIVER HEBER BOOKS

For Sunday and Cindy:
beautifully buffalo-hearted
and missed

PROLOGUE

There once was a little girl who lived in a coal miners' town with her mother and father. Their company-owned house was dusty, wooden, and plain, as were all the houses on all the streets; no one dared to paint a door bold blue or to plant window boxes of bright flowers. The girl's parents, like everyone in the town, toiled hard and ate simply. They slept deeply and rose early to repeat the day's routine. Nearly all of the town's children worked in the damp dark of the mines, but this girl was kept home and taught to read, to cook, and to sew. Her mother had spent too many years longing for a child to send hers to be smothered by coal.

Sometimes, the girl roamed the woods that encircled the town. There, she marveled at the rich colors and filled her lungs with the pine-scented air. She befriended squirrels and named trees. With her back pressed to the trunk of her favorite hemlock, she read the book of fairy tales she'd received on her eighth Christmas. The tales enthralled her: brothers who became swans, fish that granted wishes, house-nibbling Hansel and his brave sister Gretel.

But on the morning the girl turned eleven, she awoke to find that a pair of silvery gray antlers had grown from her head as she'd slept. She tossed the fairy tale book into the fire, no longer amused by hedgehog sons and wolves masquerading as grandmothers. If such things could be real, they were terrible. Yet the stories remained in her head, unwelcome ghosts, shadows without sympathy, unable to offer the smallest hint as to how to shed the antlers forever.

Never again could she carelessly wander the town without risking her life, for what would the superstitious coal mining folk do if they discovered her secret? Her mother said she'd likely be burned as a witch. The girl believed her. It didn't matter that it was the late eighteen-hundreds, or that she'd always been a sweet and obedient child. The coal towns chose their own forms of law and consequences.

The antlered child had no choice but to hide.

And so she did.

Six years have passed since then, slowly. So slowly that they've felt like centuries.

I know, because I am that girl.

SABELLA

It is Christmas, a day to be merry—or at the very least, grateful for the blessings of warmth and food upon the table. With this in mind, I do my best to ignore the bony, hand's width branches that sprang from my scalp overnight and to pretend I am an ordinary, dutiful, miner's daughter, ready to serve a special holiday meal.

I set the metal coffee pot at Father's place, near the glistening dome of fruitcake. A garland of pine stretches from corner to corner above me, lending the room the faintest whiff of the woods. On the narrow shelf near the washbasin, a red glass bottle holds a bouquet of holly. It is my dearest hope that my efforts will remind my father of Christmases long past, when we were a poor but happy family who loved each other.

Hope. Where *that* came from is as much a mystery to me as the source of my antlers. It is like a single firefly bottled up in my chest. Its light pulses, but for how long?

When I hear the clomping of Father's boots in the bedroom

above the kitchen, my heartbeat skips. The mines are closed today, so he slept hours longer than usual. I wrap my hand in a towel and take Father's already filled plate from the wood-burning stove's warming oven—a meal of crispy-edged fried eggs, fat sausages, freshly made biscuits, and a small boiled potato sprinkled with coarse salt. Just as Mother used to make on Christmas morning, before ceaseless sickness left her mostly bedridden. I straighten the knife and fork. Everything looks just right.

Father trudges down the wooden stairs with the grace of an ox. He is not a large man, but one broad with muscles earned through hard labor. His thin hair appears to be gray—but who can tell if it's truly gray, or white stained by coal dust. As he grows closer, I note that he wears fresh clothes this morning—although his shirt and trousers are also shades of gray. My body stiffens with apprehension as he steps off the last stair. My antlers weigh little, but in his presence my head feels almost too heavy for my neck.

"Merry Christmas, Father," I say with the unease of a person reaching out to pet a slumbering bear. He responds with the briefest of nods, a motion so fleeting that I might have imagined it. And then he glares at my antlers and curses.

He has not looked me in the eye in years, as if meeting my gaze might turn him to stone or doom him to perdition. But I think his heart is already a stone, a thing as black as the coal he gathers. As for perdition, he daily endures the agonies of living with a sick, shrewish wife and an antler-growing daughter—torments any devil would be glad to take credit for.

Father stomps past me. "For the love of the Almighty, could you at least try to cover the blasted things, girl?" He ignores the steaming plate of food, the perfectly set table, and the decorations. With a groan, he bends to retrieve a hand saw from inside the painted wooden cabinet. He grunts to instruct me to move to the stool in the corner, the stool I hate with a passion one ought not to waste on furniture.

A flood of disappointment extinguishes my spark of hope. The events of the day are proceeding as usual, and I was a fool to expect anything else. I lower my body onto the seat.

Rough, calloused fingers grab the back of my neck. I hold my breath. With both hands, I press my hair flat to keep it out of the way. He sets the blade at the base of one of my antlers, so close to my scalp that the coldness of the metal sends a shiver through my body. And he starts to saw. Back and forth, back and forth. The blade grunts and sighs, grunts and sighs. I inhale the dust—breathing in bits of myself that no one wants.

The antler falls to the floor. I peer down at it from the corner of my eye. It is beautiful, although I would never dare to speak such a sentiment aloud. Silvery gray and curved like a young tree limb with five short, pointed branches, its velvety surface calls out to be touched, caressed. I cannot hate it as I ought to, but neither do I feel affection for it.

Father adjusts his stance, tightens his grip, and cuts into my remaining antler. I bite my lip and bide the time until the second antler clatters against the floorboards. My head is lighter now, but Father's mood is not. Glowering, he points to the white cotton cap I left to dry on the clothesline above the cookstove.

"Cover your head and get rid of them quick," he says—as if I need reminding. "And then get breakfast for your mother. She has one of her headaches." He tosses the saw onto the table with a thud, narrowly missing his plate of congealing food.

"Yes, Father." I swallow hard, holding back tears.

He plods upstairs and leaves me alone without acknowledging my attempts to make Christmas happy. My face grows hot with frustration and indignity. Honestly, what did I expect? A miracle? The last miracle that happened here was me—a longed-for child thrust into the arms of a barren couple—and look how that has turned out. As Mother reminds me far too often, the distance between a miracle and a curse is no more than the breadth of a silken thread, and to wish for one is as good as begging for the other.

The soot-smeared kitchen walls seem to inch closer together by the second. My lungs beg for a breath of fresh air. With haste, I wind my hair into a bun. I don the cotton cap, shove my stocking-clad feet into boots, and cover my dingy calico dress with a black woolen cloak. I struggle to jam the antlers into a burlap sack. They snag on the rough fabric as if they're resisting their fate, but I persist until they're hidden within the bag. Finally, I tear open the door. A blast of frosty, pre-sunrise air chills my cheeks and nips at my earlobes. I welcome the honest, expected sting of it. I pull the hood of the cloak over my head and step outside.

My feet know the way without being reminded. I slip between the houses and climb the steep, stony bank that slopes behind the residences. Once I reach the top, I take the path my feet have worn into the ground with these daily ventures. When I was younger and played with the neighbor children, we called this brushy patch of land haunted, favoring the forest on the other end of town. The belief seems to have stood the test of time, which has been to my advantage. I have been charged by Father to be invisible. To be less noticeable than a specter.

The icy wind gusts harder. My eyes water as I shimmy through a gap between two leafless bushes. The sun has started to rise, but its pinkish-orange rays do nothing to warm the landscape. Today, I choose to head to the hidden meadow where, many years ago, Mother first taught me to bury my "disgraces." There have been plenty of places I've taken the antlers for disposal since: a glade farther up the hillside, the river when it's running fast, the dirt-walled cellar of a long-abandoned cabin near the mountaintop—to name but a few. But in unpleasant weather, I favor the places closest to town. So Mother's meadow it shall be.

The rusty shovel stands where I left it yesterday, propped against the trunk of a wild cherry tree. I take it up and look for a spot to dig. Soon, I choose a place on the western edge of the meadow. Hands wrapped around the shovel's handle, I try to thrust its point through the snow and dirt, but it's no use. True winter has arrived, solidifying the earth with her wrathful breath. I'd sooner be able to puncture stone with a hat pin. There will be no more burying until the spring thaw. Which means *more* walking in the cold, a full half-mile to the next closest disposal place, an abandoned mine shaft.

I trudge uphill and down, winding my way through a maze of bare trees, fallen branches, and ancient boulders. Snow works its way into a hole in my boot, where it melts and dampens my stocking. The relentless wind causes my teeth to chatter.

Merry Christmas, indeed.

The rotting wooden frame around the mine opening creaks as if to say hello. A few boards have fallen since my last visit. One by one, I toss them aside, making the hole just large enough to admit the antlers. My stomach grumbles as I work, urging me to hurry home to the pot of oatmeal I left simmering. Perhaps, as a Christmas treat, I'll have a slice of fruitcake with my breakfast. It's unlikely that either of my parents will notice such an indulgence— or would bother to scold me for it. That would require discourse beyond the ordinary "sit," "fetch," "cook," or "mend" commands they're used to flinging in my direction.

I dump the antlers into the hole, wad the sack in my hands, and turn toward home.

On Christmas night, my thoughts are almost as dark as my little bedroom off the kitchen. I perch on the edge of my thin mattress and, with long strokes, I brush out my hair. I remember my eleventh birthday, when I came trembling to the breakfast table with antlers sticking out of my head for the first time. How my parents' mouths gaped open as they stared. How Father swore and Mother wept as if I had died.

Ever since, I've wondered why my parents had not anticipated such an occurrence. If an old woman gives you a mysterious basket, and said basket contains the baby you've been wishing for, you might well expect the child to be unusual in some way.

And yet the antlers broke them.

When the antlers came, they broke us all.

They brought on Mother's daily headaches. The big city doctor she visited prescribed special medicine, remedies that stank of alcohol and only made her headaches and moods worse. The doctor's monthly bills consumed most of Father's meager pay. Debts piled up; Father turned sour and then bitter. I had been his delight, but the growth of my odd appendages purged all affection from him, like dysentery of the soul from which he would never recover.

I tried to imagine what excuse he gave for my absence from sewing circles and church services, but I never dared to ask. Whatever tale he told was dire enough to prevent friends, neighbors, and busybodies from stopping by with pots of soup or offers of aid.

Ever frantic, Mother knitted strangely shaped caps and sewed wide bonnets until every drawer and cupboard burst with them. The day soon came when even her cleverest handiwork was no longer sufficient to cover the antlers. For as I grew, their size kept in proportion to the size of my wide-spread hands. Finally, Father obtained a hand saw from the company store. He wielded the tool like a weapon of salvation, and I sobbed with fear as he cut off the things which were me yet somehow not me.

His victory was short-lived. The antlers returned; they always do. Their growth during daylight is slow, but after nightfall, they inch upward and outward like the branches of an enchanted tree, painlessly but persistently—whether I sleep or remain awake. (This I know because I once thought I might thwart them by avoiding sleep. Alas, my experiment resulted in nothing but exhaustion— and the usual antlers. At the time, I was equal parts disappointed and fascinated.)

And so, every morning, futile though it is, Father saws them off with neither apology nor sympathy.

The day Mother realized the antlers could not be defeated, she took to her bed. There she continues to spend most of her time, leaving me to perform all of the household duties. She drowses the day away while I endure endless cycles of cooking and cleaning, baking and washing. In my rare free hours, I find consolation in reading the four books we own, grateful that Mother took the time to teach me to read and write back when she believed I was an ordinary child.

One freedom remains mine: visiting the woods to do away with the sawn-off antlers. Rain or shine, they must be disposed of promptly, as if their mere presence might poison Mother worse than her sham medicine. This time out of doors keeps me sane. Indeed, I feel more at home wandering under a canopy of leaves than I do within the walls of my parents' shabby, company-owned house.

In spite of my antlers, I know I am blessed. Most coal miners' children suffer far more than I, forced to work endless hours underground, afflicted with lungs full of black dust and ever-hungry bellies. Yet grateful as I am, my heart dares to ask for more.

Sometimes, tucked into my narrow bed at midnight, I dare to wish for a friend. Someone to unwind the shroud of loneliness I wear. But who would befriend a girl with antlers? Who could be trusted with my secret?

Mother's old warning never fails to echo in my mind: "The townsfolk will burn you for a witch if they find out what you are." I believe her enough that I often fall into dreams of flames scorching my dress, my skin, and the silvery gray antlers that stand out from my head so brazenly.

CALDER

I watch her from the forest shadows—but not in an improper or sinister way. It's for her own good. Her protection.

Almost every day, I follow her as she walks through the woods with that ugly burlap sack in her hands. She moves like one born to the forest. Not like a lumbering bear or skittering chipmunk, but like a nimble young doe. Which is fitting, given her antlers.

I know all about the antlers.

She thinks only her parents are aware of them. She does well at hiding the bumps on her head and never removes the detached antlers from the bag unless she's deep in the woods. I'm not one for peering into windows, but I confess that, out of concern, I have done so a time or two. Or ten. If I can help it, I shall not spy on her through the clouded glass panes ever again. The sight of her sadness, the cruel-toothed saw, the severe set of her father's jaw—it is too much to be borne.

In the woods, though, I will watch her. I was given the task by my guardian and I take it seriously. This girl must be kept safe until the day she's invited to join our little family of curiously gifted folk, or the day she chooses to run away from her unkind parents.

The world is full of hateful men and women who would kill her before trying to understand her differentness. History speaks of martyrs murdered for less than wearing a set of antlers. Mankind is keen to reject and spurn rather than to embrace and love. I will not let her be jailed or burned.

When first I saw her six years ago, I was thirteen years old. It was not love at first sight. Even I know that such a thing is more mythical than girls with antlers. But when I saw her, my heart said, "I know her, and have always known her, even outside of time." That is the truth, and I will stand upon it until my dying day.

Today is Christmas, but events unfold as usual. She creeps out the front door of her wooden house, looks both ways, and then runs through the dusting of snow in the direction of the woods. To the same path she always takes. She doesn't see me. She doesn't hear me. She doesn't know that I see the wet streaks of tears on her pale cheeks, or that they wrench my heart most painfully.

I trail behind her as she steps into the shelter of the pines. We walk together, but separately. Our feet trod over dead ferns and dormant moss. I listen hard for strangers and predatory animals. No harm will come to my antlered girl if I can help it—other than the harm already done to her by parents who ought to love her.

Who might she become when she realizes that she is wonderfully special rather than a shameful secret?

The day of her liberation from them cannot come soon enough.

SABELLA

JANUARY 1, 1886

I t is the first morning of the New Year, and strangely warm
for January.

Antlers discarded, I walk along the banks of a winding
stream. Pieces of ice stick up from it like shards of glass, sparkling
in the bright sunlight. Clear water burbles and hisses as it flows
against and around the ice.

A few yards upstream, a buck bends its sleek, brown neck and
laps water. His antlers are majestic, a wild crown spreading above
his ears. I hold my breath until he ambles away.

My fingers probe beneath my woolen bonnet and find the twin
stubs of my antlers. These little nubs have no feeling, like fingernails. Less than two hours since Father's sawing, they've grown by
only the smallest of degrees. But if I tarry past sunset and into the
night, they will lift the bonnet up off my head or poke through it.

I lean over the stream, then push the bonnet back so it falls to
sag behind my neck. I squint downward to catch my reflection. My
face is milky pale, as one might expect in a girl who is a stranger to
the noonday sun. My eyes are brown flecked with green and gold.

The stubs of my antlers sit surrounded by my reddish-brown hair, almost hidden. I spread my hands over my head to imitate the buck's rack. I can only imagine what I must look like with my own antlers fully formed, since Mother forbids me to look into the mirror before Father attends to my "affliction." Might the antlers lend some beauty to my appearance?

If someone were to observe me in my true state, would they tremble with fear or sigh with wonder?

Do I hate the antlers, as Mother and Father do? Sometimes. They have cost me much and yielded only misery. But the antlers have been part of me long enough that I imagine to lose them forever would seem like losing a hand or foot. I often wonder if they were meant as a gift or a curse—or both.

A branch snaps nearby. A chickadee in the brush sounds a warning call as it takes flight. I replace my bonnet hastily and scan my surroundings. Out of the corner of my eye, I see a flash against the snowy landscape. A silhouette ducking behind a hemlock tree, a wisp of someone dressed all in black.

I freeze like a startled fawn. Nausea twists my stomach. Could the watcher perceive from afar the two small bumps on the head of this imprudent girl? I hope with all my heart that he is merely a passerby, someone who did not recognize me. As I rarely leave the house, most of the townspeople would be hard pressed to name me on sight, but still...

There's rustling in the brush, and I think I hear the soft thud of his footfalls grow fainter and fainter. I wait long minutes, hardly daring to blink until I am certain he is gone.

The man has fled, but to where? Whom might he tell if he has seen my secret?

My ruination, Mother's favorite prophecy, could be at hand.

I should run, but my knees wobble with weakness and my mouth is dry as a desert. I stoop to capture a handful of water. I drink, and the liquid's chill numbs my throat. Bitter cold spreads throughout my body as I realize the stranger has stolen something valuable from me: the peace I'd known in wandering alone. From now on, I must get rid of the antlers in haste and return home without delay.

What was left of my girlhood freedom has vanished like a vapor in the wind.

CALDER

I have made a grave and foolish error. Sabella has seen me.

I saw the terror in her eyes before I ran away from her.

Now, things will have to change. New plans must be made. Perhaps it is for the best. She has suffered isolation and disparagement for long enough, in my opinion.

The matriarch of my familial group, Delphine, has gone away and left her partner Yonaz in charge, which may be a stroke of good fortune. He is around the age of thirty and as serious as an arithmetic lesson, but his heart is tender. I think I can convince him that the time has come to bring Sabella into the fold.

As I hasten to our hidden home in the forest, I rehearse the speech I will use to persuade him to issue her an invitation.

I only hope she'll be willing to accept it.

SABELLA

The idea of someone knocking at our door is so foreign to me that it takes a quarter minute for me to connect the sound with its meaning: there is a visitor upon the doorstep. My chest tightens as if my corset strings have been yanked firmly enough to crush my lungs. Had I not already been sitting at the kitchen table, my legs might have given out.

What should I do? I wait, holding as still as a cornered rabbit. No one ever calls upon my family. It is as if some sign has been posted outside, a warning of plague or danger.

The knocking stops, and then starts again.

I stand and set my mending on the table. I linger there with my hand on the wadded fabric. I stare at the door and continue to think. Mother is dead-to-the-world asleep upstairs and Father is at work. Surely it would be most prudent to pretend no one is at home.

The visitor knocks again. Harder this time. What if it is someone coming to report that Father has been in an accident? But no, if there were a problem in the mine, they'd sound the company whistle. Wouldn't they?

A shiver of dread passes through me. I call out, "Who is it?" I must know. It is torture not knowing.

A male voice replies, muffled by the thickness of the door. "Hello? This is the Jenkins house, is it not?"

"What do you want?" I know full well that the stranger cannot see through the door, nevertheless my hands fly up to make sure my cotton cap still conceals my antlers' stubs.

"I'd be happy to explain, but I would like to get out of the cold, if you'd permit me," the man says.

I bite my lip, still indecisive. A trio of trumpeting angels couldn't wake Mother, and our nearest neighbor is stone deaf. If this fellow has wicked intentions, no one would answer my cries for aid.

A notion makes my breath catch: what if he's the man who was watching me in the woods a few weeks ago?

"Please," the caller says, sounding younger now. "It's terribly cold out here. I swear by all the saints and angels I'll not cause you any trouble."

His voice is so pitiful that my resolve to turn him away starts to melt.

"Go to the window so I can see you," I say. I must be sure he's not clad in all black, as the man in the woods was.

"With pleasure," he replies.

I adjust my cap again and peek through a tiny gap between the curtains. The caller appears to be a boy near my own age. Any local boy's face would be indelibly sullied by coal dust, but his round-cheeked face is as clean as a Sunday morning. He holds a basket of apples with one of his bare hands and grips the handles of a leather case in the other. This stranger wears a tan tweed coat and a red scarf—and not a stitch of black. His eyes are acorn brown, and the hair sticking out from under his cap is a few shades lighter. I imagine if it were spring rather than winter, the town girls would be trailing behind him, giggling and remarking upon his handsomeness.

He leans close to the glass, no doubt trying to catch a glimpse of me. His breath fogs the pane. "May I come in now, miss? Do I pass inspection?"

I step back and consider once more. It would be kind to let him in, but would it be wise? The black-clad man could have changed his clothing. Nice-looking fellows can hide hearts full of evil. The villains of fairy tales are often well-disguised. But...something about this boy convinces me to take a chance and let him in.

"Come to the door," I say. I grab a large, scuttle-shaped, green bonnet and jam it over my cotton cap before turning the lock.

"Hello there," he says as soon as the door swings open. He smiles as if he's truly happy to see me. It's like being slapped with sunshine. He glances at my oversized bonnet as he sets his leather bag on the floor. "I'm sorry. Were you on your way out?"

"No, but I have a knife," I blurt. The part about having a knife is an untruth—unless you count the dull-edged dinner knives in the drawer eight feet away. Mortification surges through me, heating my cheeks as I step aside so he can enter the kitchen. I suspect there are countless reasons for this flare of embarrassment, but I can narrow the list down to three: the shame of telling a falsehood, my lack of experience in society, and this boy's too-pretty face.

He pulls one faultless apple from the basket, his smile unfaltering. "Well, maybe you could use your blade to slice this rather than my poor skin."

"Oh," is all I manage to say. Still flustered, I take the fruit with one hand and point to the woodstove with the other. My ability to think and to speak eludes me for a moment. I am unaccustomed to surprises, especially surprises that stand in my kitchen looking pleased with themselves. I shove some words out of my mouth. Inane words. "If you want to get warm, the fire's over there."

"Thank you. This weather is cruel indeed." He sets his basket on the table and strides across the room, where he holds his open palms a few inches above the blackened top of the iron cookstove. "You don't get many callers here, do you? You look...startled."

"My mother has been ill for some time, so no, we do not get callers. I am too occupied with her care to host tea parties." Although my words sound rude to my ears, he does not flinch.

I try to remember the rules of hospitality. Ought I to offer this stranger some refreshment? He looks so pitiful rubbing his chapped hands together that I decide to err on the side of generosity. "Would you care for some tea?"

"I'd give my left ear for tea," he says. I must look befuddled—or startled again—because he quickly adds, "Not in the literal sense, of course." He sinks into Father's green upholstered armchair near the stove like he owns it, while I make tea like I've never made tea before—sloshing water everywhere, dropping the spoon, and scattering precious leaves across the counter.

Finally, after several exasperating minutes, I press a mug into his grasp. I back a few feet away from him, my arms folded over my chest. Worry simmers inside me, a roiling fear that extra-large antlers might suddenly surge forth from my skull and send the boy into the streets screaming my secret to all.

I push my fear down and try to speak calmly. "You can't stay long," I say. "My father will return soon, and he's not fond of entertaining strangers."

A playful smile appears above the rim of his mug as his gaze meets mine. "I could try to be less than entertaining, if that would help."

"Oh," I say flatly. A second passes before I realize he meant to be humorous. My already hot face grows hotter still.

I want him to go. And I want him to stay. He is too bright for this dark house. There's a ravenous sort of feeling in my belly, as if I've been physically starving for human companionship and he's the embodiment of a tantalizing supper. I think I prefer the nausea of unease he first caused to this raw hunger.

His face turns serious. Heavens, was I staring at him like he's supper?

"We've just met, but I can already tell you're a good daughter, taking care of your mother. Respecting your father. But you should still have friends. At least one person who knows and appreciates the other aspects of you. Someone who wants to share your hopes and dreams."

My mouth opens but I cannot cobble together a reply. I keep my gaze on the steam rising from his tea. It's impossible that he read my mind, is it not? But then I remember my antlers and my parents' granted wish for a daughter. Nothing is ever impossible.

He takes a few leisurely swallows from his mug, oblivious to my internal debate and mounting panic. "You make a fine cup of tea," he says. He sits up straight, cradling the mug between his hands. "Now that I'm warmed through, I suppose I should state my business."

"Business?" I scowl at him, remembering the sizeable leather satchel he dropped near the door. "Allow me to guess. You're a traveling salesman. You cajole housewives into buying overpriced soap and scrub brushes." I feel mean saying this after his kind speeches about friendship, like the spirit of my oft-cranky mother has possessed me.

"A worthy guess, but no." He stands. He pulls a letter from the pocket of his jacket and holds it out for me to take. "It's from the housing officer. I'm your new boarder."

I shake my head and take a step backward. "There's been a mistake. We don't take boarders. We never have." And then...all the blood and breath seem to leave my body. With horror, I think of how slow-moving my father has become of late. How he daily complains of backaches and leg aches. Miners are paid according to how much they produce. If Father has become less productive, his pay has fallen. And if a miner makes too little, the company places boarders in his house to make up the difference.

The young man steers me to the green chair he abandoned less than a minute ago. I sit down hard.

"I apologize, miss. I thought they would have warned you that I'd be arriving today." A wrinkle of worry creases his forehead. He crosses the room and returns with a cup of water. "Here. Drink this and try to catch your breath."

I obey. I miss the sluggishness of mind I had when I first let this young man into the house, for now my thoughts come fast, on dark and terrible wings. We cannot have a boarder. He will find out about my antlers. It is inevitable. I can be careful, very careful, but someday, I will make a mistake and he will see them branching from my head. And then I will be ruined. My entire family will be ruined, cast out of this house and this town without a penny.

The end-of-shift whistle rends the air as I gulp the water. Father will be home soon.

"Can I get you something else, miss? Another drink? Something to eat?" The young man stands close to me, watching me with more concern than anyone else has in years. "Do you need a blanket? You're shivering."

"I need nothing," I say. Something hits the floor of the bedroom above my head and I nearly jump out of my skin. My mother must have dropped her hairbrush or book. If my heart beats any faster, I will surely die.

The boisterous sound of homebound miners carries in from the street. The men are a block or two away at most. Time seems to both slow and speed up as my mind churns out images of what might happen if my father finds this boy here alone with me. None of these imaginings have happy endings.

"How about this?" the visitor says, crouching beside the chair. "I'll go, and I'll come back tomorrow instead. Give you more time to get a place ready for me and to let your parents know I'll be boarding here."

"Yes," I reply. Now I can draw a breath in. I have been granted something like a stay of execution. "Tomorrow would be better."

"Is that a smile there? I was hoping you had one of those in you," he says. He gets up. "I'll be on my way, then."

I stand and follow him to the door. He picks up his bag and reaches for the doorknob, but hesitates. He faces me again. "Forgive me. The cold must have affected my mind earlier. I neglected to introduce myself. My name is Calder Hadrian." He takes my hand quickly. In a heartbeat, he lifts it to his mouth and kisses my knuckles like a knight of old from a storybook. The gesture is outdated, but there is nothing vulgar in the brief press of his lips to my skin, only a sweet tenderness that terrifies and charms me in equal measure.

I yank my hand away as if burned. Never in my life have I so desperately wanted someone to leave and to stay at the same time. Has he cast some spell upon me?

Just outside, the miners' voices rumble as loud as thunder.

"Calder Hadrian," I say. The five syllables fall from my mouth with the heaviness of a vow and the lightness of a song. I do not understand myself. "Please go."

"Enjoy the apples, Sabella," he says. He ducks outside, leaving the door ajar. Wind keens through the opening. I rush to shove the door shut. But before I do, I peek through an inch-wide opening and watch Calder cross the still-empty street. He jogs past Mr. Driscoll's house, uphill to a patch of pine trees, and joins someone there. His acquaintance is scrawny, with wind tossed hair as black as a crow's wing—but that is not what makes me gasp.

In the place where his boots should be, the young man has the feet of a bird.

CALDER

"What happened in there?" Robbie asks when I brush past him. We've been firm friends for years, brothers in all ways but blood—but I wish he were elsewhere at the moment. I'm too disgusted with myself to be good company for anyone.

I fear I have bungled things again. Worse than before, even.

"Later, Rob," I mutter.

I hurry toward home, crushing sticks and ferns underfoot. My regrets plague me, but I can no more outrace them than I could a runaway steam engine. Robbie, too, manages to follow at my heels.

She—Sabella—makes me lose my mind. All right, it is wrong to put it that way. It is not her fault I transformed into a grinning nincompoop the instant she opened the door to me. She cannot be blamed for my overabundant, play-acted charm, or the apple-offering (am I the serpent of Eden? Good glory no!), or the falsified letter from the housing officer. Yonaz was the one who insisted I tell the new-lodger tale instead of the truth, so I suppose he is partly at fault...

Nevertheless, it is I who flitted about like a dandy from a poorly written novel. Blast me.

If I were the praying kind, I would beseech the Lord above to help me do better when I return to Sabella's house. This is no mere game. Nor is it truly about me and my personal inclinations. This is about her safety. Her future happiness.

Ahead of me stands the vine-covered wall and the entrance to my home. I bend and press my palms to my knees as I try to catch my breath. The welcoming scents of wood smoke and cinnamon cake beckon me inside. Ordinarily, I'd track down the cake like a hound on the hunt, but I seem to have misplaced my appetite.

Untrue. I know exactly whose kitchen I left it in.

The hours between now and when I can bring Sabella here—to the place where she belongs—will seem eternal. I have never been one to worry, but I worry now. What if she refuses to join us? If that were not vexation enough, I'm pining to be in her presence again. If such longing makes me a madman or a fool, then so be it. I only hope that in the end, I am the fool she chooses to call her own.

SABELLA

In a basin of suds, I slosh a rag over Father's breakfast dishes. The door slams behind him as he leaves for his shift at the mine. Across the room, Mother snores beside the woodstove. She's passed out in Father's green chair with a bottle of her special medicine clutched to her breast. Strands of gray-streaked, dull brown hair have escaped from her sloppily knotted bun to frame her sagging, sallow face. Her weakness for alcohol-laced curatives has made her old before her time.

As I continue the washing up, my mind is occupied by three things in turn: our new boarder, Calder (who somehow knew my name without being told), his bird-legged companion, and my failure to inform my parents that we are about to become a household of four. Much as I wish I could banish these thoughts, they buzz around inside my head like nagging mosquitoes.

When the dishes are clean and dried, I slide them into the wooden rack above the cupboard. Thoughts of Calder and his odd friend continue to plague me as I sweep dirt and dust into a pile. I glance at the bowl of apples on the table. If not for them, I might convince myself that yesterday was only a dream. I might quit trembling at the thought of Calder's imminent return and the perils of having a boarder. I might stop dwelling on the way he looked at me as he sipped tea in Father's chair. How his lips felt against my knuckles. I might return to sensible thinking.

He will be back, this I know as surely as I know my name. At any moment, he will knock upon the door and assault me with his smile. This time, he will stay.

Mother awakens with a snort and presses a hand to her heart. Her empty medicine bottle tumbles to the floor. "Dear me. Was I asleep?"

"Let me help you upstairs," I say as I offer her my arm. "You'll be more comfortable in bed."

She nods, but before she's on her feet, the knock comes—loud and insistent.

"Whoever could that be?" Mother asks. She swats my arm away. "Leave me be and go see, girl. No use waiting. That's a good, thick headscarf you're wearing. No one will be the wiser."

I know who's calling, but I do not say so. I wish I could run into the woods and hide. Instead, I answer the door.

"Good morning," Calder says. He wears the same tan tweed jacket and red scarf he wore yesterday, and grips the same brown leather bag. His smile is every bit as blinding as before. I glance at his boots as if to avoid damaging my eyes. "Will you not ask me in?" he says cheerily.

"Come in," I say. It sounds more like a question than an invitation. He must not mind, for he crosses the threshold and walks straight toward the cookstove—and my mother.

"You must be Mrs. Jenkins," he says, still beaming like the summer sun. He offers his hand and she takes it.

"Do I know you, young man?" Mother squints as if trying to place him, her head wobbling a little. She is far from sober, but in this instance, it may prove to be a blessing.

"Not yet, but you will presently. I'm your new boarder," he says. "Calder Hadrian, ma'am."

Mother coughs and fans herself with her hand. Her pasty complexion grows a shade paler. "Never! Sabella? Did you know about this?"

"I just found out," I say, not adding *yesterday*. My face flushes. I cannot even tell half a lie without coloring up like a wild strawberry.

Calder takes the blasted letter out of his pocket and gives it to Mother. "The housing officer sent me, Mrs. Jenkins. He should have warned you, but alas, here I am. I promise not to be a burden. I'll help with chores if you like. I can polish a stove so it's black as a crow."

Mother doesn't open the letter. She waves it in the air, gesturing for me to take it and set it on the shelf. Her hand trembles, as if the danger of the situation is dawning upon her. Her words run together as she says, "There has been a mistake. My husband will deal with the matter after his shift. You'll have to return then. Now, if you'll excuse me, I'm feeling quite unwell. Help me upstairs, Sabella."

I haul her to her feet, feeling Calder's steady gaze upon me.

"Good to meet you, Mrs. Jenkins," Calder says as I support Mother's stumbling ascent to the second floor.

In reply, Mother mutters something quite un-Christian under her breath.

After I tuck her into bed, she grabs my sleeve. "This has the makings of a nightmare. You'd best be careful, miss. That one's as clever as he is pretty, I can tell. If he sees what you're hiding—"

"I'll be careful, Mother. I promise."

She shuts her eyes and drapes a hand across her forehead. "All this excitement does my poor head no good. Fetch that new medicine from my dresser."

The bottle is blue glass embossed with the words *Jorgen's*

Elixir. When I deliver it to her, she drinks straight from the bottle. She sighs, wipes her mouth, and says, "Better."

I head for the door, but she calls out, "Wait."

"Yes?"

"Be careful, Sabella," she reiterates. "Hold your secrets close."

She's snoring before I reach the stairs.

Well, that went better than I'd expected. Father will be another matter. Mother is a faded flower, but he is a tempersome bull. His metaphorical horns and hooves are a hundred times more dangerous than my real antlers could ever be.

"Why are you not at work in the mines?" I ask Calder as I descend the steps.

He's standing by the stove, warming his smooth, unsullied hands. Skin like that has no place in a coal town. He glances at me and says, "I start tomorrow. There was paperwork."

"And your friend? Does he start tomorrow as well?" My boldness surprises me, but I give it free rein and let it gallop.

He raises an eyebrow. "Friend?"

"I saw you with a dark-haired boy. He had...strange legs."

"Robbie? No, he will not be taking employment here." He explains no further, as if bird legs are nothing out of the ordinary. He wanders to peek into the parlor. "Will this be my room?"

I nod, thinking, *Heaven forbid.*

"Nice enough," he says. He turns toward me. "Do you have anything to eat? My belly is about to glue itself to my backbone." There is that grin again. Charming, handsome, eager to amuse. I almost wish I could shake it from him. Perhaps if I were an ordinary girl, I might allow myself the luxury of enjoying his smiles and turns of phrase—but I am a girl with a weighty and dangerous secret.

"There's bread." I point to a cloth-wrapped loaf on the counter. "Or the apples you brought."

"Thank you." Calder slices an inch-thick piece from the loaf, then pulls a chair out from the table. "Sit with me?"

"I have work to do," I say, but with a huff, I sit across from him. In my lap, my fingers pick at a thread that's come loose from my cuff. I watch him eat, debating whether I should interrogate him further about his bird-legged friend or leave the matter alone for now.

He finishes the bread. "You look at me as if I'm a snake who slithered into your kitchen."

"Are you?"

"I do not think so."

My head itches around the stubs of my antlers, but I do not dare to scratch. I press my palms firmly against my thighs and say, "My father will not be pleased to have a boarder."

Calder eyes me soberly. "I think we both know that I am more than a boarder."

The room seems to sway. Could he already know about the antlers? I swallow hard. "I don't know who you are, but I think it would be best if you'd leave Miners Ridge and not return. If you want mine work, try Lindenville, a few miles east."

He leans toward me and whispers, "Tell me what you know about the basket."

"Basket?" My voice comes out higher-pitched than usual. I spring from my seat and hurry to the stove. I twist the handle on the stovepipe to open the damper, grab a stick of wood from the wood box, and feed the fire with shaky hands. I have never been more afraid in my life, because I think *he knows.*

To my back he says, "The one your parents found you in. Do you still have it?"

"Sabella!" Mother calls from upstairs as if she's somehow sensed my distress. "I need you!"

"Excuse me." I rush toward the stairs. I scale them as if Mother's a fire that requires immediate dousing. To be sure, my own guts feel as if they're being consumed by flames.

I throw open Mother's door to find her lying in bed. Of course the urgency of her call does not equal the importance of the task she has for me. She is neither on fire nor in true desperation, having only misplaced a book. My hands will not stop shaking as I search for the thing under the bed and among the blankets. Again, she warns me to be wary of Calder. She need not. I could not be any warier. I trust the boy less than I'd trust the devil himself.

When I finally creep downstairs again, he is gone. And I praise heaven for it—although I know he shall return soon. He will ask questions, but I will not answer. I do not have to, for I have something to hold over him.

If Calder Hadrian refuses to leave town, I will threaten to tell everyone about his friend, Robbie the bird-legged boy. He can leave on his own two feet or wait to be tossed out of town by burly, superstitious miners. Either way, I will be rid of him.

CALDER

I squash my hat in my fist as my feet pound the ground beneath me. Robbie's waiting for me just inside the border of the woods, or he'd say something like, "Don't punish that poor hat for your own stupidity." And I'd give him a glare or a smack for it, even though he'd be right in pointing out that the stupidity that just happened was one hundred percent of my own doing.

Will I ever encounter Sabella face to face without saying the wrong thing?

I never should have mentioned the basket. I know full well I am forbidden to speak of it. Delphine would skin me alive if she knew I'd mentioned it. Yonaz would make me chop firewood until my blisters sprouted blisters.

As much as I regret that Sabella's mother cut our visit short, it was probably for the best. My blasted tongue had gotten off its leash. Again. Next time Yonaz should write me a script rather than giving me a vague idea of what to say and do.

Now that I reflect on it, his plan was rather ridiculous. What sense was there in my pretending to be a boarder? How would that have inspired her to trust me? It feels like I've been shoveling lies into a heap and hoping they'll sprout daisies, but all the while they're just useless excrement.

"Judging by the sour look on your face, the visit did not go well," Robbie says as we head toward home. His bird feet tread lightly on the pine-needled path. The trilling of robins overhead is louder than his footsteps.

A brown frog stubbornly sits in the path. It eyes me as I step over it. I do not wish to expound upon my foolish behavior, but Robbie will pester me until I do. My face heats as I say, "I mentioned the basket to her. And also, she saw you yesterday. And by you, I mean all of you, including your feet."

"Blast it all to blazes," Robbie says. "Then we're both in big trouble. Or we will be if Yonaz or Delphine find out."

"Maybe nothing will come of our little missteps and we won't have to confess." I say this with far more optimism than I feel.

"We'll keep it to ourselves for now. No harm in that," Robbie says. "So, will you be moving in with the girl's family or not?"

I shrug. "Remains to be seen. Yonaz thought that if I formed a friendship with her, she'd be more easily swayed to join us. I'm not so sure. She doesn't seem to trust me one bit."

He casts me a sidelong glance, accusatory in nature. "You flirted, didn't you?"

"Not on purpose."

"Well, be more careful next time. She's been housebound for ages; of course she's uncomfortable with strangers. Befriend her slowly instead of proposing immediate marriage or waxing poetical about her hair."

"Hey! I don't do that."

"Pardon me?" Robbie counters. "Every blessed time Yonaz sends you for supplies, you come back mooning over some shop girl or dairy maid. Remember the girl from Coalton whose giant of a brother came after you because you asked her to meet you in the meadow?"

I shrug. "She said she liked flowers and I offered to show her flowers. It was not my fault she leapt at me and kissed me right as her brother got there. She was forward, Rob. I'd been a perfect gentleman—"

Robbie rolls his eyes. "Gentlemen do not invite young ladies to meet them alone in fields, and well you know it. The mine towns are rough but the people are not without their rules of propriety."

I roll my eyes heavenward. "You have to stop reading those etiquette books. Try a novel or something."

"Calder." He chastens me with my own name. He'd have made an excellent parson or schoolmaster if he'd not grown the feet of a chicken. Strict, but wise.

"All right. I will try to do better," I say. "Slow, sensible friendship it shall be."

"Good," Robbie replies.

The path narrows and I let him walk ahead of me. Robbie is like my brother, but I don't tell him everything. If I were to confess my strong feelings for Sabella, he would argue that they're my "typical nonsense" and will burn out fast, but I know otherwise. This is no fleeting infatuation with someone I just met, but something abiding and real that has already endured the test of years. I have been with her, although unseen by her, on sunlit days and days wet with rain or thick with snow. I have seen her tears fall in torrents and I have listened to her sing softly, contentedly, as she roamed the mountainside. I have pressed my ear to the plank walls of her home and heard her father belittle her and her mother berate her. I have stood ready to rush in and rescue her from misery more than once. Only the threat of severe punishment has kept me from acting the hero. Well, that and my firm belief that she will one day join us of her own free will.

Robbie glances over his shoulder and says teasingly, "She is pretty, though. Do you think she fancied my fine set of legs when she caught sight of them?"

I shove him off the path. He stumbles into the brush but doesn't fall. "Shut it, Rob."

He chuckles and picks leaves off his shirtsleeve. "I will take that as a yes."

"I think she'd fancy your chicken legs cooked up in a stew."

He shoves me back and cries, "Last one home is a rotten raccoon carcass!"

And the race begins.

SABELLA

The basket Calder spoke of this morning calls to me like forbidden fruit whispering into the ear of the starving. It held me as an infant when the old woman handed me over to my father, and it now sits hidden, two floors above my head. I cast a glance at the boards of the ceiling, imagining the shape of the woven hamper.

It is mid-afternoon. Atop the cookstove, stew simmers in anticipation of the evening meal. Fresh bread cools on the table, scenting the air. Usually, I would indulge myself by sampling the warm heel of the bread, but today, I am too stirred up to eat. All I can think of is that basket.

Calder has not returned. With Father at work and Mother insensible in the chair beside the stove, no one would be the wiser were I to take a peek at the basket. It would take no time at all, for I know its exact location. All my life, it's been kept in a trunk in the far corner of the attic. When I was twelve years old, Father himself showed me the trunk to ensure that I would never unintentionally disturb it or the basket within. Every year since, on the anniversary of the day he received me, Father warns me anew not to meddle with the basket under any circumstances. He is set on edge by anything to do with magic, and after my "change," it seems he became convinced the basket was ensorcelled. It is a great wonder he has tolerated its presence—and mine—for so many years. Perhaps he fears casting either of us out could cause a worse calamity to fall upon his household than mere antlers.

I go upstairs and slide the ladder out from underneath my parents' bed. I place the ladder against the wall, directly under the hatch that allows access to the attic. I think of Calder Hadrian as I climb the wooden rungs. How did he come to know of the basket, and why did he ask me about it?

With one hand, I push the hatch up and open. My head and shoulders fit easily through the hole. Hazy light streams in through the single, square window at the end of the attic. Everything here is exactly as it was the last time I dared to visit. Beside a crooked wooden chair covered in lacy cobwebs sits the trunk. Gray dust, fine as pollen, coats its lid. Its metal fittings are red-brown with rust, and mice have nibbled the leather straps into tatters. I kneel beside it and work the latches. My heartbeat thuds with trepidation and unexpected excitement.

I should not tamper with the forbidden. I should return to the kitchen and peel potatoes like a good daughter. I *should*...but this time, I will not. Is not the basket mine as much as it is Father's? And what if it holds some clue as to my origin—a note from the woman who bore me, or some keepsake she wished me to possess?

What if opening it releases the magic to cure me of recurring antlers? A miracle like that would be worth almost any risk.

Still on my knees, I open the trunk. I have done this twice before, driven by curiosity or rebellion. On both occasions, mere seconds passed before I lost my nerve and shut it again.

Not today.

An unfamiliar scent rises up to tickle my nose. Dust and old wicker, as expected, but mingled with something sweet and strange.

A flat lid sits atop the rectangular basket. A leather loop and wooden pin hold it shut. It is the perfect size to hold a picnic, but barely large enough to contain an infant. Was I unusually small when my parents received me? Their narrative about that day has never ranged beyond a few facts: on his way home from work one night, Father met a ragged old woman seeking coal in exchange for a closed-lidded basket. Out of respect for her age and pity for her wretched state, he agreed to the transaction—only to discover an infant inside after her hasty departure. He ran home, dumbstruck with joy, to present Mother with her heart's greatest desire.

How happy they were.

For a time.

I touch the wicker with my fingertips. Nothing happens. No flash of light, no puff of smoke, no sparks. It is only a basket. A simple container for ordinary uses.

Never before have I taken the basket out of the trunk, but now I lift it upward, my fingers clenching its handles, finding it heavier than I expected. Something shifts within the woven walls. A tiny squeak warns me that a colony of mice has made this their home, but I am not afraid of mice.

I set the hamper on the floor beside me and throw open the lid.

Two blue eyes stare up at me from a tiny, round face.

I gasp and fall onto my backside.

"Sabella!" Mother shouts from the kitchen. "Where are you, child? The fire has almost gone out!"

"I'll be right there," I reply. Taking a deep breath, I get on my knees again and peer into the basket. A flannel-wrapped baby coos and waves its small, wrinkly fists. There is no clue to the child's gender in its countenance, even as its expression changes from delighted to distressed.

A high-pitched wail proceeds from its mouth, building in

volume like the shrill whistle that announces the end of the miners' shifts.

"No, no, no," I say. "Hush." If Mother hears...

Perhaps, if this is a magical basket, all I need to do is shut it. The baby can return to wherever magical babies come from, and I can return to housework and forget this happened. "Hush now, baby," I say soothingly, "Go back to where you came from. Please." I close the lid and slip the pin through the loop.

I pray and wish, beg and hope.

For a moment, silence fills the attic. I sigh. And then the earsplitting shrieking resumes.

"Sabella!" Mother yells. I can hardly hear her through the baby's screams. "What in the name of heaven is that noise?"

"No, no, no," I say. "This cannot be happening." Yet I know it is. This baby is one hundred percent real, and I am one hundred percent in trouble.

I open the basket and scoop up the infant. It stops crying and rubs its rounded cheek against my chest as if it thinks I'm its mother and source of nourishment.

"Was that a cat I heard, Sabella Jenkins?" Mother shouts. "Your father won't abide a cat in the house!"

"I wish it were a cat," I mumble.

What can I do? I cannot hide this child, nor can I let it suffer hunger. I know nothing of caring for babies. I have no choice but to present this little one to my mother.

My disobedience will cost me dearly, blast it. And curse that wretch Calder for tempting me to touch the basket in the first place. I'm half inclined to hunt him down and punch him. Or to present him with this child. But he'd surely dump the poor thing off at an orphanage, and I cannot stomach that thought. The tales I've heard of the county orphanage are too terrible to reflect upon.

I clutch the baby tightly and descend the ladder, praying my trembling knees won't give way and send us both crashing to the hard floor below.

The smell of scorching stew fills the air, but I make no move to attend to the pot I left on the stove. None of us have eaten supper, and it seems as though we never will. The instant Father stepped through the door, Mother assaulted him with tears and shrieks—and the news that we are now a family of four.

Calder has not yet returned, and I pray he does not. Unless he possesses the ability to turn back time, his presence could only make things worse.

The baby sleeps in a drawer of the corner cupboard and I stand watch, overcome with an inexplicable, otherworldly calmness. Have I passed through fear and into a state of numbness? My heartbeat throbs slowly, evenly. She holds my gaze like the sun holding a planet in orbit, without a word or visible display of power.

The child is a girl. This I discovered while rewrapping her swaddling after I brought her downstairs. She is perfectly formed, with ten tiny pink fingers and ten impossibly small toes. Her cheeks are rosy and her mouth puckers as if she dreams of suckling. Standing beside her, I feel like I am on trial. I suppose I am, in truth. I sinned by disobeying Father and opening the basket, and I will suffer the consequences he metes out in judgment.

Mother occupies a chair at the table, worrying a handkerchief in her lap, moaning and muttering. Father paces the floor like a caged lion. His thinning hair clings to the contours of his head and perspiration glues his grubby shirt to his chest and underarms. Streaks of coal dust give his face a monstrous quality—which befits his terrifying mood.

"They'll say it's hers," Mother says coldly. She drops the handkerchief onto the table in order to sip tea mixed with medicine. If the drink is half as bitter as the look on her face, she ought to pour it into the slop bucket. "They'll call her a whore and we'll all be tossed out of town. You know Davy Rees will not tolerate immorality among his miners' families."

"What, then, do you propose we do, woman?" Father's voice is the low growl of a riled beast. It makes my skin rise into goose pimples.

"Leave it in the mines," Mother replies, as if the idea of murdering a baby affects her no more than the price of figs in Rome.

Tears sting my eyes, but they are tokens of anger, not sorrow. "How can you suggest such a thing? Is that what you wish you'd done with me, Mother?"

She looks away and doesn't answer. Which hurts more than if she had simply agreed.

Father stops pacing. "If we leave the child where it will be found quickly, what harm would there be in it? Yes, I think you're right, wife. Billy Jones is watchman tonight. He sleeps on the job, which'll be a grand favor to us. The new vein's our best option. Men start there at five. The wee thing will hardly have a chance to get hungry before it's passed along to another family."

A sudden, protective love for the child expands to fill my chest. "We could keep her," I say. "We could say we found her, or adopted her from the orphanage. Why couldn't we keep her?"

The look Father gives me pierces like an iron nail. "I cannot fathom raising another child tainted by magic, as this one surely is. It's too much to bear thinking of, let alone doing."

"The mines it shall be," Mother declares. In spite of all her neglect and selfishness, I have never before hated her—but I hate her now.

Tears blind me as I lift the baby out of the drawer and carry her to my room. The room is only big enough for a narrow bed and a small dresser, but I would gladly share it with her. We could be sisters, best friends. My heart aches for such companionship.

But she cannot stay.

I lay her on the faded patchwork quilt and slide the flannel blanket off her head. Her ears look slightly pointed to me, but perhaps my estimation of them is tainted by suspicion. I feel the soft spot on top of her fuzzy skull, how it throbs lightly with her pulse, and then I let my fingers explore further, searching for any hint of antler nubs. Do I hope to find she is like me? Perhaps a little. It would be a comfort to have someone in the world who could truly understand my plight.

Her head is smooth. Faultless. She smiles in her sleep, and in this moment, I know that I would die for her.

This morning, I was only myself. Now I feel that I am so much more. Someone belongs to me, and I to her. It is a burden and a blessing, terrifying and enlivening.

I lie down beside the baby and watch her breathe in and out. Was her arrival part of my destiny as someone drawn out of the basket? How many children have come out of that ordinary-looking hamper?

Impossibly, mercifully, my eyes drift shut. I sleep without dreaming. The baby's whimper startles me awake. I find my father standing over us with the look of a harried judge resigned to hanging a habitual criminal. "It's time," he says sternly.

With no other plan, I decide to accompany him to the mine. I will pretend to be in accord with his decision. To try to fight him would be folly, for he could wrench her away from me with barely any effort. I am no match for muscles built by long shifts spent hacking at solid rock. The best I can do for this baby now is to keep her close to me.

"I will carry her, Father," I say in a meek voice.

"Suit yourself. But don't forget to cover your head. Almighty, those blasted antlers grow fast at night. Hurry now. I'll wait by the door."

"Hush, baby," I say as I wrap her in my best shawl. That done, I reach up to touch my head. Father was right. Midnight has come and gone, and my antlers are spikes, inches long and budding with points. I wrap my head with a thick, woolen scarf, and cover that with my largest bonnet. I tie a shawl over the bonnet to hold it firmly in place. Next, I tear a wide strip off an old sheet to make a sling for the baby. When I slide her into it, her body curls against mine, warm and trusting. I wrap my heavy cloak around us both, and on slow and solemn feet, I go to meet my father.

My mind whirls as I try to construct a plan. Every idea falls flat. I have no money, no relatives or friends who might offer aid, and it is the brutal middle of winter. But one thing is certain: I will not be leaving this baby alone beneath the cold, black earth tonight, no matter what Father says.

CALDER

I cannot sleep for worrying, and who wants to stay up all night alone? But it isn't just that. In my bones, there's a feeling of wrongness. A strange tightness sits in my chest and shortens my breath. It all started after one of the most vivid dreams I've ever had.

I cross the hall and let myself into Robbie's bedroom. A pair of his cast off trousers tangles around my feet and I almost trip onto his bed.

"Robbie," I whisper, gripping him by his bony shoulder and giving him a firm shake. He grunts and swats at my hand, but I hold tighter and shake harder. "Wake up. Something isn't right."

His eyes flutter open. In the dark, they look solid black, like the eyes of an animal. "What?"

"Get up. We're going to check on Sabella."

"Ugh. Are you joking? It's the middle of the night." He pulls his blankets up to cover his head. I yank them down again.

"Get up anyway."

He mumbles something impolite, pounds a fist on the mattress, and sits up. "I'm only getting up because I know you'll pester me until I die otherwise."

"Correct." I pick up his trousers and toss them onto his blanket-covered legs. "Get dressed. I'll be waiting in the kitchen."

Ten minutes later, we're stumbling through the woods by lantern light. There's neither conversation nor complaining. We both know it's best to move through the trees as quietly as possible in the hours between dusk and dawn. We've had our share of nocturnal adventures, Rob and I. But I'm not reminiscing about the good times now. My current thoughts are fixed on a certain girl who grows antlers, and a dream I had of her during my brief stint of sleep earlier.

In the dream, I saw her hiding in a mine tunnel with a tiny baby clutched to her chest. The remembered image sends a mighty shiver through me. If my dream is true—and my dreams often are —things have gone from bad to catastrophic. It would mean she tampered with the blasted basket.

Which, of course, would be my fault.

Robbie breathes hard behind me. I hadn't realized how fast I was walking or that I've also started to pant. We can't rest now, though. I hold the lantern high as the ground slopes downward. Gravity helps us descend the rocky hillside. The trees grow sparse in this area near the mine, thinned mercilessly by the company's axes and saws.

A glimpse of movement stops me in my tracks. Robbie skids and collides with my back. As he rights himself, I squint into the distance. Two figures creep toward the fence that encloses the newest part of the mine: one is broad-shouldered and stocky, and the other is smaller and cloaked in black. I have no doubt these silhouettes are Sabella's father and Sabella herself.

Instinct commands me to be still and wait, but my heart urges me to run and whisk Sabella to safety. This time, I disobey my heart. Robbie sets a hand on my shoulder in a gesture of support. I glance at his face, and he nods to acknowledge that it's right that we came, and right to bide our time here.

My body buzzes as if it's stuffed with a thousand frantic bees, but I stand frozen on the hillside as the two figures slink through the gate and hurry toward the black maw of the mine.

SABELLA

My father, dimly illuminated by cold moonlight, stops walking and holds up a hand to signal me to stop as well. He stands on tiptoe to peer through a knothole in the fence that encloses Rees Anthracite's Number Four mine. The baby does not stir inside the sling as I wait, in spite of my vigorous shivering. I want to be motionless, but fear and winter will not allow for it.

The smallest sound of gravel shifting pulls my attention to the left.

Two shadowy forms crouch on the rocky hillside, silhouettes I recognize as Calder and his bird-legged friend. They are still as statues—until Calder nods in my direction. There is no time for me to question the boys' presence because Father has swung open the gate and yanks my arm. I trail him as we pass the seated, slumped, and snoring watchman.

Moonlight glances off the cautionary sign marking the mouth

of the new seam. Father reaches for the baby. "Give it here now, girl. I'll take it down."

"No. I'm going with you," I insist, tightening my hold on the child.

"You will not. It isn't safe." Father glowers at me like a cruel dictator dealing with a troublesome peasant. I've seen this look before. There will be painful consequences if I rile him further, but I cannot hold my tongue.

"And yet you would leave a helpless infant there?"

His open hand smacks my cheek quick and hard. My skin burns. Shock steals my breath for a moment. I say nothing but stand up straighter, imagining myself as stately and strong as the buck I watched beside the stream last month.

"Give me the child now," Father demands.

I shake my head and step backward. My arms wrap around the sling, forming a protective barrier between Father and the baby. "I will carry her."

"Hey!" a deep voice echoes through the site. I look toward the sound but cannot see its source. The man adds, "The sign over there says 'Trespassers will be shot.' Do you not believe in signs, sir?"

"I work here," Father blurts. "Forgot something and came back for it. I'll be off home now."

A crack of gunfire makes Father jump. He takes off running. For a moment, fear paralyzes me. Then, hearing footsteps approach, I duck into the hole carved into the hillside, the mine's dark mouth. The baby wriggles against me and I feel sick, so sick. If she cries, I'll be caught for certain. Taken into custody by the guards and dragged before the mine boss. My antlers will finally lead to my doom—and the baby's, too, if they think her my devilish spawn.

I slink along the rock-walled corridor that leads to the depths of the mine. After a few yards, a darkness thick as tar surrounds me. Without a lantern, I cannot risk venturing any deeper. I crouch against the jagged wall and stroke the baby's rounded back beneath my cloak. Silently, I pray for two miracles: first, that the watchman will feel more inclined to return to his nap than to spend time searching for trespassers, and second, that the baby will stay silent.

The glow of a lantern, a halo of pale golden light, moves toward us. I huddle down, arching my body over the baby, hoping my dark cloak will conceal us.

"I believe in signs," Calder's voice says. "And I'm good at imitating guards and shotgun fire."

I lift my head. He's standing in front of me, holding a small metal lantern aloft. Warm light skims over his face. As usual, he looks pleased with himself. This time, I cannot fault him for it.

"Come with me," he says. Since the guard or Father might appear at any moment, I nod in acquiescence. He offers his hand, and I allow him to help me to my feet.

We keep silent until we're well away from the coal yards. Calder leads me by the hand along the outskirts of town and into the woods—my woods. My other hand supports the baby in the sling. In the scant light of the moon and Calder's little lantern, the familiar trees look like the enchanted trees of a fairy story. The scent of pines and hemlocks soothes my pattering heart. Calder's firm grip makes me feel safer than I have felt in ages—which is an odd thing, considering how deeply I doubt his trustworthiness.

It doesn't matter at the moment if I trust him, for I must do whatever it takes to protect the baby. "Where are we going?" I ask. "And where is your companion?"

"Robbie will appear imminently," he says as we round a boulder. "As for our destination, I daresay we're going home."

I glance sidelong at him as we continue to walk. He's smiling as if he has a hundred brilliant secrets to share—and no intention of giving them away for free.

The baby whines and stretches against the boundaries of the sling, and Calder scrutinizes the odd shape of my cloak.

"Either you've been eating exceptionally well, or you've been up to something," he says wryly. My hackles rise. I yank my hand out of his.

"This is your fault," I snap. "All of this trouble we're in."

"My fault?"

"Do not pretend you knew nothing of this baby. You tempted me with your talk of the basket. I think you knew what would come of opening it."

"On my honor, I did not know the basket would give you a child. I never—"

"What's this? Quarreling, on such a fine, starlit night?" an unfamiliar voice says. I look up to see the dark outline of someone standing on an outcropping of rock. He drops to the ground beside me, landing squarely upon his bird feet, and performs a courtly bow. "Your servant, Robin Hallsey."

"Enough of the dramatics, Robbie," Calder says, walking away. "We mustn't linger here."

"Of course," Robbie says. He and I fall into step, side by side. From a distance, his thin frame and short stature had led me to think he was a lad of no more than twelve. Now I see he is older, fifteen or sixteen perhaps. It is hard to pinpoint his heritage as he is veiled in shadow, but I would guess one of his parents hailed from a Far Eastern land. If he has parents. Perhaps bird-legged boys also spill out of baskets. *Was* he found in a basket, as I was? I want to ask him, but it seems a rude thing to ask a stranger. Besides, I can hardly think straight after all that's happened in the last twenty-four hours.

"You are Sabella," Robbie says, holding a pine branch out of the way to allow me passage. "Calder's told me a lot about you."

I duck through. "Your friend is quite good at talking."

Robbie laughs. "That he is."

I stumble and grab a tree to right myself. The baby wriggles and whimpers, so I extract her from the sling and hold her against my shoulder. "Hush now," I whisper.

"Ah, the baby," Robbie says with delight. "The wee miracle. I overheard you and your father talking before you went into the mine. My ears are that good. Could I carry her? I promise not to drop her. Babies are fond of me. I have a way with them, I've been told."

Now that he has offered to help, I realize that my neck and shoulders pulse with pain from hours of wearing the makeshift sling. I swear the child has gained weight since I bound her to me back at home. "Well…"

Robbie clasps his hands as if in prayer. "Please?"

Something in his earnest face convinces me to trust him. I stop, and Robbie stops. Calder looks over his shoulder, groans with annoyance, and then halts as well. He waits for us, lantern raised, impatience written large on his face.

The baby cries as I pass her to Robbie, but stops when he kisses her forehead. He cradles her—and she fills his arms. She has definitely grown since the evening began. Wonders never cease—not even when you wish they would.

"We cannot keep stopping," Calder says. "Someone might see us." He leads the way across a meadow carpeted by patchy snow and dead leaves, and then into woods.

Beside me, Robbie whistles softly to the baby, trilling like an especially musical bird. She giggles and coos in reply.

My body warms as we walk, in spite of the coldness of the air. We journey farther west than I have ever ventured. Although the path we tread is new to me, it seems well traveled. There are footprints and talon prints, and someone has cleared away fallen branches. We walk and we walk, between boulders, over streams.

Now and then, I catch sight of the moon through the treetops. It inches through the heavens as if it has no reason to hurry, not a care in the universe. Calder continues to lead with confident strides. My flesh and my spirit are weary and worn. Again and again, I stumble over roots, sticks, and my own feet.

The journey grows foggy around the edges, like a dream.

When I awaken, will I regret leaving Mother? Who will care for her in my absence? I glance at the baby in Robbie's arms and remember that Mother made me leave as much as Father did. The child is helpless and blameless; I did what was right—for the baby and for me. Still, a dull ache pools in my chest. Homesickness for a place I ought not to miss.

After a while, as dawn begins to coax color into the woods, Robbie announces, "Her name is Sparrow."

I open my mouth to ask him why he's chosen this name, but what I see over Calder's shoulder renders me speechless. In the middle of this wilderness, almost blending into its surroundings, there stands a high stone wall set with a thick-looking, weather-stained, wooden door.

Calder pulls a skeleton key from his jacket pocket and inserts it in the keyhole. He pushes the door open, then wraps an arm around my shoulders. His touch drives the chill from my bones like he is the sun itself. I ought to scold him for being so familiar, but I am too tired and too flustered for speeches. Intertwined with my embarrassment, there is something I have never felt before and do not wish to feel now: a flutter of attraction.

Clearly oblivious to my discomfiture, he grins and says, "Welcome home, Sabella."

SABELLA

Within the stone walls, early morning sunlight washes over two boxy wooden houses, a small barn, and several sheds. The buildings are old, but in good repair. I imagine some family lived here long ago, staking their claim on a few acres of this Pennsylvania mountainside.

Snow has been swept off the pathway that leads to the smallest, one-story, clapboard-sided house. Slate gray smoke puffs out of the house's stone chimney. Calder leads us to the door then excuses himself, leaving me in Robbie's care.

Sparrow naps in the crook of Robbie's arm. "Told you babies like me," he says proudly, his deep brown eyes glinting. He shifts the baby so that her head rests against his shoulder before he shoves open the door. Warm, pleasant air rushes over me. The faint aroma of bread makes my stomach rumble. An oil lamp burns low in the center of a square, age-scarred table, and a cheerful fire dances in the stone fireplace.

Robbie gives me the baby and turns up the lamp. He pulls out a chair and invites me to sit, for which my spent legs and I are grateful. I watch him skitter, birdlike, about the room. He grabs a teapot from a shelf and sprinkles a handful of dried leaves into it before scampering to the hearth to fill the pot with hot water from a blackened kettle. "You'll love my mint tea. Everyone here does."

"If it's warm, I will love it," I say. In a clumsy attempt to shed my cloak, I awaken the baby in my arms. Rather than crying, she gnaws her chubby fist and stares up at me adoringly. The implausibility of the moment makes breathing difficult, as if my lungs have filled with water. Everything catches up with me at once, a churning flood of emotions and questions. I feel safe with Robbie, but am I? How in the name of heaven did I end up welcome in this snug, secluded house with an infant in my charge, when two days ago I was nothing more than my parents' shame and servant—resigned to a life of loneliness? I fight the urge to weep by biting hard on my lower lip.

With his back to me, Robbie slathers jam on two slices of bread. "Of course you're wondering about the bird legs, but too polite to make inquiries," he says. "So I'll just tell you now and get that business out of the way. What I've been told is that there's something in a spring of water not far from here that did it, a bit of magic left over from wilder days. The very same magic gave you your particular gift. It's an unsatisfactory answer, I reckon, but it's all I know."

"And are there others? More people...like us?"

Now he pours water from the kettle into a brown teapot. "There are indeed," he says. "I'll make introductions later today if you'd like. But first, you must have a bit of nourishment and a good sleep. You look as if you've been dragged backwards through a mouse's keyhole."

I cannot help but smile at Robbie's odd turn of phrase. There is something genuine and wholesome about him that calms me like a cup of chamomile. "That is exactly how I feel," I say.

Robbie scurries back and forth, delivering the bread, two mugs, and then the teapot to the table. Finally, he slides into the chair across from me. "You're welcome to remove your head covering, you know. It's plenty warm in here and I reckon you'd be more comfortable without all the wrappings. I have the legs of a songbird; I won't be repulsed by whatever you're hiding there. On my honor, I won't."

My hesitation lasts only a moment. During our overnight trek, I was forced to remove my bonnet as my antlers outgrew its bounds. As they spread up and out, they forced the scarf under the bonnet to form a strange kind of angular hat. When I reach up, I find places where they've poked through. The baby holds perfectly still on my lap as, with one hand, I work to unwind the pierced cloth.

When at last I yank it free, the scarf is all but shredded. I drop it onto the empty chair beside me. No one outside my family has ever seen my antlers. I lower my gaze in embarrassment. Nonsensically. For if anyone can understand my affliction, it is this young man.

"Ah. They're glorious," Robbie says. "Astonishing."

I look up. His smile is sincere. All I can say is, "Thank you." Never would I have imagined that anyone would appreciate the sight of my antlers. A single tear leaks from my eye, but I brush it away quickly.

If Robbie notices, he doesn't mention it. He passes me a spoon and plate and says, "By Jove, if I had antlers like yours, I'd wear them proudly. I'd invite a whole flock of hummingbirds to perch on them, that's what I'd do." He pours tea into a mug and slides it toward me. "You're ashamed of them, aren't you? That's an outright tragedy. Good thing you're with us now. People who appreciate lovely things such as what you've got there. Believe me, I know what it's like to—"

The door flies open. Calder enters, accompanied by a blast of cold air and a very fat gray and white nanny goat. "I've secured breakfast for the wee nipper," he says. "And all her meals for the foreseeable future, if Sweet Pea is agreeable to it."

Robbie scowls. "No goats in the house, Cald. You know the rules."

"Yes, yes. Just give me a chance to milk her and then I'll return her to the blinking cold shed."

"You could have milked her *in* the shed," Robbie says.

Calder shrugs. "The shed stinks. The twins must have forgotten to clean it yesterday. Anyway, see how much little Sparrow likes her?"

The baby giggles and waves drool-covered fingers at the animal.

"You are impossible," Robbie says, rolling his eyes.

"As are you, oh bird-legged one. The same could be said of our new, antlered friend and her fairy-eared babe." He eyes my antlers, his face full of wonder. "Sabella. How lovely! You really ought to do us all a favor and burn everything you ever used to cover them."

This second, fervent compliment leaves me staring at the teapot, mouth agape like a beached fish's.

Robbie stands, grabs a pail from a hook on the wall, and shoves it into Calder's arms. "Hurry and do the milking before the goat fouls the floor. Save the flirting for later."

Calder scratches the goat between the ears and looks her in the eye. "Bear with me, Sweet Pea. It's been a month of Sundays since I last drew milking duty, so I may be out of practice."

Soon, the rhythmic sound of milk squirting into a pail echoes through the room, adding one more peculiarity to the morning. But this does not hinder me from wolfing down all the bread and tea Robbie offers.

The knock at the door startles the goat—and the rest of us. Robbie leaps to his feet and rushes across the room to admit the caller.

A girl steps in and shoves back the hood of her green cape to reveal a profusion of long, copper-red curls. Her face is heavily freckled, her eyes a deeper green than her cape. She is fourteen years old at most. In her wake, a black bear cub ambles into the room and shakes snowflakes from its coat. A few days ago, such a sight would have shocked me almost senseless. I am beginning to think I should expect such things.

"What is it now, Cleona?" Calder asks from the far side of Sweet Pea. "Out of honey again?"

"I'm Branna. The bear is Cleona," the girl replies with a faint hint of an Irish accent. "And I didn't come here to bandy words with you, Calder. I've a message from Yonaz."

Calder stands and wipes his palms on his thighs. "What is it, then?"

Branna takes a folded piece of pale brown paper from inside her cloak and delivers it into his hand. "Read it yourself. 'Tis not my business, is it?" Her face breaks into a warm smile as she notices Sparrow and me. "You're the new ones? What fine antlers! And such a beautiful baby," she says. She bends over Sparrow to admire her further and the baby wriggles and coos. "Ah, look at her precious wee pointed ears. Touched by the fairies, she is."

"There are no true fairy folk on this continent," Robbie says, chin lifted.

"You think you know everything, bird legs," Branna replies, looking down her pert nose at him. "But you're wrong."

Calder stuffs the note into his jacket pocket. "Enough bickering. Tell Yonaz I'll meet him at the barn this afternoon, Branna."

"That I'll do," Branna says. She turns her attention to Sparrow again, fussing over the baby until the bear pokes her with its snout. "Yes, I know, sister. Time to go home and get the bread into the oven."

Branna bids us farewell and volunteers to return Sweet Pea to the shed. The bear cub hurries after her, and Robbie secures the door before turning to me. "Give me Sparrow," he says. "I'll change her and get breakfast into her belly." He lifts the baby from my lap. She smiles. "Da," she says. "Da da."

"That's a clever girl," Robbie says, bouncing her on his hip. "Smart as a dappled mare in a silk ball gown, aren't you now?"

I know almost nothing about babies, but I do not believe an infant less than a week old should be calling anyone "Da." Not to mention the size of her. How has she grown from a meager armful to this overnight? She must weigh nearly fifteen pounds.

Also, did Branna just imply that the bear is her *sister*? My head feels about to burst. Before I can ask Calder about the girl and the bear, he slips an arm through mine and shepherds me into an adjoining room. The warm ease I felt in Robbie's presence earlier is rolled aside by an icy tide of anxiety.

"We need to talk," he says.

The parlor is ten feet square at most, its walls painted spruce green and stamped with red and white flowers. A small, charcoal gray sofa, a round black table, and a wall of bookshelves all but consume the space. "Care to sit?" Calder asks.

"Did the note have something to do with me?" I perch on the edge of the sofa.

"Indirectly." Calder drops onto the sofa as if there is enough room for two—which there is not, unless the two persons are children under the age of five. The cushions sink and his shoulder collides with mine. "Cozy, isn't it?" he says, clearly enjoying the forced closeness. He smells like the woods and the goat.

I try to inch away but the slant of the cushion won't permit it. "A little too cozy, perhaps. Should I call for Robbie to play chaperone?"

"I swear to heaven I shall behave with decorum," he says. "Or is it yourself you don't trust?"

"Very amusing. Please say what you must so I can return to Sparrow. Or we could have this conversation in the kitchen."

"You're wound tighter than the bishop's pocket watch, Sabella. Why do you expect the worst of me?"

"Of course I'm wound up. And why should I expect the best

of you? You show up at my door, full of mysteries, and a few days later, I have a baby and I've run away from home. My life is turmoil."

"Or you've been part of a series of miracles. It's all in how you look at it." He pauses and folds his hands in his lap. There's a thoughtful look on his face as he says, "Think of it. You're free of the household drudgery now; you've gained friends. Tell me, were you happy there, locked up in forced, thankless servitude? What did you do to deserve such a sentence?"

Our eyes meet. "I thought you might know, since you're acquainted with bird-footed boys and girls with bears for sisters."

"The answer is you did nothing wrong. You were touched with magic as a baby and blessed to grow magnificent antlers. If regular folk refuse to accept them, they are the poorer for it."

I rest a palm on my forehead, trying to soothe the ache within. "I still don't understand."

"Do you have to understand everything?"

"Ugh. Do you have to be so...so perplexing?"

As if to vex me further, he smiles and bumps his shoulder against mine. "I think you like my perplexingness." Never did I imagine a person could be so charming and so exasperating at the same time.

"That is not a word, and no, I do not." I bite my lip and try not to smile. I do not want to be amused by his antics, but my self-control has worn thin and I have always been apt to giggle when exhausted.

"Much as I am enjoying this conversation, I must alter its course, and probably perplex you more."

"Must you?" I slump against the back of the sofa.

"I must. Because you're going to have to decide if you want to stay with us, return to your parents, or find another way in the world. To make that choice, you need to know a few things."

"I'm listening."

"To begin with, Delphine is our matriarch and Yonaz is her partner. Delphine has been away for a while, but you'll meet Yonaz today. He's always in charge of us when she's gone."

"Us?"

"We're called the Springborn. I don't know all the details, no one does, but I do know we were all dipped in a magical spring by an unknown benefactor and given gifts: Robbie's bird legs, the twins' ability to take animal form, your antlers. Each one of us was then given to childless parents in a basket. Sometimes Delphine is the one who presents the basket; sometimes it just appears to a couple. As far as I know, the chosen parents all live on this mountain or in the valley beside it."

"These parents never want the children when their...differentness becomes evident?"

"Sadly, they rarely do. That's why sometimes when Yonaz or Delphine hear of a spring-gifted child, one of us is assigned to watch over them. If the child is cast out or endangered, we rescue them. Make them part of our family for as long as they want to stay."

"Someone has been watching me," I mumble. I remember the black-clad man in the woods and a shiver passes through me.

Calder's cheeks turn pink and he directs his gaze to the floor. "To be precise, *I've* been watching you, at Yonaz's request."

I stand and glare at him. My blood goes cold and then hot. Everything he's told me has been disturbing, but this is the last straw. "You watched me in the woods? You were the man in the black clothes?"

Calder nods. "See. I knew you would be upset. That's why I decided to tell you now, up front. It was to keep you safe, I swear. I never meant to scare you or to encroach upon your privacy."

My feet carry me across the room and back. "You watched me," I say again. I am stunned. Angry. Confused. I want to go home, but remember that there is no such place for me anymore.

From the other room drifts laughter, Sparrow's and Robbie's. I eye the door, considering fleeing both this conversation and Calder.

"I swear, Sabella, I meant no harm. Nothing untoward. Would it help if I begged your forgiveness? I will. I do." He slides off the sofa and onto his knees. He peers up at me with hands folded as if in prayer. "I beg your forgiveness, most humbly."

I take a step backward and collide with the bookcase. "Get up. Please."

"All right." He gets up and runs his fingers through his hopelessly messy hair. "I am sorry, though. You have to believe me."

"I—"

Someone pounds upon the kitchen door as if they mean to demolish it. "Hold onto your horses," I hear Robbie say. The door squeaks on its hinges. A draft blows into the parlor.

Now Robbie says, "Yonaz. A pleasure to see you. Come in. Warm yourself by the fire."

"No time for that." Yonaz's thick accent reminds me of Mr. Cazacu, the company storekeeper who hails from Moldavia. "We go now."

"Now?" Robbie repeats.

Calder rushes into the kitchen. I follow at his heels.

"What's wrong?" Calder asks.

"So many things, I fear," Yonaz says. His gaze falls first on my face and then rises to assess my antlers. I take in the sight of him as well. He is an average-sized man dressed in a white shirt, red frock coat, and matching black trousers. His dark hair is slicked back. Heavy black brows arch above blue eyes smudged with kohl. Beneath his hawkish nose, a mustache forms curling commas. His earlobes sag with the weight of silver hoops, and a detailed tattoo of a bat with outstretched wings encircles his throat. On each of his fingers he wears a different silver ring, some plain, some jeweled.

No one in Miners Ridge looks half as fantastical. No one would dare.

He strides toward me, his gait as smooth as a cat's. "Miss Sabella Jenkins," he says with a bow. "Welcome. I am Yonaz. I regret that we have no time for further formalities. We must pack up and leave this place without delay."

"Why?" Robbie's face pales. Sparrow wriggles in his arms and whines, as if she senses his distress.

"The townsfolk have been alerted to our presence. It is no longer safe for us here. They will come, and if they see what we are, they will name us as works of the devil. And these simple mountain folk get rid of their devils in one way: with fire."

I believe him.

All my life, I have been warned that if ever a witch were discovered in our town, she would be burned. Anything resembling sorcery will neither be tolerated nor forgiven anywhere on this mountain. I touch my antlers, suddenly aware of their slight but sure weight. A memory pushes to the front of my mind from the year before my antlers grew, when I was ten years old: in the middle of the main street, a bonfire with leaping flames, men tossing books, papers, jars, and bundled herbs into it—articles belonging to the town midwife. What became of her, I do not know for certain. But I never saw her again after that day.

Robbie curses, then apologizes. "Someone must have followed us."

"But we were so careful," Calder says, shaking his head.

"I lay no fault at your feet, my boys," Yonaz says. He turns to me. "I am sorry, but I must ask you now: Miss Sabella, do you wish to come with us, or would you choose to return to the Jenkins house?"

"The baby," I say. My first thought is of her. My legs feel weak as twigs. Calder takes hold of my arm as if he knows I might fall, and I make no objection. "My parents won't allow me to...they do not want her."

Yonaz answers gravely, "The child is yours, to keep or to give into our care. It is a weighty decision, but one that cannot be postponed. Boys, hurry and pack only what you need. Blankets, clothes, food. Essential things only. We must load the wagons and leave within the hour."

"But..." The rest of the sentence eludes me.

Gently, the tattooed man enfolds my hands with his. His many silver rings chill my skin. "I do not wish to cause you alarm, but I would be remiss if I did not warn you. Whoever followed you here might have recognized you. To go back to town would imperil you, the child, and your parents. But be assured, no one is more prepared to protect you than we are."

I nod, utterly dazed. Is this a dream? How could any of this be real?

Yonaz squeezes my hands before releasing them and taking a step back. "You must decide your fate, and the babe's, trusting your heart to guide you."

Calder's arm wraps around my shoulders. He guides me to a chair as Yonaz sweeps out of the house like a mustachioed whirlwind. "Can't have you fainting now," Calder says. He presses a mug into my grasp. "Take a deep breath and drink that to the dregs."

"I don't think I can do this." My hands tremble around the mug. The room sways.

But then I glance over at Sparrow. She smiles and waves both chubby fists at me, almost bouncing her way out of Robbie's thin arms. She is beckoning me.

She wants me.

And I want her.

That is my answer. I could not be a good enough daughter once I grew antlers, but antlers cannot stop me from being a good mother to this child. Even if no one saw us with Robbie and Calder, and my parents allowed Sparrow and me to rejoin the family, our lives in Miners Ridge would be isolated, bleak, and fraught with misery. For myself, I could endure it, but Sparrow deserves better. She is new and innocent. She should be brought up among people who will cherish her. And I suspect these people, the Springborn, will do so. It seems I must at least give them a chance.

I finish the tea and set the mug on the table. "We will go with you," I say. The words feel like a vow taken rashly.

Calder smiles as if he's won the world's biggest prize. I swear his face glows.

"For the love of Saint Peter," Robbie grumbles from the fireside. "If you could stop mooning over the girl for five minutes, we have work to do, Calder. It's an emergency we're having here."

"The packing, yes," Calder says, his smile undiminished.

Robbie brings Sparrow to me. The shape of her in my arms, her weight, her milky sweetness—all of these things feel *right*, no matter that the future is uncertain. She yanks my hair and drools on my shoulder—and I fall in love with her all over again.

Calder dumps a wooden crate of kindling onto the floor and sets the empty box on the table. "Could you put any food you find in this, Sabella? Robbie and I will pack up what's in the bedroom."

"Of course."

"You're a dear," Calder says. Half a second later, he blushes at the double entendre. Even his ears turn rosy. "I mean, not the animal deer, but that you're a fine person. A good help? So, anyway, thank you." Still pink-cheeked, he follows Robbie into another room and leaves me to my task.

This flustered, uncertain version of Calder charms me more than the cheeky new boarder, more than the goat-milking jokester, more than the boy who showed up to rescue me from the darkness of the mine. If I could afford such an extravagance, this is the kind of boy I could someday fall in love with like a girl in a story, head over heels and happily-ever-after.

But falling in love is not for me. I have been made Sparrow's mother, and everything I am and have must belong to her—and only to her.

Robbie and Calder lug a trunk past me and drop it with a thud by the door. Both boys grin in my direction before returning to the bedroom. One would think they'd never seen a young lady before. Mother always said I could never hope to be more than passably pretty, but perhaps the crown of antlers I wear today lends me allure.

From the other room, I hear Robbie's voice. "Sure is nice to have Sabella's lovely face to look at instead of just your hideousness, Calder."

A loud thump, a scuffle, and a duet of laughter ensue. They are terribly jovial considering that they're being driven from their home.

I hold Sparrow closer and thank heaven she is a girl, for I do not understand boys at all.

Indeed, I find I do not understand much of anything.

What possessed me to agree to accompany a band of strangers to an unknown destination? How did the parents I loved, parents who once desperately longed for a baby, become people who would abandon an infant in a coal mine? And who in the universe decided I should be a mother?

Sparrow sneezes. One look into her small face and my misgivings fly away like frightened blackbirds. In my heart of hearts, I know I have made the right choice.

Box in arms, Robbie returns to the kitchen and offers me a sympathetic half-smile. "You look worried," he says. "But everything's going to be fine. I'm a bit of a pessimist, so I won't promise life will be all sunny days and cherry pie, mind you. But we'll see you and the little one through the worst of it. You can count on Robbie Hallsey, come flood, fire, or famine."

"Thank you." I slip Sparrow back into the sling I used to carry her into the mine. With her body held securely against me, I fill the kindling box with cheese, apples, bread, dried sausages, and a sack of raisins. So little food will not feed us long, if the journey is a lengthy one.

The door flies open, and Branna sticks her head into the

kitchen. "Hurry up, you sluggards! Yonaz has the horses harnessed."

"Can't hurry any faster!" Calder shouts from the bedroom.

"Well, try!" Branna replies. She notices the crate of food and comes to take it. "I don't have a good feeling about any of this," she mutters as she heads outside.

CALDER

Never in all my days did I imagine that being threatened with annihilation would make me happy. But as I pack boxes and load the wagon, I can hardly keep from singing aloud. I must remind myself not to grin and cause Sabella to think I am some sort of madman. Truth be told, I do not care much for moving to parts unknown. What delights me is the fact that Sabella is going with us. She has chosen us, as is right and good.

I try not to stare at her as I carry yet another box from the bedroom to the front door, but good glory, she is something to behold. The look on her face as she whispers to little Sparrow is so tender and loving, so divine, that anyone would believe the babe to be her own flesh and blood. The antlers her father despises are a silvery-gray crown upon her head. In the dancing firelight, they look like the gift they are.

"Calder," Robbie scolds from behind me. "A snail could beat you in a footrace."

"I'm going." How he still has such vigor after all this hard labor and being awake half the night, I do not know.

Once outside, we pass our boxes up to Yonaz, who crouches

under the bowed canvas roof of the wagon. Behind him, our belongings are stacked and piled. It is odd to see our lives shoved into so small a space, but also the picture of how we Springborn exist: keeping to our own little corner of the world where we do not offend the regular folk with our outrageous attributes.

When I was younger, I railed against the narrow-mindedness of the society we live outside of. Yonaz taught me that they were the poorer for not knowing us. That we are more blessed than they're capable of imagining. His words ring more true to me now than ever. If I were the king of this land, I could want for nothing more than my Springborn family—provided that Sabella were my queen.

"Mooning," Robbie mutters as we head back into the house. "You'll scare her off if you don't calm down. She could still go back to her parents, you know."

"Heaven forbid." I offer him a feigned frown. "Better?"

"No, you look more insane than before. Stop that. There's no hope for you, is there?"

"All I am is hope at the moment," I say.

"All you are is ridiculous," Robbie counters. He holds the door open and I slip past him into the warm kitchen.

I will miss this place, its comfortable chairs and use-scarred table, its pretty stone hearth, and the faint scent of bacon that always lingers here. I try to commit the scene to memory— including the antlered girl who's standing by the dying fire now, yawning and bouncing lightly to soothe the baby in her arms.

And I think she could be home to me for the rest of my days— if I don't mess this up and she's willing.

SABELLA

FEBRUARY 15, 1886
LATE IN THE AFTERNOON

Sparrow slumbers in the sling inside my cloak. With my back resting against the outside wall of Robbie and Calder's house, I watch them heft a huge trunk onto the back of one of two canvas-covered farm wagons. A few snowflakes escape the darkening sky and drift earthward. Less than an hour of daylight remains, in my estimation. I pray our safe haven lies nearby, and that it features a huge fireplace and a vat of hot tea.

"Sabella can ride with us," red-haired Branna says as she and Yonaz approach me. The plump brown owl perched on Branna's shoulder opens its beak and thrusts out its pointy tongue.

Yonaz shakes his head. "Alas, dear twins, in our haste to pack, I regret that we left no place for her to sit inside where her antlers would not endanger the canvas. She must ride beside Calder as he drives. I do hope this is agreeable to you, Miss Sabella?"

The truth is I would prefer to ride inside—protected a bit from the weather and the awkwardness I will undoubtedly feel seated close to Calder. I have yet to make peace with the idea that he has been secretly watching me—never mind that rationally, and in light of what's just happened, I understand that it was necessary for my safety. But Yonaz is right; my antlers forestall my traveling inside the covered wagon. I probably should have asked someone to bring a saw. I swallow my regret and say, "Yes. But the baby might fare better inside."

"Uncle Robbie will look after the little Sparrow," Robbie says. "I'll keep her warm as toast. I promise. The goat will be with us, too, so she'll not go hungry."

Calder joins us as I part the front of my cloak and lift Sparrow out of the sling. She giggles when I kiss her soft forehead, then shrieks with joy as Robbie scoops her into his arms. He strides away, singing to her, and a pang of sadness pierces my chest. I miss her already.

"Good. That is settled nicely, no?" Yonaz jams a furry, round hat onto his head and climbs onto his seat. His wagon's horses step in place, eager to begin the journey. "I shall take the lead," he says. "You follow close, Calder."

"I will," Calder replies. "Give me just a moment." He checks the straps and buckles of the horses at the front of the second wagon once more, humming to himself. I know almost nothing of horses, but these horses look larger and stronger than any I've seen before.

While Calder works, I lift the shawl from my shoulders and attempt to cover my antlers. The fabric catches on a point, and my tugging only makes the snagging worse. I don't notice Calder standing near me until he says, "Here. Allow me." He gently frees the shawl from the antler's sharp tip. With a flick of his wrists, he balloons the fabric and lets it settle over both antlers. His warm fingertips brush my skin as he knots the shawl's ends at the base of my throat. His eyes meet mine. The combination of his brief touch and his intense gaze make me forget how to breathe. I could kick myself for such girlish silliness.

"Done," he says, scowling as if he's just had to clean up after Sweet Pea the goat.

"Thank you," I say. "I am beginning to see the benefit of removing them each morning. I half wish we had time…"

Calder shakes his head. "Time or no time, such a thing should never be done. It's nothing short of sacrilege." An impish smile turns up the corners of his mouth. "I suppose it would be impolite to say you look rather like you're wearing a miniature tent atop your head."

"To your wagon now, Calder," Yonaz commands from his seat. "We must make haste."

I start to walk. Calder trails behind me as I say, "Whenever I think I'm beginning to like you, you never fail to remind me that it would be unwise."

"But I do want you to like me," he says, suddenly serious. "Truly, I desire nothing more." These last whispered words are so full of longing and hope that they could have been a poem.

I turn away from him and toward the front of the wagon. My heart trips in my chest, the traitorous thing. I scramble up onto the narrow seat without waiting for him to offer assistance. On the cold, hard, plank bench, I cover my legs with two heavy plaid blankets and then hunch inside my cloak. What is wrong with me? Why am I so stirred up by him, his words, his smile? Perhaps my parents' neglect has left me too vulnerable to flattery, too hungry for attention and praise.

I must squash this feeling. I must focus solely on caring for Sparrow. There is not enough of me to be shared between the two of them—even if I wanted to parcel myself out.

"I've seen that face before. You're cross with me." Calder settles onto the bench beside me and takes up the reins. "I apologize. Sometimes I speak my heart when I should not. Robbie says my mouth's as wild as a mountain donkey. Well, those are not his exact words, but as you are a lady…"

Yonaz clucks his tongue and the other wagon starts to roll, but Calder remains still, eyeing me as if he's waiting for me to speak.

I adjust the blankets on my knees. Snowflakes land on my cheeks like tiny kisses and melt away. "I'm not cross. Not really. But I will speak plainly. I am barely acquainted with you, and I have Sparrow to consider. Whatever your intentions are, I must insist that we remain within the boundaries of friendship. Treat me as you treat Robbie."

He huffs out a sigh, then shakes the reins. The horses pull us forward. "If that is truly your wish, then I will try to honor it." There is a catch in his voice, a hint that he wants to say more but chooses to restrain himself.

Snow swirls around the wagons. The wheels creak and crunch on the frozen forest road. The lanterns affixed to the wagons cast little light, yet we move steadily through the thickening darkness. Calder keeps his eyes trained on the path ahead, and I try not to think about the dangers of traveling through the woods at night. Vicious animals, uneven terrain, patches of ice, deep holes disguised by leaf litter... And what of our destination? We seek safety, but will we find it?

I cannot deny that I am afraid. The temptation to reach for Calder's hand vexes me. The warmth of his palm against mine would be a comforting thing in this wild unknown, as would the hand of any friend. But I imagine him misinterpreting the gesture, leaning closer as we both forget our pledge to be only friends, and his eyelids shutting as he draws closer and...

Good heavens. The cold must be affecting my mind.

In the morning, I will beg Yonaz to cut off my antlers so that I may ride inside with Robbie, the twins, and the baby. Where I can cover myself in a half-dozen blankets and not fall prey to foolishness. Mine or Calder's.

A wolf's howl reverberates through the woods.

"Tell me more about the Springborn," I say, ready to welcome any distraction.

"I cannot promise what I say will be absolutely true, since there are mysteries involved. Almost everything I know, I learned from Yonaz. The tales he weaves of our kind are incredible. There once was a boy who could tame wild animals with a word. Another boy had a back like a hedgehog's, all full of quills, and could roll up into a tidy ball. There was a girl, long before my time, who shot flames from her fingertips. Some of us have more modest gifts, of course: pointed ears, an easily concealed tail, eyes that can see through the darkest night. Some of us even have two gifts. A particular mine town lass, rumors say, grows splendid antlers atop her head—yet walks unaware of the beauty she possesses."

I bow my head under the burden of his praise. What is his gift, I wonder, and why does he seem to keep it a secret? I cannot bring myself to ask.

"I say this as a friend, so please don't be angry," he says. "But I think you have been told too few times that you are special—in the best of ways. Nevertheless, I'll return to the subject at hand."

"Please do." I lift my head but avoid looking directly at Calder. I believe I know what I would see there: admiration I have not earned and a longing I cannot fulfill.

Calder clears his throat and continues, his eyes now fixed on the increasingly winding road. "Yonaz thinks there have been around a dozen of us."

"An old woman gave me to my father in a basket. Do you know of her?"

"That was Delphine. Her appearance changes with the seasons. Young and beautiful in spring and summer, old and frail in fall and wintertime. She also has a talent for making green things grow, which would be grand if I appreciated vegetables. Those are her Springborn gifts." A chunk of snow falls from the branches overhead and lands squarely on Calder's shoulder. He brushes it away with a few brisk strokes of his fingers.

"That does not explain how Sparrow came to be inside a basket in the attic," I say.

Calder shrugs. "As I said, there are mysteries. Sometimes a basket isn't delivered by anyone. It just shows up on a doorstep or in a cowshed. Anywhere someone who has wished for a baby will quickly find it."

I frown. "I made no such wish. Of that I am certain."

He says thoughtfully, "It could have been a quiet wish of your heart."

And then it dawns on me. I *have* wished for a friend. Someone who could understand and love me. "Oh," I say softly, wonderingly. Somehow, strange as the basket story is, I believe it. Perhaps, if I did not have antlers and a basket-delivered baby, I would think Calder was fabricating tales, but these things testify to the validity of his account.

Sparrow was no accident. She was not sent as a test or a prank, or to punish me for disobeying my father. She is a gift. A wish fulfilled. My heart feels as if it is expanding within the cage of my ribs, growing to accommodate the love I cannot help but feel for her.

Calder passes the reins into his left hand. His eyes graze over my fabric-covered antlers, with adoration so intense it would make a stone blush.

"You are a wonder, you know. Your parents...well, they were badly chosen. No doubt Delphine was trying to be kind to them and to you, but people are unpredictable at best. Darkness can spring up in them overnight. You were meant for a better home, Sabella. I hope you'll find one with us. And I hope the same for Sparrow—although I believe you will be the best of mothers to her."

"Calder," I say in a warning tone, to remind him that he agreed to treat me as a friend.

"I know, I know. I meant that in the friendliest of ways."

"Good." An owl swoops across the road, barely visible through the heavy shadows. Still marveling at the notion of my answered wish, I say, "So Yonaz and this Delphine have been responsible for gathering the Springborn together?"

"It's been their life's work. If a child is unwanted or mistreated, they offer refuge. A place with us. When we're grown, we may leave if we wish. Some have, but I've chosen to stay. I like being surrounded by brothers and sisters. Most of the time, anyway."

"The love among you is plain, even when you're arguing. I understand why you would want to stay." A wave of drowsiness sweeps over me, and I yawn. I have a thousand more questions, but Calder has given me much to ponder, and the night is too beautiful to ignore. I look up and say no more. There are a million stars above us, clinging to the cold sky like twinkling bits of ice. Never have I seen such a thing. One does not wander the streets of a coal town after midnight.

This is a new world to me, full of wonders, unfamiliar emotions, and grave responsibilities.

I glance at Calder. Like it or not, this boy has stirred my heart. I want everything he says to be true. I want to belong to this family of Springborn. It is as if I have been whisked out of a slow-moving bad dream and into a reality where being a girl with antlers might not be such a terrible thing.

I fight to stay awake, but my head bobs. My chin drifts toward my chest. The whirring of the wagon's wheels and the faint clop of the horses' hooves are an irresistible lullaby that ushers me into unconsciousness.

CALDER

The night air is laced with frost, but I am warm as toast. At least metaphorically—for Sabella has fallen asleep beside me. Her head leans back so that her shawl-covered antlers bounce against the canvas wagon cover whenever we hit a bump in the road, but not hard enough to damage anything. Her body slumps ever-so-slightly in my direction, enough that her shoulder jostles mine. From her hair or clothes, the scent of violets or lavender emanates. I am no good at identifying flowers by smell, but the name of the bloom does not matter one fig. What matters is that the scent is nigh unto intoxicating. Or maybe it's just her nearness that's making me dizzy.

I could be wrong, but I think my explanation of Springborn matters went over well enough. She didn't shove me off the seat or scream with terror, anyway. Nothing in my speech bothered her enough to keep her awake, either. This is quite encouraging, even if she does insist we remain friends.

The road curves sharply. Sabella murmurs in her sleep and leans more heavily against me. I swear my actual heart aches with the sweetness of it. A yearning for the road to lengthen settles into the pit of my stomach. Why would I want the wonder of her nearness to end?

Tame yourself, Robbie's imagined voice chastens. But I cannot.

If I was falling for her before, I am plummeting now. It was one thing to watch her from afar, to pity her in her suffering, but in the last day, I've witnessed firsthand her selfless devotion to Sparrow, her bravery in setting out among near-strangers for who-knows-where, and her rather charming stubborn streak—and I'm moving with the speed of a shooting star toward either utter bliss or total destruction.

At this moment, I don't care about the ending. This present time with her is all I want, here on this wagon seat under the sparkling winter sky.

SABELLA

I awake shivering in the milky, early morning light, with my face turned up toward the stark, bare branches of the highest treetops. Sometime after I dozed off in the night, my head must have fallen back to rest against the outer wall of the wagon. A lightning bolt of pain shoots through my neck as I straighten it under the slight weight of my antlers. Never before have I worn them fully grown for so long.

Beside me, Calder hunches over the reins, pale with exhaustion —except for his red-tipped nose.

"You snore worse than Robbie," he reports. "Like a bear with a rattlesnake lodged in its throat."

"That's a fine way to say good morning."

"You did ask me to treat you as I treat Robbie," he says with a teasing grin—the one that makes me want to swoon and to smack him at the same time. How does he manage it?

"I suppose I did," I reply. "Will we be stopping soon, do you think?"

"We'll have to. The horses are dog-tired, if horses are capable of canine fatigue."

Ahead of us, Yonaz's wagon veers off the rutted road and onto a tree-lined lane. We follow it through several twists and turns, over a stone bridge, and then up a gently sloping, forested hill. We stop abruptly in front of a stone cottage surrounded by white birches. An unpainted barn stands behind the cottage like a plain but protective big brother.

"Who lives here?" I ask Calder as he helps me down from the seat. My legs, numb from sitting so long, buckle when my feet meet the ground. I grab his arm to steady myself. "Sorry."

"No need to be," he says simply. "I believe this is Hiram Maguire's place. Yonaz has mentioned it."

"Indeed it is," Yonaz says as he strolls over to join us. Plaid blankets are layered over his coat, and his cheeks are chapped scarlet by the cold. "Maguire is one of our own. He grows the ears and tail of a wolf when the moon is full, but otherwise lives as an ordinary farrier. You'll find him a generous and gracious host, Miss Sabella. His cider is fit for the gods, his mattresses are stuffed fat with feathers, and his fireplaces burn hot enough to singe a demon. We'll rest here for a few hours and then resume our journey."

Branna rounds the wagons with a young eagle perched on her gloved wrist. But wait. Doesn't this girl have more freckles and slightly darker copper hair than the girl I met earlier?

"Will we be stopping here long enough for Branna to stretch her wings?" she asks, confirming my suspicion that this girl is not Branna.

"Let her fly," Yonaz says.

Calder leans close to me and confides in a whisper. "The twins take turns shape-shifting. When one is an animal, the other is a girl. Branna must have taken the form of an eagle during the night, allowing Cleona to assume human form. Don't feel bad if you can't tell them apart. No one can, half the time. It drives Robbie mad."

"Fear not, children," Yonaz says, herding us toward the cottage with a sweep of his arm. "No enemies shall trespass here. Hiram's guard dogs would shred them like old paper."

Robbie scampers to meet us. Sparrow sleeps in his arms, her face pressed against his shoulder. "Passed out like a rum-drunken sailor," he says. "Only this little sailor has a belly full of goat's milk."

"Thank you." I take her and cuddle her close. The scent she exudes—sweet and pure—is most intoxicating. We have been apart for only a few hours, but I have missed the dear little thing. My stomach sinks as I note that she has grown larger in Robbie's care. What will become of her? Might she attain the sprawling height of a giantess by springtime? Or will she have the wizened body of an old woman before her first birthday?

"Let's get Sparrow indoors before she freezes," Calder says, slipping one arm around Robbie and the other around me and guiding us onward. "And before I transform into a glacier myself."

"Right," Robbie says. He lifts one of his bird feet and shakes the snow off. "At least you have boots. My toes are frozen."

I glance at Calder from the corner of my eye, trying to figure out if he is joking about becoming a glacier. If that is his gift, I prefer my antlers.

And he catches me looking.

"I know I'm handsome, but do try not to stare," he teases.

"Oh, stuff it, Calder," Robbie says. "She's probably wondering how many times your mother dropped you to make you so ugly."

"Ugly, am I? Have you seen that beak of yours lately?" Calder says, elbowing Robbie hard. Robbie lunges to smack Calder but misses—provoking Calder's laughter and awakening Sparrow. In my arms, she whines and reaches chubby hands toward Robbie, ending the battle.

"There, now," Robbie says. He kisses her fingertips. "Little Sparrow knows who's handsomest among us."

"Babies," Calder says. "Always sticking up for each other."

85

CALDER

Our host, Hiram, is a quiet man. His appearance brings to mind the wolf he becomes at the full of the moon, for he is muscular but lean. His black-and-gray beard and hair are untamed and his eyes are the color of amber. When he smiles, he displays sharp canine teeth. Astonishingly, his grin comes across as cordial rather than fearsome.

He and Yonaz must empty every cupboard in the place, for they set the table with three kinds of jam, two big loaves of bread, several tins of biscuits and dried fruits, a half-wheel of golden cheese, most of a cold, roasted chicken, a bowl of boiled eggs, and a big pot of tea. Sabella and I set out plates and cutlery while Robbie rocks Sparrow in his skinny arms.

When we're all seated, the meal is all eating and no conversation. For once, I am too tired to say anything foolish. Robbie pinches my thigh under the table when my weary gaze settles on Sabella's antlers for too long. She notices nothing, it seems, other than the food on her plate. Quite the eater, our Sabella is, and I'm glad to see it. Her mine town diet was enough to keep her alive, but I long to see her cheeks rounded and rosy with health.

Robbie pinches me once more, harder. Was I staring again?

Grinning stupidly? I'm too tired to remember. "I think I'll lie down for a while, if you don't mind," I say to Hiram.

He points to the hallway. "Second door on the right."

Somehow I convince my legs to carry me to the bed. Seconds later, I'm out like a snuffed candle.

SABELLA

In the hours between lunch and dinner, Calder and Yonaz rest in their bedrooms while Cleona and Branna venture out of doors so the eagle Branna can stretch her wings again. Our host, Hiram, heads to the barn to look after the horses—leaving Robbie and me to sprawl on matching green velveteen sofas in the spacious parlor. Sparrow sleeps in a basket, swaddled tightly, sucking her fist as she dreams. A merry fire crackles in the fireplace.

I ought to be relishing this peaceful interlude. Instead, I fret. I adjust the pillow behind my neck, mindful that my antlers could easily tear the fine fabric of the sofa. Hiram didn't bat an eye at them, but he might not think so kindly of them if they ruin his furniture.

"I do love a good fire," Robbie says, tucking one arm behind his head. His yellow-orange bird feet look comical propped on the end of the sofa. "I could stay right here forever if someone would bring me tea and cakes now and then."

"I'm worried about the baby," I blurt. "She should not be growing so fast. Have you seen this before among the Springborn?"

"I have not. We're one of a kind, so far as I can tell. I won't say it isn't a little distressing, her growth. But she's a happy girl. As long as she's happy...well, we must be content with her lot. None of us gets to choose our gift or the length of our days." He says these things gently, as if he has already learned how to lose loved ones with grace.

I swallow hard. When I was small, Mother told me tales she'd heard from her granny. One was of an enormous black dog with fiery eyes, the Black Shuck—a harbinger of impending death. I feel as though that wretched dog rests upon my chest, its great weight crushing my heart as it sucks the breath from my lungs. I close my eyes and will myself not to cry. "I cannot bear the thought of losing her."

"Then do not bear it. Do not think of it. Enjoy her. If I've learned anything from life, it's that tomorrow's not guaranteed to anyone, so we ought to treasure our friends while they're in our company."

Robbie pauses. A burning log hisses and sputters to fill the silence. In a quieter voice, he resumes speaking. "This isn't the first time we've had to flee our home. On a day that started out ordinary as porridge, two of us, Springborn called Peony and Geffen, were murdered. We lived near Ashford then, on the other side of the mountain from Miners Ridge. Someone caught sight of Peony's fox ears and followed her to our cottage, thinking she was a witch who needed killing. Geffen saw the man chase Peony into the yard, heard him call her dreadful names. He tried to stop the man to reason with him, but the man drew a pistol and shot them both. Then he set our home ablaze. We fled with nothing but the clothes on our backs."

"I'm so sorry."

"Calder took it hardest of any of us. Since then, he's been little more than a shadow of himself. Lost all his shine, even his love of a joke. Sometimes hardly said a word for days on end. Since you've been around, he's got some of his spark back." He looks at me hopefully.

"Oh, Robbie. I'm glad he's feeling better, but you shouldn't credit me. If he's one of those love-at-first-sight boys—"

"Oh, but he isn't. We've been close as brothers for roundabout five years, and I admit he's always been an incorrigible flirt, but I swear I've never seen him truly smitten with anyone before." Robbie turns and sets his clawed toes on the Turkish carpet. He watches the fire and says quietly, "Maybe, just maybe, it's meant to be, you and Calder. Sure, you've just properly met, but I do have this feeling..."

Exasperated, I sit up. "Please stop, Robbie. What I need are dependable friends, not a suitor. I've just run away from home. I'm suddenly a mother, without any time to prepare for it. I am afflicted with antlers, and heaven only knows what is wrong with Sparrow. Are these not enough tribulations for one girl of seventeen?"

Robbie stands. He is not tall, yet he seems to tower far above me, his expression dark. He clenches his hands into fists at his sides. "*Never* say that. Never say there's something wrong with Sparrow, or with you. If that is your belief, you should leave, for you do not belong in our company—antlers or no antlers."

I wince, stung by his words. "Forgive me, Robbie. I didn't mean to offend you. I'm confused. Scared. I've been hidden away in my parents' house since I was eleven years old, called a disgrace and treated as a servant. I had four books to learn about life from, just four, and one of them was about plants. What do I know of portents or fate or people falling in love?"

Robbie sinks back onto the sofa. He sighs and scratches his neck. "I'm sorry, too. I forgot how new you are to all this. I've had bird legs since I was four. I almost don't remember my parents, and how it hurt not to be wanted. They left me on top of a mountain, alone, right after I changed. I ate wild blueberries and slept covered in leaves until Yonaz found me."

"There you are," Calder says from the doorway. "I was wondering if you two had eloped."

"It would serve you right," Robbie says. "But no, we're planning a spring wedding in the south of France."

Calder flops down next to Robbie. "Is that so? No wonder Sabella has been resisting my charms. Who doesn't enjoy a tasty chicken leg?"

"Shut it, Calder," Robbie says. "You're just jealous."

"Of course I am," Calder says with utter sincerity. "I have never been more jealous in my life."

Quite stupidly, I meet Calder's searching gaze for a moment. For long enough that I feel seen and wanted in a way no one has ever seen or wanted me. Long enough that I wonder if Robbie might be right about a connection between the two of us.

Sparrow cries out from her basket and breaks whatever spell held me. Before I can move, Robbie scoops her up and shushes her. I watch Robbie cuddle and bounce the baby, but I can feel that Calder still watches me.

"Come have tea!" Yonaz shouts from another room.

"Thank the stars," Robbie says. "I'm parched." He clutches Sparrow to his chest and hurries toward the door. I spring off the sofa to follow him, but Calder catches my wrist with his fingers.

"Sabella," he says softly before he lets me go, hiding mysteries and promises in every syllable of my name.

Heaven help me.

SABELLA

"I won't do it," Robbie declares. "I can't and I won't." He removes his hand from my left antler, drops the handsaw onto the ice-glazed grass at my feet, and hugs his body. His exhalations make a series of tiny clouds in the air as he starts to pace.

I remain seated on a tree stump behind Hiram's barn, trying hard not to shiver inside my cloak and shawl. "Please, Robbie. It will take five minutes at most to saw them off, and I swear it causes me no pain. If someone sees me wearing a ridiculous headdress made from a weirdly shaped scarf as we're traveling, what will they think?"

He shrugs. "That you like strange hats?"

I release my breath in a huff. "Hat preferences aside, I want to ride in the wagon with Sparrow. She grew four teeth last night. Four! She may very well turn into a two-year-old before we next stop."

Robbie shakes his head and taps the clawed toes of one foot. "No. I'm sorry, but no."

From beyond the barn, Yonaz calls our names for the third or fourth time. His accent grows thicker as his patience thins.

"What's happening over here?" Calder asks as he comes around the side of the barn. "Yonaz is itching to leave, if you haven't noticed. And where's the baby?"

"Sparrow's with the twins. And this one," Robbie says, pointing to my head. "This one wants the antlers off, and I can't. It would be like cutting off my own two feet. No. Not a chance."

Calder's brow furrows. "Why, Sabella? Are you still ashamed of them?"

"It has nothing to do with that." I blush as if he's caught me in a lie. In spite of their assurance that the antlers are gifts, I am still uneasy wearing them. But now is not the time to examine my feelings about the antlers. This is for Sparrow. "I want to ride inside with the baby, and with these branches sticking out of my skull, it's impossible."

Calder shakes his head glumly. "I agree with Robbie on this count. It's a crime to vandalize such magnificence."

"Fine." I grab the saw and lift it over my head. "I'll do it myself."

"Wait!" Calder says. "Hold on. You'll hurt yourself." He lunges for the tool. "If you insist upon removing them for the sake of motherly devotion, I will help you. I think it's atrocious, mind you, but I would rather perform the loathsome task than watch you slice into your own scalp by accident."

"Well, I can't watch." Robbie stalks off, making tracks in the snow like a giant chicken.

Calder moves to my side and widens his stance. He sets the saw at the base of my right antler and grips my neck with his free hand. His fingertips warm my skin. "You're certain about this? Absolutely certain?"

"Do it. Please. Before Yonaz decides to leave without us."

Metal scrapes against the antler's bony base. I close my eyes. The slow rhythm, the bitter scent of the dust, the firm pressure on my neck—transport me back into my parents' kitchen.

The smell of Mother's singed griddle cakes and Father's tobacco haunts my senses.

Clear as anything, I hear Mother's late-night, inebriated humming.

I envision Father crouched in the washtub on a Saturday night, cursing as Mother brandishes the stiff-bristled brush and tries to scrub the coal dust out of his pores.

Calder gasps almost too softly to be heard when the first antler comes free from my skull. After a moment, I feel him set the blade at the other antler's root. Again, my imagination dredges up the past. I see Mother in the grips of one of her sleepwalking episodes, counting her six silver spoons over and over, fondling the last remnants of her privileged upbringing.

I relive the horror of Father's calloused fingers clutching my neck before dawn, roughly enough to elicit tears. The downward curve of his mouth. The hatred simmering in his eyes.

I remember the pain of being *not what they wanted*.

"Did I hurt you?" Calder says after the second antler falls. I open my eyes. He bends to swipe a tear from my cheek with his thumb. "I'm sorry."

"It wasn't you." I stand and straighten my cloak. Motes of antler dust float through the air when I give the material a shaking. Calder sneezes.

The shed antlers lay at the base of the stump like silver birch limbs brought down by a storm. Calder eyes them in the forlorn way one might regard an injured baby rabbit. He rubs one palm against his chest as if he's trying to soothe an ache.

I thought I would feel better, less burdened, with the antlers gone. But I do not.

"I'm sorry," he says again, cupping my shoulder with his hand for a moment.

We walk to the wagons, side by side, in silence.

CALDER

The wagon seat is cold and unforgiving beneath me as we leave Hiram's farm and set out for the main road. I deserve "cold and unforgiving" after what I just did. The memory of it sickens my stomach.

My guilty hands clench the reins. These hands were no more made to cut off Sabella's antlers than they were to shatter the windows of cathedrals. But what choice did I have? The chore had to be done and she all but begged me to do it. Blazes, my backbone might as well be made of jelly when I'm near her.

I train my eyes on the road ahead and try to forget her tears and the bitter dust the saw cast into the air, my nose, my lungs. This road is well traveled, the only route linking the mountain coal towns to the valley and then the world. I must take care, for if I steer the wagon into a ditch or break a wheel on a stone, other travelers might stop to offer aid. It is best to avoid contact with strangers. If Sabella's parents told the authorities that she ran away or was stolen, there could be trouble. And while most of us appear ordinary at the moment, we do have a bird-legged boy in our company.

Above me, the sky wears a smooth garment of gray cloud. The

sun hides, hoarding heat I wish she'd share. I'm cold, within and without.

Baby laughter filters through the canvas wagon cover, followed by Sabella's laughter. *There, now,* the universe seems to say. *Sabella would not be sharing joy and warmth with Sparrow if you had not wielded the saw. Forgive yourself.*

Sparrow laughs again and this time, I cannot help but smile. If there is any magic in the world other than that which gives the Springborn their gifts, it is surely contained in the laughter of infants.

SABELLA

Wind pummels the heavy canvas above me. There is hardly any room to spare inside the narrow wagon, even though almost all of the boxes and trunks were moved to the wagon Yonaz drives. Robbie and I sit hunched under piles of blankets. We take turns cuddling Sparrow. Sweet Pea the goat dozes at our feet, adding welcome warmth and disagreeable goat smells. Near us, Cleona sleeps. She shares several quilts with her sister Branna, who became a shaggy black dog before we left Hiram's farm.

February is an inopportune time for taking such a journey. I feel sorry for Calder, Yonaz, and the horses. They must endure the full measure of winter's unkindness to see us to the place Yonaz has chosen as the next home for the Springborn. He reckons we will arrive in two or three days, if the roads and weather offer no hindrance. And then what? We all hide together, waiting to be evicted again by superstitious, hateful mine town folk? Could we not move away from these mountains, to some sweet, uninhabited, unspoiled forest? I must save these questions to ask Yonaz later.

Robbie leans over to pass Sparrow into my arms. I stare into her face, memorizing the pert shape of her nose, the roundness of her cheeks, the deep blue of her eyes. She stares up at me as if she's memorizing me, as well. My heart thuds hard in my chest, hardly able to support the amount of love flowing through my body. When she falls asleep, peace embraces me. Is this magic, or just an ordinary blessing of motherhood? I think I could hold her like this forever.

Hours pass. I doze and wake. The wagons slow and then cease moving. When Robbie uncinches the canvas at the back of the wagon, snowflakes swoop through the opening. Beyond him, the last purplish red streak of the sunset fades away from the sky.

Robbie jumps out. I pass Sparrow down to him before I leap to the ground.

Yonaz pulls the frost-caked scarf off his mouth as he strides toward us. He says, "We must stop here for the night. I've stayed here before. The innkeeper is kind—and conveniently nearsighted. If we are careful, our gifts will go unnoticed and no trouble will befall us."

Cleona, yawning, climbs down from the wagon and snatches Sparrow from Robbie. "Did you say 'inn,' Yonaz? I do hope they allow dogs." Branna leaps to the ground and stands on four legs next to her human sister, tail wagging.

"I will pay extra for Branna's lodging, if the innkeeper requires it," Yonaz says. "I will go in to make arrangements. Wait here."

As Yonaz walks away, I look around for Calder, but he must be busy tending to the horses. In anticipation of meeting strangers inside the inn, I pull the hood of my cloak firmly over my head. My regrowing antlers are still short and well hidden by a cotton cap and a scarf, but surely it is better to be cautious than sorry. Robbie prepares, too, by bending to unroll his wide, gray trouser legs. They flare out to cover his bird feet. "Clever, aren't they?" he says.

"Hiram gave me some fabric and thread back when we were at his place, and I stayed up half the night to make them. It might become the new fashion for gentlemen of refinement. 'Hallseys,' I'll call them, after my fine self."

Something in Cleona's smile makes me wonder if she is smitten with Robbie. "They're quite nice," she says.

The trousers look rather comical to me, but it is obvious that he is exceedingly proud of them. "I like the color. And they are certainly practical in your case," I say.

"They're only for out among the ordinary folk, mind," Robbie says. "At home, my bird feet will continue to be on full and glorious display. Once we have a home again."

"You may come in now, my children," Yonaz calls from the inn's porch.

"Let's go," Robbie says, leading the way toward a sprawling brick house topped with numerous smoke-spewing chimneys. The first floor's windows glow with yellow lamplight, drawing me forward like a siren's song. I imagine blazing fireplaces and steaming cups of cider. To be warm again will be a wondrous thing.

Finally, Calder catches up to us. His gait is unsteady and his teeth chatter. The blanket around his shoulders is stiffened and starred with frost.

"Darnation, Calder. You look terrible," Robbie says.

Calder does indeed look terrible. His red-rimmed eyes leak onto his chapped cheeks.

"Are you all right?" I ask, dreading his answer.

"I'm afraid not," Calder says. His voice is raspy, and he winces as if speaking pains him. Robbie puts an arm around his shoulders and guides him onto the porch.

"A hot bath will do you good," Yonaz says, patting Calder's back. "And then a bed with warmed soapstones, if they have them."

Without warning, Calder's knees buckle. Yonaz catches him

under the arms. "Bless me, boy," Yonaz says. "You're frozen through."

The innkeeper opens the arched door, greets us profusely, and invites us to call him Edgar. With his wide, bearded face, friendly smile, and big, bespectacled eyes, he seems made for his role. When he notices Calder's ill state, he steps aside to allow Yonaz to usher him inside, and then calls out for hot water, tea, and blankets. "Get the boy upstairs and into bed, and be quick about it," Edgar says. "We run a cheerful establishment here. I'm not keen on guests dying under my roof if it can be helped."

Yonaz drapes Calder over his shoulder like a big sack of grain. He trudges upstairs, leaving Robbie to pace the floor of the large common room like a skittish hen. The claws of his feet click against the hardwood floor.

"He will be fine, Robbie," I say. I can only hope that I am speaking the truth.

Robbie nods but looks unconvinced. He wanders away from me and sets to nibbling his fingernails.

Near the wide, brick fireplace, Cleona and her bushy, black, canine sister entertain Sparrow. The baby claps when the dog stands on its hind legs and walks. Would that I felt so merry.

But my thoughts meander along a darker path. I have heard of men dying from the effects of the cold, strong men used to hard labor. One was as young as Calder, a robust miner who lost his way in the woods while hunting. What if...

The mere six days we have shared were not enough. They cannot be all we're allowed. Even if we're not fated to someday fall in love, as Robbie believes, I want his friendship. And the world needs his brightness.

Darlis, the innkeeper's tidy blonde wife, bustles about, dispensing encouragement and tea. After shepherding us to the dining table, she serves us loaves fresh from the oven and thick potato soup flecked with bacon. She refills our mugs with hot, spiced cider, and directs their servant boy to place rectangles of heated soapstone at our feet. In spite of their eager ministrations, time drags miserably.

I meet Robbie's fretful gaze. His food sits untouched on the plate. He grips his spoon as if he has forgotten what one does with such an object.

From the top of the stairs comes the innkeeper's frantic shout. "Send for the doctor, Darlis!"

Robbie drops his spoon with a clatter. He flees the room and bolts upstairs. Although I am no longer cold from travel, I shiver.

Less than half a minute later, Robbie's unearthly bellow echoes into the dining room. I am on my feet and up the oak staircase before I draw another breath. I round the hallway corner and stumble into a blue and white striped bedroom furnished with a pair of identical four-poster beds.

Beside one bed, Robbie crouches with his head bent over Calder's hand. His bird legs won't let him kneel, yet he looks as if he's pledging fealty or begging for a king's mercy—only he's weeping, not speaking.

Calder sits propped against a pile of pillows, his face barely visible above numerous layers of blankets. When he sees me, he lifts his free hand and waves. My terror melts away like snow assaulted by summer sun. I cannot decide whether to succumb to relieved laughter or tears of joy—but since Robbie appears to be doing a fine job with the crying, I offer Calder a smile.

I wish I could embrace him, kiss his pale cheeks, and tell him how pleased I am to see him alive, but I hold my body still, as would befit a well-mannered young lady.

Someone coughs and wheezes behind me. I turn to find the other bed occupied by Yonaz. His usually olive complexion is now whiter than the bed linen. Innkeeper Edgar stands beside the bed. He shakes his head and says, "This is not good at all, miss. Will you stay with him while I fetch a cool compress? His fever's hot as Hades. Could boil a pot on him, I reckon."

"Of course I'll stay," I reply. From my place between the two beds, I can keep an eye on both patients. Although it would be much more pleasant to keep both eyes on Calder—for he looks unwell, but Yonaz looks a few breaths shy of the grave. I have never witnessed a death—and I do not care to do so today.

"Oh, Cald. We thought you were...that you might..." Robbie says, still crouching beside Calder. He scrubs his shirtsleeve over his eyes before he stands up straight. "It was a dirty trick, that. I'd like to thrash you for it."

Robbie's words bring a faint smile to Calder's face. "I'd like to see you try, bird legs."

"Later," Robbie says. He sets Calder's hand on the bedclothes and straightens his body. "You won't guess it's coming, that's the thing. You'll be on the ground, seeing stars, without a notion as to how you got there."

The brotherly love between these young men is as fine a thing as I've ever seen. It is fierce and tender, pure yet natural.

A fit of coughing grips Yonaz, drawing Robbie's attention to the other bed. "Holy saints. What's happened to him?"

"A fever," I say. "It must have come on suddenly."

"He collapsed directly after he set me down," Calder says. "That's when the innkeeper called out for the doctor."

"This is bad," Robbie says, gripping his head between his hands. "We need Yonaz. He looks out for us. And we'll never find our new place without him. Oh, saints above! What if the fever is catching? Darnation, why did we ever leave home?"

"You know we left because we had to, Rob." Calder slouches against his pillows as if the brief conversation has sapped him of all vigor. "I'm sure he'll be fine. Probably needs a good nap, as I do."

Calder closes his eyes and is snoring within a minute. Edgar reappears in the doorway. "Doctor's coming. Best clear out."

Robbie and I pass the doctor on the stairs, a sour-faced bulldog of a fellow toting a huge leather bag. Not the sort of man I can imagine delivering good news.

At the bottom of the stairs, Robbie pauses and half turns.

"Perhaps I should go back up and keep an eye on things. Doctors can't be trusted. They're only after the money, you know."

"That surely isn't true of all doctors." I will not mention Mother's quack physicians and add to his worries. I slip my arm through his and steer him toward the sound of Sparrow's laughter. "Come. There's a little bird who must be missing you sorely by now."

"Well...I'll go with you for a bit, for Sparrow's sake. But if I get the smallest inkling that so-called doctor is causing either one of them to suffer—"

"We will both give that doctor a trouncing," I say.

"Exactly."

Robbie's intense devotion warms my heart—and bolsters my opinions of both Yonaz and Calder. If they have earned such loyalty, they must be special indeed.

They are a family, these Springborn. Bound together by threads of loyalty and love, even when they're squabbling. The kind of family Sparrow deserves to have. My decision to stay with them feels more right than ever.

SABELLA

My cold and clandestine trip to the innkeeper's tool shed proves fruitful when I find a small saw hanging on the wall. I set my short candlestick on the work bench and take the tool in hand. Its teeth feel adequately sharp to my fingertips. It will do. I tuck it under my cloak and head back across the snowy yard.

Overnight, as usual, my antlers have been gaining length and breadth. They must be removed before breakfast, lest the innkeeper or his guests catch sight of them. No scarf or shawl can effectively conceal them when they're fully grown.

As much as I loathed my father's saw, I welcome the weight of this one as I clutch it close. I could have saved myself the trouble of searching if I'd thought to ask Hiram for the gift of his saw—but the past is over and done. Before the break of day, I will beg one of the twins to remove my antlers. If they are too squeamish for the task, I will cut them off myself, heaven help me.

A narrow, unheated room separates the kitchen from the

outdoors, a place where mucky boots are shed and odds and ends are kept on shelves. I pause there to shake snow off my boots, and then I cautiously open the kitchen door, cursing it under my breath for its sharp squeak.

The warmth of the kitchen envelops me. I am seized by a sudden desire to lie down at the hearthside and sleep—a foolish and dangerous notion. I force my feet to carry me past the low, orange flames, toward the door. And somehow I collide with something.

Someone.

The impact knocks the candle out of my grasp and onto the floor. As the flame dies, I step backward, careful to keep the saw hidden under my cloak, praying that my scarf-covered antlers don't betray me and the Springborn.

"Sabella?" Calder whispers. "Have you been wandering out of doors?"

He's wearing a long, striped nightshirt and his hair stands up like wind-blown hay in a field. He could be mistaken for a scarecrow, if scarecrows carried oil lamps. The sight of him, combined with the shock of being discovered, tempts me to giggle.

"Is something humorous?" he asks as he sets the lamp on the kitchen work table.

"No. Not at all." I withdraw the saw from the folds of my cloak and present it. "I was on an errand. My antlers...they'll have to be seen to before breakfast."

"You should have asked me. I would have fetched that for you." He squats to retrieve the fallen candlestick and sets it beside the oil lamp.

"I'm capable of going to a tool shed myself. I'm a coal town lass, not a princess. Why are *you* wandering about at this hour? You've been ill. You should not be out of bed."

He shrugs. "Couldn't sleep. Too many naps, perhaps. Also, I'm famished." He crosses the room and flings open cabinet doors until he finds half a loaf of bread and a dish of butter. "Care for any?"

My stomach surprises me by rumbling. I suppose I can risk staying here long enough for a slice of bread. "Please."

I set the handsaw on the floor, against the wall. I shrug off my cloak and use it to cover the tool—just in case someone else happens into the kitchen. Thank heaven I took the time to put on a day dress before sneaking out of the room I share with the twins and the baby.

Calder tears off hunks of bread and coats each with a thick layer of butter. He hands me one and we sit on the stone floor, close to the low-burning hearth. The butter is salty and rich, and the loaf is soft and slightly sweet. Has anything ever tasted so good?

His acorn-brown eyes catch the firelight. This untidy, whispering Calder has a strangely soothing effect on me, like a familiar quilt. The shadowy kitchen is redolent with ghost scents of past baking and roasting, faint whiffs of herbs and soap. It feels like I always wanted home to feel. Safe and welcoming.

"Do you miss your old family at all?" he asks when his bread is gone.

"No." I answer right away, not pausing to think. Guilt washes over me as I realize I've spoken the truth. If I were a good daughter, I would miss my parents. If I were a good daughter, I would not have left my sick mother. But I was never going to be a good daughter in their minds, no matter how I tried. The antlers made it impossible. "What about you?" I ask him. "Do you miss the family you first had?" I feel more vulnerable asking this than being asked.

He reaches to grab the poker and uses it to stir the embers. "Not anymore. I was young when we parted ways. It was not what I wanted. Yonaz could have collected my tears in buckets. But time covers over the wounds of your heart, if you're lucky."

I want to ask him more about his parents, but this does not seem like the time or place for that. I say instead, "I will do everything I can to keep Sparrow from suffering such wounds."

He sets the poker aside and reaches for my hand as if doing so is the most natural thing in the world. His fingers squeeze gently, and then he lets go. "Sometimes the baskets do choose well, you know. Sparrow will have the best of lives because of you."

Affection and flattery are strangers to me. A blush heats my face and throat. Does he notice in the flickering firelight? I swallow hard.

"The innkeeper's wife will be down soon," Calder says. Outside, a rooster crows to restate the warning. He stands, picks up my cloak and the saw, and places the bundle into my arms. "Promise me you won't try to use the saw on yourself."

"I'll ask one of the twins."

"Good." He looks at me for a moment, hard, as if he means to memorize my image. "You go up first. I'll listen for your door. Wouldn't want to sully your reputation by being caught together, especially with me in my nightclothes."

"Good night, Calder," I say, forgetting morning is nigh.

"Good night, my antler girl," he replies in a whisper so faint, so full of exquisite tenderness, that I will forever wonder if I imagined it.

CALDER

Sabella turns away from me, her arms full of bundled cloak and shawl. As I watch her leave the kitchen, I almost wish we'd been caught alone in the dark by the innkeepers. I could bear the accusations of misbehavior. To be forced to marry her would bring me more joy and relief than shame. She would feel otherwise, no doubt. She might even hate me for a while, or at least resent the loss of her freedom to choose a husband.

With a sigh, I lower myself to the chilly floor. I sit and ache. I could blame it on my recent illness, but most of the pain resides in the region of my heart. It is yearning, pining, longing—all of those poetic things that sound grand until you're caught up in them. Until you think you might die of wanting and waiting.

Light peeks through the window as the rooster crows again. I haul myself to my feet and put the bread and butter back in the cupboard. I will go upstairs and lie upon my bed, but there is no chance I will sleep.

I will stare at the ceiling and try to solve the great riddle of the ages: how to get someone you love to love you in return.

SABELLA

The scents of toasted bread, fried eggs, and fried potatoes fill the air. On my lap, Sparrow babbles while banging a spoon on the edge of the long, oak table. I cherish the warm weight of her and forgive her for keeping me awake during the hours between my saw-fetching and now. If only I had a third arm with which to feed myself, I would be quite content.

Sparrow's happy wriggling causes her dress to slide up and bunch at her waist. I tug it down. This flowered, blue cotton frock was a gift from Darlis, the innkeeper's wife. The dress Sparrow had worn since we left Miners Ridge—a dress formerly belonging to Cleona's largest doll—had become too tight and short, which caused her, in Calder's eloquent words, to resemble an overstuffed sausage ready to split its casing. Mere moments after Cleona finished sawing off my antlers this morning, Darlis paid a call to our bedroom to offer me two baby-sized dresses and a bonnet. The woman made no comment regarding the baby's size, likely thinking Sparrow's growth spurt both natural and unexpected by

113

an inexperienced mother. There were tears in her eyes as she pressed the small garments into my grasp, so I did not dare to ask who had last worn them.

The morning sunlight blazes through the half-closed shutters and heats the dining room most pleasantly. It would have been a fine day for traveling, but if the doctor's predictions are correct, Yonaz will not be well enough to leave here for days—if not weeks. How will we pay the innkeeper's bill, unless one of the other Springborn has a hidden, magical talent for minting gold?

Calder strides into the dining room with Robbie at his heels. Literally. Their clothes look freshly ironed—and I suspect that Darlis should be thanked for this as well.

"I still say you ought to have stayed in bed for the entire day," Robbie fusses. "Look at you. You're pale as milk."

Pale from lack of sleep, I think, recalling our secret repast.

"I think it is better that I give Yonaz silence and solitude so he can recover," Calder says. He pulls out the chair beside mine and offers me a smile. "Besides, it will do me more good to be here among friends than to be shut up in the gloom with a sick person."

Sparrow squeals with delight and reaches for Robbie. He takes her and kisses the top of her head before he sits across the table from Calder and me. "You know where stubborn ill people end up, Cald? The graveyard, that's where."

Calder pours tea into his cup, smirking at Robbie's fussing. "Thank you for the reminder. But as I am no longer ill, I will store up your wisdom for another time."

"Where are the twins?" Robbie asks nervously. "Not stricken with the fever, are they?"

"They're perfectly well." I make sure to whisper in case Darlis and Edgar are close by. "Cleona took Branna out for a walk. She's still a dog. Or at least one of them is a dog. I suppose they could have switched roles in the night."

I glance at Calder as he grabs a slice of buttered toast from the platter. Of course he catches me looking at him.

"Are you worried about me as well?" he asks playfully. Is he flirting, after we agreed to be friends? "Because I'm fine, I swear it. It was only the effects of the cold. I have been thoroughly warmed. I feel almost tropical."

"Good." I reach for my tea cup and knock my fork off the table. The clatter of the metal hitting the floorboards does not amuse me—but it does make Sparrow giggle and clap. When I bend to retrieve the fork, Calder does the same. His forehead collides with mine while his fingers brush the back of my hand. It is the briefest of touches, but it sends my pulse racing.

Apparently, my heart is disinterested in my brain's plan to avoid romantic notions of Calder Hadrian.

He laughs and sits up, rubbing his forehead. "No good deed goes unpunished."

I force a laugh. It sounds like a donkey with a chest cold.

"Unka," Sparrow says, patting Robbie's cheek and providing a welcome distraction.

"Clever girl," Robbie says. "She's calling me 'uncle.' Did you hear that?"

Calder spoons eggs onto his plate. "They heard her in the stables, Rob. How a small girl can produce such volume is a mystery to me. Eggs, Sabella?"

"No, thank you." Lack of sleep left me with barely any appetite —and even that vanished the moment Calder entered the room. Now that I've heard him speak my name, I couldn't eat another bite. Somehow, on his lips, my name sounds like much more than the simple title my parents gave me. Like he's quoting a sacred book or the lyrics of a glorious song.

My breath hitches. What if Calder possesses a gift that allows him to manipulate others with his voice? Could he be forcing me to fall for his charms? How could I defend myself from that kind of magic? The very notion that I might have escaped my father's control only to fall under the power of another man sickens me.

"Are you all right, Sabella?" Robbie asks. "You look as if you've seen a ghost. You're not ill, are you? Feverish?"

Calder pours more tea into my cup. "Drink," he says.

"Go on. Tea always helps," Robbie adds.

I fear it will take more than a little brown liquid to assuage my fears. Nevertheless, I drink.

"Better?" Robbie asks hopefully. I nod.

Sparrow reaches for me. "Mama," she says, plain as day.

Robbie rounds the table to bring her to me. I welcome her into my arms with a kiss. She rests her soft cheek against mine. In my heart, I pledge anew to protect her. But how can I keep such a promise if I cannot even protect myself?

SABELLA

A week and a half passes. Yonaz is recovering at a snail's pace —and a lethargic snail's pace at that. The doctor says he must not leave his bed for a few more days, and ought not to travel for another week. Yonaz calls the man a ninny, but submits to his orders nonetheless.

In return for room and board, the innkeeper requires Calder, Robbie, and me to help with cooking, cleaning, and barn chores. Whichever twin is human also does her share (the innkeepers think the twins are one girl called Cleona). We take turns looking after Sparrow in between our tasks. Plump and content, she is passed from loving arms to loving arms. Thank heaven her growth has slowed, so we need not justify her unusual development to our hosts.

Daily, one of the twins saws the antlers off my head, a slow and joyless process they detest as much as I do. The pile of evidence lies wrapped in an old blanket under my bed. I would discard them or bury them in the night—were it not for fear of meeting Calder in the kitchen again. I have managed to avoid being alone with him since our early morning collision, and I mean to continue keeping my distance from him and his potentially magical voice.

Mondays are laundry days. By midmorning, my fingers wrinkle like raisins from too much time in sudsy water. The air in this windowless outbuilding is steamy, my apron and face as damp as the wrung-out linens strung across the room on the clothesline. No matter how hard I try to conjure the sensation of being knee-deep in the snow, I cannot convince myself to stop sweating.

I wipe my wet brow with my sleeve and stare at the tempting chair in the corner. If I sit, sleep will overcome me. Blessed sleep. The thing that eludes me each night as Sparrow insists on playing for hours rather than slumbering. But I must keep working, just a little longer. I must do my part to earn our keep here.

I hear footsteps as someone enters the room. "Almost done, Darlis," I say.

"It's me," Calder says behind me as I peg the last towel to the sagging line. "Edgar and Darlis are sending us to the mercantile for a few things."

My stomach sinks with dread. A trip to the mercantile with someone who might be manipulating me with his voice seems unwise. I wipe my hands on my apron and face him. My cloak, bonnet, and shawl are draped over his arm. He already wears his heavy coat, wool scarf, and knitted hat.

"Us? Need I go? I'm certain you do not require my assistance to buy nails or flour."

"Darlis insists you go. She needs thread and yard goods, and said she doesn't trust 'a male eye' to choose well. Come on, Sabella. Some fresh air and a change of scenery couldn't hurt. Anyway, we're allowed to use the horse and cart, so we'll be back before the laundry's halfway dry."

"Oh, all right." I untie the apron and hang it on a hook, for I cannot disobey our hostess. "But we must hurry. I've hardly seen Sparrow all day."

Calder points to my head. I reach up to find my cotton cap askew. I feel sick. Anyone—Darlis, or the hired help, or another guest of the inn—might have seen the short spike of my exposed left antler if I'd left the laundry shed without adjusting my head covering.

This is why my parents kept me confined to their home. One careless move and calamity could ensue.

I adjust the cap, then check its position with probing fingers just to be sure. "Better?"

"Depends on your definition of better." Calder passes me my cloak and watches me wrap it around my shoulders. "Personally, I've missed the sight of your antlers."

"Hush," I scold, whisking my bonnet out of his hand. "Someone might hear."

"Well, it's the truth. And for the record, I'm not flirting, merely stating my humble opinion. A tree without branches is just a...a big pole."

I attempt to scowl at him although I find his clumsy analogy more comical than insulting. "I resemble a pole? When you said you weren't flirting, you were definitely being honest." I take the shawl from his arm and use it to secure the bonnet in case of strong wind. Cap, bonnet, and shawl. I am fortified against even the unluckiest of weather-related circumstances.

Calder turns red as a radish—and I like this color on him. "Apologies," he says. Without another word, he escorts me through the door, his hand firm against the center of my back. Even through all my layers of clothes, I think I feel its warmth.

Whirling snowflakes surround us as we cross the yard to the waiting horse and cart. The smallest sliver of sun peeks out coyly from behind gray clouds. The frosty air feels good on my face and in my lungs. I shall not miss the hot laundry shed one bit.

"Did Edgar give you a list?" I ask as I climb onto the driver's bench of the cart—with all the grace of a minnow trying to climb a tree. Of course Calder leaps up with the ease of a young cat.

"Don't need one. It's all in here." He points to his head.

"Very reassuring."

"Your faith in me is nothing short of inspirational," he says with a wry smile. He tosses the loose end of his scarf over his shoulder and commands the horse to walk. The cart lurches forward before settling into a smooth roll.

Calder glances at me. "You'd be astounded to learn of all the wondrous workings that go on within the confines of this handsome head."

"Please do not assail me with such knowledge. The loftiness of it all might cause me to swoon."

He laughs. "Well, aren't you full of sass today? And I expected you to be gloomy company after you tried to avoid coming along."

The truth is I expected the same. I might have even intended to be. But his predictions about the effects of the fresh air and change of scenery were correct. I feel quite enlivened although still cautious. I must be wary of his charms—whether they are natural or magical in origin. And so I let silence fall between us and look for chickadees and sparrows in the roadside hedges.

"You know," Calder says as we travel around a bend, "I've been wondering about you. If you're still happy with us. It's no easy thing to leave home and take up with strangers. How are you faring?"

In spite of the frosty air, heat creeps across my cheeks. I am unused to questions of a personal nature. Certainly my parents never inquired after my feelings or opinions.

When I do not answer immediately, Calder says, "I didn't mean to offend you by asking. Friends do discuss such things."

"I'm not offended." I pause, watching snowflakes fall and cling to the horse's fluffy mane as I choose what to tell him. "I feel... different. Everything is different. Mostly better. And then there's

Sparrow. Her arrival was a shock, of course, but now…the joy she has brought me cannot be measured. Every minute we play together is precious. She loves to listen to my stories, and she even tries to sing along with the songs the twins and I sing for her before bed."

"She is a marvel, our Sparrow," he says. "You know, I think I dreamed of her once, long ago. A girl with pointed ears and an aptitude for healing."

Now that he has me talking, I cannot seem to stop the flood of words. "I only hope her aging will continue at a usual pace. It was alarming to see her growing and changing so quickly. I was afraid she'd pass me in stature before another month was out."

He is quiet. Perhaps he too fears Sparrow's life will be brief. Perhaps he *knows* it will. This is not something I want to hear, even if it is true.

"And you?" I say, anxious to change the subject and forestall the tears that well in my eyes. "Are you pleased with your life?"

"I am."

"Your gifts never inconvenience you?" I want to ask him if he does indeed possess a magical, manipulative voice in addition to his gift of prophetic dreaming, but my courage fails me.

He stares at the road ahead. "Strangely, my dreams have been scarce since we left home. Not that I mind much. A solid night's sleep is far more refreshing than seeing the future. As for my other gift…it is no bother. I learned to control it by the time I turned nine—well enough to keep it hidden. Too late to appease my beleaguered parents, unfortunately. They'd already handed me off to a mostly blind, roving tinker who used me as his servant boy. He was a cruel master. I ran away first chance I got and was lucky enough to be found by Yonaz in the woods."

I imagine him as a little boy, wide-eyed and round of face, with the same eager smile and friendly nature—yet burdened by his failure to be what his parents wanted. This pain I know.

"I'm sorry," I say.

He smiles and scratches his neck. "Well, it all worked out all right in the end. I think I turned out quite splendidly."

"But your gift. Is it so appalling that you must keep it hidden?" Inside my mind, I chide myself for assaulting his privacy—all the while imagining traits of a terrifying nature: limbs swathed in snakeskin beneath his clothes, spider-like appendages folded close to his sides, a talent for transforming into a lava-spewing demon-lizard.

Or perhaps he does possess a voice that can alter the thoughts and feelings of others.

He turns his face toward me. His smile widens and lights his face, banishing my dark notions. "My gift is astounding. But it takes up a fair bit of room, even more than your antlers—so I'm better off keeping it concealed most of the time. Would you like to see, Sabella? I'll show you if you'd like."

Part of me, the irrational part which leans toward being infatuated with him, begs me to say yes, but the sensible part of me subdues her. "We should keep going. We were given an errand to complete."

"Come on. It won't take long. Edgar will never notice if we're gone five extra minutes, and if he does, he'll assume we were mesmerized by the mercantile's baubles and sweets." He steers the horse to the side of the road, toward the edge of a tract of woods. "Whoa," he commands.

"It really isn't necessary to stop," I say. "You could just describe it."

He hops down from the seat and proceeds to tie the horse to a tree.

"Would you rather view the Sistine Chapel or hear someone speak of it? Some things must be seen to be properly appreciated."

The excitement that has crept into his voice proves irresistible. I say, "Well, I suppose, since we've already stopped."

I jump to the ground and follow Calder into the cover of the trees, ignoring the voice in my head that shouts, "Impropriety!"

and "Danger!" As if he too has chosen to ignore that voice, he doffs his coat, tosses it onto a patch of frost-touched moss, and starts to unbutton his shirt.

A hot flush of embarrassment floods my entire body and I turn away from him. "Calder, stop. I may have had a rather rough upbringing, but I do have morals."

"Oh. Sorry. I beg your pardon. I ought to have warned you. I must remove my shirt. Will your modesty permit you to look at my uncovered back?"

"If you really think it is necessary." I have seen my father's bare back on countless occasions as he huddled in the washtub and endured Mother's overzealous scrubbing, but this feels a thousand times more intimate. My stomach flutters. I should have said no.

"All right," Calder says. "Stay as you are until I tell you to turn around."

Half a minute passes. I hear Calder draw several deep breaths behind me, like he's preparing to dive into deep water. Finally he says, "You may look now."

I turn slowly, my heart pounding hard, my eyes squeezed shut. When I open them, when I behold his gift, my knees fail me, and I must grab a tree limb to remain upright. The beauty before me is too much.

Calder Hadrian has the wings of a moth.

Translucent pale green etched with veins of gold and bronze, the wings extend well beyond the edges of his back. Their gently arched tops reach just past the tops of his ears. A single circle of black, yellow, bronze, and white—like the eye of an exotic cat—decorates each upper and lower section of wing. They look soft, and I wonder what it would feel like to run my fingers over them.

"Sabella? What do you think?" He maneuvers one wing in an attempt to get a glimpse of me over his shoulder. The wing's golden veins catch the muted forest light.

What do I think?

I think he is too magnificent for words.

I say, "They're...lovely. The most beautiful wings I have ever seen."

The way he's standing, I can only perceive part of his face, but I'm sure I've never seen him look this happy and proud. "Told you my gift was astounding."

"You spoke the truth."

Again, I wonder: how could his parents have rejected him? How could they have looked at him and seen anything but splendor? Why had they not loved him enough to embrace his uniqueness? My heart breaks for the rejected little boy he was; my throat constricts as I hold back a sob.

He bends forward and grabs his coat from the ground. He gathers it to himself, covering his chest, and spins to face me. "Your antlers are every inch as special as my wings, every bit as exquisite. It's a crime you don't know that."

He takes slow steps toward me, as if I'm a fawn he might scare off. I neither move nor breathe, because I cannot. With one hand, he continues to clutch his coat to his body. With his other hand, he unties my shawl and bonnet. He lifts them off my head and then removes my cotton cap. He drops them all to the ground in a heap. Stunned, I forget that I should protest such familiarity. But without being told, my hands rush to cover the short spikes of my antlers.

"Please don't," Calder says. He takes hold of my wrists and coaxes my hands to my sides before releasing them. "There you are," he says adoringly. "That's the real you."

His eyes meet mine and suddenly I am dizzy, reeling with a fierce longing to touch him that I must resist. I drop my gaze to the groundcover of frost-crusted brown leaves. I clench my hands together at my waist.

"Sabella?" He lifts my chin with his fingertips.

"Yes," I say. The word is both a question and an answer. Because I know he understands me, has endured the same pain as I have. And because I think I could fall in love with him for it, dash it all. Honestly, it might already be too late.

"Will you trust me now that you know my gift?"

His acorn-brown eyes are guileless, but I will not answer this question without asking one of my own. "Do you have another gift? A voice gift of some kind?"

He laughs and lets go of my chin. "If you ask Robbie, he'll tell you I'm the worst singer in the world."

"Please, I have to know. When you say my name, do you add some enchantment, something to affect me unnaturally?"

"You're serious? You find my voice enchanting?" His expression takes a turn toward mischievous. I want to smack him for being overly amused by my theory, but instead I try to burn him with a glare.

His amusement fades as the implication of my question sinks in. "You think I would use magic to make you fall in love with me? I'm not that much of a cad."

"I didn't mean... I only thought..." Embarrassment renders me as hot as I was back in the laundry shed. "We should return to the road." I start to turn away from him, but his hand catches my shoulder. My senses grow strangely keener as he coaxes me to face him once more. I hear dead leaves rattling above me, feel the press of each of his fingertips on my shoulder, and inhale a hint of the hay he unbaled for the horses this morning.

"Wait," he says quietly.

All I can manage to say is, "Sorry."

His eyes. Oh, the depths of them. I see in them that he has already forgiven me, and that he would forgive me a hundred times more. I am mired in regret but full of reckless hope. He holds me with his gaze in a way that I have never been held.

The moment imprints itself on my soul, as random moments do in life. I am a girl with antlers standing before a boy with wings, and nothing will ever be the same.

He takes a deep breath, then says, "I'm trying, really trying, to behave as you wish, Sabella. To simply be a good friend. I may not be succeeding in that regard, but I swear I'd never try to trick you." He takes a step back, his fingers still resting on my shoulder. His delicate wings spread wide behind his pale body. A ribbon of sunlight stripes his dark hair. He is unlike anything or anyone I ever imagined.

His hand leaves my shoulder. Without a word, he bows to retrieve my cap, bonnet, and shawl from the forest floor before he gives them all to me in a pile. My pulse pounds as he traces my cheekbone with one cool finger. Finally, he moves to the far side of a wide hemlock, presumably to fold his wings and to don his shirt.

While he is gone, I miss him. Heavens above, I am a fool. More incautious than I ever suspected. But sorry for it? No.

Not yet, anyway.

In this cathedral of woods, I have seen a moth-winged boy. My heart still beats within my chest, but I feel as if it has given me notice of an imminent departure. My inner voice gives up warning me of danger, packs its bags, and leaves me standing here half afraid but entirely *alive*.

Calder comes from behind me, catches my hand in his, and starts to escort me back to the cart. "This is over the friendship line, I suppose?" he says.

I open my mouth to say yes, but instead I say, "It's fine," and tighten my fingers around his.

"Good," he says smugly. "I like this kind of friendship."

"Perhaps you should stop speaking before I change my mind."

"Sealing my lips."

He helps me onto the wagon seat, untethers the horse, and gets us back on the road in only a few minutes.

The cart bounces over the uneven ground. A few snowflakes flutter around us. I want to enjoy the warmth of Calder's hand and his unusually quiet presence, but I find I must speak. "Whatever may happen between us, Sparrow must come first in my life."

"Understood," he says. He smiles so broadly that it must hurt.

I think back to his earlier question regarding my happiness. I wish he would ask me again if I am happier now than I was at home, where I was trapped in a joyless house, where I spent every day trying to be good, or good enough but pleased no one.

And in spite of my jumbled feelings, I would answer without hesitation: yes.

CALDER

This cart moves far too quickly. I wish I'd chosen a less energetic horse. A half dead one would have been a better choice. Sabella's hand is in mine, and I never want this journey to end.

I steal a glance. There's a smile on her lips. The angle at which she holds her chin hints at contentment. Me, I could cry with happiness. I won't, but I could.

This afternoon has been one miracle after another. I trusted her with the secret of my wings, and I think she's starting to trust me, too.

It has been ages since I let anyone see my wings. I almost forget they exist sometimes. No, that isn't true. I never forget they're folded close to my back, rubbing against my shirt, tickling my skin. When they itch—a common occurrence in summer—it is first-rate torture. I cannot say that I am ashamed of them, but... Silly as it sounds, I do not think I have forgiven them for costing me the love of my adoptive parents.

I don't deny that my wings are pretty—at least what I've glimpsed of them over my shoulder—but I see them more as untrustworthy companions than constant friends. I would never dare to rely upon them to carry me off the ground for more than a few feet.

But who needs to leave the ground? Here on the earth, Sabella lives and breathes.

My mind rushes toward the future, but I force it to stop. This moment is enough. The cart hits a bump, and her fingers tighten around mine. The fault is probably not the horse's, but just in case, I will reward him later with the biggest carrot I can find.

SABELLA

Somehow, in a blur of time, we arrive back where we started. Calder parks the cart near the kitchen door, in the shadowy alley between the inn and one of the outbuildings. "Well. Here we are," he says with a surprising hint of awkwardness. "Shall we go again tomorrow?"

"If Darlis needs more thread, then yes." My voice sounds different to me, as if I am not the same girl I was this morning. But I think I like this girl I'm becoming.

"Good," Calder replies.

We are alone, save for the horse. We remain on the driver's bench, our fingers entwined, listening to melted snow dripping from the eaves. The pleasant scent of herb-roasted chicken mingles with the acrid stench of the nearby barn.

"Your wings," I say in a hushed voice. "I feel as if I dreamed them."

"They're real all right. As real as your splendid antlers."

"Bony gray branches are hardly 'splendid.'"

"Nonsense. But let's not argue. Arguing would be a waste of our time together. You'll be knee-deep in laundry again soon."

I nod, agreeing to a truce.

He shifts on the bench, turning slightly toward me, the reins lying loose over his thighs. Our eyes lock for half a minute, and then he leans close. His breath warms my cheek for a heartbeat before his lips meet my cheekbone. I close my eyes and forget the world. It seems such a small thing, the touch of his lips on my face, but I feel as if some of his inner light is seeping through my skin, filling me with sweet happiness.

"Darnation!" Robbie exclaims. We spring apart. "Can't a person walk through an alley anymore without seeing things he'll want to unsee?"

Calder laughs, but I shrink away from him in embarrassment.

"Since you're here, you can help unload," Calder says to Robbie. His grin contains not a hint of shame. He hops from the seat to the ground.

Robbie rolls his eyes and plods to the rear of the cart. "Just when I thought my luck couldn't get any worse."

Deep in the night, when I ought to be asleep, I lie awake clutching my pillow. For once, Sparrow sleeps soundly in the borrowed cradle, an arm's length from the edge of my bed. The twins sleep forehead to forehead, dog and girl, in their bed across the room, while I question every choice I've made in the last few weeks.

And I worry.

I worry about my ceaselessly growing Sparrow and her future. I fret over the idea of returning to the icy roads soon. The safety of our next home. Most of all, I agonize over Calder.

Are his feelings for me authentic or a fleeting fancy? And what of my feelings for him? We have known each other for such a short time, and fires that catch fast burn quickly and leave behind nothing but ashes.

I roll over. My nightgown twists and entangles my legs.

If Mother were here, she would scold me for being easy prey for a charmer. I hear her voice in my head, her words slurred by medicine: *He does not truly care for you. Boys will take whatever they can from a girl, and it's the girl who ends up maligned and ruined.*

If you think a man would ever really love the likes of you, you're a fool. You were a bad daughter; you'd be a worse wife.

You should be ashamed of yourself for allowing his advances, Sabella Jenkins.

Perhaps this apparition of Mother is right. Perhaps years of loneliness and isolation have left me all too vulnerable to kind words and adoring glances. But maybe, just maybe, she was wrong. Maybe her views of the world and of me were tainted by her own bitterness and broken dreams. Her own failures.

Am I brave enough to dismiss her apparition and to choose to follow my own heart?

I stare at the shadowed ceiling until I hear the squeak of the stairs that daily announces the housemaid is on her way down to stoke the kitchen fire. It is time to rise and dress for a new day—ready or not.

SABELLA

MARCH 8, 1886
AFTERNOON

We have bided another week at the inn, waiting for Yonaz to recover.

In my free hour after washing the dishes from the midday meal, I go to my bedroom. Sparrow toddles across the floor and collapses into my arms, squealing with delight.

She was a scrawny newborn when I drew her from the basket. According to Darlis, she is now the size of an average one-year-old. Fortunately, the innkeeper's wife would believe our dashing Calder if he told her the stars were bits of paper pasted to the sky—so she readily accepted his explanation of Sparrow's rapid development as "a family peculiarity." If we stay here much longer and Sparrow continues to grow like a well-watered weed, Darlis may lose faith in his claims.

"I am tired of this place," Cleona says, collapsing onto her mattress and staring at the plastered ceiling. Her red curls spread around her head like a spilled sunset. On the rug in front of the fireplace, Branna the dog whimpers. "See? Sister agrees. We are both utterly and completely tired of being able only to take the form of the same dog, day in and day out."

I lift Sparrow onto my hip and carry her to look out a fraction of the window not glazed with starry frost. "It is for your protection, trying as it may be. The doctor did say that Yonaz will be fit to travel within a week. Then you can change into whatever you choose."

Cleona sits up and gathers the quilt around her like a cloak. "It isn't like that, though. We don't get to choose our shape, not often. We can ask, but the magic does what it wants. Anyway, I'm going to ask to be something with extra thick fur next time. A polar bear, perhaps."

"That would surely scare off any thieves or scoundrels. You don't see many polar bears in Pennsylvania."

"Well, I don't care. I think it's a grand idea."

Sparrow presses one tiny palm against the window glass, melting a hand shape into the frost. She shivers and subsequently wipes the moisture onto my sleeve. If only she could turn into a polar bear for the journey, then I would not have to fret about keeping her safe and warm.

A knock rattles the door. Calder enters clutching something brown and furry. "Ladies," he says with a slight bow.

My insides perform a series of somersaults. Sparrow wriggles and reaches for him, so I pass her to him, exchanging her for the furred object. Thank heavens the thing does not appear to be alive.

"Bought it from a pair of peddlers who stopped by," Calder says. "The man was persuasive enough, but his little boy could sell snowshoes to a mermaid. He overcharged me for the thing, but it should prove practical."

The garment unfurls in my hands. It is a Sparrow-sized fur cape, complete with a little hood. I sigh in admiration.

"That is the most adorable thing my eyes have ever seen," Cleona says. "I'm jealous, so I am."

"You? Jealous of a bit of old pelt when you get to inhabit all kinds of fur coats?" Calder says.

Cleona scowls at him. "A cape is clothing. 'Tis not the same at all, Calder. You have no idea what it's like to be a girl."

"Thank the stars for that," Calder says. He laughs and tosses Sparrow gently into the air. She giggles profusely. After a few more tosses, he snuggles her close to his chest and says, "I bought something for you as well, Sabella."

"So romantic," Cleona teases, hand on heart. "Well, what is it? Let us have a look." Canine Branna lifts her head from her paws and sniffs the air as if searching for a clue.

"No. I'm going to save it for later. For when all the good little girls are asleep," says Calder.

"Do you imply that I'm not good?" I ask. My mother would say that indeed I am not, allowing myself to swan over a boy who convinced me to run away from home—unwed, and with a baby in tow.

"And are you calling me a little girl?" Cleona asks, temper flaring. Her hair always looks redder to me when she's riled up.

"Um...I'm going to go finish my chores now, before I get into real trouble." Calder kisses the baby and sets her on her feet. She waddles back toward the window. "Meet me in the sitting room after supper, Sabella?"

"Yes," I say.

"Is it jewelry?" Cleona asks, now sounding more curious than indignant.

"Not telling," Calder says. He ducks out the door.

"I reckon it is jewelry," Cleona says. "Goodness, I wish I had a suitor."

"You're fourteen," I say. "You don't need a suitor. It would be wiser for me not to have one, in fact."

She scowls and perches on the edge of her bed. "Who told you I was fourteen? Calder? He's forever treating Branna and me like we're babies. I'm fifteen, and I'll be sixteen in little more than a week."

"Calder is not to be blamed. I simply guessed. I'm sorry."

Cleona is quiet for a minute before asking, "Do you think I will ever have a suitor, Sabella? Since I'm an animal half the time and all? Would anyone want someone who does that and cannot stop herself?"

The mattress sinks as I settle beside her. "I'm sure you'll find someone when the time is right. Someone with a big enough heart to love everything about you." This I believe. Not long ago I thought it impossible that anyone could care for me in spite of my antlers. And then, miraculously, Calder appeared. Why should Cleona not have a miracle of her own someday?

"I do hope so. I hope he's as nice as Calder. Only I'd prefer black hair over brown. And bigger ears. Calder has strange little ears."

I stifle a laugh. "I will not tell him you said so. Besides, I rather like his ears."

Sparrow toddles to me and grips my skirt with both hands. "Up," she commands.

"Yes, your majesty," I reply.

We play pat-a-cake until the clang of the dinner bell echoes through the inn. Branna barks, Cleona declares herself utterly famished, and Sparrow claps joyfully.

I adjust my cap as I speculate upon what gift Calder will offer me later. Hair ribbons, fine soap, a woolen shawl, a tarnished silver spoon once treasured by another owner? I know already I will cherish whatever he offers me. The mere notion that he thought to choose a gift for me is a gift in itself.

"Come on," Cleona says. She lifts Sparrow onto her hip and heads out the door. "If you stand there daydreaming much longer, the boys'll gobble all the rolls."

I follow her, eager to finish a meal I have not yet begun.

CALDER

When dinner ends, Yonaz and the others leave the dining room and make their way to their bedrooms or the parlor. I linger beside the table as Sabella piles dirty plates onto a wooden tray. She blushes under my gaze but keeps working.

"If you're going to stay, you could collect the bowls," she says.

"Of course," I say. "But first..." I round the table and tug at the puffy cotton cap she wears to hide the small antlers that have pushed up from her skull since daybreak. "It was slipping."

My fingers barely graze the top of her head, but color rises on her cheekbones. She says, "Thank you," but the words are directed to the dish she's holding.

"Did I offend you?" I ask.

"No," she says to a butter knife.

"Good. Grand." I did not expect her former awkwardness with

me to return, but here it is, staining her face and making her fumble with the spoons and forks.

"You're certain? We're still friends?"

Now she looks at me with those big eyes of hers and melts my insides. "Well," she says, making the word longer than it has a natural right to be. "Maybe I'm not so certain anymore. About being friends, that is."

If she weren't smiling, I might panic. My heart gallops like a wild pony. "You mean...?"

She sets the last plate onto the tray. "I cannot make any promises, but...I think I want to possibly, maybe consider being more than friends."

At this, I take her by the arms and spin her around the room in a clumsy, joyful dance. She laughs. From the kitchen, Cleona calls out, "What in the world is going on in there? I'd like to finish the washing up before midnight, if you could be bothered to bring the dishes."

We stop spinning. Sabella holds onto my shirtsleeves. If I were bolder and braver, I might lean forward and kiss her smiling mouth. I want to. I almost do. But she releases me, steps backward, and returns to her task. She's glowing from within, I swear.

"I'll be right there," she says to Cleona.

Breathless from the dance, I help her carry the dishes to the kitchen. I've been following her for years, but darn if I wouldn't follow her anywhere, to the very ends of the earth.

SABELLA

Robbie is already lounging on his favorite sofa in the sitting room when Calder and I walk in. While we were busy working, the bird-legged boy has been busy napping. A blanket covers his propped-up avian feet.

Robbie opens one eye and peers at us. "If it isn't the love-birds," he says dryly. "In consideration of my delicate presence, I recommend that you occupy separate chairs."

"Not likely, Robin Hallsey," Calder says. He takes my hand and leads me to sit beside him on a small couch. "You may excuse yourself if you find our company disagreeable."

"I think I should stay and make sure you behave in a respectable manner," Robbie says. "Cads will be cads, as you well know." He reclines against the cushions and folds his arms over his chest.

"Cad? That's harsh," Calder says. "Well, I suppose we must pretend he isn't here, then, Sabella. Like a rash you try not to scratch."

Robbie grunts. "That's a fine way to talk about your best friend."

I scowl at the pair of them. "If you boys are going to spend the evening sparring, I will go help the twins put Sparrow to bed." I do hope they settle down, because I am anxious to see the mysterious item Calder bought from the traveling merchant.

"Very well. For you, I'll hold my tongue," Robbie says. "But I'm not leaving."

"Fine," I say. "Let's talk about something pleasant now."

Calder recounts the events of his day with the newly hired, comically clumsy stable boy. We laugh as the fire crackles and the wind rattles the windowpanes. After a while, Robbie snores.

"Finally," Calder says. He inches closer to me on the couch. "It must be eleven o'clock by now. He usually can't stay awake past nine. He can be a stubborn bird, our Robbie."

On any other night, I'd be drowsy at this hour, too. But ever since tonight's dinner ended, I've been as twitchy as a mad cat. "I should go upstairs soon," I say. "Sparrow wakes up before the chickens, and I have to help prepare breakfast tomorrow."

"Well, then." He reaches into his jacket pocket. "You must take this and tuck it under your pillow."

He places the gift in my palm. It is a wooden heart, sanded smooth and painted black, embellished with bright, shiny colors.

"Thank you," I say, staring at the tiny present. "It's lovely."

With one of his hands, he cups the back of my hand. With the pointer finger of his other hand, he draws my attention to tiny details. "There's a little deer with antlers like yours, and there's a butterfly with wings somewhat like mine. And there's a wee little hen. I reckon that stands for Robbie. And on the other side..." He turns it over before he continues. "There's a bird, for Sparrow, and another bird for whichever twin might be the wild one of the day. Pay no mind to this horribly fat porcupine eating grass. Or is it a raccoon throwing up? You could paint over that, I suppose."

"It is perfect."

"And it's the shape of a heart. To remind you that you have my heart, Sabella."

"I'm sorry, but *ugh*," Robbie interjects, eyes still shut. "How utterly unoriginal."

In spite of Robbie's interruption, my actual, non-wooden heart is skipping like a flat rock over the surface of an endless lake.

"Go back to sleep, Rob." Calder says. He tucks a stray lock of hair behind my ear. In his eyes, there is such longing. If we were alone, I think he would try to kiss me—and I believe I would allow it.

Mother's stern voice warns me inside my head: *Flee now, foolish girl.* But I refuse to heed her advice.

"I mean it," Calder says softly. "My heart is yours."

Flustered, I say, "Thank you." And it sounds more like a question than an answer. How can he offer me his heart when we know so little of each other? Yet I can no longer deny that my feelings for him are strong.

"I dislike you both very much," Robbie says. He sits up and throws a pillow at Calder. It bounces off the arm of the couch. "Separately, you're tolerable, but together you're more nauseating than Yonaz's turnip pie."

Calder tosses the pillow back. It collides with Robbie's chest. Robbie raises his arm, aims, and prepares to return fire.

I rise from the couch. "I'm going upstairs before you boys break something." I take half a step and Calder catches my hand to stop me.

"Wait. I'll see you to your door," he says.

"Good night and good riddance to you both," Robbie says.

"Good night, Robbie. Sleep well," I say.

Calder follows me toward the staircase. In my hand, I clench the pretty wooden heart. I am warm through and through in spite of the draft that whistles through the hallway like a forlorn ghost.

SABELLA

MARCH 9, 1886
MORNING

Minutes before sunrise, by candlelight and the glow of our bedroom's fireplace, Branna slowly saws away at the base of my antlers. Clearly, she has had little experience with such a tool. I grit my teeth and grip the seat of the wooden chair I'm sitting on. Cleona is more efficient at this task, but she is now the fluffy dog who sits on the floor beside Sparrow and endures her overenthusiastic patting.

Tears gather along my closed eyelids. I refuse to complain that she's pulling my hair. Her clumsy saw work reminds me of the times my medicine-addled mother did the job while Father worked extra shifts. Mother's angry grunts and whispered curses echo in my memory.

Calder clears his throat and rouses me from my waking nightmare. I did not hear him enter, yet here he is, a few feet away from me, frowning.

"Branna, I think you should let me do that," he says in a pained voice.

"Please do." She gives him the saw and goes to join her sister and Sparrow. "It makes my arms sore and the dust! I hate it. I'd rather look after the baby, to be sure."

Calder crouches before me and swipes away my tears with his handkerchief.

I rearrange the old blanket that covers my shoulders, stirring up the antler dust it's kept off my dress. "Let me do it, Calder. I can manage. I know how much you hate it." I grab for the saw but he whisks it out of reach.

"I will do it. I will do it knowing that someday soon I will not have to. Someday soon we will live in a safe place, and you can grow antlers as wide and high as you like." He stands, gripping the saw so tightly his knuckles whiten. "Now, close your eyes and listen to my voice."

I obey.

He wraps his hand around my neck and starts to cut, smoothly and capably. "Imagine this," he says. "We're walking in a white birch grove, just you and me. The birds chirp above us, a bed of moss cushions our steps, and the air is sweet with the scent of ferns. Your antlers spread above you in a magnificent silvery crown, and the hem of your silken gown brushes the tops of your bare feet. You feel safe and happy as we walk hand in hand."

"And your wings are unfurled," I add, eyes still shut. "All green and gold in the forest shade."

"Of course," he says.

I inhale sharply as one antler breaks free. He massages the base of my neck with his thumb, making my pulse quicken.

"Halfway done," he whispers reassuringly. He begins to saw the other antler. "Back to our story. My wings are spread, and the moths of the wood flutter around me, admiring them. You laugh because moths are perching on my nose and chin, and I laugh because their feet tickle. And then a strong wind blows through and carries them all away."

The second antler breaks loose. I open my eyes. He has made

what has always been torture into something tolerable, and that is as good as a miracle.

Calder sets the saw on the bed and pulls me to my feet. "There now. You may thank me."

"Thank you."

I want to say more. To tell him his kindness is worth more to me than all the riches on earth, and how I long to walk with him always—through moth-filled forests, sandy deserts, or wherever life's road leads. I want to say that if my antlers must be cut off a thousand more times, I would hardly mind at all, were he the one to always wield the saw. Of course I cannot say these things aloud. Not yet.

Sparrow, bored with harassing Cleona, waddles over to Calder and yanks on his trouser leg. "Up, up," she demands.

He lifts her and settles her on his hip. "You, my girl, weigh more than a prize piglet."

"That's funny, because I'm thinking she's hungry again," Branna says.

"I'd better get downstairs and help Darlis with breakfast before she comes looking for me," I say. I retrieve the antlers, wrap them in the blanket I'd been wearing, and shove them under the bed with their predecessors. And then I hurry for the door.

"Wait," Calder says. "Your cap, Sabella. You've forgotten it again."

"Thank you." I hurry to snatch the cap off the dressing table. I set it on my head and knot the strings too tightly at the base of my throat. Anger simmers in my stomach. Such incautiousness is unacceptable. I could have put my friends in mortal danger.

I must do better, be better.

But can I, if I continue to allow myself to be distracted by a starry-eyed, moth-winged boy? Must I take a step back from my own happiness for the safety and good of my child and the other Springborn? With all of my heart, I hope not.

SABELLA

Yonaz sits at the head of the dinner table like a tattooed, mustachioed king, a proud grin on his ashen face. I hardly know the man, but I can scarce contain my joy at the sight of him.

"Good evening, my friends," he says as we file into the room one after the other: first Calder and me, then Robbie and Sparrow, and finally Branna and canine Cleona. "How I have missed you all." I'd almost forgotten the richness of his Slavic-accented voice.

His eyes fix on Calder's hand at my waist. "I see you have not squandered your time here, Calder, my lad. Well and good, I say. Love can fashion any wilderness into a home, can it not? Even an inn where one is waylaid by ill chance."

If my face grows any hotter, I fear my hair will catch fire.

"Welcome back, Yonaz," Robbie says. "You gave us quite a fright." From Robbie's arms, Sparrow waves gleefully.

Branna rushes over to hug Yonaz's neck; Cleona wags her tail and licks his proffered hand. Conversations begin as we sit and pile food onto our plates: chicken pie, roasted potatoes, carrots glazed with honey, rolls as soft as pillows. Renewed hope makes appetites flourish. The simple meal becomes a celebration.

Time passes quickly. When the clock chimes nine, Sparrow is asleep on my lap and Branna dozes with her chin resting on her fist.

"Tomorrow," Yonaz declares, "we will resume our journey."

"But the doctor—" Robbie objects.

"The doctor has done his duty, and I am healed. Now, to bed. In the morning, we shall pack our belongings and be gone from this place before the sun climbs halfway up the sky."

Under the table, Calder finds my hand. He slips a piece of paper into my grasp. I gaze at him askance. When did he have time to pen a note? I know for a fact he spent all day repairing a wall in the barn.

Everyone stands. Calder kisses my hand and then helps a rather wobbly Yonaz out of the room. Branna takes Sparrow from my arms and, yawning, follows Cleona and Robbie upstairs. As for me, I must wash a mountain of dishes before I can retire for the night.

Alone in the quiet kitchen, I unfold the note. Calder has sketched me—poorly but endearingly—with my antlers full of little birds and squirrels. Underneath, the scrawled caption says *To My Antler Girl, from Your Devoted, Moth-Winged Admirer*.

The note brings a smile to my lips. It is a great surprise to be admired. Something like a miracle. Years spent with parents who found me repugnant did not prepare me for the possibility of being held dear by anyone, ever.

And yet, he must care deeply for me, for he has soothed me with kind words and he has worshiped me with his eyes when words could not be said. He's given me a token of his heart, and he has entrusted me with the secret of his wings. He has, in spite of his deep hatred for the task, sawn the antlers from my head to preserve my safety. What other evidence should I require as proof of his devotion?

Oh, how I want to believe we might have a future together. It would be too wonderful.

Mother's voice invades my mind—no matter that I banished it over a week ago. *You hardly know this boy. No doubt he's hiding things from you like he hides his wings. He'll be your ruin, Sabella, and you will be his. Think of your baby instead of yourself for once.*

I hide the note in the pocket of my skirt and don a sauce-splattered apron. As I wash the plates and cups, Mother's voice fades away. But for the rest of the night, I cannot shake the feeling that disaster is about to fall upon me.

SABELLA

MARCH 10, 1886
MORNING

Someone knocks on the bedroom door before dawn, and I know before the door swings open that it is Calder.

I am wide awake, washed, and dressed, but Sparrow is nestled between Branna and fur-clad Cleona. They sleep like sisters, arms and legs sprawled over one another. I should have woken them all an hour ago. Instead, I've been packing their trunk, relishing the last bit of silence before our journey. And arguing with myself about giving up Calder. My intellect demands that we revert to being friends, but my heart insists upon the opposite.

The door clicks shut behind Calder. Yes, I was awake before, but now I am more than awake. I cross the room to meet him, hardly daring to breathe lest I awaken the sleepers. He and I may not have another private moment together for a while. I should voice my doubts to him, but in his presence, my heart wrestles my good sense to the ground and pummels it unconscious.

We stand two feet apart, facing one another. His hungry look makes my pulse race. Carefully, as if approaching something dangerous, he takes a step toward me. He reaches up to trace the curve of one of my antlers. "You look like the queen of the forest," he whispers.

"I don't want to be queen," I whisper in reply.

He steps closer and cradles my elbows in his hands. He presses his forehead to mine and shuts his eyes. His breath brushes my face. His hands, still cupping my elbows, tremble almost imperceptibly. "Doesn't matter. You rule me. I can think of nothing but you all day. You and me, and the life we could share."

"I think of us, too," I confess. Perhaps I should not have, but here in the near-darkness, so close to him, I lose all good sense.

"Us," he says. His eyes are still closed, but he's smiling. "I like the sound of that." And then his fingers slide to my shoulder blades, and his head tips to one side, and I cannot think, I only want him to kiss me—but a giggle comes from the bed. We spring apart.

"Go on," Branna says. "I won't tell a soul."

"We were only talking," I say.

"Didn't look like talking to me. Looked like you—"

"Where's that saw, Sabella?" Calder interrupts. The candlelight isn't dim enough to hide the beet-red of his cheeks. I point underneath my bed, and he fetches the tool. "We'd best get on with the sawing. Yonaz is waiting for your trunks, and he's always ill-tempered when forced to rise before the sun."

I sit on the chair near the fireplace and submit to the blade, half dizzy from our almost-kiss.

"Now, good thoughts," Calder says. "Close your eyes. We're in a boat on a blue lake, surrounded by water lilies and paddling turtles..."

His voice enthralls me as he continues. I lose myself in his imaginary world. No tears slip from my eyes as he works the blade. I hardly notice when the first antler comes off.

He stops sawing. The second antler breaks free. I look up at him. He holds the saw in one hand, the silver-gray antler in the other. His face is pained and remorseful.

"Don't be sorry. It isn't your fault," I say. I stand and take the antler from him. Perhaps he's imagining how it would feel to lose his wings every morning. "It doesn't hurt me, remember?"

He looks unconvinced as he hands me the antlers. I hold them to my chest and confess, "I've been hiding these under the bed."

"I wondered. Rob and I will haul the lot out to the woods before we take to the road."

"You might have to make two or three trips, unless you find a big crate to carry them in. I should have been sneaking them out and burying them all along, but Darlis and Sparrow kept me busy all the hours heaven sent."

"No need to apologize."

Across the room, Branna yawns loudly and stretches her arms wide. "What time is it?"

"Time to leave," Calder says dryly. "Get dressed or prepare to be tossed into the wagon in your nightdress."

"Calder Hadrian! What a scandalous thing to say!" Branna says.

He points to a closed trunk. "Is that one ready to go?"

"It is," I say. "And the others will be as soon as these slugabed girls are dressed."

Calder lifts the trunk and I hurry to open the door for him. "Thank you for...everything," I say as he passes by. I'm probably blushing more than he is, but I don't care one jot.

"You're welcome for everything. And *almost* everything." He kisses my cheek and heads for the stairs. I place my fingertips over the place where his lips pressed against my skin, wishing to safeguard the kiss forever.

"Shut the door, Sabella! You're letting a draft in," Branna shouts, causing the baby and the dog to whimper.

If there is a draft, I fail to notice it. Heaven help me.

CALDER

I slip into Robbie's room, shut the door, and rest my back against its boards. He looks up from his packing and scowls.

"What's that look?" Robbie asks. "Darnation. How you manage to appear miserable and happy at the same time—it's quite a trick."

"I don't want to talk about it."

"Yet you came into my room with that face on you." He sets a pile of folded shirts into his trunk.

"Fine. I'll talk. Firstly, I think Sabella is warming up to me. Secondly, I might have done something terrible." I cover my eyes with my hand. The motion makes the envelope in my pocket crackle as if in accusation.

Robbie slams the lid of the trunk. "Tell me you didn't propose. Saints above, Calder!"

"No! No. I mean, I would in a heartbeat if I thought she would say yes." I pull the letter out and hold it aloft by a corner like it's a rotting fish carcass. "It's this."

"That is a letter. So?"

"It isn't my letter. It's to Sabella. From her mother."

"How, pray tell, did you come to possess this letter?" Robbie perches on the edge of his bed and stares daggers at me.

"A delivery man brought it earlier. He'd been searching for Sabella along the roads and byways between here and Miners Ridge for a while. I told him I would give her the letter, but I can't."

"You have to," he says in his stern schoolteacher voice.

"I cannot, Rob." I bang my head back against the door. The thud hurts in a good way, because I deserve a hurting. "I read the blasted thing."

Robbie throws his hands up in exasperation. "You are... I have no words."

"I know, I know. But if I give it to her, she'll leave. If she leaves, she won't come back. She will be lost to me, and I will just be... lost."

"Calder."

Yonaz's voice echoes through the inn. "Time to leave, my children!"

"Calder," Robbie says again. "You have to give her the letter now. Before we leave and she's even farther from home. It's her choice to go with us or go back. You know that."

"You're right," I say. I stuff the letter back into my pocket. "I'll help you with the trunk first."

We lug the trunk down the stairs and out to the wagon. I argue with myself with each step I take. I should give Sabella the letter, I should not. But in the end, I yield to my fear and weakness and decide to leave the envelope in the depths of my pocket.

Surely it can wait another day.

SABELLA

The wagons are loaded. Yonaz's is full of boxes and trunks. In the other wagon, Branna and Cleona, Sparrow and Robbie, and our reluctant nanny goat take their places with assorted blankets and a crate or two of food. Calder looks surprised when I climb onto the driver's bench beside him.

"You'll freeze," he says with a shake of his head. "I'd enjoy your company, yes, but I'd rather you were safe and warm with Sparrow in the back."

"Darlis gave me her old fur-lined jacket to wear under my cloak and shawls, and my pockets are full of hot potatoes. Sparrow is ready to nap, and she'll happily sleep in Robbie's arms." These things I manage to say bravely in spite of a gnawing nervousness in my belly.

"Truly, you need not suffer the cold on my account."

"Calder Hadrian, have I not just told you I'm dressed well enough for a polar expedition? If you do not wish for my company, please say so plainly."

He laughs and puts an arm around me. "I want your company, goose. Continually. And in spite of the fact that you're more stubborn than I imagined."

I wriggle and throw off his arm, but he only laughs.

"Ready?" Yonaz calls from the other wagon.

"Whenever you are," Calder replies. He turns toward me and says, "Would you care to drive, my antlered queen?"

"Queens don't drive wagons; they command coachmen." I tug his knit hat down to better protect his ears—and remember Cleona's opinion of their size. I bite my lower lip to forestall a giggle.

"Is something humorous, Sabella?" He rolls his eyes. "Don't tell me. One of the twins has been making remarks about my ears again."

"I cannot betray the confidences of my friends," I say.

"I'm right, then. Those twins look sweet but it's just a cover for their naughtiness."

The other wagon trundles forward. Calder shakes the reins and commands our horses to follow. The sky above us is a pretty ceiling of low, blue-gray clouds. The horses pull us merrily along the road. My thoughts ramble as we pass through a patch of woods. What will our new home be like? Will I share a room with the twins again? I have enjoyed our sisterly companionship, our late-night whispers, and sharing the care and the joy of baby Sparrow with them.

Calder keeps quiet as he drives, which is unusual. Perhaps he is simply enjoying the journey. On a day like this, it is a fine thing to ride behind a good pair of horses. The thought leads me to wonder if he's traveled without the aid of horses or wheels. Are his wings ornamental, or are they strong enough to lift him off the ground?

Impulsively, I ask, "Do you ever use your wings to fly?"

His face reddens. "Well...no."

"Never?"

"No." The syllable is clipped. He shifts on the seat. "I'd rather not speak of that, if you don't mind. It's my business and no one else's."

The startling coldness in his voice makes me cringe like a chastened child. "I'm sorry. I was just curious. You're entitled to your privacy, of course."

"Forgive me," he says formally. "I should not have used that tone. I'm a little tired. On edge about moving again, I suppose."

"It's fine," I say.

But it is not at all fine. As Mother's imagined voice has warned, this boy has secrets he's not willing to share. I shove both hands into my pockets and clutch the slowly cooling potatoes therein. Silence crowds into the space between us on the bench, an uninvited and uneasy guest. In the distance, I see storm clouds I did not notice before.

I listen to the clip clop of the horses' hooves and the faint, muffled sound of Robbie and the twins conversing behind us. If I could start the day over, I would—and I'd keep my questions about Calder's wings to myself.

Perhaps a mile farther on, Calder tries to make light conversation. He relates a story of getting into mischief with Robbie, but my worries make me an unenthusiastic audience. As the clouds thicken above us and tiny snowflakes begin to descend, he goes quiet.

Carefully, I inch away from him so that when the wagon jostles us, our bodies will not touch.

SABELLA

MARCH 10, 1886
AFTERNOON

Hours pass, and the snow falls like the harsh judgment of an angry god. I hunch under my shawls and cloak, regretting my choice to ride outside the wagon. Calder tries again to entertain me with a tale, but like the weather, my mood has been darkening since he snapped at me. He reverts to silence.

The snow becomes a stinging curtain of white. It covers the ground until the location of the road is something to guess at. The horses stumble and the wagon's wheels slip from time to time as we move into deeper and deeper layers of accumulation. But we cannot stop. There is nowhere to shelter, nowhere to warm ourselves and the poor horses.

I glance at Calder. Snow clings to his eyelashes, his hat, and his coat, and forms a fluffy blanket atop the woolen one covering our laps and legs. His scarf has slipped down to reveal that he is gnawing his lower lip with worry.

If optimistic Calder is worried, the situation must be grave indeed. Anxiety smothers the anger I'd been nursing.

"Perhaps we'll come upon a farm soon," I say, almost shouting to be heard over a gust of wind. "Or a town."

"That would be a fine thing," Calder says brightly, as if I've just suggested that the sun might burst forth and instantly render the road snowless at any moment.

Oh, for such a miracle!

The potatoes in my pockets have gone cold. I slide closer to Calder to offer, in a purely practical manner, what little warmth I can—or to leach away at his. He puts his arm around me and holds me tight against his side. This I allow, in spite of his earlier snappishness. Staying alive trumps holding onto a grudge.

Behind us, inside the wagon, Robbie and Branna sing "London Bridge" to baby Sparrow. Canine Cleona howls along. I covet the warmth of a dog's furry body on my lap, and I miss my Sparrow's sunny smile, but I am thankful that our passengers are not suffering the pelting snow and biting wind.

The sound of Yonaz's cough drifts back to our ears from the other wagon. Calder and I exchange concerned glances. The man's hacking worsens with every mile. If we do not find somewhere to wait out the storm soon, he may end up confined to bed for weeks again...or worse.

Yonaz's wagon lurches to a halt, stuck in a drift. He exclaims in dismay, a sharp word in a foreign tongue. From what I can see through the blizzard, the snow reaches halfway up his wagon's wheels, ending a few inches short of the underside of the wagon bed.

Calder tugs the reins with one hand and the brake with the other. The wagon slides a little, and I grab hold of the seat until it stops. Then Calder states the obvious. "Looks like we're stuck."

"What will we do?"

"There is nothing we can do at the moment. The way it's coming down, trying to dig a path would be like bailing water out of a sinking ship with a thimble. We'll just have to try to keep warm inside the wagon until the storm passes. Heaven help the horses. If only one of us had a gift that enabled us to shrink them so they'd fit inside the wagons."

"Poor things. We should give them a few blankets, at least."

"Yes. Good idea. You can join the others. I'll do what I can for the horses and send Yonaz to you. If someone could milk the goat, a bit of a warm drink might soothe his cough."

Calder adjusts his scarf to cover his mouth and nose, then jumps from the seat and plunges knee-deep into the snow. "Wait," he says. "I'll carry you. No need for you to get soaked to the bone in this weather."

I move to the end of the seat. He opens his arms and I drop into his embrace. He cradles me close as he trudges through the snow. Through all my layers and his, I think I feel the steady thumping of his heart against my body—but this must be my imagination. Our faces are inches apart, although his is half covered by a green woolen scarf. His nearness and the tender way he holds me wreak havoc upon my determination to doubt and disdain him.

"Don't worry," he says, his voice muffled by the scarf. He shakes his head until the fabric falls away from his mouth. "Everything will be fine. The storm cannot last forever. We have food, and we have each other. What more could a person want?"

"A roaring fire? A hot bath?"

"Overrated," he says. "As are dry clothes, feather mattresses, and warm spiced apple cider."

His pace is slow, hindered by the depth of the snow and the lashing wind. His breathing becomes labored. Still, he refuses to set me down. By the time he stops at the rear of the wagon, the sting of his previous offense fades to a distant ache.

The canvas is cinched closed, the wooden gate shut tight. "I suppose you should knock, as my hands are full," he says.

I reach out to rap on the wood, but stop short. "Promise me you'll hurry back. If you fall ill again—"

"I swear I'll be back so fast you'll hardly notice I'm gone. Now, knock before frostbite takes my toes."

I lift my fist toward the wagon again, but before I can touch the boards, Calder dips his head and kisses my forehead. The kiss is like the peck of a cold-beaked bird. It is nothing more than I would accept from any good friend, I tell myself, ignoring the fact that it makes my insides melt like an icicle in the sun.

"A token by which to remember me while we are apart," he says softly. "And to thank you for forgiving my rudeness."

I blink up at him. He looks almost pleased with the situation. "Am I to take that as an apology?"

That familiar grin of his appears. "No time for formalities. Go on, knock. Have you not noticed that it's snowing out here?"

Now I have had enough of his teasing. I wriggle. "Set me on the lip of the wagon. I'll be fine there until someone opens the canvas."

He grips me tighter. "Don't be ridiculous. I won't leave you to balance on a tiny ledge of slippery wood. Go ahead and knock."

This time, I manage to pound on the wagon gate and call out, "Robbie?"

The canvas stirs. A small, circular opening appears in its gathered center. Robbie mutters as he works to widen it. After a few minutes of muttering and struggling, Robbie pokes his head through. He squints as if he's not seen daylight in a week. "Why have we stopped? Is something amiss? Oh, my good granny! Look at all the snow!"

"We're stuck. Sabella needs to shelter with you while I take care of the horses and check on Yonaz."

"Our humble home is yours," Robbie says. "I do hope you'll find the scent of our flatulent goat agreeable." His head disappears back inside while he works to open the canvas wider.

In the distance, Yonaz coughs and calls Calder's name. I look at Calder. "Set me down and go."

"Darnation," Robbie mutters. "Ties are all knotted up."

"Take your time," Calder says. "Are you all right, Sabella? Are *we* all right? The way I spoke to you before—"

I reach to swipe a fat snowflake off his cheek. "Forgiven." I feel both relieved and as if I could be making another mistake, but he looks nothing but happy.

Our eyes meet. The longing in his gaze steals my breath. Does he see the same yearning on my face? For in my chest, such a longing arises to know him and to be known, a swelling wave of emotion that threatens to tug me out to an unfamiliar sea.

Unaccountably, his brow furrows. "Sabella, there's something we should talk—"

"Got it!" Robbie exclaims. "Are you coming in or not, Sabella? We don't need both snow *and* goat stench in here. Calder's flirtations can wait for a less bitter day, to be sure."

"Jealous, Rob?" Calder says.

"More like frozen," Robbie replies.

Calder boosts me as high as he can. Robbie grabs hold of my arms and hauls me through the hole in the canvas with a loud groan. We fall into a heap on the wooden wagon bed, narrowly missing Sweet Pea the goat.

I scramble onto my knees and crawl to peer out the opening, to watch Calder wade off through the deep snow toward Yonaz. "Back soon," he says without turning around.

"Come." Robbie tugs my cloak. "It's warmer in the middle there, with the smelly goat."

"Mama!" Sparrow exclaims, throwing herself into my arms.

I kiss her head and embrace her tightly until she squeals and begs for freedom.

The love between my child and me is vast. Too deep to measure. That should be enough for anyone. So why does my heart long so painfully for Calder's return?

SABELLA

MARCH 11, 1886

With five people, a goat, and a shaggy dog huddled inside the wagon, the air remains tolerably warm throughout the night. Or tolerably cold, depending on one's point of view. We are packed like sardines in a tin, but we are safe, thank heaven.

Dawn must be nigh, but I cannot tell for certain since not much light ever pierces the canvas roof. A gust of wind shakes the wagon. The oil lamp suspended from the curved stave above us sways. I am glad Branna convinced Robbie to leave it burning low overnight. The twin's fear of the dark enabled me to indulge my longing to stare for hours at the baby who sleeps next to me.

I lie on my side, legs drawn up, with Robbie's spare clothes bunched under my head for a pillow. Without them, my antlers would make lying down impossible. I cannot say I am comfortable, but I am content—as I have been since Calder returned in the night. On the other side of Robbie, he mumbles nonsense in his sleep. After all his trudging through the snow yesterday, it is a wonder that utter exhaustion has not rendered him still and dreamless.

I remember how he looked at me when we paused outside the wagon in the snow—how I could have drowned in his eyes. I miss him, although he is only a foot or two away from me.

As if to offer consolation, Sparrow snuggles her blonde head closer.

Since we left the inn, she has grown taller and started to speak in sentences, the little madam. She has a complete set of tiny teeth and the appetite of a fully-grown coal miner.

My heart aches at the sight of her delicate beauty—and at the thought of how short her life may be.

Robbie rolls toward me. I meet his dark-eyed gaze.

"You're not sleeping, either?" he whispers.

"Yonaz's snoring could wake all the mummies in Egypt," I reply. "My antlers have returned and my neck aches from using clothes as a pillow. And Sweet Pea needs a bath. Two baths. All I smell is goat."

Sparrow jams her thumb into her mouth and slurps.

Robbie scratches his cheek before tugging his quilt to his chin. "May I ask you something?"

"Of course you may."

"What does it feel like to be in love?"

"I think you're asking the wrong person, Robbie." My face warms, and I'm thankful the shadows will likely conceal my blush.

"Are you joking? I've seen the way you look at Calder. You love him. Did you not admit that to yourself yet?"

I fuss with Sparrow's blanket, folding the edge over her shoulder. "I admit he fascinates me. And infuriates me. And baffles me, but…"

Am I actually in love with him?

Robbie whispers, "I'm asking because…and don't laugh at me…I think I'm in love with Cleona. You're laughing at me."

"No, I'm smiling. There is a difference." I cannot help but smile. Robbie's confession is too sweet not to smile at.

I close my eyes and draw in a deep breath. I let the notion that I love Calder settle over me like a new garment. It is not quite comfortable, yet it is mine. "Well, all right," I say. "I suppose it's...it really is a difficult thing to describe. I've not even considered it until now."

"Would you try?" Robbie asks.

For a minute or two, I reflect upon my feelings, and then I look into Robbie's almost-black eyes and say, "It is like you just discovered how to breathe. Your whole life, you thought you were breathing, but you'd hardly taken in any air at all. And then, suddenly, your lungs fill up completely, and your body expands to make room. The air...it becomes part of every inch of you, blood and bone, heart and soul. Now all you want to do is breathe, deeper and deeper."

"Yes," Robbie says. "That's it exactly. That's how I feel with Cleona."

"She's very young."

"I know she looks younger, but she'll be sixteen next week. And I'll be seventeen the week after, by Yonaz's reckoning. And I didn't say we were planning to elope. That would be ridiculous. I only said I thought I loved her. Besides, aren't you only seventeen yourself?"

"I am." Robbie seems much younger and much older than sixteen, depending on the situation. Sometimes, he spouts wisdom befitting a grandfather. Currently, the way he's grinning, he looks like an eight-year-old who's been given a bucket full of ice cream. "Have you told Cleona?" I ask.

"Not yet. I only just realized it today. But if I'm honest, I think I've loved her for years. Since the day she joined us."

"That's very sweet, Robbie. Although...are you sure it's Cleona and not Branna? I couldn't tell them apart to save my life. And last I knew, Cleona was the dog."

"I'm sure. For your information, Cleona has a freckle under her left eye," he says. "And she's prettier. They did switch forms while everyone else was napping earlier, though."

"Oh, of course. Well, I hope you'll be very happy together. Any girl would be lucky to have your devotion."

Robbie rolls onto his back with a contented sigh and stares up at the arched canvas ceiling.

I remember the conversation I had with Cleona back in our room at the inn. She wanted a suitor, and a suitor she shall have. How fortunate she is to be adored by our dear Robbie. I have reason to believe that she already adores him in return. What a marvelous thing it will be if their fond feelings lead them to a happy ending. The very thought warms me through in spite of the frost-tinged draft.

SABELLA

MARCH 13, 1886
MORNING

Two days pass before the snow stops. It leaves a blanket four feet deep and so white that to look at it stings the eyes. Several times, Calder and Robbie have used long pine branches as brooms to clear the snow off the canvas roof, fearful that its weight might break the wooden staves that hold it in place.

This morning, we all sit inside the wagon. Everyone tries to remain cheerful, but I fear we will soon run out of both food and patience. The journey between the inn and our new residence was not supposed to last this long. The thick canvas is cinched tightly closed to hold in heat, but we can see our every breath. I'm grateful that I am not a horse, though—or Robbie and Calder, who ventured out into the storm a dozen times to keep an area cleared of snow for them.

The strange, muffled silence of the wintry landscape seems to have leaked into the wagon. Perhaps we are all running low on words, sapped of strength by our captivity. Yonaz and Robbie perch on our food crates, and I sit on the floor between Calder and Branna, swathed in shared blankets. Cleona, now a thickly furred, young wolf, rests at Robbie's feet. Only Sparrow moves about. Clad in the fur cape Calder gave her, she clambers over our legs and plays with whatever is at hand: the twins' hairbrush, a wooden spoon, a tin cup.

On awakening this morning, Sparrow had attained the size of a three-year-old, by Yonaz's estimation. How could this be? Dread makes my stomach roil. When Branna rises to distribute morsels of bread and cheese for breakfast, I shake my head in refusal.

Calder gives me a concerned "you really ought to eat" look but says nothing.

Branna passes Calder his portion of food. "We've been talking, Cleona and I," she says. "Next time we switch forms, one of us will try to become a hawk or an eagle so we can fly over the area and look for a town. Food and supplies could lie just over the next hill, for all we can tell in this snow."

"Brilliant plan," Yonaz says hoarsely. A fit of coughing makes him double over. This usually happens now when he speaks. It is quite worrisome.

"When will that be?" Robbie asks. His fingers fidget with his collar. I imagine that he is not enamored with the idea of Cleona flying off to parts unknown.

"Soon," Branna says. She looks at me and adds, "If no one's told you, we can only change when no one else is watching, *and* if our gift responds to our asking. Sometimes it makes us wait, and sometimes it changes us into something we didn't ask for. Once, I was stuck being a weasel for a week."

"Let's hope you don't have that kind of luck this time," Calder says.

"Indeed," Yonaz says. "I myself would have already gone out to survey the area, but I am too weak." This time, he coughs hard enough that tears stream from his eyes.

"We cannot wait here doing nothing," Calder says. "We need

food and a source of heat. Branna, you and Cleona can use the other wagon for privacy whenever you're ready to try to change. There's hardly room enough for two in there, but it's the best option we have."

Sparrow starts to sing something Robbie taught her. I watch her make the hairbrush and spoon dance. More than ever, I long for our journey to end. Not only because I am weary of the cold and the four walls of this wagon, but also because I am clinging to the hope that once settled, we will find a way to slow or stop Sparrow's rapid aging. Maybe Calder and I could search out this Delphine—the one Calder says is responsible for finding Springborn babies. She might know what to do. I refuse to give up hope and allow Sparrow to die of old age before she has a single birthday.

Branna crouches beside Robbie and Yonaz, and they further discuss the twins' plan. Calder crawls to sit beside me. The cold has us all practically piling up like puppies to keep from shivering, so even modest Robbie could not object to our closeness.

He lifts my hand to his mouth and kisses my knuckles. His gaze drifts to my antlers. "You look magnificent this morning," he whispers. In spite of his crookedly buttoned coat and matted hair, he is as luminescent as he was the day he first waltzed through my kitchen door in Miners Ridge.

"Magnificent" I am not. My clothes are unkempt and my hair is doing its utmost to escape the braids I've pinned into a knot behind my head. Inside this small space, my fully grown antlers feel wider and more cumbersome than ever, although they are, as usual, only as large as my splayed hands. And I can only imagine what I smell like. Probably diapers and goat.

"Could I please have my hand back?" I speak softly, hoping no one else will hear.

He lets go. His brightness fades by a degree or two. "You're still offended."

"I am generally out of sorts. How would you feel if your wings were sticking out at their full breadth and devouring extra space?" I ask.

He frowns. "Devouring? That is harsh. They're not that big. Besides, no one here resents your antlers. Not one of us had the luxury of choosing our gifts. As for how would I feel with my wings on display...I daresay I'd feel better. Keeping them folded flat for days on end becomes quite painful, if you want to know the truth. Imagine having your arm strapped to your side all the time —and multiply that discomfort by four."

"I'm sorry. I did not realize the wings caused you torment."

"I am used to torment. I grow more used to it all the time." There is that yearning look on his face again, the one that makes the butterflies in my stomach whirl and swoop madly. The one that frightens yet thrills me. I turn my face away without a word.

The serious discussion with Yonaz must have ended, because Robbie throws a balled sock to Sparrow. She laughs as it bounces off her head, but Robbie's expression is grim.

"Your Sparrow is a real gift," Calder says pensively. "I've never seen Robbie take to anyone like he's taken to her."

"He and Sparrow loved each other at first sight."

"Robbie has a big heart inside that skinny chest of his." His moody expression gives way to a mischievous grin. He leans close enough to whisper in my ear. "Speaking of that particular heart, you do know how Robbie feels about a certain red-haired someone?"

"He told me. He's worried she might be the one to fly out in this weather, I can tell."

Calder shrugs and settles back against a crate. "He worries about everything. It's who he is. He'd fret if she was bitten by a mosquito. If Cleona wants to go, there is nothing he can do to stop her. She and her sister can be as wild and unstoppable as hurricanes when they take a notion to do something."

An idea occurs to me. It feels dangerous to mention, given our recent unpleasant exchange about his wings, but concern for

Robbie and Cleona emboldens me. I hug my knees and turn my face to Calder. "May I ask you a question?"

"That depends," Calder says. He packs a dramatic amount of dread into those two words.

"Could you not try to fly out instead?"

He answers in a heartbeat. "No, it isn't possible. In this cold, I doubt blood would circulate well enough through my wings to support flying. I'd get no farther than a literal stone's throw from here at best, and probably end up face down in a snowbank."

Robbie abandons his seat on the crate and crawls over the sleeping wolf to us. "You two look quite cozy. Do I need to sit between you? Or should we ask Yonaz to perform a quick wedding?"

"Ha," Calder says. "As grand as those things sound, we've been as platonic as a pair of old nuns over here. We're only sitting close for warmth."

"Is that what you're telling yourself?" Robbie teases.

"You just wish you had someone to stay warm with." Calder gestures with a toss of his head toward the wolf, Cleona. Robbie raises his fists.

"Enough arguing, boys," Yonaz says from across the way. "Calder, help the twins to the other wagon." Another fit of coughing overtakes him.

"The sooner we find help, the better," I say. "Yonaz needs a doctor."

Robbie gnaws his thumbnail as worry wrinkles his brow. Cleona nuzzles his side with her wolf snout as if to offer him comfort. He pets her head but looks no happier.

"I'm going with you and the twins," Robbie says firmly to Calder.

"Fine with me," Calder says.

From behind a food crate, Robbie plucks what appear to be two oddly shaped sacks made from a plaid woolen blanket and lined with shearling wool. He slips his bird feet into them. Calder and I look at each other with bemusement, and Robbie catches us. "Have you never seen boots before?" he snaps.

"Not like those." Calder coughs in a feeble attempt to cover a laugh.

"Where in the world did you find them?" I ask.

Robbie blushes furiously and stands. His head smacks into the low roof before he remembers to bend his neck. "Cleona made them recently, if you must know. She's talented with a needle, and kind enough to worry about me going barefoot in the cold." He works his way to the door, stepping over and around blankets, supplies, and Sparrow's playthings. Branna and the wolf trail behind him. "Are we going now, or are you planning to stand here blathering all day?"

"We must melt more snow for water," Yonaz says. "Fill the buckets while you're out."

The boys and twins exit the wagon one by one.

Right away, Sparrow cries for Robbie, her favorite, to come back. She runs to me. I enfold her in my arms and hum the Irish lullaby the twins use to calm her.

"You are a good mother." Yonaz's voice is now barely more than a croaking whisper. "The baskets, they often choose badly. But Sparrow, she is one of the fortunate."

"Without Robbie and the twins' help, I fear I would be a poor mother indeed."

"You doubt yourself too much."

"Perhaps."

He wipes his nose with his handkerchief and clears his throat. With a fatherly smile, he says, "I am happy to see you and Calder growing close. He is a clever boy with a good heart—in spite of his impudent streak. Ah, I see that I embarrass you. Forgive me."

"There is nothing to forgive." I cuddle Sparrow closer and pull a blanket up to cover us both. Her body molds to mine as she surrenders to sleep.

Yonaz coughs a few times. Once he catches his breath, he says,

"Yours is a gracious and forbearing heart. Now, I will rest, and give you respite from my foolish tongue." He slides off the crate and onto the floor in front of it. He stretches his legs out before him and closes his eyes.

In the dim light, I examine the bat tattoo encircling his throat. What might it signify? Perhaps he hides a pair of bat wings as Calder hides the wings of a moth. I imagine Yonaz unfurling a pair of night-black wings and launching himself into a starry sky. I picture Calder joining him to swoop above the treetops.

Sparrow sighs in her sleep and my daydream dissipates. I relish the goodness of her. The slow rhythm of her breathing is more comforting than any words could be. I let go of my worries and breathe with her, in and out, in and out, memorizing this tract of time that will exist but once in all of eternity.

I fall asleep until the muffled sound of Calder and Robbie's conversation seeps through the tent to awaken me. I shiver and draw Sparrow closer. Since the boys and the twins departed, the temperature inside the wagon has dropped by several degrees.

Which brings to mind a question I dare not entertain.

How long will we survive here if the twins' plan to find help fails?

Several hours slog by.

Calder and Robbie play checkers by lamplight, using a crate for a table. I sit on the floor next to Calder. Beside me, Sparrow whispers to her sock doll. Breezes ruffle the canvas over our heads. I try to think hopeful thoughts and to forget the worsening cold.

"Your move," Robbie says to Calder. "It's checkers, not the governing of a small nation."

"Patience, patience," Calder says. He reaches for a piece but stops at the sound of someone knocking.

Robbie bolts to the end of the wagon, bent double and tripping over blankets as he goes. With flying fingers, he works to open the canvas. He wastes no time in reaching out to pull one of the twins up over the gate and into the wagon. When the girl pushes the hood of her cloak back and Robbie sees it's Branna and not Cleona, his face darkens with disappointment.

"What news?" Yonaz asks from a cocoon of blankets. He drops the book he's been squinting at for the last hour.

Branna kneels on the floor next to Sweet Pea and gives the goat a scratch on the neck. "The magic was merciful. It made Cleona into a falcon. They have excellent eyesight. When the changing started, and she could feel it was her, she asked me to tell you not to worry, Robbie. She'll not be gone long."

Sparrow drops her sock doll and rushes into Branna's arms. Branna embraces her and kisses the top of her head. "A fine welcome, this is."

"Still your move, Cald," Robbie says miserably, staring at the game board. He chews an already too-short fingernail.

"Cleona will be fine," I say. "Falcons are fierce creatures."

"I hope so," Robbie says, but he does not sound hopeful in the least.

Calder slides a black checker forward. It's a terrible move that will allow Robbie to easily win the game. This simple kindness endears the moth-winged boy to me more than any compliment he has ever paid to me, more than his hand-holding, more than his scrawled notes.

My heart plots rebellion against my better judgment, and there is little doubt which one will win the war.

CALDER

After I let Robbie win and he fails to crow about his brilliance, I realize something must be done to distract him from his worries. "Let's go out for some air," I say cheerfully.

"I'd rather not," Robbie says.

"Come on, Rob. A change in scenery will be good for us all." I stand as well as I can in this blasted wagon, and tug him by the jacket. He grunts and murmurs but gets to his feet.

"I'll come along, if you don't mind," Sabella says.

Near the door, Robbie stoops to shove his feet into his silly boots again. "Please do, Sabella. Calder will only tease me to no end about Cleona if you don't."

I press a hand to my heart in feigned bafflement. "When have I ever?"

Robbie opens his mouth to answer, but Sabella says, "No more of that, boys." And we obey her.

And so Robbie, Sabella, and I venture outside. Sweet Pea the goat comes along, and immediately goes to work nosing hedges and gnawing off twigs, while Branna remains inside the wagon, minding sleeping Sparrow and sickly Yonaz.

Not a cloud mars the sky. Beyond the paths Robbie and I shoveled, snow drifts range from knee-high to shoulder-deep. The afternoon light makes the snow sparkle like spilled treasure. I suck in a deep breath for courage and reach for Sabella's hand as we follow Robbie along the short pathway to the snow-walled horse corral. When her mitten-covered fingers clasp mine, happiness lights up my insides like I swallowed a star.

"I'm sorry," she says. And I can scarcely believe my ears.

"For what?"

She darts a glance at me before returning her gaze to the landscape. "For being nosy before, and irritable. You have every right to talk, or not talk, about your wings."

"Let's leave all that behind, shall we? This is much better." I squeeze her fingers. I'm smiling like a fool, but I do not care one jot.

"A hundred times better," she says. There's contentment in her voice, and relief.

I slow my pace to buy us more time to talk and to be as alone as we're likely to be anytime soon. The distance between us and Robbie lengthens. A chickadee lands on Sabella's antlers but quickly changes its mind about its choice of branches. It dives off and lands with a squeak on the snow. Sabella's laughter spills out to sweeten the world like honey.

"I've missed you. And us," I say. "Blazes, I never want to get into an actual fight with you." The thought of losing her, the very thought, is as dreadful as imagining the fire and brimstone of Doomsday.

She laughs again. "Never fighting might be too lofty a goal."

"Nothing wrong with aiming for the stars."

Boldness strikes me like lightning. Or maybe it's recklessness. Regardless, I let the words gush out of my mouth. "I know you've said you have to put Sparrow first. And maybe I haven't been much help with her up until now, but I want to help more, if you'll allow it. When we reach our new home, we can have a new beginning, the three of us."

"I would like that, if it's possible."

"It is! Let me prove it to you."

She shakes her head and says, "It isn't you I doubt. I meant if it's possible for Sparrow. If she keeps aging so quickly, in a few months she could be...gone."

"If I can do anything about that, you know I will," I vow. "Anything."

"I know that."

"Worrying won't add an hour to her life or to yours," I say. "At least that's what Yonaz tells Robbie ten times a day."

"I do not deny it's true, but..."

"It isn't easy." I let go of her hand and wrap my arm around her. My palm settles on the curve of her waist. She leans her head over so her cheek brushes my shoulder as we walk. Somehow she does this without poking me with her antlers.

I think, *I would do anything for you*. But this sentiment I keep to myself. I hoard it along with the other sappy things I plan to say to her in the future as I hold her in my arms—in a warmer place.

A gust of wind ruffles my coat. The paper envelope in my pocket crinkles enough to remind me it is still there. Guilt sours my stomach. I should give the letter to Sabella. Right away.

I just can't.

SABELLA

hen we reach the corral, Calder must take his hand from my waist in order to work. It is like surrendering a bit of happiness. But I am still happy. All is well between us. The day is bright, and I am determined not to worry about Sparrow—for as long as I can manage such a feat.

Winter birds serenade us as we gather fallen branches and build a fire in the far corner of the corral. We'll melt snow into water for drinking once the flames settle down. Perhaps we could brew some pine needle tea, as well. It might do Yonaz some good. Mother used to dose me with this simple brew when I had a cold as a child.

The shrill cry of a falcon rends the air. I lose my grip on a handful of sticks. They scatter onto the snow, dark slashes of gray and brown on white.

We tip our heads back and peer toward the bright heavens.

Robbie waves both arms over his head. "Cleona!"

The bird swoops to land on a tree branch, a few feet away from us. She blinks wise, black eyes at Robbie. "It's her," he says. "I'm sure of it."

"I'll fetch Branna," I say.

But Branna must have heard her sister's call, for she is already jumping down from the wagon. She runs along the hard-packed path, her cape flying behind her.

Calder claps a hand on Robbie's shoulder. "See? Cleona is fine. Quite a pair of bird legs she has, too. If you fancy bird legs, that is."

"I don't know why we're friends. I really don't," Robbie says, but his face conveys nothing but joy. "And I do fancy that sort of thing, if it's any of your business."

Branna offers an outstretched arm and the falcon swoops to perch there. "Sister," Branna says. She kisses Cleona's feathered head and lays one hand on her back before she closes her eyes. Her face is still and peaceful, as if she is praying.

"They're speaking without words," Robbie whispers. "They can always communicate like this, animal to girl and girl to animal. It's part of their gift."

I have lived with the twins long enough to know this about them, but I simply nod, not wanting to break the silence.

Branna turns to face us. The falcon remains steady on her arm, a majestic and dangerous- looking adornment. "Sister says there's a town about three miles to the west, as well as a farm a little farther to the north," Branna says. "All the roads are still too snowy for the wagons, but the terrain looks fairly flat between here and the farm. A horse could probably manage a journey there. But going to the town would mean hiking a steep mountain pass."

"That settles it," Calder says. "I'll ride Mervyn out and find the farm. If I leave right away, I could arrive there before nightfall. If all goes well, I might even return tonight with provisions."

"Yonaz is worsening," Branna says. "I think he should go with you. If the farmer has any goodness in his heart, he'll let the man stay and warm his bones for a day or two."

Robbie steps forward. "I'll share a horse with Yonaz and help keep him steady. I don't weigh much, so Mervyn won't mind. You'll have to ride Maeve, Cald. She likes you best, anyway."

"True enough," Calder says. "I'll ready the horses if you go prepare Yonaz."

Cleona launches herself from Branna's arm and flies above us in a wide circle. "I'll help with Yonaz, too," Branna says. She and Calder head toward the wagon. I follow Calder and, boldly, catch him by the hand.

"You are going to miss me," Calder says, swinging my arm.

"So you can read my mind as Branna reads Cleona's?"

"I'll never tell."

The four horses lift their heads and snort. Perhaps they hope we're bringing their supper. Calder has been rationing their feed, but I doubt much remains.

"At this precise moment, for example," Calder says, "you're thinking you want to kiss me goodbye properly while no one is looking." He spins me around so we're face to face and wraps his arms around my back.

I look into his smug, handsome face, loath to admit that he is right. "Am I now? I thought I was thinking how arrogant you are, and wondering why in the world I would ever entertain the attentions of such a person. In truth, I was going to tell you to hurry back so that the rest of us won't freeze or starve."

"No." He cocks his head and moves a step closer, close enough that I can see the clouds of his exhalations. "You wouldn't bother thinking any of that nonsense because you know full well we'll leave you with plenty of firewood and all that's left of the food. And you know that we'll be back so fast you'll wonder if we've used magic."

On the trees and the ground, the snow sparkles like a million tiny diamonds. The sky is a startling shade of bright blue. The breeze seems to hold its breath. In a nearby hedgerow, a few little birds sing. One of the horses snorts. Everything feels a hundred times more real than usual, as if perceived through an enormous magnifying glass.

"Honestly?" I brush an eyelash off his cheekbone with my

mitten. Can I say it? I shush the imaginary, scolding voice of my disapproving mother and inch closer to him.

"Yes. Always."

My cheeks burn with blushes. I look at his chin instead of his eyes. "I would not mind if you kissed me goodbye."

"You're sure, Sabella?" I would still almost swear he adds magic to the syllables of my name, if not for the endearing hint of insecurity in his tone. It was in his voice when he asked me if I wanted to see his wings—something little-boyish and sincere.

"Yes," I say.

He rests one hand on the base of my neck and draws my mouth toward his. I shut my eyes and anticipate the kiss. Instead, he rests his forehead against mine. "Absolutely sure?"

Enough. I stand on tiptoe and press my mouth to his. At first, he laughs. And then he pulls me closer. The kiss is everything I'd hoped for, all sweetness and yearning. I am full of starshine and poetry, a million shared possibilities and aspirations. My palms cradle his face and I kiss him more fervently, losing all track of time and place.

He steps back and ends the kiss. "Whoa there," he says softly. He rubs his lower lip. "I think you did me an injury."

"Oh, no! I'm sorry."

Calder grins. "I'll live."

"I shouldn't have—"

"Please don't be sorry," Calder says. Rarely has he looked more serious. "Don't regret what was probably the most perfect kiss in the history of the universe." He gathers both my hands in his and holds them to his chest. His eyes are hazy as he gazes into mine. "I love you, Sabella."

My breath catches. Seeing his wings stunned me less than hearing these words.

"Calder! Hurry and bring the horse," Robbie shouts from behind us. "Yonaz is ready."

Unable to meet his gaze, I focus on the scarf at his throat. "Calder…"

"I mean it, Sabella. I love you. You don't have to answer in kind. In fact, I don't want you to say it until you know it's true."

"Calder Hadrian, let that poor girl go and bring the darned horse over here before the blasted sun goes down!" Robbie demands.

"Keep your ridiculous bird boots on!" Calder replies. He kisses my forehead and takes a few steps toward the horses. "Lead Maeve for me?"

"Of course."

Maeve and I follow Calder and Mervyn. My knees quake in the aftermath of the kiss and his confession. Why was I so taken aback by hearing him say those words aloud? And why could I not find it in me to respond likewise?

I am in love with him, but is that the same as actually loving him?

I stare at the back of his heavy tweed coat, searching for evidence of his wings but finding none. Am I drawn to him because of them, because I know he understands how it feels to be different? Or is it because he cherishes me—when no one has ever valued me before? Or because his kisses—even the chaste, bird-peck ones—melt whatever sense I have?

Or, might I love him for himself, as I rightly should—and as he deserves?

I squint up at the sun, searching for an answer it will not give.

SABELLA

MARCH 14, 1886
BETWEEN MIDNIGHT AND DAYBREAK

Within the canvas-covered wagon, the twins and I listen for the returning horses until long after midnight. Beside the goat, Sparrow sleeps like a caterpillar in a plaid wool chrysalis, warmed by stones Branna and I heated around the fire before dark fell.

"They must have decided to stay at the farm for the night," Branna says, stroking the feathered head of her falcon sister.

"Well, if they are spending the night inside a snug house and filling their bellies with hot food, I will try to be happy for them." I lean against a crate and sigh at the thought of sipping hot tea in a room without incessant cold drafts. That thought glides into another, an imagined scene in which I nestle beside Calder on a velvet sofa. We stare into an enormous stone fireplace. He plants a kiss on my head, near the place from which my antlers sprout.

Branna snorts derisively and says, "Yonaz I would forgive easily; he's unwell. As for Calder and Robbie, I think not. If they come back bragging about hot buttered rolls and roasted ham, I shall behave quite violently."

"If they mention clean sheets and feather mattresses, I will throttle them," I declare.

"If they speak of roaring fires and drinking brandy by the hearth, I will stuff snow down their trousers!"

"Branna! My heavens!"

We giggle until we're breathless. Sparrow reaches out for me in her sleep. With one chubby hand, she grabs onto my sleeve. I slide away from the crate and lie down beside her, mindful of my antlers. She smells milky-sweet—far better than any of the rest of us. She is so good, so lovely, that my heart overflows with love for her.

I look up at the arch of canvas and thank heaven for the blessings I've been given: a beautiful child, dear friends, and Calder's devotion. For the first time in a long time, I can envision a future in which I will be happy and fulfilled.

After a while, Branna sighs and sits up straight. She shoves a lock of red hair out of her eyes as she looks down at me. "To be sure, I am not as forgiving as you are," she says seriously. "You must have forgiven Calder in a heartbeat for not giving you that letter right away. You never even seemed angry with him. If anyone were to send me a letter—not that anyone ever would—I would be mad as a wet hornet if it was kept from me for even an hour. Was it good news, then?"

"Letter? What letter?" Now I sit up. My stomach sinks as if it knows bad news is coming.

Branna picks at the blanket that covers her legs. "A man delivered it to the inn. I saw Calder take it from him. He told me he would give it to you in a day or two, after things calmed down with Yonaz and all. He thought the letter might upset you and—"

"Start from the beginning, please, Branna." A wave of dread crashes over me and I start to tremble.

"Did he not give it...? Oh, no." Her hands fly to her cheeks. "I think you should ask him about it. I don't want to meddle."

"No, he did not give me the letter, and no, I will not wait to ask him about it. Please start again, from the beginning. The letter came...how?" *Please*, I beg the universe, *let her be mistaken about this*. But in my heart, I know she's been speaking the truth.

The lantern light is dim, yet it's plain to see that Branna has turned a shade paler than usual. "I'd rather we pretended I didn't mention it."

"Branna, you must tell me."

She makes her confession slowly, carefully. "It was a sometime last week, I think. There was a knock at the door. Calder was the one who answered it, but I watched from across the room. The delivery man wore a bluish-gray coat and hat. He said he'd been looking for you for a while, and that your mother had paid him extra not to give up before he found you. He thought you might have stopped at our inn, as there aren't many along the one and only road around the mountain. I saw him hand the letter to Calder."

"And then?"

"Well, you'd taken Sparrow to bed, so I offered to bring the letter to you. But Calder said no, that it could wait a day or two as you'd had enough trouble already that week, what with the baby appearing, and your running away, and then he and Yonaz falling ill. I assumed he'd given it to you as he said he would... Don't be angry, Sabella. Please. He only meant to protect you, I'm sure."

"He had no right to keep it from me," I say. "It was not his property, and neither am I."

All the warmth drains from my body. I might never be warm again.

"Please, Sabella. He loves you, I'm sure of it. You cannot—"

"Be quiet, Branna. I need to think."

A tear trickles down her cheek. Too angry and confused to offer her consolation, I turn my body away from her.

What could Mother have said in that letter? The woman never wrote letters, not even to her only sister. Did she miss me after I left? Was she sorry I'd gone? Or had she written to call me vile names and to declare me forever banished from her home?

I could not know which, if any, of these things were true without reading the letter.

But Calder has known for days and days if he was bold enough to open it. He's known *and said nothing.*

What game has he been playing with me, stealing my affection, beguiling me with compliments? And why?

My stomach clenches. I run to the wagon gate, lean through the opening in the canvas, and throw up onto the snowy ground.

The lamp fails in the night, out of oil or extinguished by a strong draft. I stare into the darkness until it becomes a living thing, roiling and expanding in waves of gray above my head. I listen to the steady drumming of rain on the arched roof, thanking heaven that it is not more snow. And I wait.

Time ticks by in interminable seconds.

When morning brightens the canvas over my head, I crawl out of my blanket nest, careful not to rouse Branna or Sparrow. For once, my child sleeps past dawn. With trembling fingers, I attempt to smooth the wrinkles out of my dress. I comb my hair and knot it tightly at the nape of my neck. I rewrap my cloak and drape my antlers with a shawl.

I am as ready to face Calder as I will ever be.

More waiting. I milk the goat and cover the pail with a cloth. This will be Sparrow's breakfast and noontime meal. I have no appetite for food of any kind—even if I were inclined to take what rightfully belongs to my child.

Finally, I can no longer endure being shut inside.

The clip clop of approaching hooves greets me as I leap off the wagon. My eyes widen in surprise as I survey the scenery. The vast whiteness is gone. The ground is brown with mud and decayed leaves. The weather has taken a turn, as it does when spring is nigh. If only my life had also taken a turn for the better overnight...

The returning horses are laden with bulging packs. Calder and Robbie beam with pride as they halt a few yards from where I stand. Falcon Cleona circles overhead, shrieking a greeting. My heartbeat flutters feebly in my breast like the wings of an injured bird. Goose bumps rise along my arms in spite of the morning's mild temperature.

"We brought food, Sabella," Robbie announces joyfully. "And cider, and fresh blankets. The farmer's wife is tending Yonaz, you'll be glad to know. He's already greatly improved." He hops down from his horse. "Where are the others? Inside?"

I nod, and Robbie walks away, leaving me to face Calder. I feel a dozen conflicting things at once, but grab hard onto the anger.

Calder leaps from his horse like a storybook prince. He strides toward me wearing that reckless smile of his. I hold up my palms in front of me to signal him to stop, but he does not. He takes hold of my shoulders and tries to kiss my cheek, but I angle my face away.

He steps back, his smile fading. "Are you angry we stayed away all night? I wanted to head back, but the farmer—"

I step out of his grasp. "Where is the letter, Calder?"

"Uh oh," Robbie mutters. I glance over my shoulder to see him scrambling into the wagon as if I'm an imminent thunderstorm.

"Letter?" Calder rakes his fingers through his hair and does a terrible job of trying to look innocent.

"Do not pretend with me. I want the letter from my mother. How could you keep it from me?"

He pokes a rock with the toe of his shoe. "I wanted to spare you pain, Sabella. You cannot go back there. They don't love you. You deserve—"

"I will decide what I deserve. Give me my letter."

He reaches inside his coat and pulls out the folded, crumpled paper. I snatch it from his hand and walk away.

"Sabella, wait," he says, voice cracking with anguish. "I'm sorry."

Without answering, I step off the road and enter the woods. Dead, wet leaves shift under my boots as I seek solitude among the trunks of silver birch and pine. A boulder provides a suitably uncomfortable seat.

Dampness has smudged the handwriting but I recognize Mother's slanted script.

February 21

Dear daughter Sabella,

Your father and I regret the disagreeable manner in which we parted company. He has fallen gravely ill and asks for nothing but your return. You are welcome to bring the wee cousin in your care, should it be necessary. Only come back, daughter. I fear your father may not live if you do not. I pray you will forgive us as we have forgiven you, and that you will choose to be a dutiful daughter who remembers to honor her parents as the Good Book commands.

Your Mother.

Tears course down my cheeks and splatter onto the page. My

parents have forgiven me, but for which offense? Running away? Discovering Sparrow? Growing antlers? In the end, does it matter?

At least on paper, Mother offers me another chance to be a good daughter, and Father, who is deathly ill, has expressed a longing for my return. They seem to want me, finally. It is no small miracle, being wanted by them.

If Calder had given me the letter instead of hiding it, would I have chosen to go home? I cannot say. Crushed by the weight of his deceit, I see no other option. I cannot abide his presence. I cannot stomach the hundred apologies he will offer before lying to me again.

Lying is the way of men. Mother was right all along.

We will go home, Sparrow and I. There, we will have a roof over our heads and food to eat. She and I will keep to ourselves, live quietly, and avoid the townsfolk, as has been my habit for all the years of my antler-growing. We will be reasonably safe.

At the sound of a twig breaking, I turn my head. Calder stands still beside a sapling, arms hanging limp at his sides, head cocked imploringly.

I rise from the boulder. The letter falls to the ground but I do not retrieve it. "I want you to take me home, first thing tomorrow morning."

"Please, no," he says. "You cannot..." A sob interrupts his words, and he covers his face with his hands. "Blast, Sabella."

"My father is ill, and my mother needs me. If you won't take Sparrow and me, I'll find another way."

"I will do whatever you ask of me," he says, and then he turns to walk toward the wagons with slumped shoulders and slow footsteps.

The light shifts and makes me remember the hour we shared in the forest. His green wings unfurling, the pale slopes of his bared shoulders, the vulnerability in his face when he peered back at me.

That look in his eyes I mistook for love.

My heart, already broken, breaks again, shattering into even smaller, sharper shards.

At home, within the drab walls of my parents' rented house, I will be protected from ever falling in love again. And at this moment, it seems like a blessing.

SABELLA

MARCH 15, 1886
MORNING

I sit astride the mare, Maeve, with Sparrow in front of me. The recent removal of my antlers has lightened my head, yet I feel like the entire world is pressing down upon me. To my left, Calder waits on Mervyn's broad back. Above us, the early morning sky is choked with flat, gray clouds. The birds hardly chirp at all, as if they suspect something is amiss.

Robbie comes to my side. He reaches up to grip my hand with both of his. The fiercest rainstorm could not have left his face any wetter. But I am empty of tears, numb in every part of my being.

"Please don't go," he pleads. "Sparrow needs us."

"I'm sorry. She must be with me, and I have to go."

"It was a misunderstanding. Can you not try to forgive him?"

How can I explain that the misunderstanding was so much more? That his best friend is an untrustworthy schemer? If I were to try, it would only further distress him. "My parents need me," I say. "It's my duty to take care of them. Perhaps someday, when Father is well, Sparrow and I can visit you."

"You know very well that some of us will not last until 'someday.' Look at her. She's gained two more years overnight, maybe three. Darnation, Sabella. You cannot do this. I don't think I can bear it." He wipes his nose and eyes on his already sodden shirtsleeve. I make the mistake of glancing downward and see that his bird feet glisten with fallen tears. My numbness lifts enough to allow a pang of sadness to pierce my chest.

Cleona, now in the form of a girl, walks to Robbie's side and rests a hand on his shoulder. "Come, Robbie. She must do what she thinks is right."

He shakes his head. "But it isn't. It isn't right."

"We need to leave," Calder says flatly. "The journey will be a long one."

Robbie leans closer. He cradles Sparrow's little foot in his hand and kisses it. And then he turns away from us. His shoulders shudder as he weeps. Cleona takes his arm and guides him toward the wagons.

When they're gone, Calder asks softly, "Are you sure?"

I do not look at him, fearing I might lose my resolve. I clutch the reins and say, "Let's go."

Calder commands Mervyn to walk, and soon thereafter, coaxes him to trot. I hold Sparrow tight to me as we follow on Maeve. We travel at a steady speed, under an ash-gray sky as smooth as a plastered ceiling. Sparrow points out things which delight her along the road: a pair of tan and white cows, a house with pink shutters, a huge black crow atop a copper weathervane. Her speech has lost most of its babyishness, much to my sorrow.

Will Mother and Father be surprised to see that the infant I left with has grown into a five-year-old child? They did raise a daughter with antlers, so perhaps they will not even blink at the change in Sparrow.

After a while, we stop alongside a stream to allow the horses to drink and rest. Calder and I stand a few feet apart. The silence that haunts the space between us is unfamiliar and unsettling. Sparrow picks up pebbles from the bank and examines them carefully before tossing them aside.

"I'm going to find a diamond," Sparrow says. "Uncle Robbie told me they're rocks that sparkle like glass, only you can't break them."

"That's a grand idea," Calder says.

I glance sidelong at him and accidentally meet his gaze as Sparrow skips away.

"Listen," he says. "I know keeping the letter was wrong, and I'm sorry. But it does seem as though you're angry with me for much more."

"You do not need me to list your offenses, Calder. I imagine you know them better than I do."

"I know I'm guilty of many things, but I love you. With all my unwise, unruly heart, I love you."

"Deception and dishonesty are not love."

"Sabella, I..."

I fold my arms over my middle and turn to face him. "Tell me the truth then. The entirety of it. From the first time you saw me until you hid the letter. I want to hear everything. Heaven knows you have nothing to lose by telling me now."

He bites his lower lip and shifts his weight from one foot to the other. He could not look guiltier if he tried.

I shake my head. "You see? I knew you were keeping more secrets from me."

"The truth, then." He stares out over the stream. The horses raise their heads to soak in the warm sunshine. Sparrow flings handfuls of pebbles onto the bank again and again.

"The first time I saw you," he says solemnly. "You were eleven, or maybe twelve. Yonaz asked me to keep an eye on you when you went to bury your antlers in the woods every morning. He thought it unsafe for you to be out all alone on a tract of land between two mining towns full of rough men. It was summer, and you wore a blue dress with the sleeves rolled to your elbows. Your hair was loose and chestnut brown. I wasn't much older than you, but I *knew*. Even if I had not dreamed of you, I would have known without a doubt that we were meant to be together someday."

I must not let his romantic notions get the better of me. I focus on what was wrong with the situation he described. "You spied on me and allowed me to believe I was alone."

"Yonaz gave me an assignment and I carried it out. I wanted to, truly, because it was important to me that you were safe. So often I almost approached you. You looked so sad much of the time. I know it sounds sinister, the watching, but it never was. I wanted only to protect you."

"And then what? You decided I was finally ripe for the picking and came knocking at my door, impersonating a new boarder?"

"I was glad to go, to finally speak to you, but the decision was Yonaz's. For a while, he'd been hearing mutterings in the town, rumors that your parents were hiding you because you were witch-marked. He'd started to worry that harm would befall you—and then, when you saw me in the woods, he decided the time had come for us to meet. I was supposed to slowly let you know who we are, so maybe you'd choose to join us. You can make it sound lewd and wrong, the spying. But I loved you with a pure heart all along, I swear it."

I step closer to him and lower my voice so Sparrow will not hear. "You tempted me to look into the basket. You gave me Sparrow to trap me. Admit it."

"That is completely untrue. I swear on every holy thing in the world that I had nothing to do with Sparrow's appearance. Either the basket or Delphine made that happen."

My cheeks and neck burn. My pulse races. "You blame Yonaz and Delphine for almost everything, but I think it was all you, all along. *You* felt it was time to make me join you, so you helped concoct a situation that would drive me from my home. *You* wanted me. *You* 'rescued' me. You made me fall in love with you. Everything has been about you. Your desires—and never mine."

"I beg to disagree. Think, Sabella. Were you happy with your parents? Did you enjoy living as a prisoner? Your father hacking off your antlers every day? Your mother's drunken insults? It broke my heart to see you living in such circumstances when we could offer you a better life among people who would love you."

"You can make it sound pretty, but it still reeks of treachery. I cannot trust you, Calder. That is what it all boils down to. And if I cannot trust you, there can be nothing between us, not even friendship."

Sparrow tugs at my sleeve, startling me. Consumed by the argument, I did not hear her approach. She tugs again. "Mama, please don't be cross with Uncle Calder. Look. I brought you a pink rock."

"Thank you, my love," I say. "It's very pretty." I drop the pebble into the pocket of my cloak and it clinks against the wooden heart Calder gave me. The urge to cast his love token into the water is strong, but Sparrow would ask too many painful questions if I threw it away in her presence.

"Uncle Calder, are you crying?" Sparrow asks, her brow furrowed.

He sniffs. "Probably coming down with a cold, little one. Not to worry."

"Back onto the horse," I say to Sparrow with false cheer. "We aren't home yet."

She slips her hand into mine. "You mean our new home with Uncle Robbie and everyone?"

"A different home."

Calder gently yanks one of her corn silk-gold braids. "Don't worry, Sparrow bird. Your mama will take good care of you wherever you go."

"But I want Uncle Robbie," she whines. Her lower lip trembles. Fortunately, an owl swoops overhead and captures her attention. "Look!" she says, forgoing her sadness—at least temporarily.

As it is the wrong time of day for owls to venture forth from their nests, I suspect this creature is one of the twins.

Calder boosts me onto Maeve. He sets Sparrow in front of me and gives me the reins. His hand brushes my leg, and for a moment, longing for him stirs anew within me, but I will not entertain it any more than I would entertain the temptation to rob a bank.

"Let's go, horse," Sparrow says, bouncing.

"Hold on, little one," Calder says. He mounts his horse with athletic ease. "Patience is a virtue."

Is he spouting a proverb to let me know that he will wait for me to forgive him? If he chooses to hold out hope that I'll fall back into his arms, he will be wasting his time.

CALDER

As the sun threatens to set, I spot an abandoned, half-collapsed, log cabin along the road. The space behind it appears to be flat and grassy. It's as good a place as we're likely to find to camp for the night. We're still miles from any inn I remember, and hours out of Miners Ridge. I steer Mervyn off the road and Maeve follows.

I dismount. My legs almost refuse to hold me. I've rarely ridden horseback so far in a day, and never under such unpleasant circumstances. Never while feeling like a fish that's been gutted alive.

Blazes, I hate myself. Hours of reflection on the errors of my ways have done nothing to improve my disposition.

"I'm hungry," Sparrow says as I approach her. She leans over and falls into my arms. How does she still smell sweet after all of our traveling, the dust, and the creek she waded in? The weight of her in my arms will make a terrible memory.

I set her on the ground and put on a smile. "We have a little food left. I'll get it out while you gather sticks for a fire."

"Yes! I love campfires." She runs off and starts picking up sticks.

Sabella dismounts on the opposite side of Maeve. Her feet hit the ground with a thud.

"I would have helped you," I say.

"I know that." She doesn't look at me, but at least her tone is more tired than angry. She shakes out her skirts and then follows after Sparrow, limping a little, obviously pained by the length of the ride.

I have caused her this injury and too many others. I want to undo all of my mistakes, or perform some penance to earn her forgiveness.

I remember my promise to Sparrow and pull the sack of food out of my saddlebag. There's a knot in the tie that keeps the food sack shut, one that mysteriously formed as we traveled. I pick at the tight tangle until it becomes clear that it will never yield to me, and then I get my knife. It's easy enough to solve this problem with a swift stroke of a blade. But some things can neither be unraveled nor cut out.

SABELLA

Miners Ridge looks no different than it did when I fled its confines: rows of board-sided houses with bleak windows, dour women and thin, dirt-smudged children trudging home from the company store with their baskets. They stare at the novelty of three visitors riding horses into town at midday.

I adjust the shawl and bonnet that cover the stubs of my antlers. My head throbs as I remember how a few hours ago while Sparrow still slept, Calder shed silent tears as he cut the antlers short. I straighten my shoulders and dismiss the thought. I cannot allow myself to be moved by him.

"I think it would be best if we did not go straight to the house. People would see, and talk," I say to Calder. "I mean, some of them have already seen us, but..."

"I know a path through the woods the horses won't mind. It ends near your parents' house."

Naturally he knows all the paths in those woods as well as I know them. For years, I roamed them as he kept watch over me. That is not a subject I will broach now. Calder turns Mervyn sharply to the left and through an alleyway between buildings. Maeve follows without being asked.

As we ride into the trees, Sparrow hums some merry tune the twins taught her. I pick a piece of brittle straw out of her hair, evidence that we spent our second night away from the Spring-born in a barn. It may be my imagination, but I think she's grown another inch since we set out. She may be bigger, but I feel smaller somehow.

Although we have traveled for many miles, it seems all-of-a-sudden when Calder halts his horse in the little clearing where I used to catch butterflies. I bring Maeve alongside him and stop as well. My stomach sinks and perspiration dampens my forehead. Should I be happy to be almost home? For I am not.

Calder says, "This is as close as we can ride to the house without drawing the neighbors' attention. I could walk you to the door, though. Please let me walk you to the door, Sabella."

I shake my head. "It would be better if you did not. Mother might see and think us...that you and I..."

"Indeed. She might think that we are to each other what we might have been, if only I were not such a fool." He pauses and fusses with the reins in his hands. "Are you certain this is what you want?"

The thought of never again seeing him or the other Spring-born fills me with anguish, but I shove those feelings aside. My choice is made. "Help Sparrow down?"

He dismounts, his face as grim as a rain-soaked funeral. Sparrow falls into his outstretched arms, giggling. He hugs her tightly, desperately, until she says, "You're squashing me, Uncle Calder."

Calder sets her on her feet, then he reaches up for me. I open my mouth to insist that I am fully capable of dismounting without his assistance, but the tears in his eyes render me speechless. I allow him to grip my waist and swing me to the ground.

For a moment, we stand face to face. In his visage, I see both a humbled man and a chastened boy. He takes my right hand politely, as if he never carried me close through drifts of snow, as if he never whispered adoration into my ear, as if I never marveled at the sight of him with wings of green and gold unfurled. As if we are meeting for the first time—although this may be the last time our paths ever cross.

"Sabella." He bows his head and presses his lips against my knuckles.

My heart stops. The world stops. All of my emotions converge and collapse into a vast, absolute emptiness.

I regret nothing and everything as he tethers the horses together, mounts Mervyn, and rides away. Sparrow slips her hand into mine and we make our way down the steep, pebbled hill toward the house. She is quiet, too quiet, but I cannot form a sentence to reassure her. I cannot meet her gaze and offer a supportive smile. In this moment, I must concentrate on a single task: putting one foot in front of the other until we reach our destination—for my legs can hardly hold me after the long ride.

The house has no back entrance, so we must round it and go to the front. With every step, my heart pounds harder and Sparrow's grip tightens on my fingers.

"Sabella?" Mother calls from the doorway. The full basket dangling from her arm suggests that she has just returned from the store. Perhaps her health has improved in my absence. "Lord in heaven! Is that you, girl? Come in out of the cold. Hurry now."

I take a deep breath and lead Sparrow inside.

Nothing here has changed. The kitchen is still small and dingy, the table strewn with an assortment of crumbs. My old, stained apron still sags from its hook. The wash basin is full of dirty dishes, bits of food, and gray water. Empty medicine bottles crowd the top of the cabinet. I eye its lower door, knowing the despised saw will be there when I seek it tomorrow morning.

"And who is this?" Mother says, fists on hips. "Traded the baby in for an older brat, did you?"

"This is Sparrow, Mother. She is the same child I left with. She has a condition that causes her to age faster than most children."

"More fiendish magic. The devil's work. Call it what it is, daughter. You'll just have to keep her inside with you. We can't have the neighbors seeing her and getting ideas."

"Mother," I scold, a little surprised at her cold welcome—but only a little. "Your letter said we would both be welcome. Now, where's Father? Has he improved?" He is not dead, because if he were, Mother would have already been forced to move out of this house to make room for another miner's family. The mine bosses show widows little mercy.

"He's down the mine. Where would you expect him to be at noon on a Tuesday? Lounging about nibbling sweets and having his feet rubbed by the servants?"

"But your letter said he was dying."

"That was nigh on a month ago, wasn't it? Thought you might have turned up then, but you had to wait until it pleased you. It was naught but a chest cold after all, thank the good Lord. Now, my head is fit to burst, so I'll lie down a while. See to the dishes, would you? And make some bread. We've only a heel left, and with another mouth to feed..."

"Yes, Mother," I say, gripped by a desire to flee. To return with Calder and forever escape this den of misery. But it is too late. He is far away by now. Unreachable.

"She isn't a happy lady," Sparrow whispers as Mother grumbles her way up the stairs.

"Some people never are." I grab my grubby old apron and slip it over my head like a noose. My limbs tingle with the shock of being thrust back into my old life, and at the bitter realization that I have made a terrible mistake in returning to this.

What is worse: in my haste, I have torn my child away from those who cherish her, to bring her here to be unloved and isolated.

Penniless, utterly exhausted, and without a horse, we cannot escape today. It will take time for me to plan and prepare, but I swear by all the stars in the universe that I will find a way for us to start a new life in another place. If I have to work a miracle, I will.

I conjure a smile for Sparrow. No need to worry my little bird. "Come. I will teach you to make bread." She skips behind me to the counter and watches me measure flour into Mother's chipped earthenware bowl.

"Mama, can we take some to Uncle Robbie? He likes bread."

"Not today, my love," I say as merrily as I can. I reach for the jar of starter and the salt box, the old routine taking charge of my movements. My eyes smart as tears obscure my vision. I did not expect to miss the bird-legged boy so fiercely and so soon.

"Tomorrow?" Sparrow asks.

"Well, there will be lots and lots of tomorrows, so perhaps on one of them, we will visit Robbie."

On my tongue the words taste bitter, like lies.

SABELLA

MARCH 18, 1886
MORNING

S parrow sleeps in my childhood bedroom, and I pray that she does not come seeking me now. My antlers overshadow me as I sit on the familiar, much-hated stool in the corner of the kitchen. Waiting. Dreading.

Last evening, when Father returned from the mine and found me at the cookstove stirring the soup, he offered no welcome. Not even half a smile. After he shrugged out of his jacket, he said gruffly, "Button's loose on this," and sat down for supper.

Now, the clomp of Father's boots echoes on the steps. He trudges across the room, takes the saw out of the cupboard, and stands before me. It should be impossible, but I think he has aged more than Sparrow has since the day we parted. The lines in his face have deepened into furrows. His eyelids droop. His breaths are raspy and rapid as he grabs my neck hard to steady me. He sets the blade at the base of my right antler and I bite down on my lower lip.

He thrusts the blade back and forth, muttering blasphemies as he works. Tears leak from my closed eyes. Dust fills my nostrils. The metallic taste of blood seeps from my lip onto my tongue. I try to imagine lovely things, but in the absence of Calder's soothing words, my mind floods with darkness.

"Quit your whimpering," Father says as the first antler collides with the floorboards. His grip on my neck tightens. "Why did you come home if this doesn't suit you? Let me venture a guess. You used your wiles to seduce some hobbledehoy, and he tossed you out when he found out you're cursed."

I grip the edges of the stool hard enough to numb my fingers. "Please, just finish it."

"Don't sass me, girl, or you'll be on the street with that abomination of yours. Alone and scrabbling for a crust of bread. What man would marry you now, with a fatherless brat in tow, even if he could get over the sight of the blasted antlers?" He hacks into the second antler and manages to free it in a few swift strokes.

He's wheezing like he ran a mile as he drops the saw to the floor. He jabs one finger toward the fallen antlers. "Get those out of my house and see to breakfast."

He stomps up the stairs. I pluck the antlers from the floor and clutch them to my chest.

These silvery branches...Calder called them magnificent. Robbie declared them marvelous, my crown of glory. I had almost come to accept them as something good. Now I am forced to cast them away like something loathsome, to bury them quickly like evidence of a vile transgression.

I cannot stay in this place. I cannot raise Sparrow in this house of degradation and shame. In my distress over Calder's deception, I'd forgotten the reasons why I left.

I remember now.

CALDER

Confession: I spent the night in the woods just outside Miners Ridge instead of rejoining the other Spring-born. A nest of leaves is a grand thing for a squirrel, but it's less than an ideal bed for a person. Even if I had been warm, I would not have slept. That expression on Sabella's face before she turned her back on me to return to her parents' house—it was so devoid of feeling, so empty of hope... I cannot seem to keep it from floating before me like the hazy image of a ghost. I would rather remember her raging at me with flashing eyes and flushed cheeks than standing there sallow and surrendered to insensibility, but my mind does not let me choose.

Before the first light of morning stains the sky, I leave the horses tied to a tree and walk to Sabella's house. I peer through the window of the sad, old kitchen. I watch Sabella sink onto the detestable stool in the corner. I watch that hateful man hack off her beautiful antlers and with every bit of my being, I want to pummel him into the earth with my fists.

When he goes upstairs, she gathers the antlers in her arms like they're a hurt child. Her body is angled away from me, and I am thankful. I do not think I could bear to see the look of agony that surely defiles her face.

A dog barks in the distance. One rooster crows and inspires another. The miners will exit their houses soon. I cannot stay here or I will be seen.

I slump to the ground and bury my face in my hands. This is terrible. The hardest thing I have had to do in my life. For so many years, it's been a rare day in which I did not see her. How will I survive it?

All I have left is a single thread of hope. It's filthy and fraying, but I hold onto it like it can tow me out of this swamp of misery I've created. Life is long—at least if we're lucky. Maybe someday, she'll forgive me. Want me back, if miracles exist.

A door creaks open nearby and heavy boots tromp across a wooden porch. I stand and run for the cover of the woods.

SABELLA

APRIL 29, 1886
MORNING

S pring came on the appointed day in March but waited until April to burst forth in all its glory, greening the trees and muddying the ground. Now, with May only days away, Sparrow and I delve into the forest to throw away my antlers and to forage for mushrooms and ramps.

My daughter's head is now level with my shoulders, and her figure is beginning to blossom with the curves of womanhood. Some weeks, she matures little. Other times, she'll age years in a single night. The process is less predictable and more vexing than the weather.

When we venture out, we take care to go early, while the other mine wives are still occupied with morning chores. Always, I cover Sparrow in layers and scarves so that anyone catching a glimpse of her might mistake her for Mother and not a girl aged twelve or thirteen. She copies Mother's slight limp and assumes an old woman's hump-shouldered posture until trees surround us and the only eyes watching belong to squirrels, rabbits, and birds.

An eagle screeches over the treetops, and I lift my gaze in hope. If it is one of the twins, perhaps she carries a message from Robbie or Yonaz. I confess that I long for news that my friends are safe and settled again.

Sparrow points skyward. "Mama, is that one of the twins?"

The eagle circles once more before soaring out of sight. "No, my dear. It was only an ordinary bird."

"Do you think our friends have forgotten us?"

"No, never." I crouch and pluck a few ramps from the ground.

"I hope you're right." Sparrow lowers the basket to receive the leaves and says no more.

Bit by bit, we fill the basket, taking what joy we can from the fresh air, the whispering leaves, and our companionship.

We are ready, Sparrow and I. Ready to flee my parents' hateful stares and cruel words. Ready to escape endless, thankless scrubbing and cooking. As Father reminds me almost daily, matrimony is not an option for a person like me. Which is fine, because the thought of marriage sickens me. The life I'd inherit as a miner's wife would differ little from the life I live now, all scrimping and coal dust—and the terrifying probability of bringing one hungry baby after another into the circle of suffering. I imagine a dozen hollow-eyed children staring up at me, begging for scraps, and I shudder.

Sparrow and I have better plans.

Unbeknownst to my parents, we have earned and saved handfuls of coins by peddling foraged woodland plants to neighbors and taking in mending. Early in the day, before my sawn antlers inch up, I do the deliveries while Sparrow hides at home. She has even started a little business venture of her own, concocting cough syrups and soothing balms from local herbs, drawing on some innate knowledge that must be part of her Springborn gifts. Mother's daily alcohol-induced naps and Father's long shifts have made our pursuits possible. The tin tucked under my mattress contains almost enough money to enable us to strike out on our own.

"Tell me again how it will be in our new home," Sparrow says as we start back toward town.

"Soon—next week or the week after—on a good, dry morning, we'll set out after Father leaves for the mine. We'll go through the woods, skirt around Black Rock Corners, and make our way to the train station at Cairntown. We'll buy tickets to Lancaster and find a boarding house to live in until I find a good job. After that, we'll rent a little place of our own. We'll have bread and cheese for supper whenever it pleases us. We'll sit up late and tell tales, and no one will shout or curse at us ever again."

"And you can have antlers when you please," Sparrow says. "I do miss your lovely antlers."

"On days we stay in, yes, I will keep the antlers. And you can spend hours decorating them with paper birds and bows if you like."

"I can hardly wait." She smiles and reaches for my hand. She holds on tightly until we're standing on the doorstep of my parents' house.

As I reach for the doorknob, she tugs the scarf away from her mouth and leans over to kiss my cheek.

"How did I earn that fine gift?" I ask.

"By being the best mother in the world," she says sweetly.

The door swings open. Mother slouches over the table, snoring with her cheek pressed to the scarred wood. Inches from her head, stand a neat row of blue bottles labeled "Doctor Purcell's Curative Elixir." Beside them, the little tin in which I hid our savings lies on its side, its lid pried off.

Emptied.

Sparrow gasps and grabs my arm hard.

I turn and pull her close as sobs shake her thin frame. "Hush, dearest. We will start saving again right away. Summer will bring us so many berries and greens to sell that we'll be rich as kings in no time. Our plans are not ruined forever, only delayed. Hush now."

She feels small in my arms, and yet too large. Too near womanhood. Too close to elderliness, decline, and death. I hold her tighter, breathing in her sweet, clean scent, desperate to stop her from aging her way into the grave before we can escape this place.

SABELLA

Upstairs in my parents' gloomy bedroom, I scrub vomit from the floorboards with a stiff brush. Mother moans in her bed as if death is imminent. As her suffering is self-inflicted, I feel little pity for her. The window curtains sway as wind whistles through the two-inch opening she deemed acceptable on this balmy, first afternoon of June.

The scent of fresh bread wafts up from the kitchen to almost overwhelm the sick smell, thanks to Sparrow. She does all of the household baking these days, delighting in it far more than I ever could. Aside from baking and the clandestine walks we share, mine town life offers her few pleasures—yet she rarely complains. Sparrow is a joyful creature, one who has surpassed me in height and could be mistaken for a young woman of twenty.

As Sparrow daily matures in her rapid, unnatural way, Mother and Father increasingly ignore her existence. She lives as a quiet phantom, unaddressed. Or like a maidservant of such low caste that her existence is not worthy of acknowledgment. When we first arrived, she tried hard to win their approval with cheerful obedience and hard work. Now, unjustly chastened by their meanness, she seeks to please only me and to lighten my burden of unending housework.

A knock downstairs catches me by surprise. I stop scrubbing and lift my head to listen.

Sparrow knows not to open the door for anyone other than Father. To my knowledge, the neighbors have not caught a glimpse of her without her Mother-impersonating disguise since we arrived. Which is good, for not even heaven could help us explain the magic that has transformed Sparrow from a little girl to a shapely woman in less than three months' time.

The creak of the kitchen door turns my insides to jelly. I drop the scrub brush and hurry to the top of the stairs. "Sparrow, no!" I shout too late.

"Sparrow," a man says.

"Uncle Calder?" she replies.

My heart stops and then restarts. It takes off racing. Dizzy, I grab the banister to keep from falling. Somehow I navigate the stairs and end up standing a few feet behind Sparrow. Her head rests on Calder's shoulder. His eyes are shut tightly as he embraces her with both arms. His nut-brown hair is charmingly wind-tousled.

My eyes ache at the sight of him; the air in my lungs feels impossibly heavy. It turns out that I am not immune to him, as I'd expected to be by this time. Seeing him is like seeing a woodland elf or a silver unicorn—some mythical creature I believed in as a child but later doubted the existence of.

I retain enough presence of mind to circumnavigate their reunion and close the door before the neighbors can garner any fodder for gossip. I stand still, my insides churning, my back pressed to the door. "Why are you here, Calder?" I ask.

He steps out of Sparrow's arms and turns to meet my gaze. His eyes are red rimmed, as if he has not slept in days, yet—oh saints and angels help me—he is more handsome than I remember. I want to throw myself into his arms, but I fight the inclination. Where is my former anger now that I need it?

He pales as he confesses, "It's Branna. She's been taken."

"What? Why?" I ask.

"I think it was Delphine."

"That makes no sense. Why would she steal a Springborn child? I thought she was our protector."

"As did we all. But if she was, I don't think she is anymore."

"Shouldn't you be searching for Branna instead of coming all the way here to tell us?"

"Robbie and Cleona set out yesterday to try to find her. Yonaz is quite ill again. He stayed home with some boys who joined us recently. I came to you because I'm afraid you're not safe here. Whoever took Branna could take you as well."

"We're fine, as you can see. Thank you for coming to warn us. We are always mindful of strangers, and we'll continue to be."

He takes one step closer. "Come with me, please. I will not go back without you."

"You cannot stay here, Calder."

"Do you want me to beg, Sabella? I'll get on my knees and grovel if necessary."

"Please do not," I say emphatically. There is an odd look on his face, something akin to guilt. Half of me does not wish to know why, but I say, "What have you left out of this story?"

He almost smiles but his eyes remain dim with sadness. "You know me too well," he says. "I confess I had a dream. I can't remember much of it, but it was bad. Very bad. It left me with the impression that we all must band together in order to survive. You and Sparrow included."

"How do I know you're telling the truth and not simply trying to trick us into going with you?"

"Oh, Sabella. If only I knew how to win back your trust, I—"

"We should go with him," Sparrow interjects. "We had plans to leave anyway, and now I'm frightened to stay. We could live with Uncle Calder until Branna is found, then go to Lancaster. Why not, Mama? It makes sense."

I speak without pausing to think. Shock and worry have made me reckless indeed. "We will go on one condition. You must promise that after Branna is found, you will help me look for a cure for Sparrow's aging."

"Of course," Calder says. I think he would agree to anything to get us to go with him. There's a desperate look in his eyes.

"You will keep us safe, Uncle Calder?"

Calder places a hand on her arm and says, "No one will harm you as long as I'm breathing."

I try to dredge up the strong bitterness I felt toward him for hiding the letter, but seeing him again, his penitent gaze, his kindness toward Sparrow... I find it hard to remain angry with him. Perhaps he'd been right to withhold the letter. If he'd kept it forever, I would not have brought Sparrow back here.

"What is your answer, Sabella? Will you come with me?" He waits beside Sparrow, allowing me the time to consider. But truly, what is there to think about? We are desperate to leave this house, and clearly Sparrow is unhappy here. Have I not sworn to protect and nourish her always? Even if it is uncomfortable for me to be near Calder, for Sparrow's sake, we must go with him.

An acrid smell seeps into my nostrils. "The bread," I say, and Sparrow rushes to the oven, leaving me alone near the door with Calder Hadrian.

With his head slightly bowed, he looks at me through the fringe of his dark lashes. His voice comes in a whisper. "I've missed you."

"Sparrow and I have missed you all, as well," I reply—as if I do not understand the true meaning of his words.

Hands wrapped in tea towels, Sparrow tosses the metal bread pans onto the top of the cookstove. A puff of dark smoke billows toward the ceiling. The tops of the loaves are slick and black. "Darnation," she says, using Robbie's favored expletive.

"Leave it," I say. "Pack a basket with some food for the trip, and I'll fetch our clothes. Stay here, Calder." The last thing I need is for him to follow me into the bedroom. Father's shift will end soon, and were he to find Calder in my room, someone might need to scrub blood from the floorboards afterward. Mine, Calder's, or Father's—or perhaps a combination of them all.

Calder reaches out and touches my arm. His eyes brighten. "Does this mean you'll come with me?"

"Yes," I say, and I bound toward my little room.

Five minutes later, I rejoin Sparrow and Calder near the door. Sparrow drapes a shawl around me and covers my cotton cap with my dark green, coal scuttle-shaped bonnet. She ties it tightly under my chin as if she's the mother and I'm the child.

"Ready?" Calder asks.

"Wait," I say.

With a shudder of revulsion, I grab the despicable handsaw from the cabinet and stuff it into my bag. Who knows how long we will be traveling? Come morning, the thing will be necessary.

A vivid memory of Calder removing my antlers plays in my mind. I almost feel his gentle hand on my neck and hear the echo of his tender words. Blushing from head to toe, I tie the bag shut.

In the distance, the whistle blares to announce the end of the miners' shift. Soon, the street will be full of men—some weary, others ready to cause mischief after hours of confinement under the earth. It is no time for young ladies or strangers to linger on the streets.

"We should hurry," I say.

Calder opens the door wide.

SABELLA

The swaying of the train car puts Sparrow to sleep after only a few miles, somehow besting the novelty of the experience. She has always had a talent for falling asleep easily—even without the strain of hiking through woods for hours and then along the road for much of the night, as we have just done with Calder. Her body leans heavily against mine; her head rests on my shoulder. An observer might mistake us for sisters and assume that she is the elder by four or five years.

I adjust my big, clumsy bonnet. My hand rests on my neck in the place where Calder's hand lay not long ago. I remember how carefully he sawed off my antlers in the red-gold light of the sunrise, how his touch lingered after the second antler fell, and how I did not mind but should have.

Now, Calder sits facing me, straight backed and vigilant. He squints out the window almost constantly, as if danger might appear along the tracks at any moment.

So many questions tumble through my thoughts that I cannot choose which one to ask first.

He catches me staring at him and I wait for him to tease me as he used to, to make some remark about his irresistibility. Instead, he smiles sadly and shifts in his seat as if he cannot endure much more travel.

"Branna is a fawn," he says, voice thick with sorrow. "A helpless fawn, of all things. She and Cleona and Fabian, one of the new boys, were walking in the woods near our farm when someone wearing robes and a mask grabbed her and ran off. Fabian is four years old and scared of his own shadow. All he could do was scream while Cleona tried to catch up with the kidnapper. But the fiend just disappeared. I've asked myself a hundred times why one of the twins could not have been a lioness that day, or a bear, or..."

"The twins are not seers," I say. "They had no way and no reason to prepare themselves for such an attack."

"What you say is true," Calder says. "But the facts give me little comfort, Sabella."

"I'm sorry." It is a useless remark, but all I can offer.

His gaze settles on my sleeping Sparrow. "She is much changed, and yet much the same." His mouth curves into a faint, fond smile. "We have missed her. Robbie misses her most of all, of course. When he sees her...do you think he will laugh or cry?"

"I think he will do both at once, and so shall she. I regret that I separated her from Robbie and the twins. From all of you. Almost daily I ask her to forgive me. Without fail, she embraces me and swears there is nothing to forgive."

"You did what you thought best," Calder says. "She surely knows that."

"Let us hope so."

A wrinkle of concern forms between his eyes. "Was it bad for you in Miners Ridge? As bad as ever?"

"I'm afraid it was."

"I'm sorry things were not better." His regret sounds sincere.

"You did not make my parents who they are." My heart patters, goading me to speak difficult, apologetic words. "I realize now that you were right to keep the letter. You were protecting me. Did you dream what would happen if I read it?"

"I wish I could blame a dream for my actions, but no. My own selfishness made me keep it, because by doing so, I believed I could keep you. I wanted you so much that I lost all sense of right and wrong. I'm sorry, Sabella. More than I can say."

"I'm sorry, too." I cannot bring myself to say that I forgive him, although I think I do. If I were to speak words of pardon, I am afraid he would gather me into his arms or break into tears. We must avoid making a scene here on the train, runaways that we are.

He nods soberly and resumes his window-watching.

I pick at the frayed edge of my cuff, realizing how tattered I must look to the other passengers, especially seated in proximity to Calder. In all the fuss and flurry of running away from home, I noticed little about his clothing until now—other than its newness. As surreptitiously as I can, I take a moment to study his outfit. His well-cut navy-blue coat and trousers must be worth a month's wages. His boots shine like they were carved from polished coal. The whiteness of his starched collar stings my eyes. Nothing in a coal mining town is ever that white, not even freshly fallen snow.

As if he notices my appraisal of his clothes, he clears his throat and tugs at his collar. His eyes fix on my bonnet, his expression lightening by a degree or two.

"The twins ordered the suit," he says. "They've become quite obsessed with fashion. Speaking of which... That hat is..."

"Practical?"

"Is that what you call it?" His mouth slips into a devilish smile.

This is the Calder I remember. The one I have denied missing every day for the last few months.

I roll my eyes heavenward. "Go on. Say it."

"That hat was meant for a curmudgeonly German governess whose diet consists solely of thistles and boiled radishes."

"Perhaps I enjoy boiled radishes."

"That, Miss Jenkins, is a ridiculous suggestion. I know for a fact that you despise radishes. And turnips. And orange marmalade. In addition, you loathe Chaucer and pointy-toed boots. Also, strangely yet passionately, you hate yellow waistcoats. Did you think I would have forgotten these things so quickly?"

I shrug. "I suppose I did. Why retain the memory of such trivialities?".

He replies with silence and a lingering look that almost cracks my wall of resolve. The look says he has forgotten nothing that transpired between us, not one glance, not one whisper.

Neither have I forgotten these things.

I turn my face toward the window. "Could we begin again as friends and leave the past where it lies?"

"Of course, *Fraulein*," he says with excessive cheer. "Let us bury the past six feet deep. To be your friend would be an honor."

I do not quite believe that this is everything he wishes for, nor do I know for certain what I wish for in regard to our relationship. But we are starting again, and there is every reason to hope for the best.

CALDER

The train ambles steadily along, but in the presence of Sabella and Sparrow, I feel as though I am already home. They sit on the bench opposite me, near enough that I could reach out to touch Sabella's soft cheek if I were allowed such a privilege.

Blazes, I have missed her. Her stubborn streak, her kind heart. How she bites her lip when she's thinking. Her ridiculous hats. The way her hand fits into mine.

I want to hold her, to tease her, to feed her until she loses that hungry mine town look again. I want to make her laugh loud and blush hard. I want to meet her in midnight kitchens and to take her on long afternoon rambles through the woods. I want her to trust me again, enough that she'll want to plan a future for both of us.

I'm still worried about Branna, of course. The worry simmers in my gut constantly. She is my sister in all but blood, and I cannot imagine life without her.

Why would someone take Branna? Had this kidnapper been spying on us Springborn for an age, waiting for a chance to snatch one of us? Or was the crime a random thing—a case of someone wanting a small deer for a pet and no more?

In my bones, I feel that there's some riddle to be solved here. When we reach the farm that's now our home, if Robbie and Cleona's search was unsuccessful, I'll play detective and interview the other Springborn. One of us might have seen or heard something that could help us find Branna.

Sparrow slumps against Sabella, fast asleep. The train rounds a sharp curve, and Sabella holds her grownup-looking child tightly to her side to keep her from slipping off the seat. The love between them is so strong, I swear I can almost see it glimmering. The scene really should be the subject of a painting or a poem.

I try to compose a verse in my head but soon abandon the idea. Instead, I force myself to look out the window. In truth, all I want to do is stare at Sabella, but if I do, she'll scold me. "We're friends," she'll say with that little scowl that makes me want to kiss her so badly it hurts.

Blazes. Friendship is starting to sound more like a trial than a pleasure.

Just as I wonder how much longer this journey will take, the train whistle hoots and the station slides into view.

SABELLA

S parrow and I follow Calder to the rear of the red brick train station where horses, a farm wagon, and a pair of closed black carriages stand waiting. There, other passengers are already reuniting with their families or friends.

A man in a black top hat sits atop the driver's seat of one of the most well-appointed carriages. He is draped in a heavy cloak and a thick scarf, garments far too warm for the season. His eyes, the only exposed part of his face, are encircled with kohl.

"It's Yonaz," Sparrow says. She releases my hand and runs to him like the little girl she remains in her heart, skirts flying in her wake. She scampers up the side of the carriage and nearly pushes him off the seat with the force of her greeting.

"That will do him more good than all the medicine he's choked down in the last couple months," Calder says as we approach at a more dignified pace. "I must warn you. When Yonaz removes his cloaks and scarves, you'll find there isn't much left of him but skin and bones. He's tried everything. Doctors and wise women, potions and poultices. Still he coughs from dusk to dawn and withers away before our eyes."

"Do you poison Sabella's fair ears with foul words, Calder Hadrian?" Yonaz calls from his seat. Sparrow is sitting beside him now, holding his hand and beaming.

"Nothing I could ever say is worthy of her ears, as well you know," Calder replies.

Yonaz's answer is supplanted by a hacking cough. When he finally catches his breath, he says, "Get in, or we will not make it home before supper."

"I want to ride beside Yonaz," Sparrow says. "May I, Mama?"

"If he has no objections," I say, trusting his judgment in the matter.

His reply is hoarse but resolute. "Few things would bring me more joy."

Calder opens the carriage door and waits for me to climb inside. A wave of heat spills out as I peer in. Asleep on one bench like a pile of puppies are three young boys, all under the age of five by my reckoning. Two are identical, cherub-faced, and brown-skinned. The other child has golden freckles and hair the color of buttercups. He rolls over but does not wake as I settle onto the opposite bench.

Calder slides in beside me—which cannot be helped, as the boys occupy all the space on the other seat. I inch away from him as subtly as I can until my shoulder collides with the wall. It is too warm in here for closeness, and besides, I do not wish to test the boundaries of our new friendship.

"Their names are Fabian, Tiberius, and Rhys," Calder whispers as he sheds his blue jacket to reveal a waistcoat of burgundy silk. "And I'll be horsewhipped if I've seen them this quiet once since Yonaz brought them home."

Each little boy is beautiful. Each one, I know, hides some gift their parents deemed unacceptable.

Calder leans back and crosses his ankles. "The farm is about ten miles from here. Some of the road is rough, but Yonaz is a capable driver."

"Unless we encounter three feet of snow," I say.

"Keep talking of snow, I beg you. You could roast a goose in here." He starts to roll up his blindingly white shirt sleeves. The sight of his bare forearms, unfortunately and ridiculously, causes a hot blush to spread over my face and throat. When he's finished fiddling with his sleeves, he looks directly into my flushed countenance and says, "For the love of all that's holy, take that coal bucket off your head or you'll end up fainting." He leans across me and yanks the window shade halfway down. "There. Now no one could see the top of your head if they tried."

My fingers struggle to untangle the knotted ribbon under my chin.

"May I be of assistance?" he asks.

"No," I say too loudly. One of the twins sighs in his sleep and throws an arm over his brother's belly. "I mean, thank you, but I can manage it myself," I whisper.

He frowns. "If we're going to be friends, you're going to have to stop behaving like I have the plague. Friends sometimes touch each other, you know, for purely platonic and helpful reasons."

I drop my hands into my lap and lift my chin in surrender. "Fine. But I fear this knot will only be undone by scissors."

"Knots are a specialty of mine," he says. He leans in closer. Eyes narrowed with concentration, he picks and prods the ribbon. His fingers brush my neck and I realize he was right that I might faint from the heat. I cannot draw in a full breath with him so close. I shut my eyes and pray for the ribbon to cooperate quickly. But is that what I truly want? The scent of his soap and the brush of his breath on my chin tempt me to lean toward him. It would be easy now to place my hand behind his neck and to...

The knot unfurls. The bonnet loosens. He lifts it off and sets it on the seat between us, a barricade built from a hideous hat.

"Thank you," I say. I fan myself with my fingers. Can one perish of sunstroke when not in the sun?

"At your service," he replies with a grin.

Without the hat, I am not a single degree cooler than I was with it.

Three Stars Farm is surrounded by a ten-foot-high stone wall. Yonaz drives past a pair of stone barns and onto a curved lane leading to the biggest, grandest house I have ever seen. Built of the same gray stone as the wall and barns, the front of the house boasts no less than twenty leaded glass windows. The roof is scalloped with slate shingles and crowned with numerous chimneys.

The boys, as if sensing that the tedious trip has ended, yawn and stretch themselves into wakefulness.

"Who're you?" the blond one asks, squinting at me like he cannot tell if I'm a dose of castor oil or a spoonful of maple syrup.

"This is Sabella," Calder says. "And mind your manners, Fabian. She is our friend and guest—and a proper lady."

"Darnation," one of the curly-haired twins says. "Another girl."

"Rhys," Calder says sharply. "Should I tell Yonaz you boys require another course of etiquette lessons?"

"Hades, no," the other twin, Tiberius, says. The shifting light reveals two short, gray horns among his curls. I glance at his brother, Rhys, and find the same goatish protuberances.

Calder laughs. "They're wee heathens, the lot of them." He reaches for the door handle and shoves the door open. Glorious fresh air rushes in—which makes me more anxious than ever to escape the confines of the carriage. I grab my bonnet and shove it over my short antlers before stepping out onto the pebbled driveway.

"No need for the hideous hat here," Calder says, eyeing my bonnet with a scowl. "Everyone here is Springborn, with the exception of the servants, and they've taken an oath of secrecy."

"I never have liked this hat," I say as I tear it from my head. I let it dangle from its thick ribbons as I take in the scene. Everything here contrasts with the grays and blacks of the coal town I called home. I almost need to shield my eyes from the brightness of it. The trees are wealthy with late spring leaves of a hundred different greens. Blooming white rose bushes and squares of dandelion-spotted green lawn surround the house. In front of me, in the center of a blue-tiled water fountain, a six-foot-high marble seahorse spurts crystalline water from its open mouth.

In response to my stunned silence, Calder says, "Whoever abandoned Fabian in the mountains left a great deal of money with him, along with a note begging the fairies to take him back. As if fairies take cash bribes."

Sparrow comes alongside me. The ride in the fresh air has somehow added to her prettiness. She slips her hand into mine. "Am I dreaming? This house is like a palace from a storybook."

"Oh, it's real," Calder says. "You'll realize how real when Yonaz presents you with your list of household chores. I, for one, am glad you're here. With Robbie and the girls gone, it's been a nightmare keeping up with the dusting."

Sparrow's eyes widen. Dusting is the chore she most detests. I squeeze her hand reassuringly. "Perhaps you've forgotten that Uncle Calder is a terrible tease," I say. "I'm quite certain he hasn't done a minute's worth of dusting in his life. Also, he mentioned servants."

He winks at me. "You hang on my every word, obviously."

"You wish," I counter. There, we are arguing like he and Robbie do. Perhaps friendship will be possible after all.

Yonaz walks away from the carriage stiffly, as if every part of his body aches. He is clearly far from well. He instructs the boys to fetch the stable hand. "Come inside, my dears," he says to Sparrow and me. "See your rooms and take time to refresh yourselves before dinner."

"Rooms?" Sparrow says with delight as we follow Yonaz. "We have *rooms*?"

Calder sneaks between Sparrow and me and puts an arm around each of us. "Rooms bigger than the entirety of your old house, crammed full of dresses and slippers and porcelain bath-tubs. Beds with pillows so deep your head gets lost in them. And lots of girlish fripperies I couldn't name if I wanted to. Cleona and Branna chose everything for you when we moved in. They insisted you'd return someday, and wanted you to feel welcome when you did." His voice cracks with emotion, a heart-piercing reminder that we have not been brought here for enjoyment but for protection.

Calder politely allows us to pass through the wide front door before him. It bothers me to see him unsmiling. I want to tell him everything will be fine, to have faith that our little family will soon be restored. I want to say I would help him search the world round for Branna, but the words stick in the back of my throat, unuttered.

CALDER

Yonaz leans heavily on me as we scale the stairs to the second floor after dinner. He would not make it up alone, no matter that he spent most of the day simply sitting on the carriage seat. His skin is sallow, his eyes glassy. I would almost believe he suffers from Sparrow's condition, for he seems to have aged a decade in a week.

He did a good job of hiding his poor health while Sabella and Sparrow were with us earlier. He coughed a few times during the meal and his voice was rough and gravelly, but he also told a few stories and managed to eat everything on his plate. Perhaps he should have pursued a career as an actor.

"Have you given any more consideration to the idea of sending for Delphine?" I ask him as we pause for him to catch his breath. "She knows a great deal about magic, does she not? Maybe she has a recipe to improve your health."

His grip tightens on my arm and he says hoarsely, "We must not summon her. Promise me you will not, no matter how ill I become."

I stare at him like he's grown an extra head. "What? She's your partner. Your wife, practically speaking. You've always said she was your true love."

"There are things I cannot share with you. She has set a guard over my mouth. I can only caution you to be wary...and beseech you not to send for her." His black-rimmed eyes bore into mine.

"I won't send for her," I say. He is too ill to be argued with, and besides, I respect him as if he were my father.

He exhales with relief and his fingers loosen their grip on my arm. "Good lad."

It takes another five minutes to reach the top of the staircase, and five more to get him into his room and onto the bed. When he lies down and shuts his eyes, he makes a good approximation of a corpse. I wish I hadn't promised not to send for Delphine, for I do not think he will recover without her aid.

As I'm leaving the room, his voice follows after me. "Be wary, Calder."

"I will," I reply. But it would be easier if I knew why.

SABELLA

JUNE 3, 1886
MORNING

In the stillness of the early morning, I roll over to find Sparrow asleep in my bed. She must have crept in during the night. She did seem nervous when we retired to our separate (although connected) rooms last night, for rarely have we slept more than a few feet apart since the day I found her in the basket. I am most surprised that I did not awaken when she crawled under the covers beside me. Running away from home must have fatigued me more than I knew.

She sighs in her sleep. There are little lines on her forehead and fanning from her eyes that were not there yesterday. Along her hairline, silvery white hairs intermingle with the flaxen strands. How old is she now? Thirty? Thirty-five?

If she ages five or ten years a night, how long will she remain alive?

My heart sinks as I realize she has never seen Christmas, and probably never will. Why this makes the short span of her life seem crueler, I do not know. Perhaps because she, of all people, would love bedecking the rooms with greenery and singing sweet carols.

The old panic of losing her returns with a vengeance, making my pulse surge and my body tremble. I take deep breaths to try to calm myself, but it does little good.

Sparrow's eyes open. "Mama? Why are you shivering? Are you unwell?" She does not wait for an answer before sliding closer and wrapping her arm around me. Her warmth and familiar scent bring both comfort and deeper pain. I cling to her as if she can save me from drowning in sorrow.

A bloodcurdling wail echoes through the house.

We sit up, breath bated. Again, the sound rents the air.

"Oh heavens," I say. "That was Yonaz, I think. Quick, Sparrow. Get dressed."

I vault from the bed and pull a new dress from the wardrobe. Too rushed to fuss with laces and tiny holes, I leave my nightgown on, forego a corset, and step into the lavender-and-white-striped cotton frock. The row of buttons vexes my trembling fingers, but in the end I claim victory over them.

"Sabella!" Calder shouts outside the door. He knocks so hard that I think he'll have bruises from it later. "Sabella? Are you awake?"

I rush to open the door. Calder's eyes are wide with panic. One side of his cotton night shirt is stuffed into his trousers and the other side droops to his knees.

"Rhys has been taken," he says, gripping the doorframe like it's preventing him from falling off the earth. "Yonaz is beside himself. If someone cannot calm him, I fear his heart might give out."

"Do you have the medicine chest we traveled with?" I ask.

"I think it's in the pantry. I'll fetch it." He turns to go.

"Meet me in his room. Oh, heavens. Where is his room?"

Halfway down the hallway, he calls to me, "Second floor. First door on the left from the landing."

"Hurry," I say, although he's already gone.

Sparrow tugs my sleeve as if she were five years old. "Button me?" She has thrown on a pale pink gown. She spins to show me her back.

My voice shakes as I say, "Did I ever tell you how much I despise dresses that button up the back? Who has time for such nonsense?" Calder's terror-stricken face and Yonaz's miserable howls haunt me as I struggle to force a row of pea-sized mother of pearl discs into the proper holes.

"I'm sorry, Mama," Sparrow says. "All of the other dresses were too small."

I spin her to face me and kiss her cheek. "I am not displeased with you, dearest. Only worried for our friends. Now, come. Yonaz needs care, and you have a talent for medicines."

"Hawthorn or lavender may help," she murmurs as she follows me into the hallway. "Or perhaps a tisane of celery seed and tassel flower."

"Thank heaven for you," I say. I take her hand and we run.

SABELLA

"How did it happen? Were the doors unlocked?" I face Calder in the narrow, white-walled dressing room adjoining Yonaz's bedroom. Over his shoulder, I watch Sparrow spoon a freshly-made herbal tonic into Yonaz's mouth. The patient grimaces but swallows.

Calder rakes his fingers through his hair. "Fabian said they all snuck out during the night to look for whippoorwills. The boys have a bit of an obsession with the birds—my fault, I confess. But they know better than to go outside the walls unaccompanied by an adult. They've been told a hundred times. A thousand."

He looks so plagued with guilt that I feel compelled to comfort him. "Little boys will have their adventures. You cannot blame yourself for that. Did they see the person who took Rhys?"

"Fabian described her. I have no doubt it was Delphine."

"Delphine? I don't understand. She's one of our guardians. Why would she steal children?"

245

He shakes his head. "I understand no more than you. I have a suspicion she can't come inside the farm's walls, though. Both abductions happened in the woods outside the property."

"Those poor boys. She must have been lying in wait for the chance to snatch one of them."

"Her hiding place must be nearby." His face pales and he curses under his breath. "Robbie and Cleona are looking farther afield for Branna by now, where they'll never find her."

"Can you send them word somehow?"

He shakes his head. "I haven't the slightest idea how that could be done. For all I know, Delphine could have already captured them, too."

"We must go, then, and try to find Rhys and Branna ourselves."

The smallest shadow of a smile coaxes the corners of his mouth upward. "I should have expected you to say that, but I do like it when you surprise me," Calder says. "We'd have to leave Sparrow here to look after Yonaz and the other boys. Could she handle them?"

"I have every confidence that she could. She's become a most remarkable young woman."

"She takes after her mother," Calder says. His countenance grows more serious. "We must avoid getting into any altercations with Delphine. Yonaz has always said she's powerful beyond words. It would be best if we could reclaim our friends when she's not paying attention."

"I agree."

"Good." When his gaze fixes above my forehead, I remember that I carry fully grown antlers.

"Must you stare? They're just antlers. We have to stay focused on our mission, Calder."

He lowers his gaze as his cheeks turn pink. "Sorry. I forgot myself for a moment. I haven't slept much lately."

Now that I recall their presence, the weight of the antlers, although slight, makes my head ache. I consider asking him to saw them off, but to do so suddenly seems as personal as asking him to kiss me—and *that* is not going to happen in the foreseeable future.

I look past him to Sparrow. She dabs Yonaz's forehead with a damp cloth and whispers reassurances to him. Calder may want to avoid confronting Delphine, but we may have to. Rescuing Branna and Rhys is important, but I must also ensure that my daughter will remain safe from harm.

"Tell Sparrow the plan," I say. "I'll fetch my shoes and meet you downstairs."

If not speaking the whole truth is the same as lying, I am guilty, for I neglect to tell Calder that when I reach my room, I will use the saw I brought from home to remove the antlers from my head. It would be foolish to leave the farm with them in place, a glaring sign to anyone we might meet that I am no ordinary girl.

CALDER

I t's like taking an unexpected punch to the gut, seeing Sabella waiting by the front door without her antlers. It's as if she's standing there missing one of her arms. My mouth gapes open. Meanwhile, she looks unconcerned as she ties a blue and white kerchief behind her neck to secure it as a head covering.

"Don't scold me. It had to be done," she says, grabbing a satchel from the floor.

"I would have helped." I'm sure I look miserable, because I feel wretched.

"I did fine myself."

"Did you?" I reach over and touch a dark, spreading spot on the kerchief. I show her the red stain on my fingertips. "You're bleeding."

"It's hardly more than a scratch. It will heal."

"Sabella."

"Calder," she replies impatiently. "Let's go." She is all business now, and it is true that we ought not to waste time debating while our friends are in danger.

She grabs my hand when I do not move quickly enough. She tugs me out the door and down the lane, and keeps tugging until we're outside the stone walls of the farm. The whole time, I'm wondering when she'll let go, and dreading the thought of my hand being just mine again—and not a sacred connection to the girl I cannot stop loving.

You're friends, Calder, I remind myself.

And then I tighten my hold on Sabella's fingers in a quiet act of rebellion.

SABELLA

In the woods beyond the stone wall, Calder discovers footprints in the mud, just where Fabian said the kidnapping occurred. They were made by narrow boots with pointed toes. A woman's boots. Delphine's boots.

"You can let go now," I say, unsuccessfully trying to free my hand from his. I only meant to hurry him out of the house, and I ended up holding his hand for half an hour. Half an hour!

"It's only friendly hand-holding," he insists. "A sensible measure to ensure that we don't become separated in the woods." His imitation of innocence would not fool even the most gullible child.

I yank harder and fail again. "Well, we've been friendly enough for one day."

"Fine. I surrender for practical reasons." He lets go and points to where the trail of footprints leads. "That path between the rocks looks a bit treacherous. You'll need both hands to grab onto trees where it gets steep."

Without waiting for him, I follow the tracks. They go on for a while, first up a slope, then winding between sharp-edged, red-brown boulders, and finally through a grove of young silver birches. In a place where the ground is strewn with pebbles, the footprints become indiscernible.

Calder curses under his breath. He turns red when I look over my shoulder at him. "Sorry," he says. "But now what will we do?"

"We will not give up. Delphine is not a ghost who can simply disappear. There will be more tracks somewhere." I point to the left. "You search the ground along the edge of the rock face that way, and I'll check in the other direction."

"No." He plants his feet and crosses his arms. "I am not moving more than ten feet away from you. Delphine is young and strong this time of year. She has some magic, too. She could take you before you even sensed her presence."

"I appreciate your concern, but I promise I'll be careful. Besides, she could just as soon snatch you."

"Say what you like. I'm not leaving you. Two are better than one, as the saying goes."

"Your stubbornness is not helping Rhys and Branna."

"Neither is yours."

"Fine," I say. "We'll stay together, although I hold to the opinion that it isn't at all necessary." I trudge toward the edge of the rocks and he follows me like an overgrown puppy.

My skirt snags in a thicket of thorns. I am caught like prey in a trap. I pull at the fabric, but it only seems to make the thorns grip harder. Of course nature would prove Calder right about our need to stay together within five minutes of his declaration. I wriggle and jerk the fabric furiously. If I were one to curse, the words I'd say...

"Wait," he says behind me. "Let me help. I swear, you become more stubborn by the minute."

Now he's next to me. He takes a folding knife out of his pocket and starts to cut the offending branches while I stand still and brood. His nearness and his slightly musky scent fluster me. My pulse quickens. He's done nothing but vex me for the last half hour, and yet my puerile mind reminds me of every detail of our long-ago kiss. Blast and darnation.

The fabric tears, and my skirt is free. "There," Calder says, looking pleased with himself. "The thorns left a few holes, but they can be easily mended, I imagine."

I must be scowling because his smile shifts into a grimace. He sets his fists on his hips. "So I still have the plague, do I?"

"I wouldn't say that."

"Your face would." He stuffs his knife into his pocket and steps back. "All I did was to help untangle you. Like a gentleman."

"Well, there was the hand-holding." I regret saying the words as soon as they leave my mouth.

"Blazes, Sabella. You are impossible. Was I the one who started the hand-holding? I clearly remember otherwise, Miss Let's-be-friends. You know, I think you were right. Searching separately is a grand idea."

He turns his back to me and rips a dead branch off a fallen tree. I watch him walk away in silence, his head bowed as he uses the branch to overturn leaves and flip stones, looking for signs of Delphine. My chest constricts with sadness because there is such misery in the slump of his shoulders and the angle he holds his head. Because I have hurt him.

"Calder, please." I begin to follow after him. "I didn't mean—"

He does not turn but raises the stick in his hand as if to signal me to stop speaking. "Let's leave it, shall we? We need to find Branna and Rhys right now, and frankly, I'm tired of whatever this is between us."

"Very well." Tears sting my eyes. I quickly wipe them away with my sleeve, glad he's not looking in my direction to witness it. I asked him for friendship instead of romance, but it seems I may lose both.

SABELLA

JUNE 3, 1886
EARLY EVENING

As dusk veils the woods, my hopes wane.

We have found no sign of Delphine since we lost track of her footprints, and to make matters worse, I am fairly certain we are lost.

Few words have passed between Calder and me since our misunderstanding, all of them practical. "Be careful there," or "watch out for that." Things a person would say to a stranger.

Calder stops to pick something up. He turns and shows me a yellow silk handkerchief embroidered at its corner with a fancy letter D.

I open my mouth to comment but he lays a finger on his lips. He cocks his head to the side, listening intently. After a minute or two, he points up the steep, rocky slope to our right.

She's up there? I mouth.

He steps close to me and whispers into my ear. "There are caves in the rock face. I'll climb up and look for signs of Delphine. You wait here."

"I'm going, too."

"You can't scale the rocks in that cumbersome dress, and I don't think you want to go without it."

I cringe at the idea of abandoning my frock in order to climb in my nightdress and knee-length drawers. He is correct. I may not be the most modest of maidens, but I will not appear before the man in my undergarments.

He accepts my silent concession and whispers, "I'll be back soon."

Calder climbs with the deftness of a mountain goat, hardly pausing as he ascends to a jutting ledge. Once atop it, he disappears from view.

The woods grow dim as time slogs along. I sit on a fallen tree trunk and try to occupy my thoughts with memories of gathering fiddlehead ferns and mushrooms with Sparrow, but worries intrude all too quickly—concerns for the stolen children, for Calder, and for my own safety.

Soon, night will clothe the forest with heavy shadow—if not utter darkness. The moon tonight, if I remember rightly, will be three-quarters lit, but the sky is already roiling with thick clouds which promise to obscure its light.

An owl hoots nearby. Leaves rustle, stirred by an opossum or raccoon—I hope. Insects hum and buzz as the air cools. A sprinkling of stars peeks through a gap in the clouds.

I wait and wait.

Calder has been gone too long.

SABELLA

J udging by the regrowth of my antlers, midnight is near, but I am wide awake. And still alone. I stare into the forest's shadows, praying morning will come on swift wings so I can search for Calder. I do not know if I will be able to help him if he's been captured, but I must try.

I rise from my seat on the fallen tree trunk, ready to pace along its length, as I have done at least twenty times in the last few hours.

A rope slips over my head and shoulders. Before I can react, it clenches tight around my body, binding my arms to my sides. Fear expands within me as a sharp tug tightens the rope.

"Sabella Jenkins," a female voice says. "How lovely to see you." I cannot turn to see the woman's face, but I can guess who is speaking.

"Let me go!" I strain at my bonds but it proves futile. The rope is strong, and so is the woman who wields it.

There is a faint rustling as she walks, the sound of fallen leaves being crushed by her slow footsteps combined with the swish of her skirt. "Not a chance, my dear. Calder Hadrian sends his greetings, by the way. Not quite a hero, is he, leaving his lady alone to face the perils of the forest?"

"I'm no one's 'lady,'" I say. I continue to squirm. The rope constricts. I look down to discover it is not a rope at all, but some sort of vine. A living thing.

Delphine steps into view. "It could be argued that you're mine now, but I prefer not to waste my breath."

Yonaz once said that she could make men fall in love with her with a mere glance, and I believe it. This springtime version of Delphine has smooth skin the delicate golden-brown of dried wheat. Her eyes are a startling blue-green that almost glows in the dim light of the forest. Her figure is curvaceous, her bearing regal. She wears a short, plain black cape over an unremarkable, earth-colored dress, yet she is as stunning as a woman bedecked in velvets and silks. On her forehead, she wears a miner's headlamp. Somehow she makes even this humble piece of equipment look elegant.

Just as I take in her appearance, Delphine takes in mine, assessing me from my antlers to my shoes. She tugs the dark, purplish green rope that spirals from her left hand to my body. "Come."

I am tethered like a disobedient dog, so I follow her. If she is taking me to Calder, perhaps we can think of an escape plan together. At the moment, I am too stunned and angry to think clearly. I should have been more careful. More alert.

Rather than dragging me up the rocky slope Calder climbed, Delphine leads me along a path we'd missed. It winds steeply up a hill clad in wiry grass. Her headlamp illuminates the ground ahead.

There is something menacing about the thick-stemmed vine between us, something that seems more animal than vegetable. In all my forays through the forest, I have never seen anything like it. Where it encircles my body, I think I feel its throbbing pulse.

Ahead, a boulder as big as a barn looms. Delphine jerks the

rope. I stumble before increasing my pace to her satisfaction. As we come around the side of the boulder, the smell of wood smoke drifts into my nostrils. A moment later, I spy two dimly lit windows set into the front of a steeply gabled house built of dark timber. Vines embellish its face like an overabundance of Christmas garlands.

"Do you like my pretty little house?" Delphine asks as she strides forward. "It is no palace, but it is certainly better than anything in the mine towns."

I stumble again, this time over a stone. I grab the vine to steady myself. I say to her back, "Why are you doing this?"

"We will speak of that later."

"I would prefer to know now."

Over her shoulder, she sneers at me. "Your preferences mean nothing to me, child."

She keeps walking. The light from her headlamp spreads onto the face of the house. Thousands of leaves cringe as they catch the light. Each one is attached to purplish-green vine identical to the one binding me. Now I can see that entwined by tendrils of vine, there are metal bars on the windows. This is not a house but a prison.

Delphine stops to throw open a wide door spackled with moss and lichens. I follow her over the threshold, tugged along by the vine. My eyes scan the single large space that appears to serve as the kitchen, dining room, and sitting room. A steep set of wooden stairs abuts one wall. A few oil lamps and an open fireplace illuminate the sparsely furnished room. Every windowsill and shelf is crowded with plants of different shapes, sizes, and colors. Some flaunt flowers, blossoms of blood red and honey gold. The scent of damp soil and moldering leaves troubles the air.

"Sabella," Calder says from the far side of the room. "Blast it."

Had he imagined I would rush in to slay the proverbial dragon and rescue him? How I wish. He is covered in dirt and a bruise swells on his cheekbone. He looks frustrated, angry, and weary all at once—feelings I share, especially as I note the odious vine that twines from his neck to his ankles to secure him to a chair. This chair is wedged into the corner of the kitchen area, a spot readily observable from any point in the room.

"No idle chatter," Delphine says. The vines around Calder creak as they tighten their hold, and he winces.

Delphine unravels my vine leash from her arm and tosses the end of it toward the wall. It snakes forward to fasten tendrils to a metal hook. At her command, the vine loosens enough for me to work my arms free. My unbound muscles tingle and ache as the vine adjusts itself into a stiff belt around my waist.

Delphine points to fireplace where a tarnished copper kettle hangs over a pile of orange embers. "Feed the fire and brew some tea, Sabella."

It feels dangerous to ask, but I cannot hold my tongue one second more. "Where are the others? Where are Rhys and Branna?"

She presses a hand to her chest and does a poor job of feigning astonishment. "Why, they're upstairs tucked into their beds. I am not ignorant. I do know that children need their rest."

Branna is hardly a child at fifteen years of age—and as far as I know still a fawn—but if being viewed as a child earns her mercy, it is a good thing.

Delphine removes her short cape and drapes it over the back of an armchair before taking a seat. She reclines like a queen enthroned.

My hands tremble as I take a tin of tea leaves and a silver tea pot down from a shelf. I do not ask where I might find the other things I need to prepare the tea. Instead, I use this opportunity to rifle through drawers and cupboards. If asked, I can claim I'm looking for spoons. In reality, I'm searching for a blade to slit my bonds. I find only a dull, dainty butter knife before Delphine says with a yawn, "Is all well over there?"

"Fine," I reply. Disappointment weighs heavily on me, but I

have not given up hope of finding a knife. She has asked me to make tea; surely she will ask me to cook something else soon. There must be some sort of cutting tool here somewhere.

Across the room, Calder shifts in his chair and draws my attention. *Are you all right?* he mouths.

I nod and pause from my work to take in the sight of him. Despite our recent quarreling, and notwithstanding our present trial, his presence consoles me.

"Midnight," Delphine says from her chair across the room. "I always feel it in my bones when it comes, stirring like an earthworm among newly cast roots. Do you feel it, Sabella, in the marrow of your antlers?"

"No. I am usually asleep at midnight." I say no more, wary of this woman who commands vines and kidnaps children. She is likely sifting my every word for information to use against us. When the tea is ready, I deliver a cup to her, my pace hindered by the vine around my midsection.

Delphine offers me a small smile in exchange for the cup, but it is as false as a paper flower. "You must be tired after such a long day of walking. Sit with me while I drink. When I have finished, I will show you to your room."

I take a seat across from her, forced to sit up uncomfortably straight by my antlers, the vine, and the stiff wings of the high-backed chair. She sips while perusing my antlers with obvious curiosity. "However do you manage to sleep with those atop your head?"

"It is not easy," I reply. I try to stifle a yawn but fail. This tiredness is inconvenient to say the least. I should be spending every moment trying to solve the problem of our captivity. I pinch myself hard but it does no good.

Delphine's cup clinks against the saucer as she sets it onto the small table at her elbow. "It is clear that I will wrest no brilliant conversation from you this evening. Let us retire upstairs."

"What about Calder?" I glance over at him, noting his puffy

eyes and sunken cheeks. The neck-to-ankle constricting vines give him the appearance of an exhausted mummy propped in a chair.

She dismisses my concerns with a wave of her elegant hand. "He will be fine where he is."

"He needs to lie down," I argue. "He looks ill."

Delphine's eyes widen with surprise. A wry smile curves her mouth. "You're a bold creature. Very well. He can sleep by the hearth, tethered as he is. I'll see to him after you're settled."

"Thank you." It irks me to offer her gratitude, but I am relieved to know Calder will be allowed some rest.

"Do not mention it. Only a fool refuses a request inspired by true love."

My face heats. "I asked because I'm concerned for his health."

Delphine peers down her nose at me, accusing me of lying without saying a word. She turns and flicks her wrist toward the vine that holds me. It wriggles and unhooks from the wall. The end slithers toward Delphine like an eyeless serpent. She gathers a portion of the vine with her hands and wraps it around her wrist. At the same time, through some silent magic, the vine shortens until it becomes a taut, three-foot-long rope between her wrist and my waist.

"Come," she says.

With a slight nod, I bid Calder an unspoken good night and follow my captor up the creaky wooden stairs.

CALDER

Delphine descends the stairs slowly, stiffly. I can hardly believe this is the same woman who bandaged my scrapes and tucked me into bed with a kiss when I was younger. I cannot imagine this Delphine laughing in Yonaz's arms on a picnic blanket as the little boy versions of Robbie and me chase butterflies and catch toads. There is no warmth in her face. She might as well be sculpted of marble.

"You could make this easy," Delphine says as she pulls her chair close to mine. She sits and leans toward me. I try not to meet her gaze. There is too much power in it, and I have never been more tired.

Although I'm exhausted, I have enough vigor left to be furious. I stare at the fire and say, "Easy is the road to hell, so I understand how that might appeal to something who steals and terrorizes children. I, however, am not interested in being your accomplice."

She laughs. "Such wit. But be careful. I do not need you to accomplish my plan, Calder. You're nothing but an implement of torture in my hands. If you cause too much trouble, you'll find yourself in a shallow grave. Is your antlered paramour good with a shovel?"

"Who are you?" I blurt. "What happened to the kind, motherly woman you were? The bright, giving woman Yonaz adored?" She was not always with us, but when she was, she made our lives a joy with her affection and generosity.

"I am many things, as all women are. You are too much of a child to understand." She leans back in the chair and examines her fingernails. "Do you think the others will come looking for you soon, or must I venture out again?"

A shiver runs down my spine and spreads from there to chill every inch of my skin. "What do you need them for?"

"I commend you for your curiosity, but you will have to wait and see."

"I'll make a bargain with you. If you release the others, I'll do anything you ask for the rest of my days. You know I'm clever. We could make quite a mark on the world together, you and I."

She leans toward me again. She places her palms on my cheeks and says, "Oh, sweet boy. I do confess there was a time when such an offer from a handsome, winged gentleman would have made me swoon. But the past is the past. I am interested only in the future." She kisses my forehead like she did when I was small, but the kiss is colder than a snowflake on my skin. My anger slips and fear takes its place.

What could she be planning? I feel certain that some of us Springborn will not live to see the results of her scheme. I think I dreamed as much, but I sure as blazes do not want to remember that now. The situation is distressing enough.

The fire hisses and pops in the hearth. Delphine stands and does something to the vine-restraint to make it loosen. She pulls me to my feet, and when my legs buckle, she clutches me to her. Just as I remember, she smells of the forest: its pines and birches, its rare flowers. The scent makes me ache for the mother she was to me.

"Please, Delphine," I say. "It isn't too late to stop this. Come back and be a family with us. We can all start over and be happy together."

She shoves me to the floor and my heart breaks. The vine tightens around me again, a cocoon of slick greenery.

"Sleep," she says. She walks away. I listen to her footsteps on the steps, then the soft thud of a door closing upstairs.

I rest my head on the cool stone of the floor. I'm tempted to weep, but I cannot waste time grieving or trying to unravel the mystery of Delphine. There are people upstairs who need my help to escape before she can do something worse to them than holding them captive.

SABELLA

R obins chirp merrily outside the bedroom window to announce that morning has dawned. Rhys's arm is thrown over my chest and his small body nestles against my side. He sleeps deeply, his breaths slow and even. I remember climbing into bed with him last night, how he grabbed hold of me with both hands and sobbed until sleep overtook him.

The red-brown, spotted fawn Branna rests atop the blankets near the foot of the bed. Her ears flick now and then as if she's dreaming of bothersome flies.

I might have slept for an hour all told. Delphine was correct in her assumption that sleeping is difficult when stiff antlers branch out from one's head—especially when one is also secured to the bedpost by an unyielding vine, and bedmates with a restless boy and a fidgety deer.

A dew-dampened draft of air wafts into the musty bedroom. Delphine left the windowpane raised a few inches, trusting the bars beyond it and the vine tether to prevent my escape. The sound of flapping wings quickens my heartbeat as I imagine Cleona visiting in the form of an eagle or raven. That daydream dissipates when I remember the twins cannot change unless they are together —and that one of them must always be human. They cannot be fawn and bird, only fawn and girl.

A yellow flower bursts open on the vine where it crosses my ribcage, a poorly placed ornament on my filthy lavender and white dress. The flower makes me miss Sparrow more than I already did. Her fascination with botany is deep—although she would not appreciate this particular plant's habit of holding people captive.

Delphine knocks once and enters without waiting to being invited. "Time to rise, Sabella. I must say I am quite looking forward to having someone else cook my breakfast."

She unfastens the vine from the bedpost and holds it like a leash while she waits for me to get up. I gently lift Rhys's arm and set it on the pillow, determined not to wake him. My antlers scrape the headboard as I roll off the bed and scramble to find my feet, but Rhys does not stir. Branna eyes me forlornly and then rests her dainty, furred chin on Rhys's foot.

"Graceful you are not." Delphine taunts me with a grin as I struggle to regain my balance. What does she expect from me after scanty sleep and almost a day without food? It takes all my willpower not to scowl at her.

We go downstairs. The big room is quiet save for the faint crackle of the fire. My eyes scan the room for Calder. Until I see him, I hold my breath. But there he is, sitting perfectly still on the floor near the fireplace. The vine that binds his wrists swoops up to encircle his throat on its way to an iron hook meant for the hanging of a kettle. He stares at the coals in the hearth. I imagine he's spent the night wracking his brain for some notion of how to get out of this predicament.

"Get up, Calder," Delphine demands. His body jerks like she's startled him. "There's a spring house at the edge of the back garden. Fill the buckets and bring the water into the kitchen. The vine will allow you to go only that far, so do not attempt any foolishness. Death by choking would be a gruesome way to start the day."

"Could I perhaps borrow the use of my hands if I'm to carry buckets?" Calder asks in a strained but polite tone. Delphine waves her hand and utters a few syllables. Part of the vine unwinds from his wrists then reattaches itself as a cuff on his left upper arm.

Calder's gaze passes over me as if he's looking for signs of injury. Our eyes meet for half a second—long enough to strengthen my resolve to get all of us out of this mess. There is so much I want to say to Calder, to shout at him, to whisper to him. He abandons his makeshift bed and walks toward the door, the vine at his throat lengthening with each step to accommodate his movement.

"Sausage and eggs are in the pantry," Delphine says to me. "Summon me when the meal is ready." She leaves me to my task, scaling the steps with slow grace. I hear her bedroom door shut, and I sigh. Her absence is a relief.

As Delphine's kitchen has no cookstove, I must try my hand at fireplace cookery. I hang a shallow, cast iron pot from one of the hooks dangling over the fire and wait for it to heat so I can fry the sausages and eggs. If Delphine expects a fine, well-cooked breakfast, she is about to be greatly disappointed.

Calder returns with buckets sloshing. "My word, I'm hungry," he says—as if that were our worst problem. The buckets clunk against the stone floor when he sets them down.

"I hope you like burnt sausages and charred eggs, then," I say, glancing over my shoulder at him before dropping a glob of butter into the pot. It hisses and bubbles. The scent of it makes my stomach grumble.

"Where's Delphine?" Calder asks.

"Upstairs."

He crosses the room to join me by the fireplace. "Have you come upon any cleavers or hatchets to use on these blasted vines?"

he whispers. "If she hadn't taken my pocketknife, I could have gotten away the first day." he whispers. Frowning, he scratches the red welt the vine has left on his throat.

"No. I've checked the entire kitchen." I tip the dish of raw sausages into the pot and they sizzle alluringly.

"I saw nothing useful in the back garden, either." He peers into the pot as if it contains a leprechaun's golden bounty rather than a few morsels of meat.

"Rhys and Branna aren't tethered," I say, rolling the sausages over with a long-handled fork. "But there are vines securing the doors, and bars on all the windows; they could not escape any easier than we could."

"There has to be a way out. Think. How can we use our gifts to thwart hers?"

The sound of Delphine's footstep on a creaky step brings our conversation to an end. "Why is breakfast not yet on the table?" she says. "Does the boy distract you too much, Sabella? Need I tether him elsewhere?"

"Sausage takes time to cook," I say as matter-of-factly as I can. I bustle over to fetch the bowl of brown eggs from the table—and make no reply to her comments about Calder.

"Say what you will, I think you're dawdling," Delphine says. "Calder, go upstairs and wake the children or it shall be noon before we eat. Clearly, this girl finds your charms overwhelming."

I clench my fists as I stare into the fire. The woman is exasperating in every way.

After Calder leaves the room, Delphine gives me a threatening glare. "Did I interrupt your plotting when I appeared? Do not think you'll leave this place unless I allow it. Every plant and tree within a mile of here is under my command."

I whack one eggshell hard against the rim of the pot and then another, expressing my frustration in a way that will not buy me more trouble. Unfortunately, I believe she is telling the truth about the plants. We may be well and truly stuck here.

Yonaz might be able to find and rescue us—if Sparrow has had success in healing him. He has known Delphine for years. He knew her when she was the guardian of the Springborn instead of a threat to them. To *us*.

But hoping for rescue feels as futile as wishing on a distant star.

SABELLA

Two days later, and still we have neither seen nor heard from Yonaz. I have begun to doubt he shall ever come.

Fully adopted as Delphine's cook and housemaid—much to my displeasure—I hang freshly laundered sheets from a clothesline in the unnaturally lush garden. Rhys carries a small basket of wooden clothes pegs and hands them to me as I need them. Branna, still a fawn, sleeps in the shade of a row of blackberry bushes. Looming behind the bushes is a wall of hedges riddled with needle-tipped, two-inch-long thorns and prickly triangular leaves. No one could pass through them without being sliced to ribbons.

Calder paces along the edge of a vegetable patch prolific enough to feed all of Miners Ridge with beans, cucumbers, and squash for a month. His plodding footsteps and grim face bear witness to his frustration. I long to see the return of his impertinent smile almost as much as I long for my own freedom.

A little bat swoops low, stirring the air inches above my head. I duck. When it circles back and brushes the top of Calder's hair, I am tempted to run for the house. The creature must be ill or mad. A normal bat would never venture out in broad daylight.

But instead of fleeing, Calder holds out an open palm. The bat lands there and Calder grins. "I was beginning to think you'd never come," he says.

Rhys runs toward Calder. I toss aside the sheet I'd been clutching and follow him. By the time I reach Calder, Rhys is already standing on tiptoe to peer at the bat.

"Someone you know?" I ask. I scan the entire garden, looking for Delphine but not seeing her. Good. She must be in the house.

Calder strokes the bat between its pointy little ears. "It's Yonaz. Did no one ever tell you of his gift?"

"No, I never had occasion to ask," I say, a little stunned—although this news should not surprise me. "I was always busy working for the innkeepers or trying not to freeze during a blizzard."

"Fond memories," Calder says wryly. "Yonaz can become a bat when the moon is full if he wills it. The trouble is once he changes, he's usually stuck as a bat until the next full moon."

"I heard a strange fluttering outside the window not long ago. It could have been him." I lean closer and inspect the bat for similarities to Yonaz. I find none save the dark rims of his eyelids.

"Whatever medicine Sparrow gave him must have cured him quickly," Calder says. "If we're lucky, this means help is on the way."

The bat Yonaz nods emphatically. Rhys laughs and says, "Do that again." Yonaz obliges.

"Is Robbie coming?" Calder asks our visitor.

The bat dips its head.

"Today?" I ask, and this time, the bat shakes his head.

"Tomorrow?" Calder asks.

The bat nods. Hope floods my soul.

"We'll be ready," Calder says. "I wish you could stay, but you should leave before Delphine sees you. She will not have forgotten your gift, and we don't want her to capture you or suspect anything."

Without hesitation, Yonaz takes off. We watch him fly until his silhouette fades into the blue sky.

I meet Calder's gaze. The lively glint has returned to his eyes. My cheeks hurt from smiling so broadly.

"You're going to have to go back to looking miserable or Delphine will most certainly suspect something," Calder says.

"With all the cleaning I've been assigned, that should not be difficult," I say. But this turns out to be untrue. Throughout the rest of the day, I must stop myself from smiling again and again. I don't know how it will happen, but soon we will be free and safe. I'll return to the fond company of Sparrow, Robbie, Cleona, and the boys. I'll sleep for a full week in my glorious soft bed at the farm.

The hours pass slowly. Afternoon leans into evening. Calder stacks wood beside the fireplace. His ability to wait calmly is enviable. I feel coiled tightly as a spring and can hardly keep my hands steady as I struggle to slice potatoes and carrots for supper with a butter knife.

"Hurry," I whisper to the universe.

CALDER

I toss a log on the fire, although it's hot as the devil's ankles in here. But that's how Delphine likes it for some reason. I have foregone trying to figure her out, for the most part. I think she might be better off unknown, anyway. Like all the parts of the devil that come with his ankles.

Across the room, Sabella stands at the counter, her back to me as she hacks some helpless vegetable with a butter knife. Her hair is in a knot, revealing a few inches of skin on the back of her neck. If I were not bound by these blasted vines, the temptation of that pale and narrow terrain might overcome whatever good sense I have left.

One might think a person trapped in a house by a madwoman would not squander time imagining the act of kissing a fellow captive, but one would be quite mistaken. I have been full of such imaginings. In fact, I grab onto them like they're the precious driftwood that will keep me afloat on this sea of perilous unknowns.

Sabella looks over her shoulder at me. "Didn't Delphine tell you to help Rhys wash up before dinner? He and Branna are still in the yard."

"I can hear that." Squeals of delight echo through the open

windows as the boy and deer play tag. At least Delphine allows them to roam the grounds as she waits for whatever it is she's waiting for. I try not to consider what might happen to us if she loses patience before Yonaz and Robbie return to rescue us. In my efforts to forestall such thoughts, I entertain romantic notions of Sabella's neck. It works out rather well, I think.

"Where is Delphine?" I ask Sabella as I take a seat in our captor's favorite armchair. The movement causes the vine around my upper arm to cut into my skin, and I cringe at the pain.

"In the garden doing something. Probably cursing weeds to die or talking apples into growing to be the size of your head." She scoops up chopped carrots with her hands and drops them into a bowl before she starts in on a defenseless potato.

I ignore her jab at my hat size and appreciate what I can see of her left earlobe. If she had any idea the power she wields over me just by *being*... Honestly, she has ruined me. And it is wonderful indeed. Or will be, if the universe has any mercy upon me in the future.

My foot pokes at an ant, pointing it toward the open door. My mouth says without asking my brain, "This would be nice, if not for that woman. This house in the woods. Us together." Regret makes my face a bonfire. I brace myself for another reminder that we are only friends.

Sabella turns toward me. She rests her hip against the counter. Her dress is rumpled and her forehead is speckled with perspiration. A lock of hair hangs down, barely falling clear of her left eye. A maple leaf clings to one of her antlers, evidence that she ventured outdoors earlier. Apart from the worry line between her eyebrows, I would not change a thing about her.

"You certainly have a good attitude today," she says.

I shrug off her comment. Compliment? "Well, we did see a bat recently."

"I hope we see him again soon. I thought my mother worked

me to the bone, but Delphine... Why are you looking at me like that?"

"Um, there's a leaf on your antler," I say, hoping she believes me. What must my face look like? Is the longing for her written across my features in huge letters? I try to adjust my expression to a neutral one.

She runs her fingers over the silvery branches of her antlers until she locates the leaf. After she plucks it off, she presses it flat in her palm and stares at it. "I want to apologize," she says. "Back in the woods, before we were captured, I hurt your feelings. I know you were just trying to help me."

"Apology accepted," I say. "We will figure this out, Sabella, how to...get along." I don't want to talk about being friends. I need to be allowed to hope for more—at least until we can return to the farm.

"We will," she says, meeting my gaze. "I know we will."

In a perfect world, I would cross the room now and give her a friendly embrace, something completely cordial and platonic and warm, but not warmer than she would appreciate, but this prison is not a perfect world. The vine around my arm tightens as if to remind me to behave.

And then Delphine calls my name. Before I go, I give Sabella the best smile I own. When she smiles back, I feel as though I could fly all the way to the moon without using my wings.

SABELLA

T toss the sodden dish towel onto the counter and brush a damp lock of hair out of my eyes. With some kind of enchantment, Delphine keeps her home as humid as a greenhouse, *and* I've just finished washing the dishes from the midday meal in a basin of steamy suds. I feel as if I'm actually melting—yet slumped in her chair by the hearth, Delphine dozes, unbesmirched by a single drop of sweat.

Rhys and Branna were sent to play in the shade of the apple trees after lunch, and I envy them greatly. If I hurry to put the dishes away, I might be able to join them for a while before Delphine assigns me more work. There could be a breeze out there. How I long for a nice breeze.

Over at the table, Calder mutters something. I glance in his direction. A small, yellow blossom has burst forth from the vine encircling his upper arm. Its color is jarring and out of place in this cheerless kitchen. Calder doesn't notice, as he's busy scowling at a spoon while scrubbing at it with a gray cloth. Before him, a pile of tarnished flatware awaits his attention. At this rate, he might not finish before Christmas.

Through the open windows, I hear a male voice calling out from a distance.

Delphine does not stir, but Calder drops the spoon and jumps out of his chair. "Sabella," he says breathlessly. "It's Yonaz. It has to be."

I freeze in place. "What should we do?"

The man shouts again. This time, his accented words are intelligible. "Delphine! Come out and show yourself!"

Delphine awakens with a snort. She sits up straight. "Who woke me?"

"Delphine!" Yonaz calls again.

She inhales sharply. For half a second, she looks surprised, but then her face hardens. "Stay here," she commands Calder and me, as if our vine restraints would allow us to do otherwise. And then she strides out the front door with her head held high, like a queen on her way to meet her inferiors.

"What should we do?" I ask Calder again. My heart races so fast that I feel sick.

Calder shrugs, a gesture which does not inspire confidence. "Hope Yonaz can reason with her? I have no idea beyond that. Without a way to sever these vines, we're stuck."

An idea strikes me. "Let me try," I say, reaching up to test the sharpness of one of the points on my antlers. Perhaps I could use it to break through the vine. I lift my vine-shackled wrist and incline my neck as I attempt to align the point and the plant.

"Brilliant idea," Calder says. "Here. Let me help." He holds my hand and directs the angle of my antlers. I feel the point puncture the vine. Pain shoots through my neck as Calder yanks and maneuvers the antler, but now is not the time to complain of discomfort.

After a minute, he lets go. "Blast. It isn't going to work. The plant keeps healing itself somehow. Now what?"

I straighten and rub my aching neck. "We must keep thinking.

Trying. Meanwhile, I'm going to the orchard to tell Rhys and Branna that Yonaz is here. They need to be ready to flee if the chance comes."

But they must have already heard Yonaz's voice, for they scamper in through the back door, tracking mud all over the wooden floor with bare feet and hooves. Rhys skids into Calder. "Yonaz is here," he says. "I heard him. We're saved!"

"Whoa," Calder says. "It might not be as easy as that. You must stay calm and pay close attention to whatever instructions Sabella and I give you. Can you do that, Rhys? It's very important."

The joy in Rhys's face shifts to somberness. He nods his assent.

I pat the soft black curls between his tiny goat horns. "Try not to be afraid. Yonaz is clever. He will do everything he can to help us. Now, why don't you sit down and I'll get you a slice of cake?"

The boy climbs into a chair at the table. He watches me fetch the cake, his head cocked like he's pondering something important. Branna lies at his feet like a watchdog.

"Do you think my horns will get as big as your antlers?" he asks as I set the plate before him.

"I do not. But if they do, you'll get used to them."

"Are you finally used to them?" Calder asks me. His tone is so gentle and sincere that it prods all the butterflies in my gut awake —butterflies I worked so hard to evict. A resurgence of girlish infatuation is the last thing I need at this moment. My skin goes cold and then hot.

I do not know how to answer.

I am used to my antlers in the sense that my neck has become accustomed to bearing their meager weight. I am used to them in that I can sometimes forget their presence atop my head. But am I used to them being always there? Could I live every day of my life from now until death without once wishing them gone, never again begging someone to saw them off? Even if I were not in a state over Yonaz's appearance, I do not believe I could rightly say.

"Is there any milk?" Rhys asks.

"A little." I hurry to fill a tin cup, thankful for an excuse to delay answering Calder's question.

Calder walks past me to the open window and angles his head, trying to catch the sound of Delphine and Yonaz's conversation.

The butterflies begin to settle down. I hand the cup to Rhys, then cross the room to stand behind Calder at the window.

He says, "It's hard to see anything through the trees. I only catch glimpses. They're awfully quiet, whatever that means."

"Look." I point over his shoulder at Delphine and Yonaz. "They're coming this way." Yonaz is dressed in a suit of burgundy silk, with a black cravat knotted at his throat—as if he is paying an afternoon call rather than staging a rescue.

Calder glances back at me again. "Um... Perhaps you could step aside so I might move away from the window? Delphine probably would not appreciate being spied upon by her prisoners."

I am suddenly aware of how close I've been standing to him. He's all but pinned to the windowsill. Mortified, I take a huge step backward, catch my foot in the hem of my dress, and fall hard onto my posterior.

Now doubly mortified, I clench my eyes shut and wait for Calder's laughter. Instead, I hear him ask, "Are you all right, Sabella?"

When I open my eyes, he's crouched next to me.

"I'm fine," I say.

"Good. You frightened me for a second. Your face went white as milk. May I help you up?"

I nod. He cups my elbows with his hands and pulls me to my feet—as Delphine strides into the room. "Dancing, are we?"

Calder releases me and steps away. "She fell."

Delphine sneers. "Of course. Conveniently into your arms. You need not tell me tales, Calder. I'm well aware of the little romance between you." Yonaz comes alongside her. She gestures in our direction. "Here are your friends, safe and sound."

Rhys rushes to Yonaz, embraces him hard, and sobs. Yonaz pats his dark curls. "You're safe now. No need to cry." The fawn, Branna, totters over and rubs her cheek on Yonaz's side.

"Untie Sabella and Calder immediately," Yonaz demands. "They could not breach your enchanted hedges if they tried."

"You know I will do almost anything you ask, my dearest, *after* you deliver the last of the three, as agreed," Delphine says.

"I have changed my mind," Yonaz says.

"You would betray our pact and our plans? You would betray *me* after all this time?"

Yonaz's face and neck redden as everyone in the room eyes him. His accent grows thicker as he says, "I am choosing not to betray the children. There is a difference."

Rhys must sense the burgeoning tension between Yonaz and Delphine, for he abandons Yonaz to cling to Calder. Branna scampers after the boy.

"It matters not whether I take the girl or you bring her willingly, dearest." Delphine's voice is soothing, her smile gentle. "I will see the plan to fruition. Let the burden of it be upon my soul, if you must. In the end, you and I will be together. You will forget the children as you bask in my glory and our love." She moves closer to Yonaz and lays a hand on his arm. "I have missed you."

He looks unmoved by her speech, but I am utterly baffled. According to Calder, Yonaz has long been the caretaker of the Springborn. Delphine was touted as their oft-absent guardian and matriarch. It appears something darker is afoot, and has been for some time.

Yonaz says, "Prove your love to me by this: remove the bonds from Calder and Sabella and let them take the little ones home. We will find another way to—"

"There is no other way!" Delphine tears her hand away from him. In anger, she loses none of her beauty, but gains the cold visage of an empress ready to lop off her enemies' heads with her own sword.

She heaves a dramatic sigh, then says coyly, "Come, sit with me, Yonaz. Let us take a moment to compose ourselves. You may use the time to reconsider, my darling. To remember what has been between us and what will be—when you come to your senses once more."

Delphine strides across the room and perches on a settee near a window. She takes a black lace fan from her pocket and flicks it open. She proceeds to fan herself languidly. I think she believes Yonaz will yield to her yet, and help her do whatever terrible thing she has in mind.

Calder and I exchange troubled looks. He scratches his neck under the edge of the vine there—which makes me notice the itchiness in my own vine-clad wrist.

Instead of sitting with Delphine, Yonaz starts to pace. Droplets of sweat glisten on his creased forehead. His lips move but no sound comes from them. Is he deciding whether or not to yield to Delphine, or is he trying to think of a way we all can escape her? Not knowing makes my stomach churn.

The air in the room becomes unnaturally still, and I swear I can hear the faint creak and crackle of the vines growing around us as Delphine broods. Even the vines tethering Calder and me lengthen and stretch looping tendrils along the floor.

Rhys pulls Calder close to me. Branna follows. The boy and the fawn are both trembling and wide-eyed.

"It will be all right," I whisper to Rhys. "Let's all go into the garden and make Branna a crown of dandelions while we wait for Yonaz." The longer vines will allow Calder and me to wander outside without asking Delphine's permission.

If we are lucky, Robbie is out there waiting to escort us away from this place. Yonaz got past the hedges somehow, so there must be a way for us to breach them and flee.

Slowly, as not to draw unwanted attention, we creep toward the door.

CALDER

I can breathe again once we're outside and well away from whatever is happening between Yonaz and Delphine. The air actually moves out here, and the birds hop about on the grass as if there's not some colossal, life-or-death conflict going on. They don't care about betrayal or botched plans, just worms and berries—and I am a bit jealous.

Sabella is biting her lip. I've never seen her so unsettled—but I've never been this unsettled, either. Her eyes survey the edges of the property.

"I don't see Robbie," she says quietly. "Shouldn't he be here by now?"

"He'll come," I say. I take her hand and squeeze it. "Robbie is the most reliable person I've ever known."

"Unless he *can't* come. What if—"

"Stop," I say. "We cannot 'what if' right now. Not in a negative way, at least. Let's keep walking and looking for clues. Maybe a message, or a hole in the hedges."

The vine tether scrapes against my skin. Blazes, I hate vines. I might have been able to fly us all out of here ages ago if not for the stupid plants.

Rhys tugs at my sleeve. "Yonaz put something in my pocket," he says. "Not candy, though. Paper this time."

At the farm, Yonaz often sneaked small gifts or treats into the pockets of the boys' jackets—with all the deftness of a pickpocket, only in reverse. He doted on the boys like a good father. But was he? Delphine has made me wonder if he's been playacting all along, keeping us together to be used by her for who-knows-what wickedness.

"May I see it?" Sabella asks, and Rhys passes her a small, folded envelope. A message. It's too small to explain everything, but maybe the right size to explain enough.

SABELLA

I open the envelope and take out a slip of paper. While I squint at the tiny handwriting, Calder moves so that anyone looking out from the house will not see me reading the message. Rhys and Branna watch me with expectant eyes.

"What does it say?" Calder asks.

My pulse quickens. "Sparrow and Robbie are waiting on the other side of the hedge. They've broken through Delphine's enchantment and made a tunnel. It's on the north end of the garden."

Calder points to a dark gap close to the ground, near the tool shed. "There."

In my excitement, I grab his arm. "We're going home."

He grins. "We are. As soon as we get loose from these confounded vines."

"This should help." I pull a tiny packet out of the envelope. "Sparrow made this. The note says it's a powder to rot the vines."

"Glory be," Calder exclaims. "We're going home."

I tear open the envelope and sprinkle black powder onto my vine-leash. An inch-wide piece of the plant dries up, shrivels, and breaks free from the rest of the stem, releasing me from bondage.

Calder offers his arm. I dust his vine with the powder. "Thank you, Sparrow," he says as the plant withers and drops off.

We join hands with Rhys, and with Branna beside us, we sprint to the hedge. Toward freedom.

The outer part of the hedge is still dark green and densely foliaged, full of sharp thorns the color of old bones, but from the edges of the tunnel, limp, blackened leaves dangle. Side by side, Calder and I kneel and peer into the opening. The passage is only high and wide enough for one person at a time to pass through on hands and knees. Shadows lurk near its beginning and obscure the view of its ending.

My antlers could be a problem in such a small space, but I refrain from voicing that concern. Heaven knows we don't have the time or the tools to cut them off.

We sit back on our heels. Calder says, "I'll go first to make sure the way is clear of those nasty thorns. Once I'm through, I'll whistle." He takes my face between his hands and kisses my forehead. "Wish me luck."

He turns and plunges into the tunnel's mouth. "Good luck," I say to his disappearing feet. I draw in a deep breath and stand up. Worry rises inside me, a river threatening to flood, but then Rhys tucks his small hand into mine. He needs me to be strong.

"Why did Uncle Calder leave us?" he asks. With his free hand, he strokes Branna's neck.

"He's making sure the way is safe, and then we will join him. Everything will be fine."

The boy nods. Together with Branna, we wait. Every second feels like an hour.

No sound comes from beyond the hedge. Fortunately, no sound comes from the house, either. Against my side, Rhys trembles like a frightened puppy. I wrap my arm around him to reassure him, to encourage him not to lose hope—although my own hope is wavering. What if something has happened to Calder inside the tunnel? He might be caught by thorns or ensnared by another enchanted vine. Perhaps I should venture in and check—but who would watch over Rhys and Branna then? I could take them with me, but if the way is dangerous…

A shrill note comes from beyond the wall of vegetation. Calder's whistle. Relief washes over me.

"Go on now," I say to Rhys. "You crawl in with Branna, and I'll follow you." The look of terror on his face suggests he will need to be shepherded along.

"I can't," he says. His eyes brim with tears. "It's too dark. The thorns…"

"Rhys, you must. If you want to go home to your brothers, this is the only way. Calder whistled to tell us it's safe. He's waiting on the other side. It isn't far."

The boy bites his lip. One tear plummets to the grass before he nods bravely, kneels, and crawls into the hole.

"Branna," I say to the deer. "You're next."

She motions with her chin as if to insist that I go before her. I will not waste time arguing with a fawn when, at any moment, Delphine might catch us in the act of escaping. And so I fall to my knees and enter the ominous passage.

The way is not easy. The heavy foliage obscures almost all light. Again and again, my knees catch in my skirt as I crawl. Finally, I pause to gather up the fabric and tuck it into my waistband. This done, I crawl faster. My antlers brush against long thorns and sharp leaves. Now and then I must stop to untangle them. I pay for this in blood when thorns score my hands and wrists.

I hear Branna moving slowly behind me, mewling as if in pain. As a deer, she cannot crawl on her knees, nor can she bend low enough to avoid all the thorns. Perhaps that is why she bade me to go first, so her faltering progress would not impede mine.

Finally, I see light. Calder pulls Rhys out. I scramble forward onto soft grass.

Before Calder can help me to my feet, Delphine's angry shouts echo over the hedge.

I stare back into the tunnel but see nothing but blackness. "Branna is still in there," I say. Panic spreads through me, ice water in my veins.

"I'll get her," Sparrow says. I see her then, standing with Robbie a few feet behind Calder. Her hair is shockingly white and her body is bent with age. I have but a second to marvel at the sight of her before she dives into the hole like the heroine of some legend.

"Wait!" I call after her. But it is too late. She is gone.

The entire hedge shudders and groans. Branches spread to cover the opening, sprouting wicked thorns and razor-edged leaves. Rhys cries out and throws himself into Calder's arms.

My heart shatters. This sudden, violent separation from Sparrow is too terrible. I grab Robbie's shoulders hard. "Open it again. Please. We must help them."

Robbie's face pales. "I can't. Sparrow's the only one who knows how." Despair cracks his voice. "Oh, saints. Poor Branna. What will I tell Cleona? Her sister..."

"They're not dead," Calder says with conviction. "Delphine would not have killed them. She has plans for them, remember? You heard her, Sabella."

The world grows eerily silent, and then under our feet, thunder rumbles. The sound swells; the earth convulses. We stumble away from the hedge and cling to one another. Just beyond the hedge, a stalk half an acre wide erupts in a mighty rush, moaning like a great monster. It bears Delphine's house on its back as it climbs skyward. Farther and farther the monstrous plant ascends, until it is a sleek green tower that reaches the clouds. Branches sprout from its trunk; leaves spring from these until the thing resembles one of Delphine's unnaturally-lush bean plants.

With a shudder, the stalk stops growing. Its lowest branches loom a hundred feet or more above us, untouchable. Clouds obscure its highest branches and the house.

Branna and Sparrow are halfway to the sky.

If ever I wished that I could fly, it is now.

SABELLA

C alder sits on the moss beside me in the shadow of the giant plant. I'm trying to make sense of what just happened, but of course there is no sense in any of it. How can this be the same world in which I lived before? How can it be that only a few miles away, people are mining coal, or baking bread, or laughing? Laughing, and not fretting over loved ones stolen by a vegetation-wielding witch.

"Your hands are bleeding," Calder says. He pulls a crumpled, formerly white handkerchief from his pocket. "It looks ugly, but it's clean. May I?"

I hold out my wounded hands, beyond caring about anything but the plight of Sparrow and Branna. He dabs gently, staining his handkerchief with red blood and brown dirt.

Robbie sits on the ground, facing me, with his arms full of Rhys. "What can we do? There must be something. We cannot leave them up there with that madwoman."

Rhys lifts his head from Robbie's shoulder. "Calder has

295

wings," he says. "He can fly up and save them, then we can all go home."

Calder grimaces and continues blotting my cuts.

I picture Calder's wings in my mind, their delicate, almost translucent beauty, and I wonder if they can bear his weight for longer than a few seconds. "Can you fly far, or are your wings mostly decorative?" I ask him.

Head lowered, shamefaced, he meets my gaze. "I don't know. I've rarely flown, and never more than a few yards."

"How could you not know?" I blurt. "You've had wings for well over half your life and you've never once tested their strength?" I do not know why this angers me, but it does.

"My wings and I have a complicated relationship," he says.

"What he means is he's always been afraid to use them," Robbie says. "He doesn't trust his gift."

Calder scowls and throws his hands up. "Oh, that's nice, Robbie. A true show of loyalty. Shall we tell all our personal secrets now and be done with it?"

"Boys, please," I say. "You can bicker later. Let's focus now on how we can help Branna and Sparrow."

"Sorry," Robbie says. "Maybe Yonaz will think of something up there. Unless Delphine has him tied up, or worse."

"He's probably fine," Calder says. "But we don't know for sure whose side he's on anymore."

Robbie's eyes widen with surprise. "What?"

"We'll explain later," I say. "Calder, will you try to fly? For Branna and Sparrow?"

He blows out a breath before acquiescing with a grim nod.

I lay a hand on his forearm. "Thank you."

Calder stands and walks away from us. We follow him into a small meadow. With his back to us, he slips the buttons of his shirt through their holes one by one. In silence, he shrugs his way out of the garment. He shuts his eyes and inhales until it seems his chest could expand no farther. And then, slowly, his wings unfold behind him, fern-green edged with bright gold. They look both insubstantial and strong. They look like a miracle.

The wings begin to move, a measured opening and closing that stirs the air ever so slightly. I hold my breath, captivated by their beauty, and I pray they will be strong enough to lift him high above the earth—and strong enough to the bear his weight combined with that of our friends.

His face is full of determination as he takes one step forward and then another. He breaks into a run and pushes off the ground with both feet. His wings catch the breeze like a pair of sails and he rises above the ground. He leans forward so his body is parallel to the grass, expertly, as if he has done this a thousand times before. The wings beat against the air, holding him aloft. And then he swoops back and forth above our heads.

Calder Hadrian is flying.

Robbie cheers and Rhys lets loose a peal of laughter. I am almost too full of wonder and hope to breathe.

After a minute, Calder descends in slow circles. His feet brush over a patch of daisies before he touches earth and stumbles to a stop. Tears streak down his beaming face. "I had no idea," he says. "It felt like... I can't even say what. But it was amazing."

I step toward him, possessed by a sudden determination. "Carry me up to the house. Please. Sparrow needs me."

"No, Sabella. It would be too risky."

"You might not trust your wings, but I do."

A pained look erases his smile. "Sabella, please. I just can't. How could I live with myself if—"

"No, Calder. It isn't your job to protect me, but it *is* my job to protect Sparrow. She is my child. I have missed decades of her life in the last few days; if there is anything I can do to buy one more day with her, I must do it."

With a sigh of resignation, Calder opens his arms. "Far be it from me to keep one of the world's rare good mothers apart from her child."

I step into his embrace. He lifts me, supporting my knees with one hand and encircling my waist with the other. He has never held me as tightly as he holds me now. My heart beats wildly as he takes a few running steps. His feet leave the ground and my belly lurches. The heat of his bare torso seeps through the fabric of my dress and I am all too aware that my hand is clutching his unclad collarbone. Mother would be mortified—but I do not want to think of her. This marvelous moment belongs to me—and to this moth-winged boy who chose to trust his gift for the sake of his friends.

I hold my head still, afraid that in moving, my antlers might wound him. We rise higher and higher, circling the huge green stalk that undergirds Delphine's house. I glance down at Robbie and Rhys. They look like dolls waving.

Dizziness makes me clench my eyes shut. I've never been so far above the ground. Too many feelings crowd my breast: the sheer joy of flying, fear for Sparrow's safety and Branna's life, gratitude for Calder's kindness, and a reckless, brazen longing to never again leave his arms.

Calder lands gently this time, hardly jarring me as his feet settle onto a strip of grass on the windowless side of Delphine's house.

"You can let go now," he whispers. "Not that I object to having you cling to me like a barnacle."

I push away from him and attempt to ignore both my embarrassment and his smirk. He lifts a finger to his lips as if I need to be reminded to keep silent. Together, we creep around the perimeter of the house.

We crouch in the tall grass under the kitchen window and listen.

"I will never change my mind," Yonaz says. "I am sorry to have to make the choice, but I must choose the children over you."

"I could force you, you know. I could make you love me again." Delphine's voice sounds taut, as if her temper is a mean dog straining at an overstretched leash.

"You could try," Yonaz replies calmly. "But I know enough of magic and my own strength of will to be sure you would fail."

"Now, now," Delphine says soothingly. "Let us both take a moment to regain our composures. Perhaps a cup of tea?"

Calder whispers into my ear, "We should sneak in the back door and surprise them."

"Is that the entirety of your plan?" I had hoped he had some secret, infallible scheme in mind.

"At the moment."

I bite my lip and say no more. Fussing and fretting will not improve our odds of success. I try to think of a better plan as we crawl to the other side of the house. There, we stand to walk along the wall.

"Have you thought of another approach?" Calder says when we stop.

"Not yet," I reply.

"My plan it is, then. Follow me. Stay low when we get inside. It sounds like they'll be at the table in a moment, so we'll each hide behind one of the big chairs near the fireplace. We'll wait there until...well, until the right opportunity presents itself."

"Which would be...?"

He shrugs. "We'll know when it happens. Trust me."

I envision my headstone: *Here lies Sabella Jenkins, age seventeen. Died of trusting Calder Hadrian.*

Calder darts through the door and ducks behind the bigger chair. My knees quake as I follow in his footsteps. On my way, I catch a glimpse of Delphine sitting at the round table, her back to the hearth. She's watching Yonaz pour steaming water into the teapot. Sparrow is seated beside her on a stool, with Branna curled up at her feet. They appear to be untethered, and for this I am thankful.

I crouch behind the chair and peek around its edge. My eyes fix on Sparrow. She is an old, old woman, snowy-haired and wrinkled of face—but she is alive, my daughter.

"Shall I pour you a cup now?" Yonaz asks Delphine in his everyday, polite voice. I can only hope he's trying to buy time by playing along with her. Maybe he has a plan better than Calder's current "wait and see" strategy.

"Yes," Delphine says. "And do sit beside me when you're done serving. Remember how you used to entertain us in the evenings long ago, the children and me? The tales you made up. The shadow plays..."

"I have not forgotten."

"And do you remember the day we met, Yonaz, my love?"

Yonaz sets the tea pot on the table and sits across from her. "It was high summer, and you were at the height of your seasonal beauty, as glorious and full as a well-tended garden."

"You were emaciated and sunburned. Hardly more than a child. And so replete with sadness those first weeks that it hurt my heart to look at you. But then, little by little, I brought you to blossom."

"For this I will always be grateful."

"Show it, then. Help me to always be that woman you fell in love with, young and strong and unblemished by age. Help me stave off the winter crone forever."

"Your obsession with youth poisons you. I would have loved you through all seasons, no matter the face you wore."

"It is fate, not a mere obsession. This curse was made to be broken. Remember how many nights we spent puzzling over the words the fairy woman spoke when she gave me my gifts and charge of the spring? 'To break the hold of winter's curse, these three 'til death you must immerse: One with horns and eyes of gold, an antlered girl both brave and bold, a child who is both young and old.'"

"She was a fairy, Delphine. Full of trickery and absurd beyond any human understanding. Do you truly believe she gave you the riddle to help you?"

"You have not endured what I have every winter: the indignities of age, the pains, the ugliness. I will suffer it no more. I have waited too long for Springborn with the needed gifts to appear. You failed to deliver them to me as you'd promised. Now two of them linger below, and one is here in this room. You must convince Sabella and the goat-horned boy to meet me and the old woman at the spring before death claims her. Just bring them, my love. I'm not asking you to do the drowning. You owe me this much."

The cold, queenly gaze she casts upon Yonaz sends a shudder through me. He sits still and makes no answer.

"Do not complicate things, my darling," she says sweetly. "If it is more Springborn children you want, I will bring you more. A dozen, if you wish. We'll raise them together this time, all the year 'round."

Calder sneaks a look from behind his chair. He retreats and meets my gaze. *Be ready*, he mouths. *I'm going for Delphine.*

There is no time for me to ask him to explain his intentions, for he launches himself from his hiding place and barrels across the room. He tackles Delphine, knocking her off her chair and onto the wooden floor. Yonaz stands, pales, and drops to the floor in a faint. Was there something in that tea?

I cannot help everyone. I choose Sparrow and Branna. I hurry to Sparrow's side. "Come," I say as I pull her onto her feet. "We must go."

Sparrow gasps in pain. "My knees," she says. Branna nudges her skirt with her black nose. "The tunnel did some damage to them."

I turn around and crouch. "Get onto my back. I'll carry you." She can weigh no more than a child, frail as she is. As she climbs on, Calder and Delphine struggle on the floor. He's trying to pin her down, but she fights like a wild animal.

They roll apart and get to their feet. Panting and bedraggled, they stare at one another.

"Stupid boy," Delphine says. She raises her hands and shouts, "Root and stem, vine and tendril, come now to my aid!"

A vine snakes in the window and whips toward Calder. Yonaz, awake now, scrambles to grab a small shovel from the rack of fireplace tools. He whacks the plant until it lies flat and motionless. But another vine comes, and another, and he cannot fight them all.

One winds its way up Calder's leg, around his belly, his arms. Delphine punches him hard enough to knock him off his feet.

I rush toward the door and trip over a vine. My chest hits the floor. Every bit of air is expelled from my lungs. Sparrow rolls off my back. Branna bleats beside us, urging us to hurry out the door.

"Stop!" Sparrow cries as she gets to her feet beside me. "Delphine, you must stop. Let me help you."

Blood runs from Delphine's nose and seeps from a cut above her left eye as she stands over Calder's plant-entangled, prone body. "Help me? What help could you possibly offer me?"

"I can heal you," Sparrow says. "That which is broken in you need not remain broken."

Delphine sneers. "You look like a woman, but you understand no more than a babe. I am well enough. And soon I will be stronger than you can imagine."

"I can sense the sickness in you," Sparrow insists. "My gift—"

"I have no need for your gift. You will be part of the cure, but not my healer."

There is no fear in Sparrow's eyes. Although her back is crooked, she stands with a warrior's confidence. "You refuse my help, then?"

"I said *shut up*." More vines slither into the room, splitting and spreading over the furniture and up the walls. She waves her fingers and the vines constricting Calder's body send out shoots toward Sparrow and me.

We need to run. Once Sparrow is safe, I'll rescue Calder somehow.

I get to my feet and grab for Sparrow, but she says, "Wait." She takes a glass vial out of a little satchel hanging at her hip. She uncorks it and a pale gray wisp swirls toward the ceiling. The vines thread around our ankles.

I claw futilely at the plants as they reach tendrils toward my knees. "Sparrow!"

Quickly, she proclaims, "By the power of this elixir, in the name of goodness and mercy, I claim dominion here. Every plant here shall obey only me, every sprout, every vine, every bush, every tree." Turning in a circle, she flicks her wrist and flings liquid out of the vial. Silver drops roll toward the four corners of the room. The globules grow then divide as they move. The vines turn to soot at their touch.

Delphine stands as if frozen to the floor, mouth hanging open in shock. Calder leaps to his feet. He shakes black ash from his arms and advances on her. But as he reaches to grab her, she seems to regain her wits. She dives across the floor, sliding through the soot as if it's snow. Lightning quick, she seizes Branna and scrambles out the door.

Calder, Sparrow, and I chase after them, all the way to the narrow strip of grass at the very edge of the property. Beyond this land, there is nothing but air and clouds. Delphine stands perilously close to the precipice. Branna squeals with distress and wriggles in her arms.

We stop a few yards short of them. Never in my life have I felt such raw fear.

"Don't move," Calder says to me—as if I could. Or maybe he is addressing Delphine.

"Put her down, Delphine," Yonaz says as he approaches from the house. He must have awoken from his faint when I was too occupied to notice. "Let us work this out peaceably."

"I will put her down," she says. "Where she lands is your choice."

"No," Calder says.

Delphine does not acknowledge Calder. She smiles grimly at Yonaz. "I do believe it is time for you to agree to my terms. Unless you'd prefer that I toss this creature to earth?"

Sparrow clutches my arm and whispers, "Should I send vines to bind her?"

"No. She might panic and drop Branna."

Behind Delphine, chunks of soil break free and plummet to the ground. She takes a single step forward, gesturing to Yonaz with a motion of her head. "Come, darling. Say you will help me. Be true to our old vows and our sacred love."

He walks toward Delphine slowly, cautiously, and stops within an arm's length of her and Branna.

"Now, a kiss to mark the renewal of our pact," Delphine demands. "It is not too late."

Yonaz is shaking. Hesitating. He looks more ill now than he did when near death at the inn.

"Come, darling. I want us to be together in this, but I am growing tired of your indecision."

The air roils, thick and sulfurous. The ground rumbles and quakes underfoot. Are these things side effects of Delphine's fury? Will we all die before this day ends?

Calder moves close to me. I reach for his hand and entwine my fingers with his. My other arm wraps around Sparrow's bony back.

Delphine leans forward. With one hand, she grabs Yonaz by the shirtfront and yanks him to her. She presses his mouth to hers. It is an ugly kiss, a thing laced with greed and magic that makes the air vibrate. Yonaz whimpers and slumps against her.

Fawn Branna, half freed from Delphine's grasp, twists to bite down on her arm. Delphine cries out in pain and stumbles backward. Yonaz's body leans heavily against her as she struggles to regain her footing. She reels, still clutching Branna. Her feet meet crumbling dirt—and then nothing at all.

Delphine disappears over the edge, taking the fawn and Yonaz with her. Sparrow cries out to command vines to catch them, but swift as the vines are, they're no match for gravity's pull.

A sickening thud comes from far below.

CALDER

Sparrow weighs little in my arms. Too little, like a hollow-boned bird instead of a girl. She offered to command the stalk to sink and deliver us to the ground, but Sabella thought it might endanger our friends below. And so I will supply transport. Sparrow first, and then Sabella.

Down toward the ground we glide in circles, borne by my wings and a gentle breeze. Sparrow holds onto me, but not desperately. She trusts me. And I wonder why I have not trusted myself all this time, why I never trusted my wings before today.

I am too tired and too sad for deep introspection. Branna is lost to us. Yonaz, my foster father and friend, is surely dead. He passed into eternity without once seeing me fly. I think it would have brought him to happy tears. He was a weeper, always smearing that black stuff around his eyes with shows of emotion.

One last circle around the huge stalk brings Sparrow and me almost to the earth. The fresh air rushes over my wings. I imagine this is how moths and butterflies feel when they finally break free of their chrysalises. Like they unfurl more than just their bodies and are ready to be something else. They endure darkness and a kind of death, and come out new.

At the moment, I cannot fathom how all this death and pain could better me.

My feet meet the ground. When Sparrow leaves my arms, she all but falls into Robbie's. One of them sobs, and then the other. I have to turn away. I still have work to do. No time to indulge my grief.

Now I will fly again. Up quickly to claim Sabella, and down slowly—to keep her in my embrace for as long as possible. Certainly there can be nothing wrong with savoring the sweet when one is presented with so much bitterness and sorrow.

SABELLA

With slow beats of his wings, Calder carries me earthward in his arms. He descends with quiet grace, as if he has mastered the art of flying after only a few flights. One of his arms curves behind my back and the other supports my legs. My arms encircle his warm neck. I can feel the steady, fast thud of his heart in the place where our bodies meet. It comforts me, this throbbing evidence that he still lives. He is not a hallucination crafted by a weary, careworn mind.

If I had lost him today with the others, how could I have borne it?

When we reach the land, the first sight I see is Sparrow in Robbie's embrace. How small and ancient she looks. Rays of evening sun stream through the treetops and graze their bowed heads. There is something strangely beautiful in their shared sorrow.

Rhys sleeps nearby at the base of a tree, blessedly unaware of the tragedy that has befallen us. Loath to disturb him, Calder and I choose a place to rest among the gnarled roots of an old oak. He cries without making a sound, his knees drawn to his still-bare chest, wings folded flat against his back. Through my own tears, I spy his abandoned shirt on the ground. I fetch it and wrap it around his shoulders. He reaches up to pat my hand in thanks.

The shadows are shifting here in the woods. Nightfall must not be far off. Sparrow breaks the silence, saying, "We should go home. Cleona is waiting there with the other boys."

"Let me find Branna first," Robbie says somberly. "Cleona will need to say goodbye to her sister." He walks off and Calder follows him.

When he returns after perhaps a quarter hour, Robbie carries the body of a red-haired, fifteen-year-old girl. She's been dressed in Calder's shirt, and they've folded her fair hands upon her chest. The long fall left no mark on her freckled face. If I did not know otherwise, I might think her asleep rather than dead.

Where is Calder? Did he stay in the woods to grieve privately for a time? I want him here with me, where I can see he is safe. Our recent peril has left me ill at ease with separation from loved ones.

Robbie looks straight ahead as he walks past me. Perhaps to gaze at Branna would be too much for him, as she and Cleona share almost identical features. With such a slight twist of fate, Cleona might have been the sister to die.

As if rough handling could break her, Robbie slowly lowers Branna onto a patch of moss. Sparrow kisses her forehead; her gnarled fingers smooth the girl's hair. "Rest well, little one," she says. "Your brave, kind heart will never be forgotten." She tucks a white, star-shaped wildflower into the girl's hand.

Something makes me look back into the woods. There is Calder, stumbling out of the trees with Yonaz's body draped over his shoulder.

"I think he's still alive," Calder says. "Though barely." He lays Yonaz on the ground and collapses next to him.

Sparrow rushes to them and falls to her knees beside Yonaz. She digs in the satchel at her hip and pulls out a surprising assortment of small bottles and paper envelopes. She arrays them on the ground before selecting a few. These ingredients she funnels into a water flask.

I kneel beside Calder as he lies staring at the treetops. "Are you all right?"

"I will be." He sits up and runs a hand through his hair. Exhaustion has left purple crescents under his eyes and his cheeks are sallow. "And you?"

"The same."

"Hold Yonaz's mouth open," Sparrow says, and Calder obeys. She pours her concoction into Yonaz's mouth. He coughs and moans. His eyelids spring wide open. Panic and fear show themselves in his expression and the twitching of his limbs.

Calder presses down on his shoulder. "Hold still now. You're safe."

Yonaz's teeth chatter. Sparrow whips off her shawl and covers his chest with it.

"I'm going to die," Yonaz says. There is blood on his lips, blood seeping through his clothes and from the side of his head.

"I've done all I can," Sparrow says. "I'm sorry."

"Branna. I..." His voice weakens as his skin fades to an impossible shade of white.

Gently but with authority, Sparrow says, "You are not to blame for what happened to Branna. That is on Delphine's soul, if she has one."

"Still... I am sorry. So sorry. Tell her sister..."

"I will."

Only then do I notice Robbie returning again, this time with Delphine in his arms. He places her on the ground a few feet from Yonaz. "She's alive, though not for long, I reckon," Robbie says.

This Delphine is far different than the one I saw before the fall. She is still touched by springtime beauty, but she no longer commands awe. She is like the dried husk from an ear of corn, an empty, powerless thing. Her eyes stare blankly skyward. Her chest rises and falls slowly.

Yonaz turns his head toward her. "I forgive you," he says. He seems to sink closer to the ground. A second later, he breathes his last.

Sparrow crawls from Yonaz to Delphine and lays a hand on her forehead.

"Ah," Delphine says. "The little Sparrow with healing in her wings. You cannot save me."

"I would try, if there were any hope at all." Sparrow takes a tiny box of salve from her collection of treatments and moistens Delphine's lips. "Would you like something for the pain?"

"No. No. Too late for that. I will make my confession. Long ago, there was a fairy woman. She ruled these mountains. I angered her. She ensorcelled me...to live three hundred years but to change into a crone every winter. Gave me dominion over the magical spring. She said... I had to use it. Or perish in agony. No choice. I had to...wash foundling babes whenever...the magic demanded. Make them...rare and wondrous. Give them to the barren women of the mountain...to bless and to trouble them."

"Why?" Robbie asks. "It makes no sense."

"She...did not give reasons. Fairy folk...are not sensible creatures." She shuts her eyes, and struggles to draw a few raspy breaths. "To stop becoming the winter crone...required a sacrifice of...three particular Springborn."

"You wanted to stop being the crone at any cost. Yonaz was supposed to help you, I gather," Sparrow says.

"Do not blame him for...my transgressions. He was blinded... by love for me...for a time. But in the end...he regretted...refused."

"Rest now," Sparrow says. "What is done, is done."

"Come close," Delphine says. Sparrow leans over so Delphine can whisper into her ear.

When Sparrow sits back on her heels, the life is gone from Delphine's eyes.

Calder helps Sparrow to her feet. Robbie brushes leaves off her clothes and offers his arm to steady her when she sways a little. She says, "Before we leave this place, I must do one thing." From a pocket, she pulls out a vial like the one she used to poison the vines inside Delphine's house. "You must all move a fair distance from the stalk. I will command it to come down gently, but one cannot be too careful."

Robbie, with Rhys in his arms, leads Calder and me up onto the mossy knoll where Branna's body rests. From there, we watch Sparrow fling a potion onto the base of the huge plant's stalk. The ground grumbles and trembles. Leaves fall from the trees like snow. Sparrow hastens to join us as, inch by inch, the stalk sinks down into the dark soil from which it grew. When the house touches down, the earth opens wide and swallows it whole, along with the lifeless bodies of Delphine and Yonaz.

Dirt rises like water from an underground spring to fill in the hole. Everything settles. The woods look as if nothing happened there apart from the ordinary. It has nothing to remember and nothing to try to forget.

I glance over at Branna. It is good that she was not swallowed by the earth like the others. She deserves to be kissed goodbye by her sister, and to be given a proper burial thereafter, with songs and flowers and memories.

Why did Delphine take her? She was not even one of the three needed to break the curse. Was Branna nothing more than a lure to draw Sparrow and me into her trap? We will never know—and such painful, unanswerable questions should not be dwelled upon.

The sky above the treetops is graying quickly. Nighttime insects are starting to buzz and chatter in the trees and bushes.

"We ought to head toward home," Calder says.

"Yes," Robbie says. "I do not want to spend another hour here."

"Are you in agreement?" Calder asks me. "There should be a little moonlight to navigate by, and we do not have to hurry."

"What about Sparrow and Rhys? I do not think their legs will carry them far."

"I'll carry Sparrow," Calder says. "Robbie can carry Branna, and you can carry Rhys. If we need to stop to rest, we will."

"All right," I say. Heavens, I'm tired. I cannot imagine walking half a mile, let alone the four or five forested and rocky miles that must lie between here and the farm.

Robbie passes the still-slumbering Rhys to me. He is a slender child, but I know before long it will feel to me as if he's stuffed with stones.

Sparrow hobbles to me and Rhys. She lays her hands over his ears, murmurs something, and slips a bit of crumbled herbs into his mouth. "There," she says. "He should sleep until morning. He can learn of Branna's passing when we are home and he is safe in the company of his brothers."

After watching her treat the boy, I want to ask if she knows of herbs or incantations to restore her youth, but I already know what her answer would be. She'd say her gifts are her own, including the one that ages her, and she is at peace with them. She has always been at peace with them, in a way I fear I never shall be.

I want to scream at the universe and demand a long life for her. Indeed, I would ask that she would outlive me and spare me the sorrow of ever standing over her grave.

The press of Calder's hand on my back halts my rambling thoughts. I turn to look at him. He's draped one of Sparrow's big shawls over his shoulders, crossed it over his belly, and knotted it behind him to replace the shirt he gave to Branna. I recognize it for the kindness it is, an act of consideration for my modesty, and Sparrow's, that he need not have bothered with in these circumstances.

"Ready to go home?" he asks. "You looked far away there for a moment."

"I'm ready." I wish I could cast myself into his embrace and cry. I long to linger there and to take whatever comfort he might offer, to let him soothe the sting of death that pains me, but time will not allow for such an indulgence. Instead, I lean into him for a handful of seconds, my arms full of Rhys. My shoulder presses into his chest. I hold my head at an angle so as not to poke him with my antlers. Too soon, I force myself to straighten and separate from him. I miss the warmth he radiates seconds later. Although it is June, the woods become chilly and damp when the sun sinks.

He turns toward Sparrow and opens his arms to her. "If you will allow me, Sparrow?"

"Thank you, Uncle Calder," she says, sounding like a little girl again.

He lifts her as if she weighs no more than an actual sparrow. She wraps her thin arms around his neck and lets her head rest against his shoulder. Right away, she falls asleep.

Shadows overtake the woods as we begin our journey. Robbie clutches Branna close to his chest as he walks. Now and then, he sobs or sniffles, adding bruises to my already sore heart.

SABELLA

Hours pass. Clouds move in to obscure the moonlight. It is too dark to continue walking. There are too many roots and rocks to trip us, too much risk of falling off an unseen ledge or into a hole or ravine. We could be lost already, for all I know.

We stop without discussing it. A black silhouette of Robbie slouches against a blacker silhouette of a tree trunk. Calder's shadow sits on either a stump or a boulder. Although I squint hard, I cannot tell for certain.

Rhys yawns and wriggles in my arms. Sparrow's medicine has worn off too quickly. "I want down," he says. Once I set him on his feet, he looks around. "Where are we?"

"We're in the forest, on our way home," Calder says in a kind, reassuring voice. He comes near and squats before the boy. "Do you think you can walk now, like a big lad? You must keep hold of Sabella's hand, though."

"It's awful dark," the boy says as he folds his fingers around mine. "And I'm hungry."

"Food will have to come later, but I have the stub of a candle in my pack," Robbie says. "Not that it'll help much. It's just that I hate wasting time waiting here for morning. We need to be home. Branna needs to be home."

"I'll carry the candle," I volunteer. Their arms are full, and mine are empty—although they still throb from holding Rhys.

Somehow, without setting Branna aside, Robbie maneuvers the candle and a tiny box of matches out of the bag slung over his shoulder. "Here."

Once I light the candle, I take the lead, holding it aloft. Rhys's small fingers cling coolly to my other hand. The homey scent of beeswax calms me, while the scalding wax that runs down my arm does not. I can endure the pain for the sake of the light.

In silence, we advance. Wildcats, wolves, and bears likely lurk nearby. They do not frighten me half as much as they might have half a year ago. Now, I would not hesitate to fight any wild beast to the death to protect Sparrow and my friends.

The trees grow sparser. We step into a meadow as the candle sputters and threatens to revoke its light. Ten does lift their heads, distracted from their supper of grass. A few fawns scamper toward me. Are they drawn by my antlers? I stop. The others must stop behind me, for the sound of their footsteps ceases.

I hold still while the fawns sniff my ankles and rub their faces against my knees. They accept me as their own. Delight and sorrow mingle in my breast, for Branna lost her life while wearing the delicate form of one of these sweet creatures.

Now the does draw near and circle me. They bow their sleek heads as if they take me for their queen.

I am not one of you, I want to tell them.

I am not one of anything—other than myself.

I will never be anyone but myself: a melding of daughter,

mother, and friend. One who is loved and is still learning to love in return.

Is that enough? In my heart of hearts, I think it could be.

To the deer, I say, "My name is Sabella. Thank you for your welcome."

The deer amble back to their grazing spots. Hundreds of fireflies spark in and above the grasses. Perhaps the last flickering of the dying candle draws them out; perhaps some unknown part of my gift beckons them. Whatever commands them, they obey, swarming around my head like a miniature galaxy of stars. One by one, they settle on my antlers. More of them fly to me, emerging from the forest in ribbons of light. I cannot watch them as they land, but I can tell they're perching on the branches and points above me, for their pulsing glow soon becomes a steady, spreading illumination. I stand statue-still, afraid I might scare the insects away.

The candle in my hand hisses as the flame dies. A better light remains.

"Glorious," Robbie says, his voice full of wonder. "Your antlers..."

Calder comes alongside me. Sparrow's sleeping head lolls against his shoulder. In his eyes, I glimpse my reflection. Robbie was right. They are glorious, my antlers. Not something to scorn or regret, but something lovely and yes, even useful. "How did this happen?" I ask. "Why did the fireflies come?"

"Yonaz used to say, 'Sometimes we do not know the value of a gift until long after it is given,'" Robbie says.

"I bet they can tell how good you are, and love you like we do," Rhys offers.

"I think you're right, Rhys," Calder says. He casts me a fleeting look of adoration that makes my stomach flutter before he adds, "We shouldn't waste the light. Lead on, Sabella?"

I straighten my neck, relishing the slight weight of my antlers, savoring the sensation of balancing them like a fine silver crown covered with living gold. I hold my head high, bearing the light my friends need—the light I need—to find my way through the woods.

To lead us home.

The deer stare as we cross the meadow and continue on the path lined with ferns, briars, and mushrooms. How long we walk in the fireflies' glow, I do not know. But I start to recognize the landscape as sunrise brightens the sky. When the farm's stone walls and curlicued iron gates finally come into view, the fireflies lift off my antlers and stream away.

As they disappear into the woods, I call out my thanks.

"Thank goodness we're home," Robbie says, clutching Branna's body closer to his. "I'd run straight in without wiping my feet if I had any feeling left in my lower half. Bird legs weren't made for all-night hiking." In the blink of an eye, his expression shifts from relieved to stricken. His voice trembles as he says, "She's there, waiting."

Cleona peers through the tall gate. Her smile beams like the sun at midday. A pang of sorrow pierces my soul. "You've come back!" she shouts. She shoves the gate open and runs to meet us.

And I wish that her heart was not about to be broken.

CALDER

There are many beautiful things in this world, and some are through-and-through beautiful, to be sure. The sight of Sabella's firefly-covered antlers, how her face glowed with their gentle, golden light, the graceful way she led us through the forest, striding over roots and rocks as if she were more fairy than girl...

And then there are beautiful things that are also terrible. Things you cannot look away from but wish you could because they will leave indelible marks on your soul. They will be scars you lift your shirt to look at later, because you cannot help yourself and because the getting of them was important and should be remembered.

Here is Cleona, running faster than she's ever run in all her days to meet her long-missed sister. Here is Robbie, shaking with sorrow to the very claws of his bird toes. Here is Branna in his arms, forever asleep, as pretty as the sunrise that's creeping up over the barn.

The image cuts deep, as it must.

In my arms, Sparrow asks sleepily, "Are we home?"

But my throat has seized up with sorrow and I cannot form the words to answer.

SABELLA

JUNE 8, 1886
MORNING

Cleona's feet are a blur of motion as she runs toward us.

"Wait," Robbie says. His pained tone makes Cleona stop. She sees the unmoving girl he clutches to his chest. Her hand flies to cover her mouth as her face pales.

Calder sets Sparrow on her feet. She whispers a prayer as Robbie steps forward to meet Cleona. Rhys tugs my sleeve, but I shake my head, and he understands he must be still.

Robbie approaches Cleona slowly, solemnly, his arms quaking from the weight of his precious burden. Cleona falls to her knees. Robbie crouches before her and places Branna onto the soft grass.

"She is not a fawn," Cleona whispers. She touches her sister's face with her fingertips, tracing her freckled cheekbone. "I already knew she was gone. I felt it. Still, I hoped..." She starts to weep quietly, as if loath to bother her lifeless twin.

Rhys wails now that he realizes Branna is gone. Sparrow gathers him into her arms and pats his back.

I turn away and hide my face against Calder's shoulder. He

embraces me, shushing softly as my tears saturate his shirt. A few minutes or half an hour later, he says regretfully, "My legs will not hold me much longer. Robbie is taking care of Cleona. Shall we go inside and rest?"

"Yes." I back away from him and wipe my eyes with my dirty sleeve.

He reaches out to brush my cheek with his thumb. "You missed one," he says. A little pink stains his face, but Rhys has wandered over to draw his attention. Calder lifts the boy and gazes at him with unhindered love. "Ready for bed for once, Rhys?"

"Just this one time," the boy answers.

We start toward the house, slowly. "Sorry about dampening your shirt," I say. I do not know what else to say.

"It will dry." Calder's eyes tell me he wants to say more but knows better. Now is not the time for grand speeches or declarations. It is time to grieve, to rest, and to try to make sense of all that has happened. Everything else can wait.

We enter the house through the grand front door. The place looks bigger and more opulent than I remember. Its straight lines and spotless surfaces stir in me a sharp longing to return to the forest's leafy wildness. My legs could never carry me back there now. Indeed, when we reach the foot of the winding staircase, I cannot convince my feet to climb it.

I grip the banister to keep from sinking to the floor and tell Calder, "Go without me. I must sit for a moment."

"I can carry you up after I put Rhys to bed," Calder offers, and I am too tired to discern if he's flirting or merely being kind.

"We could rest in the blue parlor," Sparrow says from behind us, startling me. "The couches there are as soft as beds."

At the word "bed," I yawn. "If I can make it that far, it will be a miracle."

She slips her arm through mine and steers me into the parlor adjoining the entrance hall. Her description of the furniture proves true. I sink into plump, indigo velvet cushions with a sigh—and seconds later, find myself stricken with terror that if I close my eyes, ugly scenes of violence and death will replay in my mind. And so I stare at the painted ceiling, a delicate pale blue expanse embellished with puffy clouds and images of birds in flight.

In spite of my fear, sleep overcomes me like an unexpected storm sweeping over a mountain.

SABELLA

Three days ago, we buried Branna at the far end of the rose garden. The little boys stacked a cairn there in memory of Yonaz. Fond words were said, along with tearful words of farewell. The days since have been spent in somber silence, staring at walls or aimlessly wandering the gardens.

And then, as evening falls, the little housemaid, Evaline, delivers messages to everyone in residence: Come to the hay barn without delay. She refuses to say who summons us, but if her barely contained giddiness is any indication, this assembly will not be of a solemn nature.

Sparrow leans heavily on me as we trail behind Rhys, Tiberius, and Fabian. Her shuffling gait is no match for their excitement, but they stop now and then to politely wait for me and "Granny Sparrow" to catch up. In their waiting, the boys jostle and joke. They have set aside their sorrows with childish ease, and I envy them. Grief hovers about me with the tenacity of a buzzing mosquito.

The path to the hay barn takes us through the apple orchard

and past the horse stable. And then I hear music. A fiddle plays scales then moves on to something lively. Sparrow gives me a questioning look. "Go ahead," I say to the boys. They cheer and race to the barn door.

Just as they arrive, the door slides open and Calder steps out. He wears his widest grin and a bright blue velvet jacket with matching trousers—something so outlandishly fancy that I know the twins are to blame for it. He bows low and declares, "Welcome, dear ones!"

The boys dash into the barn. Good smells waft out of the building—not the expected sweet scent of dry hay, but the aromas of sausages, fruit pies, and spiced cakes. I peer over Calder's shoulder into the lantern-lit room. On a platform built of crates, a young man sits with a fiddle tucked under his chin. He was Yonaz's valet, if I remember rightly.

I bite my lower lip. Although Yonaz's true intentions remain a mystery, he was good to me, and I miss him. Tears crowd my eyes, and I do not want them. I must take a deep breath in and let it out slowly before I can ask, "What is this?"

Calder's face lights up like it used to before our shared tragedies. "This, dear Sabella, is a surprise birthday party for the boys. Of course, we have no idea when they were actually born...I just thought we could all use a bit of fun after...everything." He places a hand on my shoulder and gives me a knowing look. "Before you scold me for not properly observing the mourning period, Cleona and Robbie approved of the idea. Branna would have wanted us to remember what joy is."

I lean in and kiss his cheek. "What a puzzle you are, Calder Hadrian."

"A puzzle. I like that," he says in a way that warms me to my toes. He moves a step closer. "Have you forgiven me now? Am I finally free of the plague?"

Behind me, Sparrow clears her throat. "I'll go in, if you don't mind." She sidles past us.

"Sorry," Calder says to her. His eyes meet mine. "So?"

"Mostly." It is the best I can do. I'm afraid to admit I have completely forgiven him for the letter incident. What might he do if I say the words? What might I do? Heat rushes to my face and spreads down my neck as I imagine the possibilities.

"Good enough," Calder says. He takes my arm and drags me toward a table laden with platters of food and pitchers of lemonade.

"Thank you," I say. "The boys need this. We all do."

"You can thank me by dancing with me. After we eat, naturally."

"Oh, naturally," I say. "Stomachs first, as all the great poets say. Even Shakespeare."

He gives me a squinting, quizzical look. "Truly? Shakespeare?"

There is such delight in teasing him and seeing him fall for one of my jests.

"Shakespeare?" Robbie says with a mouthful of something as he joins us. "A birthday party is no place for schoolish talk." He smiles but the circles around his eyes are almost as dark as the black mourning bands tied around his shirtsleeves.

"Agreed." Calder snatches a piece of cheese from the plate in Robbie's hand.

"Hey, get your own!" Robbie tries to slap Calder but he leans out of range. At least grief has not stolen their brotherly banter.

"Care to dine?" Calder takes an empty plate from the table and offers it to me. Suddenly, I am ravenous.

"We cannot let all this food go to waste," I say.

And so I eat biscuits, cheese, sausages, cakes, and pie until I cannot swallow another bite. Afterward, Calder and I dance with the three little boys, skipping and twirling across the floor to jigs and reels sawed out by the fiddling valet. Cleona and Robbie watch from chairs along the wall with one of the black-and-white farm dogs curled at their feet. Robbie clutches her hand. From time to time, he lifts it to kiss her knuckles. In spite of his affection and the boys' antics, she remains somber.

The boys declare imminent starvation and scamper to the food table. The valet retunes the fiddle and then begins to play a slow, sweet melody. Calder bows to me. "May I have this dance, madam?"

"Yes. But I must warn you, I have never before waltzed with a gentleman."

"Well, you know I am no gentleman," he jests. "Waltzing is easy enough. You just meander around like you know what you're doing. Besides, this is no ballroom; no one will judge your missteps, least of all me. And let us face the facts. If anyone is ridiculous here, it's me in this gaudy suit." He tugs at the thick sleeves. "This thing is as stiff as a dead woodchuck."

"I like your suit. You might be mistaken for an actual grownup, dressed in such finery."

He tilts his head and narrows his eyes. "Not fair, Sabella. I don't know whether to feel complimented or insulted."

"I do like the suit," I insist. "Very much. Now, is this how it's done?" I rest my left hand on his shoulder as I remember seeing a lady do at a mine town dance before I grew antlers.

"Perfect." He places one hand on my back and clasps my right hand with the other. His hazy-eyed gaze makes my stomach somersault. "And now we glide."

We do not glide. Our time on the dance floor is replete with stumbling and giggling. My heart drums a rhythm far faster than the song's. If the music were to never end, I would remain happy here in Calder's arms, under his adoring gaze. Adoring him in return.

All of my past grievances with him have fled. I acknowledge to myself that I do not want to be his friend. I want to be much more. Later, if the opportunity presents itself, I will tell him. At this moment, we are dancing and I will take joy in it—as Branna would have wanted me to.

As we whirl, I catch sight of Sparrow. She sits in the corner with a cup of tea in her wrinkled hand. Her smile is sweet and serene.

This is happiness, this here-and-now. I wish I could bottle it, or press it between pages like a flower so I might keep it always.

The song ends. Calder rests his forehead against mine and closes his eyes. He looks as contented as I feel. He continues to hold me as if we're dancing, with his fingers clasping mine and his other hand lingering at my waist. I do not dare to move. He whispers my name in a gruff way that makes me shiver most pleasantly.

"Yes?" I answer.

"Promise you'll stay with us. With me."

I start to reply but someone tugs the back of my dress.

"Dance with me now," Rhys demands, his face upturned and charmingly serious. "Granny Sparrow says I have to go to bed after this song."

His face and sleeves are smeared with pie, but I cannot resist the boy. "Of course I will dance with you."

"Well, then. We'll talk later," Calder says. He takes a step back. "I must claim a dance with Sparrow before the dancing's done."

But when he approaches her, she refuses with a shake of her head. I watch Calder escort her out of the barn as Rhys swings my arms and hops on my toes. Sparrow's gait is slow and shuffling—worse than it was yesterday. My heart sinks from great heights to a terrible depth.

The final note fades. Rhys skips away to join the other boys, who are stuffing their faces with sweets while the valet puts his fiddle into its case. I should help clean up leftover food and dishes, but they can wait.

I rush toward the house and my age-stricken daughter. How many more times will I tuck her into bed with a kiss before...before she will no longer live on this earth. The thought is too much to bear.

CALDER

"Good night," I say to Sparrow as I leave her on the couch in the sitting room that adjoins the bedroom she shares with Sabella. I shut the door and lean back against it. The clock in the downstairs hallway bongs ten times as I stare at the shifting shadows that play in the second-floor corridor.

What a night it has been.

Blazes, if I had not been in love with Sabella before, I would be now. She dances like a three-legged pony and could out-eat a lumberjack. Her laughter is as pure as a child's, but some of the looks she gave me this evening could scorch the fur off a muskrat. I suspect those glances said more than she wished them to. She'd blush scarlet for a solid month if she knew how badly they made me want to kiss her breathless.

Ah, but Yonaz did raise me to be a gentleman. Whatever he was guilty of, he did a proper job of that. And so I will not kiss Sabella—for as long as she insists we remain friends.

"Calder," Sabella says, and I jump. She's just to my left, at the top of the staircase. She holds a candlestick. The light flickers over her features, rendering her ghostly yet stunning.

"You scared me. Well done. Robbie will be jealous." I stand up straight and notice the soreness of my feet. When I was dancing with Sabella, my feet were the last thing on my mind. Now I curse these stupid, fancy shoes.

"Why are you standing there? Is Sparrow unwell?" she asks with a frown.

"She's fine, but tired."

"Good. But you didn't answer my other question."

The truth of the matter falls out of my mouth. "I was waiting to say good night to you, I suppose."

"Calder."

I cannot tell if this quiet utterance of my name is meant to admonish or encourage me. I wait for her to say something else.

She says, "I think you should go." But she doesn't sound altogether certain, and the candlestick quakes a little in her grasp. I move a step closer to her.

"You think I should go?" My hands settle on the curve of her waist. Her breath catches. "Now?"

Her eyes close. Blazes, she's beautiful. The side-to-side movement of her head is so subtle that anyone might have missed it, but I see it. Gently, I tug her closer.

"Uncle Calder?" Fabian's voice echoes down from the floor above. "There's a mouse in our room! Come quick!"

I say a word that would have earned me a mouthful of soap from Yonaz. Sabella laughs rather than scolding me.

"You swear like a coal miner," she says.

"I should go," I say.

This time, she nods and moves out of reach. My hands fall to my sides. It was a grand *almost*, I think as Fabian hollers my name again.

SABELLA

"Why are you still awake?" Sparrow whispers from the other side of the bed. The room is deeply shadowed, but her hair is so white it almost glows.

As usual, she has eschewed her own room to be with me. It is better this way. We belong together. Whoever ultimately decided to send her to me—Delphine, the magical basket, or the universe—did the right and proper thing.

"Too much cake, perhaps," I say.

"Could it be because you're in love with Calder?" she asks with a hint of mischief.

"Sparrow!"

She giggles like a young girl. I roll onto my back and cover my head with the blanket. She yanks it away.

"My eyes are weak but I have seen the way you look at him," she says. "And the way he looks back. Will you marry him? I would very much love to be your bridesmaid."

If she were anyone else, I would refuse to continue this conversation. But every second we share is a precious thing. "Oh, Sparrow. So much has happened. I do not think we should rush into anything. To be honest, he doesn't even know how I feel."

She reaches out to press a cool palm to my cheek. Her expression is grandmotherly, full of kindness and affection. "Time is not something we should waste, and neither is love. But I'm suddenly very tired. We can talk more in the morning." She rolls over and burrows under the blankets.

"Good night, my sweet girl," I say. She snores softly. A single tear leaks from my eye as I imagine the bed without her in it. I swipe it away and turn my mind to remembrances of the party. The dancing. Calder.

I remember the way he looked at me as we danced, and the sure pressure of his hands upon my waist as we stood at the bedroom door. Such a longing stirs in me that I fear I might never sleep again.

SABELLA

After Sparrow and I share a quiet breakfast of eggs and toast in the dining room, we rise from the table and leave the house. The sun is bright enough to make us squint. The birds sing riotously in every tree, but all of the other residents of the house are still abed recovering from last night's festivities.

Side by side, Sparrow and I amble along the herb garden's paths. Today, her gait is punctuated by limping steps. She grips my arm for support. I gaze down at the fuzzy crown of her head. Weeks ago, she was taller than me, but no more.

Age has stolen her height, the roses in her cheeks, and the fullness of her lips. In an unfair exchange, it has left her with a bent back, a wrinkled face, and cloudy eyes.

To me, she is as beautiful as ever, my Sparrow. My basket babe.

The heat of the day coaxes rich scent from the herbs. A hummingbird zips past us while bees hum and bob over the flowers. Sparrow plucks a green stalk and tucks it behind my ear. "Rosemary for remembrance," she says.

I pat her gnarled hand where it holds tight to my arm. "Might it not be better to forget the past and start anew?"

"You do not truly wish to forget all of the past, Mama. It would be a great shame to forget the times you whispered stories to me under the quilt we shared, or the times we waded in the streams outside Miners Ridge. Or that time the billy goat got loose and chased us through the woods."

I smile as we resume walking. "Or seeing you smile for the first time. Or hearing your first baby laughter."

"Even times of sorrow have their worth and their lessons." She bends and picks a twig full of tiny green leaves. "Thyme for strength and courage."

Our eyes meet. In hers, I see certainty untainted by fear.

"No, Sparrow."

"Before the next month passes," she says. "I feel it in my marrow." She slips the sprig of thyme behind my other ear. "I am old, Mama. Ready to go to my rest."

"You're a healer. Can you not add length to your life with some concoction? You have not yet had one year with us." The heaviness in my chest grows, a lead weight of agony that threatens to crush my soul.

She lifts my chin with her knobby fingers and forces me to look into her eyes. "Before I came, why did you wish for me?"

"Because I was lonely and unloved. Because no one understood me or wanted my affection."

"You needed me then. But now you have others. A family. People who love you, antlers and all. The devotion of a good-hearted young man. I came for a season, and that time is nearing its end."

"I will always, always need you."

"And I will always be your Sparrow, whether I stand beside you or sleep under the earth." She embraces me for too short a time before pushing away from me. She points across the garden. Calder, Robbie, and the three boys have appeared on the lawn.

The boys take turns dragging a kite over the grass by its string as Calder and Robbie watch from the shade of a maple.

"Look there," Sparrow says with amusement. "Should we remind them they need a strong wind for such a pastime?"

I sniffle and dredge up a smile. "Some things are better learned firsthand."

She pats my arm as if she is the mother and I am the child. "There you are. There you are. Such is life."

I nod.

But I do not know how I will live a single day without her.

"Come," she says, pulling me toward the boys.

I want to ask her what Delphine whispered to her before she died. Was there some clue in it that might lead me to a cure for Sparrow's unnatural aging? She has made peace with death, but I refuse to let her go without a fight.

The asking will have to wait, though. This sunny, joyful moment among friends should be savored for as long as it lasts.

Calder offers me his widest smile, and I push my worries away like a child shoving a paper boat into the current of a swift-moving stream. Unlike the boat, the worries will certainly return.

CALDER

After lunch, Sparrow slips her arm through mine and steers me into the house's library. The boys' school books are scattered on the floor and the table. My heart sinks as I realize Yonaz will never teach them again. He did love tormenting his foster children with mathematics and long spelling words.

A tutor will have to be hired soon, before the boys turn altogether wild. Heaven knows I'd make a dreadful teacher—and Robbie would be no better.

Sparrow shuts the door firmly behind us and gives me a serious look that makes me feel all of five years old. I'm about to break out in hives like I did when I was small and anxious. I scratch my face and ask, "Am I in trouble?"

"I need your help," she says. She sits on the sofa and pats the cushion to invite me to join her. "Before Delphine died, she whispered something in my ear. She told me you know where the spring is."

I stop scratching my face to scratch my neck instead. I fix my eyes on a cobweb hanging in the corner. "I, uh…"

She grabs my non-scratching hand with her thin fingers. "I

have no time for games, Calder. You cannot pretend you don't know."

"But—"

"No questions, no debate. This is important. Will you take me there?"

A spark of hope leaps to life inside me. "Did Delphine say the waters could heal you?"

"I cannot tell you the secrets she told me. An enchantment prohibits my mouth from speaking them. All I can say is that I must go, and you must take me as soon as it can be arranged."

The woman should take up gambling. Her face is inscrutable. Now I can't decide if I should be optimistic or sick with dread. My innards vote for sick. "I will take you," I say.

Blast it all, Sabella is going to hate me for this, I just know it.

"Help me up," Sparrow says. Once she's on her feet, she stands on her tiptoes to kiss my cheek—which only makes me feel worse. Is this a pre-goodbye kiss or a simple thank you?

I scratch my arms. Both of them at once.

"Come to the kitchen with me," she says. "I have a balm to soothe that itch."

SABELLA

JUNE 13, 1886
EVENING

The sun is inching down the red-orange sky, and the air is warm and weighted with the scent of honeysuckle. A few fireflies spark in the grass and trees. The world is a pretty place in this twilight hour, one in which I can almost forget my cares for a while.

Almost. Sometime before we return to the house, I plan to ask Calder to help me find a way to prolong Sparrow's life. She is resigned to her fate, but I am not. And if given the chance, would she not choose to remain longer with us here?

Calder takes my hand and pulls me toward the hedge maze behind the house. I've seen the outside of the structure from the garden, but I've never ventured inside it.

"Does that remind you of Delphine's terrible shrubberies, as it reminds me?" I ask.

Immediately, he stops walking and frowns. "For the love of... I did think it would be a romantic place to stroll—before you brought that up."

One corner of his mouth quirks, so I can tell his annoyance is purely theatrical.

"It was a nice idea, I suppose." Boldly, I lift our clasped hands and kiss his knuckles.

He grins rather wickedly. "It seems your ideas might be superior. What other thoughts have you been entertaining under those fine antlers?"

I pull him along the path. "I think of hats, mostly."

"You, Miss Jenkins, are a dreadful liar."

"I gather your thoughts are of a better quality. Greek architecture, the meaning of life, and such."

We enter the maze. The walls are seven feet high and composed of some sort of fragrant evergreen. A path of white pebbles crunches under our feet. Nearby, a mourning dove coos.

I expect Calder to continue our banter, but he says seriously, "All of my thoughts are of you, if you want the truth of it." He gives me a sidelong glance before returning his gaze to the corridor of greenery. "You with fireflies on your antlers, you whispering to baby Sparrow in the wagon, you in the inn kitchen at midnight with breadcrumbs stuck to your chin. Your face when you first saw my wings, all wonder and fascination. The scowl you wore when you first hated me in your parents' kitchen."

My heart beats wildly as we round a corner. The path narrows so my shoulder brushes against his as we continue moving forward. The air feels warmer although the sunlight is disappearing fast. I try to steer him back to the banter by saying, "I didn't hate you then. That came later."

He looks grim and replies, "Darkest days of my life."

"Mine, too."

"Because I do not want to revisit those days, I think I should tell you something." He steps in front of me so we're face to face. "Sparrow asked me to take her to the spring. The one Delphine used to give us our gifts."

"You know where it is?"

He scratches his neck and looks guilty. "I do. It's a fair distance from here. Delphine took me there when I was ten or eleven. She made me memorize the way, then forbade me from returning there. I never did figure out her purpose in it."

I throw my arms around his neck and hug him tightly. "This is wonderful news. Don't you see? If the waters can give gifts, maybe they can take them away. Maybe we can cure Sparrow by washing her in the spring."

When he steps out of my arms, he looks far less happy than I expected. In fact, he looks glum. He says, "I hate to squash your hopes, but I have a feeling the spring doesn't work like that."

"We have to try."

"I know." He takes my hand and leads me to another sharp turn in the maze. "Well, the good news is that Sparrow has already asked me to take her. The bad news is that I can only take you when the moon is full. Certain markers appear then, spots on trees that glow along the path. Delphine didn't need them for guidance, but I don't have the magic she did."

Disappointment unsettles my stomach. "It will be weeks before the next full moon."

"I'm sorry, Sabella. Truly. In the meantime, we'll do everything we can to keep her strong and in good spirits."

I do not have a chance to answer before he leads me around another bend. The center of the maze comes into view. The sunset's last red-orange light stains the scene. The space is larger than I'd expected and features a blue-tiled water fountain encircled by curved, stone benches.

Robbie is sitting on one of the benches. He startles when he sees us.

"I thought you'd gone to bed," Calder says. "You're not looking well, my friend."

"Oh. I just came here to think," Robbie says as he stands. "I'll go now." His sharp cheekbones remind me of jutting cliffs, and dark crescents underscore his eyes. His bird feet have lost their bright color. We are all grieving the deaths of Branna and Yonaz, but he seems to be suffering most.

"Stay," I say. "Tell us how we might help you."

Robbie sits again, his posture slouched. Calder and I take places on either side of him. "Cleona changed," he says to the ground. "Somehow she did it even without Branna beside her. And I'm worried she won't change back this time."

"Oh, Robbie." I put my arm around him.

"She is a mourning dove now," he says. "She was on my windowsill when I woke up this morning." A small sob escapes him.

"She just needs time, Rob," Calder says. "She'll be a girl again when she's ready, I'm sure of it. She loves you."

Quietly, he weeps into his open palms. Calder gives him a handkerchief, pats on the back, and supportive silence. He sheds a tear or two of his own.

As we sit, I stare at the darkening sky above our heads. The stars come out one at a time, like shy children taking their places on a stage. It strikes me how much of life is change and loss. It creeps up on us warily or falls on our heads like an unexpected storm.

A bird flies over. I shield my eyes with my hand and recognize it as a dove. Our Cleona. She swoops to land at Robbie's feet. I hold my breath as I wait for his response.

He sniffs, wipes his face with the handkerchief, then leans over and offers his hand. She hops into his palm. Her black eyes shine as she coos.

"She is beautiful, Robbie," I say.

"Always has been," he replies.

"I'm hungry," Calder says—and I can tell by the look on his face that this comment comes not from insensitivity but compassion. Robbie might stay here all night unless we coax him into the house. "Did you know the cook made gingerbread cake today, Rob? We should get some before the boys gobble it all."

Robbie does not resist when Calder takes his arm and helps

him stand. Instead, he cautions, "Slowly. I don't want to scare Cleona away."

"Right," Calder agrees. "You set the pace."

The dove launches herself from the ground to Robbie's shoulder. He runs a finger along her feathers. "Let's go."

I trail behind Robbie and Calder as we navigate the turns of the maze. Calder regales Robbie with tales of their past adventures. Now and then, I think I glimpse a smile on Robbie's drawn face. And by the time we emerge from the hedges, I am so full of love for this kind, concerned Calder that I do not think I will be able to eat a single bite of the cook's excellent cake.

"I will wait for her if it takes a hundred years," Robbie vows just before we reach the house.

"Of course. I'd do the same if I were you," Calder says. He looks over his shoulder and gives me a tender look I will not forget for a hundred years, or if heaven allows it, an eternity.

CALDER

I have become a proper author, or close to it. This is hard to believe, as I have always detested any task requiring pen and ink. Monkeys probably have better penmanship than me.

Of late, I find I cannot stop writing notes to Sabella. I press them into her hand when we pass in hallways. I slip them under her door before dawn. I tuck them into the pockets of her dresses as they flap on the clothesline. I ask Sparrow to hide them under her pillow.

This morning, before breakfast, I left a note under her teacup. All this waiting for the full moon has left a permanent wrinkle in her forehead and made her laughter a rarity. These things are almost intolerable. Also, since our walk in the maze, we have not spent five minutes unaccompanied by little boys or needy friends.

While Robbie and Sparrow discuss berry picking plans and nibble toast, Sabella unfolds the note in her lap, reads it, and then nods in my direction. I push my plate away. The very thought of being alone with Sabella is enough to wreck my usual voracious appetite for bacon and eggs.

And then, after what seems like an age and a half (less than two hours, in reality), I find myself waiting for her behind the hay barn.

By "waiting," I mean pacing and biting my nails as my pulse does ridiculous sprints. The note I left was simple enough: a brief request for her to meet me in the hours between breakfast and luncheon. If I had spelled out my intentions, would she be walking toward me now, smiling sweetly as her skirts swish through the clovers?

"Hello," I say. The word sounds stupid, but it is all I have at the moment.

"Is something wrong?"

I step closer to her and tuck a strand of hair behind her ear. "I've missed you."

"You have made that quite clear with your fifty-three notes."

"I wrote fifty-five. Some must have gone astray. Blazes, is that why the cook has been looking at me like that?"

"She does blush whenever you're in the room."

"Want to fly?" I blurt. "Just over the next hill? There's a stream, and a little waterfall."

"Yes," she says without hesitation.

"Good. Well..." I turn my back and unbutton my shirt. This is scandalous behavior, of course. But I have a new and brilliant plan to lessen the immodesty of the situation. I slip my arms through the shirt backwards, as if it's an apron.

I close my eyes and breathe deeply. I let my wings unfold and use oft-neglected muscles to move them. Flutter them. Strength spreads through their veins. I turn back toward her and open my arms. "Ready?"

Seconds later, I lift her off the ground. Her arms are around my neck. She holds her head back a little, as if she's afraid she'll harm me with her antlers. Blazes, I could take the injury of it—and much worse—for the joy of holding her so close.

We do not fly high, for I am wary of being seen by people wandering the countryside. But we are well above the ground, kissed by a light breeze and warm sunbeams. Below us spreads a field of wheat speckled with blue cornflowers. Even with the air rushing past, I catch the scent of Sabella's soap and whatever it is she washes her hair with (lavender or rosemary?). The sound of her laughter makes me weak in knees I'm not even standing on.

"I see it," she says, pointing at the small waterfall surrounded by pines and ferns.

My feet touch down on a flat rock overlooking the stream, but my heart is still soaring. I release her from my arms—not without a pang of regret. We are inches apart. She reaches up and attempts to straighten the collar of my backward shirt. I catch her hand and kiss it.

"You're shaking," she says in a voice barely louder than the rushing water. "Did the flying tire you?"

"Are we still friends?" I ask.

She shakes her head. "I do not think it's possible."

"I agree. You drive me to distraction." I'm swimming in her eyes. Drowning.

I cannot say she's smiling, but there is a glow about her, as if she's a saint in an old painting—but one who's gazing at me in a way unfit for church. "If you brought me here to kiss me, I think you should get on with it," she says.

"You coal town girls are forward creatures," I say.

"Lucky for you."

Blast if she doesn't put a hand behind my neck and pull my mouth to hers before I can move to kiss her, just like the last time. I feel the kiss to my toes, to the ends of every one of the hairs on my head. Her mouth on mine is bliss. Perfection.

I pull her closer. Her fingers tangle in my hair. She makes a sound between a sigh and a whimper.

I take a half step away and ask, "Are you all right?"

"Yes, but we should go home."

"We should."

Again, we kiss. Slowly this time, tenderly. I might shed a tear for the beauty of it. When she pushes away from me, some of the worry has left her face. As for me, I have never been happier. Never.

"We should go," she says again. "We really should. The wind is picking up." As if it's in some secret alliance with her, a strong breeze pummels my wings.

"Wait." I take her hands in mine. "I want to say...you mean everything to me, Sabella. I told you before that I love you, but what I felt then was nothing compared to this. I love you so much that I can barely tolerate my own company."

Here is a moment I swear I will never forget, not even after I'm dead so long there's nothing left of me but dirt: the wind toying with a loose lock of her hair, tree-filtered sunlight dappling her rosy cheekbones, the slow smile that teases the corners of her freshly kissed mouth, and her sure words, "I love you, too, Calder Hadrian."

SABELLA

Sparrow is as frail and weak as a newborn kitten. It takes me almost an hour to help her to dress, for she requires me to stop every few minutes because of pains in her joints or bones. Not even her best remedies relieve her aches—which concerns me more than I can say.

The hall clock chimes nine as I help her into her favorite chair by the bedroom window. She gazes over the gardens while I needlessly rearrange the books on the bookshelf.

"A moment, miss?" Hazel, our housekeeper, says from the doorway. She is a round, motherly woman with apple cheeks and a baffling fondness for polishing doorknobs. She rarely speaks unless spoken to.

I hug a volume of Shakespearean sonnets to my chest as I turn to face her. "What is it?"

Something in her somber expression unsettles me before she says another word.

"I've just returned from Miners Ridge. My brother lives there with his wife and baby." She pauses, and anxiety rises from my chest to my throat.

"Yes?" I say.

She continues. "While I was there, I heard your name mentioned in the shop. Miss, I'm sorry to tell you, but your mother has died. The funeral is tomorrow afternoon, should you wish to attend."

I stumble backward and land on the edge of Sparrow's bed. I grip the quilt with both hands. Words fail me, so I nod.

"Master Calder can take you in the wagon, miss. He's already hitched it. You'll need to leave soon to make it there in time for the service."

Numb, I say, "Thank you."

Hazel comes to me and pulls me into her arms. I hold onto her as if she's the only plank within reach after a shipwreck. She smells of starch and beeswax polish and baking, like one would want a mother to smell—rather than alcohol infused medicine and sour bedclothes. When I finally release her, she pats my cheek and says, "I'm sorry, love. If I can do anything, come find me." She sweeps out of the room, and I sink onto the mattress again.

"I'm so sorry, Mama," Sparrow says from her chair. "I would go with you if I could. But I fear the trip would be the end of me."

"I know, my dear."

I get up to pace, suddenly unable to hold still a second longer. "I'll need to find a black dress. Do I have a black dress? And oh, heavens! My antlers. I cannot go there with antlers."

I wander into the dressing room. In the recesses of the wardrobe, I find a plain black gown with jet buttons and a simple lace collar, something fitting for the funeral of a miner's wife. How had the twins known I'd need such a garment?

My thoughts are molasses-thick as I change and put on black boots. My fingers tremble hard enough to make tying the boot-laces a long ordeal.

My mother is dead. She loved me in her way, I think, as much as she could. And now, she is dead.

The day promises to be hot, but I grab my black shawl from the shelf and slip my fingers into a pair of black lace gloves I found in my dressing table. I kiss Sparrow goodbye. When I open my door to leave the room, Calder is there, hand raised to knock. "I'm sorry for your loss," he says. "I have the wagon ready if you really want to go. I never got the hang of driving Yonaz's monstrosity of a carriage, and there are no more trains today, so…"

"I need your help first." My voice sounds foreign to me, a thin, tight imitation of my real voice. "I need you to cut off these antlers."

He blanches and shakes his head.

"You know I cannot travel like this."

"I do know, but I hate knowing." He groans with exasperation before he relents. "All right. We'll have to go to the barn to do it. It isn't something the boys should witness."

"Fine."

Each footstep reverberates inside my head as I trail behind Calder. Once within the barn, he turns and bars the door. He takes a saw from the work bench and faces me. His face is pasty and glistening with sweat like he's fallen ill with a fever.

"Are you sure?" he asks. "After all this time, to…to go back to *this*." He scowls at the toothy blade with such loathing that the metal should melt. "Does it not feel wrong to you?"

"I feel nothing right now, Calder. Nothing at all. Please, just do it. We need to get on the road or I'll miss the funeral altogether."

"After this trip, I will never do it again. I'd just as soon set fire to a cathedral. It isn't right."

"Calder." I close my eyes and grit my teeth.

He swears under his breath and then releases a loud, huffing sigh. He rests a hand on my neck, holding hard enough to keep me still but gently enough not to hurt me. I hear the grinding of the blade. I smell the dust. After a minute, the first antler breaks free with a faint crack. A strange sound comes from Calder, a choked sob or a grunt of anger. I keep my eyes shut as he sets the blade on the other antler.

The second antler breaks free. I open my eyes to find Calder has fallen to his knees before me. I take his face in my hands. He looks up at me with such stark remorse that I feel something for the first time since Hazel brought me the bitter news. This unnamable emotion churns inside my belly, sadness and gratitude and love and regret all mixed together like one of Sparrow's pungent, medicinal teas.

"Never again," I promise him.

My hands are folded in my lap, and he covers them with his. "You don't have to go to this funeral," he says. "It can do you no good. They were never worthy of you, your parents."

"I do have to go." I cannot explain why, not even to myself.

Silently admitting defeat, he stands. "I'm going with you then. And I don't mean just driving you there and waiting. I will not leave your side for one solitary minute."

I, too, know when I am defeated. I stand and brush silvery gray antler dust off my mourning dress. "In that case, you had better hurry and fetch a change of clothes."

SABELLA

In the dandelion-carpeted cemetery behind the brick church, Calder and I watch from the rear of the small crowd as the hunch-shouldered pastor murmurs a psalm over Mother's open grave. We arrived just in time for the service, after journeying until nightfall, spending the night in the woods (I slept in the wagon bed and Calder camped on the grass under it), and then hurrying the horse over the last few miles to Miners Ridge Cemetery.

Perspiration trickles from under the edge of my black bonnet and down the slope of my forehead as Father tosses a handful of soil onto the simple pine casket. The sound of the dirt hitting the box scrapes my heart like a dull knife. The world seems devoid of air. Is it possible to drown on dry land?

Grimly, Father eyes me from the other side of the grave. He folds his coal-stained hands over the mound of his belly. A dozen mourners line up to offer him handshakes and sympathetic words before they disperse, one by one. When the last parishioner traipses away across the short, dull grass, he comes to me.

Purple, sagging skin bunches under his eyes. Smudges of coal dust stain his earlobes and throat, evidence that Mother no longer aids him in bathing.

"Sabella," he says flatly. "Is this the boy you abandoned your mother for?"

Calder tenses beside me as he takes a small step forward. I know he's ready to defend his honor and mine. I give him a look that says *no*. I can defend myself.

"This is my friend Calder, Father."

"You have my sympathies," Calder says politely.

Father grunts, refusing to shake the hand Calder offers. "If you're sorry Mother's gone, girl, you can come home and try to be the good daughter she spent her every breath trying to raise right. Last time you ran off, she told the neighbors you'd gone to visit an aunt in the country. So as long as we say this here boy they've seen is a cousin, no one need know you've been living in sin. Unless there's to be…consequences?" He gestures toward my waistline.

"Sir!" Calder says. His fingers ball into fists at his sides. "There's no need to be crass. Sabella is a respectable—"

"Please," I say, stepping into the space between them. "This is no place for fighting."

Father grunts again. He kicks a pebble. "You have a carriage, boy?"

"A wagon, sir. May I drive you home?"

"Much obliged," Father says without actually looking into Calder's face or sounding genuinely thankful.

"Should I bring the wagon to the gate?" Calder asks, meeting my gaze. Behind these words is another question. He's asking if I'll feel safe alone with my father.

"That would be appreciated," I reply.

As Calder strides off, a cloud covers the sun. I adjust my gloves, unable to think of a single thing to say to my father. A murder of crows lights on the ridge of the church roof and fills the air with rough caws.

Father kicks another pebble with his scuffed shoe. "House is a right mess. It'll take you a full week to straighten up, I reckon. Your mother was bedridden from the day you left until she passed, and I had extra shifts to boot."

As if he would have lifted a finger to help with the housework, mine or no mine.

"I will stay for the afternoon to help get things in order," I offer. The very thought makes my chest feel as if a fully loaded coal car is rolling over it. I follow him toward the gate and try to think of something besides the soul-sickening notion of going back home with this man.

"You will stay until you find a proper husband or bury me," he says sternly. He swings open the gate. "You owe me that much, child. Have I not kept a roof over your head and put food on the table for you since the old witch gave you to me?"

"You have," I say, wanting to remind him that he did it without love or tenderness. My head itches, and I imagine I can feel my antlers growing, slowly, slowly, even as I remember how he hacked them off every single morning.

Calder halts the horses and slides across the bench to pull me up onto the seat beside him. Instead of climbing into the wagon bed, Father clambers aboard and settles next to me. Squashed between the two men, I ponder their differences. Where Father is taciturn and irritable, Calder is witty and kindhearted. Father is motivated by a desire to survive while appearing respectable, but Calder is driven by his love for life and his Springborn family.

The wagon slows as we approach the house where I grew up.

"What was she like, the woman who gave me to you in the basket?" I ask Father. I need to hear this from his mouth, for I may never see him again after today.

"Old," he says. "Old and wrinkled as an apple gone bad. But a body could tell she'd been comely in her day. Her eyes...I've never seen their equal. Green-blue like the river on a fair day."

"The winter Delphine," Calder says quietly.

The horse stops and the wagon sways. Father jumps to the ground and offers his hand to me. "Come on, girl."

I grip the bench hard. "Tell me, Father. Did you ever love me at all?"

His eyes mist over—which is a surprise. "Aye. You were a pretty little thing, sweet as the day is long."

"But then I grew antlers."

His expression hardens as he peers up at me. "We prayed for a child, not a curse."

"I was still the same child, *your* child, no matter what grew out of my head."

"Is that why you're hesitating there? Because of the bedeviled antlers? It's no matter. No trouble we can't solve every morning with a saw and a few minutes of toil."

"My antlers are not *trouble*. They are part of me as much as my hands or feet."

He spits on the ground. "Words. I'll not quarrel with you over words. I'm a miner, not a scholar."

Calder squeezes my arm reassuringly, bolstering my courage.

"Goodbye, then, Father." Tears veil my vision as I turn my face away from him.

With a shake of the reins, Calder commands the horses to carry us away.

CALDER

As the wagon bears us home, I hate Sabella's father so much that my innards feel like they contain an overflowing bowl of lava. He is a monster. I should have punched him. I would have if Sabella had permitted it.

Her tears do not last for more than a mile or two, but I half wish they would have kept falling. It is worse to see her storing up the pain for later, staring into the distance with that blank look on her face.

I swear by all that's holy that I will love her hard enough to make up for all the love that despicable man and his cold wife never gave her. There is nothing in heaven or on earth that will stop me.

SABELLA

S parrow's breaths come too lightly as she naps on a small couch in the herb garden, barely causing her chest to rise and fall. Robbie and Calder brought the couch out early this morning so Sparrow could enjoy the plants and the sunshine —and they carried her out as well.

The dove Cleona preens her ever-present mourning gown of somber gray feathers as she perches near Sparrow's feet. As I sit on a bench not far from them, I wear mourning, too: a black gown and an invisible cloak of sadness. I turn Calder away with a shake of my head when he offers to sit with me, but Robbie ignores my rejection.

He sits beside me on the bench and tucks a stray strand of my hair behind my ear. The tender gesture only deepens my misery. "Is it your mother you're missing? Because it is a waste to mourn the living," he says. "And not what Sparrow wants of you."

"I grieve for both of them. I cannot seem to help myself, Robbie."

"I have something here that might distract you a little." He sets a book on his lap. Has he been holding this all along? The only thing I am certain of is that I am drifting on the edge of reality, where focusing and remembering are difficult things to do.

I stare at the book. It is cloth-bound, dark blue, and an inch thick. "Hazel found Delphine's journals inside a desk. Four in all. She kept a record of every one of us—where we were found, the parents she gave us to, our specific gifts. This one mentions you near the beginning and Sparrow near the end."

How can I answer this? Do I want to know these things? Will knowing make things better? Robbie must sense my ambivalence, for he says, "I think it might help you to hear about Sparrow's first days. May I read it to you?"

"Yes," I reply.

Robbie opens the book to a bent-cornered page. He reads, "'February 12. Today I found a girl child abandoned behind the mercantile in Miners Ridge, bloody and naked, squealing with distress. The mother ran from where she hid in the shadows, a girl barely old enough to bear a child. And then I took the babe to be washed and blessed by the fairy waters.'"

The words bring tears to my eyes. I never gave a thought to Sparrow's first mother and what she might have suffered. Did her parents lock her away in shame when they found she was with child, or did she manage to hoard her secret until she gave birth, alone and afraid, in a dirty alleyway? Was the young mother someone I knew as a child?

"Sparrow probably would have died if Delphine had not found her," Robbie says. "The world would have been a poorer place for it."

I nod and run my gaze over my sleeping daughter. "I do wonder who she might have become if someone else had found her and Delphine had not washed her in the spring."

Robbie shuts the book. "That we'll never know." He wriggles his bird toes in the dust and adds, "I will say this, not in Delphine's defense, but because it is true. These experiences—with wings and antlers and bird feet and such—they have made us stronger than we would have been without them. We are better people because of our struggles. You cannot deny it."

"Of course you are right, Robbie. I know I can live with my antlers. What I cannot live without is Sparrow." My hands lay open and empty in my lap. I stare at them and wish they could do something to help my child live.

"I could say that you can and will live when she is gone, but that would not help," Robbie says. "Just know that I love you as my sister, and I will do everything in my power to see you through." He kisses my cheek with a quick, birdlike peck. "Here's Calder. I'll go."

Calder's feet make hardly a sound as he approaches. There's a little crease between his brows, a small, endearing token of his concern for Sparrow and me.

Robbie and Calder pass each other on the path between the garden and the house. Cleona swoops after Robbie on quiet wings.

Sparrow mutters and stirs but remains asleep on her couch as Calder sits beside me on the bench. "It is a pretty morning," Calder says.

"I suppose you heard what Robbie read to me."

"Watching over you is a hard habit to break," he says. He picks up my hand and entwines his fingers with mine. "The full moon is tomorrow night. Are you sure you want to go to the spring?"

"If Sparrow is going, I am going."

"You still think the waters might heal her?"

"We have to try, Calder."

"There will most certainly be consequences, Sabella. They might not be good."

"It is a risk I must take." I refuse to entertain thoughts of failure or harm.

"All right, then. We'll take the rest of today to prepare. We can take the wagon partway, but it's a hard climb up the mountainside after that. Wear something practical. Oh, and I think we should ask Robbie to go along, in case I need help carrying Sparrow."

"Thank you," I say. "This means everything to me, you know."

He kisses my cheek. "I would fly you both there if my wings could bear the weight of it," he says. These words are a better declaration of love than any other I have heard. I rest my head against his shoulder, close my eyes, and breathe in the scents of sun-warmed herbs and his freshly laundered shirt.

Hope, that thing which had fallen into a deathlike sleep within my soul, stirs and stretches.

SABELLA

I stand between Robbie and Sparrow in front of the house. The sunshine is pleasant this afternoon, tempered by a gentle, blossom scented breeze. It is a good day for a journey.

My fingers fumble at my nape to tie a fresh knot in my dark green headscarf. I cut my antlers off myself after the midday meal. A half inch of growth remains atop my head, but it was the best I could do. To trouble Calder with the chore seemed too much. He is already tasked with guiding us up a possibly perilous mountainside this evening, by the light of the full moon.

Calder halts the wagon close to the front of the house, where Sparrow, Robbie, and I stand waiting. He hops down to help Robbie lift Sparrow into the back. Last night, I piled pillows and blankets there to cushion her frail bones for the first part of our journey. When Sparrow is settled, he glowers at the space above my head. "You cut them yourself again, didn't you?"

My face burns. "We could meet strangers on the road. I did what needed to be done. You don't have to like it."

"At least you're not bleeding this time," Calder grumbles.

"Now, now," Robbie says. "Play nice, children." He climbs into the wagon bed with Sparrow and covers her with a thin blanket. "Sabella, you ride beside Calder and try to enjoy his company," he says cheerily. "We will be fine back here."

Calder rounds the side of the wagon and stops short when he gets a full view of my attire. "Whoa, Nellie," he says, his face alight with barely contained hilarity, "What in the name of the saints are you wearing? Wait. Are those *my* striped trousers?"

Hands on hips and straight-faced, I reply to his accusations. "This is a riding costume the twins gave me, Calder Hadrian, and no, they are not your trousers. If you own trousers resembling these, Branna and Cleona were playing a joke. And for your information, I thought it practical to eschew cumbersome skirts when going hiking in the mountains."

Robbie snorts with laughter. "Darnation," he says. "I'd pay money to see you in that outfit, Cald. I might fall in love with you myself!"

"Stuff it, Robbie." Calder scowls as if he's irritated with his best friend, but we all know he is not.

Robbie is still snorting with laughter as we pull away from the house minutes later.

As the wagon carries us through the wrought iron gates of Three Stars Farm, anxiety grips my heart. Things will change today, for better or worse. There is a chance that Sparrow will not return home alive.

Beyond the gates, the road loses its smooth straightness. The trees grow thick around us. Shadows play on the ground. Squirrels and robins leap from branch to branch as we pass. I spy a deer among the ferns. She blinks shyly at me.

"They're nice, now that I've had a chance to get used to them," Calder says out of the blue. When I give him a questioning look, he adds, "Your striped trousers. They're rather becoming." He doesn't laugh when he says it, so I believe he's at least trying to mean it.

"Thank you."

His smile appears, warm and boyish in the green-tinted forest light. He leans forward a little, reins held loosely in his hand, the picture of a young man taking a pleasant Saturday drive.

"Do I have something on my face?" Calder asks, eyes fixed on the road. "Jam or something?"

"Not that I can see," I say. My cheeks flame because he's caught me staring. "You do have a freckle on your earlobe, though." I tell myself to be quiet and look at trees. I'm only worsening the embarrassment by admitting I've taken notice to a freckle no bigger than a poppy seed.

"Hmm," Calder says. I don't have to look at him to know he's grinning.

Half an hour later, as the sun sets, Calder reins in the horses. Beside us, the mountain rises steeply. Patches of ferns are interrupted by boulders and stubborn, spindly pines. "The footpath up the mountain starts a short walk from here," Calder says. "The markers should appear on the trees as soon as the moon is a little higher."

I jump from the wagon to the ground. Calder ties the horses to a tree, and Robbie brings them pails of water and a little hay. These chores are done in silence, as if we're in a church and not the woods. The moon inches up the sky.

As the shadows thicken, Calder grabs a tin lantern from the wagon bed and lights it with a match. He gives the lantern to me and says quietly, "You'll have to carry this unless your firefly friends come to call. I don't expect the moon will light everything well under the thick trees."

"Is it time to go?" I ask. I am filled with equal measures of excitement and fear.

He points to a tree marked with a slash of glowing, yellow-green fungus. "It is."

Robbie climbs into the wagon. From there, he transfers our drowsy Sparrow into Calder's arms. How small she looks curled against his chest. Were it not for her snowy hair and wrinkled face, one might mistake her for a child. She wraps one arm around his neck, lays her cheek against his shirt, and falls back to sleep.

Our hike begins. The path turns from earth and rock to all rock as it steepens. Even though he bears the weight of Sparrow, Calder is as surefooted as a buck. My head regularly grows the antlers of a deer, yet I am as clumsy as an old cow. I stumble, bruising my knees and shins again and again, and scraping skin from my hands. The lantern stays lit but bears a dozen new dents.

"How much farther?" I ask, panting, when we stop atop a level rock.

Calder points. "Up that way, and then across a ridge and down into a little valley. Half an hour's journey, perhaps."

"Darnation," Robbie says. "My bird feet weren't made for scaling rocks. I'll be in bandages for a week."

"Stop grousing, chicken legs," Calder says. But a few minutes later, Calder stops again. He waits on an outcropping of rock, still clutching Sparrow to his chest. She slumbers soundly, unbothered by the climb.

"Are you all right?" I ask him.

"Hale and hearty. And you? You've spoiled your fine outfit, I fear."

"Yes." I glance down at my torn, dirt-smeared trousers and stained blouse. "It is a pity."

We both erupt into laughter. Our tiredness must be getting the better of us.

Robbie raises one eyebrow. "You're quite the pair. Shall we continue and get this loathsome trek over with?"

Soon, we descend into a narrow valley. Soaring hemlocks and pines surround us. The sound of water spilling into a pool teases my ears long before the spring comes into view. Save for this and the rustling of evergreen branches overhead, no other sounds sully the air. Not one bird trills; not one chipmunk chatters. This place feels holier to me than the chilly sanctuary of the Miners Ridge church ever did.

Calder leads us toward a dip in the earth. Here, water gushes from a crack in the rocks at the base of a tree and cascades into a dark, round pool an arm's length wide. "The fairy spring," he says reverently. "Sabella?"

I know what he asking. "Yes," I say. I am certain but shaking.

"Help me get her into the water, Rob."

"Sparrow, you mean? You said we were bringing her to see it, not..." Robbie looks as if he might throw up. "Are you sure you want to tamper with the spring's magic? I have a bad feeling about this. More than one bad feeling, to be honest."

Sparrow awakens and lifts her head. "Did someone say my name? Have we arrived?"

I nod at Calder, and he lowers Sparrow to the ground. She leans back against the rough bark of a pine. Lantern in hand, I crouch beside her with my heart hammering. She will not like what I have to say.

"We've brought you here to wash you in the water. To see if the spring will revoke the magic. It's the only chance we have to break the enchantment. To save you."

"You cannot save me by taking away my gifts. I would not be myself without them. You must understand, Mama. My gifts of aging and healing are vital parts of me as your antlers are a vital part of you."

Tears course down my cheeks. Calder sets a hand on my shoulder.

"I'm sorry, Sparrow," I say. "Forgive me. I have never wanted you to be anyone other than yourself. You know that, do you not?"

She holds my face in her soft, wrinkled hands. "I know you love me. That you have always loved me. And that is more than enough."

Robbie sniffles behind me, the poor, tenderhearted boy.

"Now, since we've come this far, I would like to see the fabled spring," Sparrow says too cheerfully.

"It is a sight to behold," Calder says. "Come." He helps Sparrow to her feet. He and Robbie take her elbows and support her as she hobbles along the narrow strip of rock that leads to the pool.

Midnight-dark water bubbles and swirls in a basin of dark stone. It smells like creek water sweetened with honey. It is beautiful, but not what I expected. Perhaps Delphine brought Calder here to feed him a lie for her own amusement, and this is not *the* spring.

A single brown-edged birch leaf falls to float on the surface. The leaf bobs and spins, turning silver, then gold, and then dissolving in a flash of eye-stinging light.

"To think," Robbie says with awe. "That bit of water there once changed my boy legs to bird legs, when it could have melted me to nothing just as easy."

"That's one small mercy," Calder says.

"I need a moment of silence," Sparrow says. "Alone."

"Anything you want," Calder says. He takes my hand and we follow Robbie until we are several yards uphill from Sparrow and the spring.

When I turn back, I see her fling something into the water. The water rises, boiling and steaming, glowing green and then orange. It leaps into the shape of a huge flame and flashes more brightly than lightning. With a thunderous boom, the flame goes out. The mountain trembles and small stones tumble down its slope to fill the hole that once held water.

"Come," Sparrow beckons. "The spring is no more. I have fulfilled Delphine's last wish, and now I am truly at peace."

Her words make me shudder. If she believes her earthly work is done, her death is nigh.

With the tenderest of care, Calder bears Sparrow down the mountainside. Robbie and I trail behind, saying nothing. I fall too many times to count, bedeviled by slanted rocks and tear-blurred eyes. I lose grip of the misshapen lantern and watch it tumble end over end and off a cliff.

This was not the way I expected the visit to the spring to end. I'd envisioned Sparrow coming out of the water as a young girl, or even a baby, healthy and full of promise. I expected joy. Instead, our return to the wagon feels like a funeral procession.

SABELLA

N ight peeks through the windows of the abandoned, two-room cottage. Calder brought us here earlier when it became clear that Sparrow was too ill to travel all the way back to the farm without stopping. Hundreds of stars wink at me before I turn away from the panes to check on Sparrow.

I lift the candlestick from the table and tread softly across the room. My feet are bare but the floorboards are smooth. On a pallet of blankets near the fireplace, Sparrow still breathes—albeit shallowly. Not far from her, Robbie and Calder doze on the floor without blankets. I love them both dearly for giving all the blankets to Sparrow.

Crickets chirp both outside and in. I am heavy with fatigue yet so wide awake that I wonder if I will ever sleep again. I set the candlestick on the mantel and walk around the edges of the room, accompanied by my ceaseless thoughts and worries. Keeping watch as mothers have surely done since the very dawn of time.

I think back to how we came to be here. Calder parked the wagon alongside the road. This time, Robbie carried Sparrow as

Calder led us past a grove of ancient evergreens and through a knee-deep creek. We traipsed through a grassy clearing, a neglected apple orchard, and an overgrown flower garden. The stone cottage was half hidden by ivy and brush. I wondered how Calder knew of its existence, but did not ask. Perhaps Delphine brought him here as a child.

In spite of all its dust and cobwebs, I fell in love with the cottage the instant I saw it. Perhaps I had some foreshadowing dream of it long ago, for it feels familiar to me.

Sometime before dawn, I settle into a rocking chair near the hearth.

When next I open my eyes, the brightness of the morning startles me. My eyes seek out Calder. He's sitting on the floor beside Robbie, who's still asleep. He shakes his head as if to caution me. When I look for Sparrow, the familiar shape of her body has vanished.

Upon the wrinkled blankets and empty clothes perches a tiny brown and white bird. A perfect sparrow.

For a moment, I cannot breathe. Cannot move.

The sparrow, *my* Sparrow, flies toward the door. She lands at the threshold and waits, plaintively eyeing me and Calder in turn. Finally, he rises and walks toward her.

His hand clutches the doorknob. He looks in my direction, but I doubt he can see through his tears. "Sabella?"

The little bird cocks her head to one side as she waits for my answer. I want to beg her to stay, to change back. But this is not about what I want; it is about what she needs. I hold tightly to the arms of the chair and say, "Let her go."

Calder opens the door. Sparrow takes wing.

"Goodbye, my dearest," I whisper.

CALDER

Everything I have dreaded has come to pass.

She has left me, she who I guarded and treasured and dared to love without stint. If I always expected it, if I saw it in nightmares, if I once stole a letter to try to prevent it, that is no balm to my broken heart.

Broken, ha. Destroyed, decimated, torn to bloody shreds, more like.

To be truthful, I was the one who did the leaving this time. Sabella stood on the doorstep of that blasted cottage and watched Robbie and me slog away. She watched me run back to her and fall on my knees to beg her to come home. Her fingers grazed my bent head but she said no, not now, not yet.

Was it a mistake, my leaving her there? Should I have picked her up, thrown her over my shoulder like a sack of potatoes, and carried her to the wagon? Would she have kicked and screamed, or would she have let me love and support her through her grief? I will never know.

Robbie drives the wagon over all the bumps in the road. I blame his tear-dimmed eyes and his general lack of skill at driving. All the jostling makes my stomach almost as sick as my heart.

"It will all turn out right in the end," Robbie says with a mighty sniff. "That's what Yonaz always told us."

A moth flutters past and I remember flying with Sabella in my arms. The sun, the breeze, her clutching hands. I remember how she kissed me by the waterfall, the bliss of resting my fingertips on the curve of her waist. The arrow-sharp ache of perfect happiness.

"Yonaz was good for a tale," I say. For I cannot imagine how I could ever have a happy ending without Sabella to love.

SABELLA

I could not return to the farm with Calder and Robbie back in July, after the spring vanished and Sparrow transformed. I would not go with them, no matter how they begged and bargained.

It was time, I told them, for me to face life on my own. To nurse my wounds in silence and solitude, to discover what was left of me without Sparrow or my parents. To learn who I might be now.

And so they left. They returned the next day with food and supplies, and then left again—neither of them looking pleased that I had not changed my mind about staying. Calder kept his feelings bottled until they were out the door, but through the cracked window glass, I saw the quaking of his shoulders as Robbie shepherded him away. I felt then as I feel now on dark days: like the ashes of the girl I once was.

After their departure, I swept and scrubbed every inch of the house's insides. Next, I weeded and dug until the gardens and orchard could be called tidy—or at least reasonably well-tended.

This is my world now, this cottage and these gardens. It makes for a cozy home, bordered by maples and pines, hemlocks and oaks. The two hens Calder and Robbie brought me lay golden-brown eggs almost every day. My well yields as much cool, clean water as I need. The forest and my garden provide a wealth of fruits, vegetables, and herbs.

Sometimes, a little sparrow watches me from the branches of an apple tree or the edge of the roof. I leave her breadcrumbs and bits of cake, hoping she is my Sparrow paying a visit.

When the tide of my grief ebbs, there is room in my heart for missing Calder. I compose letters to him in my mind. I draft apologies, love letters, records of my days, musings on life and nature and magic. Does he still think of me fondly, or have I ruined what we had by choosing to be here instead of with him? I could not blame him for trying to forget me—or for seeking comfort in the arms of another.

On this first day of October, the dear little bird sits on a nearby twig as I fill a basket with speckled yellow pears. She lifts her head, puffs out her brown and white feathered chest, and trills brightly. Her song pushes aside the curtain of my lingering sadness to let in some light.

When my stomach complains that I ate too little for breakfast, I head for the house and plan a noontime meal of leftover egg and mushroom pie. But as I enter through the back door, someone knocks at the front.

My pulse gallops. I set my basket down and cross the room. After all this time, I still sometimes foolishly imagine my father coming to steal me back to a life of coal-town drudgery.

When I open the door, Robbie and Cleona are standing on the doorstep like a pair of miracles. They pull me into an enthusiastic embrace before I have a chance to speak.

I step out of the hug and grin at Cleona. "You're not a dove anymore."

"I won her back," Robbie says. "I knew she wouldn't be able to resist me forever."

A blush spreads over Cleona's freckled cheeks as she slips her arm through his. "I was a field mouse for a time, and then a gray rabbit. Once I took a notion to be a girl again, I found I could shift easily. I can be anything I choose now, whenever I like. The magic yields to me."

"Comes in handy when you need a fresh horse," Robbie says. She swats his arm playfully, and he adds, "Didn't say I don't prefer the girl, did I? I'm not so dumb as that."

"Come inside," I say. "And tell me all the news from the farm."

We sit at the table. I serve them mint tea and applesauce.

Robbie's persistent smile warms me like sunshine. He takes a bite of applesauce before beginning his report. "Well, the crops were excellent this year. We've enough potatoes, pears, and apples to feed an army of giants. And...let's see. Calder brought home a new girl. She's probably the last of us, if Delphine's records are right. She's sixteen and part tree. Twigs and leaves grow in her hair and out of her shoulders, but she's awfully pretty. Not as pretty as Cleona, of course. I think she's sweet on Calder, the way she carries on. Ow!"

From the look on Cleona's face and Robbie's reaction, I reckon she's kicked one of his bird legs under the table.

"Anyway," Robbie continues. "The boys burned down the tool shed not long ago, but no one was hurt. The roan mare had a foal last week, and Rhys named it after you even though it's a colt and not a filly." He stops to catch his breath and slurp his tea.

"Everyone sends their love and best wishes," Cleona says. She reaches into the purse in her lap and takes something out. "For you. Fabian carved it and Rhys painted it."

She presses the present into my palm: a length of twine connected to a roughly carved wooden pendant, a heart painted blue and decorated with a splotchy daisy. I tie the string at the nape of my neck, remembering the wooden heart Calder gave me long ago. I have often regretted leaving it behind in my dressing table when Sparrow and I fled Miners Ridge.

"Thank them for me," I say. "It's lovely."

"You ought to come thank them yourself," Robbie says.

Cleona gives him a withering look. "Maybe she's not ready, Robbie."

"Fair enough," Robbie says. He adds timidly, "Do you ever see Sparrow?"

"I believe I do. There are dozens of sparrows here, but one in particular stays close. There's a sparkle in her black eyes that's quite familiar."

"That's lovely," Cleona says.

I glance out the window at a few sparrows hopping along the bare branches of a maple tree. "It comforts me, having her close."

Cleona pats my arm. "Of course it does. All of us miss her at the farm."

"Oh, I nearly forgot," Robbie says as he rummages in his coat pocket, "Calder sent this." He slaps a letter onto the table. "He has terrible handwriting, so don't be surprised if you can barely read it."

I stare at the folded paper, wanting it desperately yet fearing its contents. Robbie slides it closer to me. "Go on. It's only a bit of paper. It won't bite, you know."

Cleona stands. "Why don't we take a wee walk while you read your letter? Robbie's been telling me about the unusual coloring of your hens."

"That really isn't necessary," I say. "I'll read it later."

She kisses my cheek. "Nonsense. A letter's best enjoyed fresh, to be sure."

They're out the door in seconds, leaving me alone with Calder's letter. I carry it to the rocking chair by the fireplace and sit down.

This paper he touched, these pen strokes he fashioned with his hand.

Drawing in a deep breath, I unfold the page.

Sabella,

All I will say is this: I miss you.

For if I say more, you might accuse me of trying to coerce you to return to the farm. If I say more, you might know that the sun shines less brightly since you left, that food tastes like dirt and ashes, that music makes my ears itch, and that I sleep too much—always hoping to see you in my dreams.

Were I to say more, you might discern all the secrets of my heart, and that simply would not do.

I remain, as ever,

Your Calder

When I look up from the page, Robbie is watching me from the doorway. "Cleona lost her bracelet," he says. He bends to claim a slim bangle of silver that lies just over the threshold. "Found it. Are you all right?"

Unable to speak and contain my tears at the same time, I nod.

He comes close and crouches beside my chair. "No, you are not. You're miserable. And do you know who else is miserable? Calder Hadrian, that's who."

My tears drip onto the letter in my lap. Robbie takes my hand between his. "This, my dear, is ridiculous. Does it give the two of you joy, this suffering and pining? Can you not find a way to be together again?"

"I'm only crying because...because he still loves me. I thought I'd ruined everything. But he loves me. And I love him."

Robbie jumps up and whoops like he's won a prize.

"What in the world is going on?" Cleona asks from the doorway. She laughs and shakes her head at Robbie's bird-legged jigging.

"I'm the world's best matchmaker, that's all," he boasts.

"You are delusional, that's what you are," Cleona says with a laugh. "You no more made this match than I made the mountains. They never stopped being in love, you dolt. A few miles of separation cannot kill real love."

"I do love a spring wedding," Robbie says, jigging his way toward his own beloved and spinning her around. "Perhaps we'll make it a double wedding."

"Dream all you wish, Robbie Hallsey," Cleona says saucily. "It will be a good many springs before I marry the likes of you."

"Oh, really?" Robbie takes hold of her face and kisses her squarely on the mouth.

"We shall see," I say, but I do not think they hear me.

Before they leave, I pen a message for Robbie to deliver to Calder: the most beautiful two words I have ever put to paper.

CALDER

T
he floor along the front wall of the entrance hall has developed a new squeak. I think the boards have grown tired of my pacing and are voicing their dismay in the only way they can. My feet throb, expressing a similar sentiment—but I turn on my heel and continue to tread upon the petulant planks.

How could it be possible that Robbie and Cleona left here to visit Sabella only this morning? It feels like I have been waiting weeks for their return.

I stop to stare hard and hatefully out the window at the darkening clouds. The heavens fling down rain in silver-gray ribbons that endlessly unspool and unspool. I can smell mud without lifting the pane.

When I finally see Robbie and Cleona dashing through ankle-deep puddles to reach the front door, I rush out to meet them. My shoes fill with water, but I don't care. They have been in Sabella's company. If anything of her clings to them, a vague scent or a single thread of her clothing, I want it. I want proof she still exists in this world.

Robbie slips his arm through mine and we run back to the house, to take cover from the rain on the wide porch. "Barely made it here. Every stream is overflowing, and the mud almost tore the horse's shoes clean off, it's that thick."

"Is she...?" I start to ask.

Cleona smiles knowingly—which makes me half sick with giddy excitement. She says, "I'm going to dry off and make tea. You two can stand here and drip if you like."

Once the door shuts, Robbie reaches into his vest pocket and pulls out something gray. He offers it to me with all the reverence of a holy man handling a sacred relic. It's paper. A note. A very wet note. Robbie leaves me, but I hardly notice.

I unfold the sodden message with fingers that refuse to stop shaking.

The ink is smeared to near illegibility. There are only two words, but they are enough. They are beautiful in their simplicity yet full of fathomless possibilities. My heart leaps in my chest at the sight of them.

Come soon.

These eight letters form a command I would not dream of disobeying.

I jam the note into the pocket of my trousers and fumble with the buttons of my shirt. I curse them and all buttons. Who invented buttons, anyway? Such a device of deviltry! A few fly off as my frustration escalates. I shrug so my shirt falls onto the porch and then I run across the gravel lane and into the grass.

My wings unfold behind me as I gulp the air. A sudden gust of wind almost knocks me off my feet. Raindrops, hard as hailstones, pelt my naked shoulders. I spread my arms to steady myself and call upon the muscles in my back to move the wings. Cold seeps through my wet skin and makes me shiver. I think every warm thought I can—sunbeams, bonfires, kissing Sabella—but it's no use. My body is too cold to allow for full and proper movement of the wings. I cannot get off the ground.

Water made us what we are, Sabella and me, and now it's water holding us apart. Water and miles of mud and trees and rocks, blast them all to oblivion.

I throw my head back. Rain runs into my mouth and ears to spite me. I utter a sound between a groan and a shout—in case anyone in the heavenly realms gives a fig about the actual, physical pain in my chest I have from perpetually longing for Sabella.

Someone tugs at the waistband of my trousers. It's Rhys. His two foster brothers stand alongside him looking serious as a bishop's funeral. "Cleona says you are to come inside right away or she'll come out for you and make you sorry for it," Rhys says.

"It's getting dark, besides," Tiberius says.

Fabian squints at me as he steps closer. "Are you crying?"

"Not at the moment," I reply. But if this rain does not soon cease, I have no doubt I will weep enough to fill jars, tureens, buckets, and troughs. I am miserable and happy to such an extraordinary degree that it surely must leak out of me somehow.

The boys take hold of my arms and tug me into the house. There, Cleona shoves a mug of tea into my hand and Robbie shrouds me in blankets. But I am still chilled through and I swear I will never be warm again until I find myself in Sabella's embrace.

There is no version of soon that will be soon enough.

SABELLA

OCTOBER 1 AND OCTOBER 2, 1886

An hour after Robbie and Cleona leave, the rain begins. It is no gentle pattering of drops, but rather an assaulting downpour that leaves me soaked to the bone two seconds after I step outside. Water blinds me as I make my way to the shed to feed the chickens. I stumble through puddles and slide across mud. I fear I might drown standing up before I get back into the cottage.

All night, the sky pelts the roof with rain. In my bed, I lay awake and worry about the two creeks running close to the house. Surely they will overflow their banks if the storm continues. My little homestead sits atop a small hill, unlikely to be washed away—but I will become cut off from the world should the creeks rise too high.

How could the sky hold so much water? Did it somehow absorb an entire ocean, an ocean which now insists on pouring its entire contents on the patch of earth I inhabit?

And how will Calder come to me now? Even if he wants to fly, his delicate wings could not bear him through such a violent storm. If he desired to come on horseback, he would be forced to wait for the creek waters to subside. That could take days. Weeks.

It is silly, of course, for me to fret and fuss over possibilities and probabilities. Calder will come when he is ready and able—and no sooner.

SABELLA

OCTOBER 4, 1886
AFTERNOON

S tuck indoors for the third day in a row, I clean until there is nothing in the two rooms that does not shine. I bake until the flour supply runs dangerously low. I eat too much bread and too many sweet cakes, and I sit by the fireplace and think of Calder.

His voice, his hazelnut-brown eyes, his unruly laughter. His steadfastness, his stubbornness, the way he looks at my antlers—as if they're more beautiful than the moon and stars combined.

I think of his wings, green and gold, and what a pity it is that he keeps them folded flat and covered with shirts and waistcoats.

And I have an idea.

While rain pummels the windowpanes, I tear open the seams of the blue calico dress Cleona sent when Robbie and Calder dropped off provisions months ago. While showers drum wet fingers against the roof, I measure and cut the cloth carefully, loath to make a single mistake.

Night encroaches. I light two lamps and bend over my work at the kitchen table, stitching as neatly as I can. Admittedly, I have never been a good seamstress, but I have never cared as much about a garment as I do this one.

When I awaken with my head on the table next to the halfway assembled shirt, I hear only silence. The rain has ceased at last. I rise and stretch, put the kettle on for tea, and resume my sewing. Every stitch is a word of love, a memory of an embrace, a whisper of hope.

SABELLA

The storm stripped every bright autumn leaf from the trees and bushes, but the long-missed, golden sunshine returns now to clothe the bare branches with a becoming sheen. The maple tree closest to the house hosts a flock of merrily twittering sparrows, fine replacements for the absent foliage. In the distance, the creeks whoosh and splash, boasting that they have left their beds like a pair of naughty children.

As I peg the last of the towels to the clothesline, one of the hens scurries past me. She's splattered with mud and clucking excitedly, obviously thrilled that she's escaped the coop.

"Silly bird," I scold. "You'll be a fox's dinner if you wander off. Come here now. Here, chicky." I approach her with caution, but she panics and dashes into the orchard. I give chase, tripping over my own feet, dousing my dress and apron with muck and puddle water.

Finally, I corner her near the house. I dive headlong onto the grass and catch her by the legs with a victorious cry. She responds with distressed squawks and flailing. A few reddish-brown feathers flutter to the ground as I adjust my grip on her round middle.

Gloating over my achievement, I get to my feet. I hold her fat body away from my chest, hoping in vain to spare my soiled clothes from further sullying. Mother would be horrified to see me in such a state.

The squelching of footsteps in the mud startles me. I pull the hen close and turn toward the sound.

"Hello," Calder says, his fingers fumbling to button his shirt. His grin is flame-bright. Eye-stingingly bright. "Sorry if I frightened you."

I cannot breathe. Oh, heavens! He is here and I am all happiness and no words.

The chicken wriggles and squawks, objecting to the increasing tightness of my embrace.

"You said to come, so I flew here as soon as I could." He takes a few steps toward me, his brow wrinkled with worry. "Did you change your mind? Please say no."

"No," I say too loudly. He is close now, close enough for me to see bronze specks in his irises. The tender longing on his face bestirs the butterflies in my belly. They plummet and soar, waltz and jig.

Calder's smile turns mischievous. "Do you enjoy washing clothes since moving out here?"

"No, I do not," I say. The hen pecks my arm but I hardly feel it.

"Well then, I am sorry," he says, brushing his fingertips over my cheek to remove a tear I shed unknowingly. "Because I do believe this shirt I'm wearing is about to become completely filthy." He wraps his arms around me, sandwiching the muddy hen between us, and kisses me. I kiss him back, and soon I cannot tell who is kissing who, but nothing matters other than the fact that I am in his arms, finally. Finally.

We kiss until the bird's cackling escalates to an earsplitting volume. Calder pats the unhappy chicken's head and she snaps at him with her beak. "She's feisty, like her mother."

"I hardly consider myself this chicken's mother. And as I am neither your mother nor your maid, I am not washing that shirt, Calder Hadrian."

"Fine. But what will Robbie think I've been up to when I come home in such a state?"

"He'll think you're nothing but a slovenly cad. Which he already knows full well."

"I love it when you call me names. Did you know that?" Flushed and mud-smeared, he looks far more impish and irresistible than a person should be allowed to.

"Stuff it," I say, borrowing Robbie's expression.

He cups my elbows in his hands and frowns. "Now is that any way to talk in front of the poultry?"

I fix my eyes on his. "I have missed you."

He kisses my forehead. "Let's never fight again."

"Oh, Calder. Always wishing for the impossible."

"Why not? I like impossible. My wings, your antlers, Robbie's ridiculous lower extremities. Impossible is a grand thing. I would go so far as to say that I love it. But there is nothing in the world I love more than you, Sabella. I hope you don't mind that it's still true and always will be."

"If you do not mind hearing me say that I love you as well, I believe I can bear it."

"That's settled, then. Now, let's put this unsightly bird away and find something to eat besides chicken. Flying makes me famished."

We return the disgruntled hen to the coop. Filthy water drips from my hair onto my shoulders and my shoes squish like full sponges as we walk toward the cottage, but these things do nothing to diminish my joy.

Tugging Calder's arm, I say, "I have a gift for you."

"Saucy wench." He laughs and then adds, "I know, I know.

'Stuff it, Calder.' I'm hoping it's food, actually." To emphasize his point, his stomach growls like a bear.

"The gift is quite inedible, but I'll feed you soon, I promise."

We shed our soggy shoes at the door and I wipe my hands on the least dirty part of my apron. My pulse thuds with anticipation as I fetch my handiwork from the basket near the fireplace. Just this morning, I sewed the last stitch into the blue shirt and folded it neatly, as if something in me sensed that today would be the day Calder would arrive.

"What's this?" he asks as I place the rectangle of folded cloth into his grasp.

Blushing, I watch him unfold and examine it. When he turns the shirt over and discovers the slits in the back, he shakes his head in amazement.

"You, my love, are a genius." He starts to unbutton his mud-stained shirt. I blush harder and I turn to face the wall.

A long minute passes before he says, "Modesty restored. Behold the rewards of your labor."

I turn, acutely aware of the swish of my skirts, the damp warmth of the room, and the pattering of my heart.

Thanks to the slits, Calder's green and gold moth wings spread wide behind him. Their colors seem magnified by the sky-blue fabric. He fiddles with the cuffs and bites his lower lip as he awaits my appraisal.

"What do you think?" he asks.

I think that he is glorious indeed, this wonderful, exasperating young man. I think that I want to spend the rest of my life with him—but I will keep that notion to myself for now. So I say, "I think you should never hide your wings again. And I also think you should fly every day, weather permitting. Such a rare gift should not be wasted."

"If that is what you wish, I shall do everything within my power to obey. My wings and I have come to an understanding of late." He sets his hands on my waist and glances over my head.

"You know what I shall ask in return: to see antlers always atop your head, rain or shine. Day and night."

With both hands, I reach up to touch the velvety branches that extend from my head. I run my fingers along their curves, find their points with my fingertips. They seem weightless to me now, no more a burden than the air in my lungs.

"Well? What do you say, Sabella?"

"Yes," I say to him.

And then I say it again more loudly, this time to myself.

Yes, to all that I am, to all that I have been, and to all that I will become.

Acknowledgments

Books might seem to appear in the world like a poof of magical smoke, but as far as I know, this is not a frequent occurrence. This book has been part of my life for almost six years. I have wrestled with it, given up on it, revised it repeatedly, cried and laughed over it, and noticed surprising parts of myself tangled up in its pages. Writing is hard—but I could never love another job as much. Like farming, it requires tons of toil, faith, and fortitude that go unseen. You can easily pick up a tomato or a book with no consideration for the effort that preceded them. That being said, I have many people to thank for being the nourishing sun and rain to my little story farm.

Firstly, thank you, dear reader, for spending time with Sabella and Calder and the rest. I hope you count them among your imaginary friends, as I do.

Thank you to early readers Joanne Brokaw, Roberta Gore, Janeen Ippolito, and Jenny and Hezekiah Brown. If you had not loved The Antler Girl, this book would not exist.

Thank you, Laura Zimmerman, beta reader extraordinaire, top-notch Realm Makers roomie (the 6 a.m. weeping!), and founding member of the Calder Hadrian fan club.

Thank you, Marybeth Davis and Sierra Shipton, for your valuable suggestions.

Thank you to my husband for the unfailing support and love, for believing in my dreams, and for never complaining when I work ridiculous hours and slap leftovers onto the table. You're a gift from God.

Thank you to Christine Doty for being the very best buffalo a person could ask for. Words cannot express how much you mean to me.

Many thanks to Tanya, Alaina, and everyone at Oliver Heber Books. I'm grateful for all you do!

Thank you, Jeff Wheeler, for supporting me since the start of my career, and for nudging me onto this exciting new path.

Because art inspires art...thank you to Andrew Hozier Byrne for "I, Carrion (Icarian)," the song that gave my moth-winged boy his heart.

And always, always, I thank God for his constant, unfathomable love, and for giving me the gift of words.

Now, get out there and be brave and kind—and use your special gifts to make the world a more beautiful place.

ALSO BY CARRIE ANNE NOBLE

The Springborn

The Gingerbread Queen

The Mermaid's Sister

The Gold-Son

Gretchen and the Bear

The Peddler's Reward

About the Author

Carrie Anne Noble writes fantasy fiction infused with fairy tales and folklore, including *The Mermaid's Sister*, winner of the Amazon Breakthrough Novel Award for YA Fiction, and the Realm Award for Book of the Year. She resides in the Pennsylvania woods with her frolicsome half-Corgi but can be lured out with chocolate or a nice cup of tea. Connect with Carrie online at www.carrienoble.com.